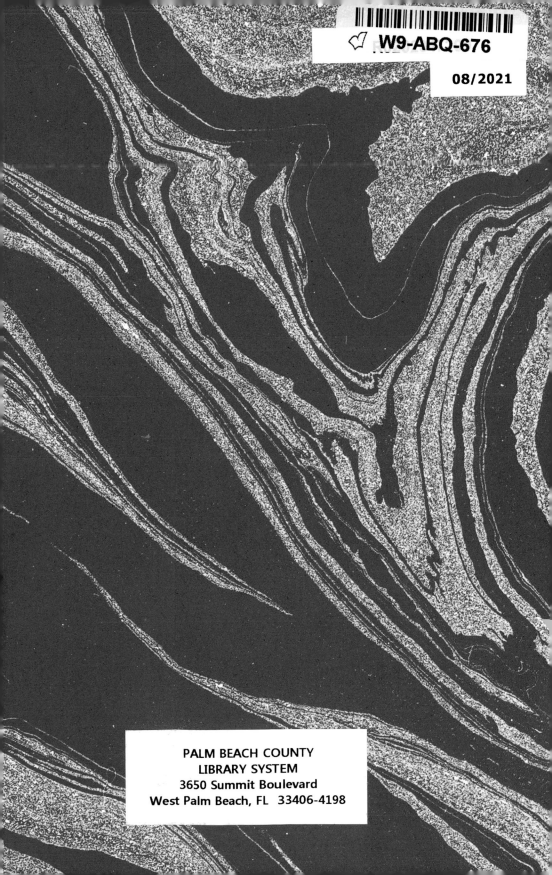

PRAISE FOR THE
GRISHAVERSE

"A master of fantasy." —*THE HUFFINGTON POST*

"Utterly, extremely bewitching." —*THE GUARDIAN*

"This is what fantasy is for."
—*THE NEW YORK TIMES BOOK REVIEW*

"[A] world that feels real enough to have its own
passport stamp." —*NPR*

"The darker it gets for the good guys, the better."
—*ENTERTAINMENT WEEKLY*

"Sultry, sweeping and picturesque . . .
Impossible to put down." —*USA TODAY*

"There's a level of emotional and historical sophistication
within Bardugo's original epic fantasy that
sets it apart." —*VANITY FAIR*

"Unlike anything I've ever read."
—VERONICA ROTH, BESTSELLING AUTHOR OF *DIVERGENT*

"Bardugo crafts a first-rate adventure, a poignant
romance, and an intriguing mystery!"
—RICK RIORDAN, BESTSELLING AUTHOR
OF THE PERCY JACKSON SERIES

"This is a great choice for teenage fans of
George R. R. Martin and J. R. R. Tolkien."
—*RT BOOK REVIEWS*

RULE
OF
WOLVES

Also by Leigh Bardugo

The Shadow and Bone Trilogy

Shadow and Bone

Siege and Storm

Ruin and Rising

The Six of Crows Duology

Six of Crows

Crooked Kingdom

The King of Scars Duology

King of Scars

The Anthologies

The Language of Thorns

The Lives of Saints

RULE OF WOLVES

LEIGH BARDUGO

{Imprint}
MAKE YOUR MARK

NEW YORK

[Imprint]
MAKE YOUR MARK

A part of Macmillan Publishing Group, LLC
120 Broadway, New York, NY 10271

RULE OF WOLVES. Copyright © 2021 by Leigh Bardugo. Jacket art © 2021 Leigh Bardugo.
All rights reserved. Printed in the United States of America.

Library of Congress Control Number: 2021900009

Our books may be purchased in bulk for promotional, educational, or business use.
Please contact your local bookseller or the Macmillan Corporate and Premium
Sales Department at (800) 221-7945 ext. 5442 or by email
at MacmillanSpecialMarkets@macmillan.com.

Book design by Ellen Duda
Map art by Sveta Dorosheva
Imprint logo designed by Amanda Spielman

First edition, 2021

ISBN 978-1-250-14230-6 (hardcover)
5 7 9 10 8 6

ISBN 978-1-250-81651-1 (international edition)
1 3 5 7 9 10 8 6 4 2

ISBN 978-1-250-81771-6 (special edition)
ISBN 978-1-250-82168-3 (special edition)
ISBN 978-1-250-80966-7 (ebook)

fiercereads.com

If you scale the cliffs on the coast near Os Kervo, you may find a cave
said to once be the lair of a dragon. Though the dragon's existence is debatable, the
damp is not. Steal or deface this book and you will spend a perpetually moist eternity
shivering in that cave, eating toadstools, and praying for a bit of dragonfire to warm you.

To EDA, who helped me find my place among the wolves

THE GRISHA

Soldiers of the Second Army
Masters of the Small Science

Corporalki
(The Order of the Living and the Dead)
Heartrenders
Healers

Etherealki
(The Order of Summoners)
Squallers
Inferni
Tidemakers

Materialki
(The Order of Fabrikators)
Durasts
Alkemi

THE WANDERING ISLE

THE BONE ROAD

JELKA

VILKI

NOVYI ZEM

WEDDLE

Reb Harbor

Eames Harbor

SHRIFTPORT

EAMES CHIN

COFTON

SOUTHERN COLONIES

The True Sea

KETTERDAM

BELENDT

KERCH

THE
DEMON
KING

I
QUEEN
MAKHI

MAKHI KIR-TABAN, BORN OF HEAVEN, was a queen from a long line of queens.

And they were all fools, she thought, her pulse quickening as she read the invitation in her hand. *If they hadn't been fools, I wouldn't be in this predicament right now.*

No rage showed on her face. No blood rushed to her smooth cheeks. She was a queen and conducted herself accordingly—back erect, body poised, expression composed. Her fingers did not tremble, though every muscle in her body longed to crush the elegantly lettered paper to dust.

King Nikolai Lantsov, Grand Duke of Udova, sole sovereign of the great nation of Ravka, and Princess Ehri Kir-Taban, Daughter of Heaven, most Ethereal of the Taban Line, would welcome Queen Makhi Kir-Taban to a celebration of matrimony in the royal chapel of Os Alta.

The wedding would take place one month from now. Enough time for Makhi's servants to pack the appropriate gowns and jewels, to assemble her royal retinue, to ready her contingent of the Tavgharad, the elite soldiers who had guarded her family since the first Taban queen took the throne. Plenty of time to make the journey over land or in the new luxury airship her engineers had constructed.

Plenty of time for a clever queen to start a war.

But right now, Makhi had to perform for the ministers arrayed before her in the council chamber. Her mother had passed only a month ago. The crown could have returned to Makhi's grandmother, but Leyti Kir-Taban was nearly eighty and was done with the troubles of running a nation. She wanted only to prune her roses and rusticate with a series of wildly handsome lovers, and so she had given Makhi her blessing and retired to the country. Makhi had been crowned scant days after her mother's funeral. Her reign was a new one, but she intended to ensure it was long. She would usher in an age of prosperity and empire for her people—and that required the support of the royal ministers currently gazing up at her, their faces full of expectation.

"I see no personal message from Ehri," she said, leaning back on her throne. She rested the invitation in her lap and allowed her brow to furrow. "It is a concern."

"We should be rejoicing," said Minister Nagh. He wore the dark green, brass-buttoned coat of the bureaucrat class—as all the ministers did, the two crossed keys of the Shu pinned at their lapels. They looked like a forest of stern trees. "Is this not the result we hoped for? A wedding to seal an alliance between our nations?"

The result you *hoped for. You would have us cower behind our mountains forever.*

"Yes," she said with a smile. "It is why we risked our precious

4

Princess Ehri in such a savage land. But she should have written a note to us in her hand, given some sign that all is well."

Minister Zihun cleared her throat. "Your Most Celestial Highness, Ehri may not actually be happy, but only resigned to this. She has never wanted a public life, let alone a life led away from the only home she has ever known."

"We are Taban. What we want is what our country needs."

The minister bowed her head respectfully. "Of course, Your Majesty. Shall we pen your reply?"

"I will do it myself," said the queen. "As a sign of respect. It's best we begin this new partnership on the right foot."

"Very good, Your Majesty," Nagh said, as if Makhi had executed a particularly fine curtsy.

Somehow the minister's approval made Makhi prickle even more than his opposition.

She rose and, as one, the ministers took a step back, following protocol. She descended from her throne, and her Tavgharad guards fell into step behind her as she made her way down the long hallway that led to the queen's sanctuary. The silk train of her gown sighed against the marble floor, as fretful as one of her advisers. Makhi knew exactly how many steps it took to reach the privacy of her rooms from the council chamber. She had made the walk innumerable times with her mother, and her grandmother before that. Now she counted down—fifty-six, fifty-five—trying to release her frustration and think clearly.

She sensed Minister Yerwei behind her, though the sound of his slippered feet was masked by the rhythmic thump of Tavgharad boots. It was like being pursued by a ghost. If she told her guards to slit his throat, they would do it without hesitation. And then when she was tried for murder, as even a queen could be in Shu Han, they would give testimony against her.

5

When they reached the queen's sanctuary, Makhi passed beneath a gilded arch and entered a small receiving room of pale green marble. She waved off the waiting servants and turned to the Tavgharad. "Do not disturb us," she instructed.

Yerwei followed her through the sitting room and on to the music room, until they reached the grand parlor where Makhi had once sat at her mother's knee, listening to stories of the first Taban queens—warriors who, accompanied by their retinue of tame falcons, had come down from the highest mountains in the Sikurzoi to rule the Shu. *Taban yenok-yun*, they were called. The storm that stayed.

The palace had been built by those queens, and it was still a marvel of engineering and beauty. It belonged to the Taban dynasty. It belonged to the people. And for this brief moment—just a few measured steps in the march of the Taban line—it belonged to Makhi. She felt her spirits lift as they entered the Court of the Golden Wing. It was a room of gilded light and flowing water, the slender, repeating arches of its terrace framing the groomed hedges and burbling fountains of the royal gardens below, and beyond them, the plum orchards of Ahmrat Jen, the trees standing like a regiment of soldiers in tidy rows. It was winter in Ravka, but here in the Shu Han, in this blessed land, the sun still shone warm.

Makhi walked out onto the terrace. This was one of the few places she felt safe talking, away from the prying eyes and curious ears of servants and spies. A green glass table had been set with pitchers of wine and water and a platter of late figs. In the garden below, she saw her niece Akeni playing with one of the gardener's boys. If Makhi didn't conceive daughters with one of her consorts, she had decided Akeni would one day inherit the crown. She wasn't the oldest of the Taban girls, but even at eight years old she was clearly the brightest. A surprise, given that her mother had the depth of a dinner plate.

"Aunt Makhi!" Akeni shouted from below. "We found a bird's nest!"

The gardener's boy did not speak or look directly at the queen, but stood silently beside his playmate, eyes on his battered sandals.

"You must not touch the eggs," Makhi called down to them. "Look but do not touch."

"I won't. Do you want flowers?"

"Bring me a yellow plum."

"But they're sour!"

"Bring one to me and I'll tell you a story." She watched as the children ran toward the southern wall of the garden. The fruit was high in the trees and would take time and ingenuity to reach.

"She is a good child," said Yerwei from the archway behind her. "Perhaps too biddable to make a good queen."

Makhi ignored him.

"Princess Ehri is alive," he said.

She grabbed the pitcher and hurled it down onto the paving stones below.

She tore the curtains from the windows and shredded them with her fingernails.

She buried her face in the silk pillows and screamed.

She did none of those things.

Instead she tossed the invitation onto the table and removed the heavy crown from her head. It was pure platinum, thick with emeralds, and always made her neck ache. She set it beside the figs and poured herself a glass of wine. Servants were meant to attend to these needs, but she didn't want them near her right now.

Yerwei slithered onto the balcony and helped himself to wine without asking. "Your sister is not supposed to be alive."

Princess Ehri Kir-Taban, most beloved of the people, most precious—for reasons Makhi had never been able to grasp. She wasn't wise or beautiful or interesting. All she could do was simper and play the *khatuur*. And yet she was adored.

Ehri was meant to be dead. What had gone wrong? Makhi had made her plans carefully. They should have ended with both King Nikolai and Princess Ehri dead—and Fjerda blamed for the assassinations. On the pretext of avenging her beloved sister's murder, she would march into a kingless, rudderless country, claim its Grisha for the *khergud* program, and use Ravka as a base for waging war with the Fjerdans.

She had chosen her agent well: Mayu Kir-Kaat was a member of Princess Ehri's own Tavgharad. She was young, a talented fighter and swordswoman, and most importantly, she was vulnerable. Her twin brother had vanished from his military unit and his family had been told that the young man had been killed in action. But Mayu had guessed the truth: He'd been selected to become one of the *khergud*, inducted into the Iron Heart program that would make him stronger and more lethal, and not entirely human. Mayu had begged that he be released before his conversion could take place and returned to service as an ordinary soldier.

Queen Makhi knew the process of becoming *khergud*—of having Grisha steel fused to one's bones or mechanical wings attached to one's back—was painful. But there was talk that the process did something else, that the soldiers brought into the program emerged changed in terrible ways, that the *khergud* lost some fundamental part of themselves through the conversion, as if the pain burned away a piece of what had made them human. And of course, Mayu Kir-Kaat didn't want that for her brother. They were twins, *kebben*. There was no closer bond. Mayu would take her own life and the life of a king to save him.

Queen Makhi set down her wine and poured herself a glass of

water instead. She needed a clear head for what was to come. Her nursemaid had once told her that she'd been meant to be a twin, that her brother had been brought into the world stillborn. "You ate his strength," she'd whispered, and even then, Makhi had known that she would one day be a queen. What might have happened had her brother been born? Who might Makhi have been?

It made no difference now.

Ravka's king was still very much alive.

And so was her sister.

This was bad. But Queen Makhi couldn't be sure of how bad. Did Nikolai Lantsov know of the plot against him? Had Mayu lost her nerve and told Princess Ehri of the true plan? No. It couldn't be. She refused to believe it. The bond of the *kebben* was too strong for that.

"This invitation feels like a trap," she said.

"Most marriages are."

"Spare me your wit, Yerwei. If King Nikolai knows——"

"What can the king prove?"

"Ehri might have much to say. Depending on what she knows."

"Your sister is a gentle soul. She would never believe you capable of such subterfuge, and she would certainly never speak against you."

Makhi swatted the invitation. "Then explain this!"

"Perhaps she fell in love. I hear the king is quite charming."

"Don't be absurd."

Princess Ehri had taken Mayu's place in the Tavgharad. Mayu had masqueraded as Princess Ehri. Mayu's task was to get close to King Nikolai, murder him, then take her own life. As far as Princess Ehri knew, that would be the end of it. But in the invasion that would ensue, lives would invariably be lost, and the Tavgharad had orders to make sure Ehri was one of the casualties. They had been assigned to Ehri's household, but they followed the queen's orders alone. Makhi's ministers would never know of the plan she had put into place. So what had gone wrong?

"You must attend this wedding," Yerwei lectured. "All of your ministers will expect it. This is the realization of their plans for peace. They think you should be thrilled."

"Did I not seem thrilled enough for your liking?"

"You were as you always were, a perfect queen. Only I saw the signs."

"Men who see too much have a way of losing their eyes."

"And queens who trust too little have a way of losing their thrones."

Makhi's head snapped around. "What do you mean by that?"

Only Yerwei knew the truth—and not just the details of her plan to murder the Ravkan king and her own sister. He had served as personal physician to her mother and her grandmother. He had been a witness on her mother's deathbed when Queen Keyen Kir-Taban, Born of Heaven, had chosen Ehri as her heir instead of Makhi. It was the right of a Taban queen to choose her successor, but it was almost always the oldest daughter. It had been that way for hundreds of years. Makhi was *meant* to be queen. She had been born for it, raised for it. She was as strong as a member of the Tavgharad, a skilled horsewoman, a brilliant strategist, cunning as a spider. And yet. Her mother had chosen Ehri. Soft, sweet, beloved Ehri, whom the people adored.

"Promise me," her mother had said. "Promise me you will abide by my wishes. Swear it on the Six Soldiers."

"I promise," Makhi had whispered.

Yerwei had heard it all. He was her mother's longest-serving adviser, so old Makhi had no idea how many years he'd been on this earth. He never seemed to age. She'd looked to him, to his watery eyes in his wizened face, wondering if he'd told her mother of the work they'd pursued together, the secret experiments, the birth of the *khergud* program. All of that would end with Ehri on the throne.

"But Ehri does not want to rule—" Makhi had attempted.

"Only because she has always assumed you would."

Makhi had taken her mother's hand in hers. "But I should. I have studied. I have trained."

"And yet no lesson has ever taught you kindness. No tutor has ever taught you mercy. You have a heart hungry for war and I do not know why."

"It is the falcon's heart," Makhi had said proudly. "The heart of the Han."

"It is the falcon's will. That is a different thing. Swear to me that you will do this. You are a Taban. We want what the country needs, and this nation needs Ehri."

Makhi had not wept or argued; she'd only given her vow.

Then her mother had breathed her last. Makhi said her prayers to the Six Soldiers, lit candles for the fallen Taban queens. She'd tidied her hair and brushed her hands over the silk of her robes. She would have to wear blue soon, the color of mourning. And she had so much to mourn—the loss of her mother, the loss of her crown.

"Will you tell Ehri or shall I?" she'd asked Yerwei.

"Tell her what?"

"My mother—"

"I heard nothing. I'm glad she went peacefully."

That was the way their pact had been formed over her mother's cooling corpse. And how a new queen had been made.

Now Makhi leaned her arms on the balcony and breathed in the scents from the garden—jasmine, sweet oranges. She listened to the laughter of her niece and the gardener's boy. When she'd taken her sister's crown, she hadn't realized how little it would solve, that she would be forever competing with kind, oblivious Ehri. Only one thing would end that suffering.

"I will see my sister wed. But first I must send a message."

Yerwei moved closer. "What is it you intend? You know your ministers will read the note, even if it is sealed."

"I'm not a fool."

"One can be foolish without being a fool. If—"

Yerwei's sentence broke without warning.

"What is it?" asked Makhi, following his gaze.

A shadow was moving over the plum orchards beyond the palace wall. Makhi looked up, expecting to see an airship, but the skies were clear. The shadow kept growing, spreading like a stain, speeding toward them. The trees it touched toppled, their branches turning black, then vanishing, leaving nothing behind but gray earth and a curl of smoke.

"What is this?" Yerwei gasped.

"Akeni!" the queen screamed. "Akeni, get down from the tree! Come away from there right now!"

"I'm picking plums!" the girl shouted, laughing.

"I said right now!"

Akeni couldn't see beyond the walls, this black tide of death that came on without a sound.

"Guards!" the queen yelled. "Help her!"

But it was too late. The shadow slid over the palace wall, turning the golden bricks black and descending over the plum tree. It was as if a dark veil descended over Akeni and the gardener's boy, silencing their laughter.

"No!" Makhi cried.

"My queen," said Yerwei urgently. "You must come away."

But the blight had stopped, right on the edge of the fountain, clear as the mark of high tide on the sand. All it had touched lay gray and wasted. All that lay beyond was lush and green and full of life.

"Akeni," the queen whispered on a sob.

Only the wind answered, blowing in off the orchard, scattering the last, faint tendrils of shadow. Nothing remained but the sweet smell of flowers, happy and unknowing, their faces turned to the sun.

2
NINA

NINA TASTED THE SALT AIR on her tongue, letting the sounds of the marketplace wash over her—the call of vendors hawking their wares, the gulls in the Djerholm harbor, the shouts of sailors aboard their ships. She glanced up to the cliff top where the Ice Court loomed above it all, its high white walls gleaming bright as exposed bone, and she restrained a shiver. It was good to be out in the open, away from the cloistered rooms of the White Island, but she felt as if the ancient building was watching her, as if she could hear it whisper, *I know what you are. You do not belong here.*

"Kindly shut up," she muttered.

"Hmm?" said Hanne as they made their way down the quay.

"Nothing," Nina replied hastily.

Talking to inanimate structures was not a good sign. She'd been cooped up too long, not just in the Ice Court but in Mila Jandersdat's body, her face and form tailored to keep her true identity secret. Nina cast another baleful glance at the Ice Court. Its walls were said to be impenetrable, never breached by an attacking army. But her friends had breached it just fine. They'd blown a hole in those grand walls with one of Fjerda's own tanks. Now? Nina was more like a mouse—a big blond mouse in too-heavy skirts—nibbling away at the Ice Court's foundation.

She paused at a wool vendor's stall, the racks crowded with the traditional vests and scarves worn for Vinetkälla. Despite her best intentions, Nina had been charmed by Djerholm from the first time she'd seen it. It was tidy in the way only a Fjerdan town could be, its houses and businesses painted in pink and blue and yellow, the buildings snug against the water, huddled close together as if for warmth. Most cities Nina had seen—how many had there been? how many languages had she spoken in them?—were built around a town square or a high street, but not Djerholm. Its lifeblood was salt water and its market faced the sea, sprawled across the quay, shops and carts and stalls offering fresh fish, dried meats, dough wound around hot irons and cooked over coals, then dusted with sugar. The stone halls of the Ice Court were imperious and cold, but here there was mess and life.

Everywhere Nina looked there were reminders of Djel, his sacred ash boughs woven into knots and hearts in preparation for the winter parties of Vinetkälla. In Ravka, they would be readying for the Feast of Sankt Nikolai. And for war. That was the knowledge that sat heavy on her chest every night when she lay down to sleep, that crept up to twine around her throat and choke the breath from her every day. Her people were in danger and she didn't know how to help them. Instead she was browsing nubbly hats and scarves behind enemy lines.

Hanne was beside her, bundled in a thistle-colored coat that made her tawny skin glow despite the overcast day, an elegant knit cap tucked over her shorn hair to avoid drawing attention. As much as Nina hated the confines of the Ice Court, Hanne was suffering even more. She needed to run, to ride; she needed the fresh smell of snow and pine, and the comfort of the woods. She'd come to the Ice Court with Nina willingly, but there was no question that the long days of polite conversation over tedious meals had taken their toll. Even this little bit of freedom—a trip to the market with parents and guards in tow—was enough to bring color to her cheeks and shine to her eyes again.

"Mila! Hanne!" called Ylva. "Don't go too far."

Hanne rolled her eyes and lifted a ball of blue wool from the vendor's cart. "Like we're children."

Nina glanced behind her. Hanne's parents, Jarl and Ylva Brum, trailed them by only a few yards, drawing admiring glances as they walked along the quay—both of them tall and lean, Ylva in warm brown wool and red fox fur, Brum in the black uniform that filled Nina with loathing, the silver wolf of the *drüskelle* emblazoned on his sleeve. Two young witchhunters followed, their faces clean-shaven, their golden hair worn long. Only when they had completed their training and heard the words of Djel at Hringkälla would they be permitted to grow beards. And then off into the world they would merrily go to murder Grisha.

"Papa, they're setting up for some kind of show," Hanne said, gesturing farther down the quay to where a makeshift stage had been erected. "Can we go watch?"

Brum frowned slightly. "It isn't one of those Kerch troupes, is it? With their masks and lewd jokes?"

If only, Nina thought glumly. She longed for the wild streets of Ketterdam. She'd take a hundred bawdy, raucous performances of the Komedie Brute over the five interminable acts of Fjerdan opera she'd been forced to sit through the previous night. Hanne had kept jabbing her in the side to prevent Nina from nodding off.

"You're starting to snore," Hanne had whispered, tears leaking down her cheeks as she tried to keep from laughing.

When Ylva saw her daughter's red face and wet eyes, she had patted Hanne's knee. "It *is* a moving piece, isn't it?"

All Hanne had been able to do was nod and squeeze Nina's hand.

"Oh, Jarl," Ylva said to her husband now. "I'm sure it will be perfectly wholesome."

"Very well." Brum relented and they made their way toward the stage, leaving the disappointed wool seller behind. "But you'd be surprised at the turn this place has taken. Corruption. Heresy. Right here in our capital. You see?" He pointed to a burned-out storefront as they passed. It looked like it had once been a butcher shop, but now the windows were broken and the walls stained with soot.

"Only two nights ago, this shop was raided. They found an altar to the supposed Sun Saint and one to . . . what's her name? Linnea of the Waters?"

"Leoni," Hanne corrected softly.

Nina had heard about the raid through her contacts in the Hringsa, a network of spies dedicated to liberating Grisha throughout Fjerda. The butcher's wares had been thrown into the street, the cupboards and shelves stripped to unearth hidden relics—a finger bone from the Sun Saint, an icon painted in an amateurish hand that clearly showed beautiful Leoni with her hair in coiled braids, arms raised to pull poison from a river and save a town.

"It's worse than just the worship of the Saints," Brum continued, jabbing a finger at the air as if it had personally offended him. "They're claiming Grisha are the favored children of Djel. That their powers are actually a sign of his blessing."

Those words put an ache in Nina's heart. Matthias had said as much. Before he died. Her friendship with Hanne had helped to heal that wound. This mission, this purpose had helped, but the pain was still there and she suspected it always would be. His life had been stolen from him, and Matthias had never had the chance to find his own purpose. *I served it, my love. I protected you. To the very end.*

Nina swallowed the lump that had formed in her throat and forced herself to say, "Hanne, should we get a honeywater?" She would have preferred wine, maybe something stronger, but Fjerdan women weren't permitted alcohol, certainly not in public.

The honeywater seller smiled at them, his jaw dropping when he caught sight of Brum's uniform. "Commander Brum!" he said. "Some hot drinks for your family? To fortify you on this chilly day?"

The man was broad-shouldered and thick-necked, with a long ginger mustache. His wrists were tattooed with circles of waves that might have indicated a former sailor. Or something more.

Nina felt a strange sense of doubling as she watched Jarl Brum shake the vendor's hand. Nearly two years ago, only a few yards from where they stood now, she had fought this man. She had faced the *drüskelle* commander as her true self, as Nina Zenik, the drug *jurda parem* thick in her blood. That drug had allowed her to take on hundreds of soldiers, had made her impervious to bullets, and had forever altered her Grisha gift, granting her power over the dead rather than the living. She had spared Brum's life that day, though she'd taken his scalp. Nina was the reason for his bald head and the scar that ran across the base of his skull like the fat pink tail of a rat.

Matthias had pleaded mercy—for his people, for the man who had been a second father to him. Nina still wasn't sure if she'd done the right thing by granting it. If she had killed Brum, she would never have met Hanne. She might never have come back to Fjerda. Matthias might still be alive. When she thought too much about the past, she got lost in it, in all the things that might have been. And she couldn't afford that. Despite the false name she bore and the false face she wore thanks to Genya's expert tailoring, Nina was Grisha, a soldier of the Second Army, and a spy for Ravka.

So pay attention, Zenik, she scolded herself.

Brum tried to pay the honeywater vendor, but the man refused to take his coin. "A gift for Vinetkälla, Commander. May your nights be short and your cup always full."

A cheerful burst of flutes and drums sounded from the stage, signaling the start of the performance, and the curtain lifted, revealing a painted cliff top and a miniature marketplace below. The crowd burst into delighted applause. They were looking at Djerholm, the very city where they stood, and a banner that read THE STORY OF THE ICE COURT.

"You see, Jarl," said Ylva. "No lewd japes. A properly patriotic tale."

Brum seemed distracted, checking his pocket watch. *What are you waiting for?* Nina wondered. Diplomatic talks between Fjerda and Ravka were still proceeding, and Fjerda had not yet declared war. But Nina felt sure battle was inevitable. Brum would settle for nothing less. She'd passed on what little intelligence she'd been able to gather eavesdropping at doors and over dinners. It wasn't enough.

Cymbals crashed to start the tale of Egmond, the prodigy who had designed and built extraordinary castles and grand buildings when he was only a child. The acrobats pulled at long skeins of silk, creating a towering mansion of gray spires and glittering arches. The audience clapped enthusiastically, but an actor with a haughty face—a nobleman who didn't want to pay for his fanciful new home—cursed Egmond, and the handsome young architect was bound in chains, to be dragged off to the old fort that had once stood on the cliff top above the harbor.

The scene changed to Egmond in his cell as a great storm arrived on a roll of thundering drums. Blue ripples of silk cascaded over the stage, embodying the flood that had engulfed the fort with the king and queen of Fjerda inside it.

Working undercover wasn't simply a question of mastering a language or learning a few local customs, so Nina knew her Fjerdan myths and legends well. This was the part of the story where Egmond was meant to place his hand on the roots of a tree that had poked through his cell wall, and with Djel's help, use the strength of the sacred ash to buttress the walls of the fort, save the king and queen, and build the foundation for the mighty Ice Court.

Instead three figures walked onto the stage—a woman engulfed in red paper roses, a young girl in a white wig with antlers around her neck, and a woman with black hair in a blue gown.

"What is this?" growled Brum.

But the gasp from the audience said it all: Sankta Lizabeta of the Roses, the Sun Saint Alina Starkov, and—an excellent touch if Nina did say so herself—the Stormwitch, Zoya Nazyalensky, had entered the play.

The Saints placed their hands on Egmond's shoulders, then against the prison cell walls, and the twisted bits of fabric meant to symbolize Djel's ash began to expand and unfurl, like roots uncoiling through the earth.

"No more of this," Brum said loudly, his voice carrying over the crowd. He sounded calm enough, but Nina heard the edge in his voice as he stepped forward. The two *drüskelle* followed, already reaching for the clubs and whips at their belts. "The weather is turning. The play can continue later."

"Leave them be!" shouted a man from the crowd.

A child began to cry.

"Is this part of the play?" asked a confused woman.

"We should go," Ylva said, trying to herd Hanne and Nina away.

But the crowd was too close around them, pushing toward the stage.

"You will disperse," Brum said with authority. "Or you will be arrested and fined."

Suddenly, thunder sounded—real thunder, not the tinny drums of the performers. Dark clouds moved in over the harbor so quickly it seemed as if dusk was falling. The sea was suddenly alive, the water forming whitecaps, rolling in swells that set the ships' masts swaying.

"Djel is angry," said someone in the crowd.

"The Saints are angry," called someone else.

"You will *disperse!*" Brum said, shouting over the rumble of the oncoming storm.

"Look!" a voice cried.

A wave was racing toward them from the harbor, looming higher and higher. Instead of breaking against the sea wall, it leapt the quay. It towered over the crowd, a wall of seething water. The people screamed. The wave seemed to twist in the air, then crashed down onto the quay—directly into Brum and his soldiers, sending them sprawling across the cobblestones in a rush of water.

The crowd gasped, then burst into laughter.

"Jarl!" cried Ylva, trying to go to him.

Hanne held her back. "Stay here, Mama. He will not want to be seen as weak."

"Sankta Zoya!" someone yelled. "She brought the storm!"

A few people in the crowd went to their knees.

"The Saints!" another voice said. "They see and they protect the faithful."

The sea roiled and the waves seemed to dance.

Brum stumbled to his feet, his face red, his clothes soaked with seawater. "Get up," he snarled, yanking his young soldiers to their feet. Then he was in the crowd, pulling the penitent up by the collars of their shirts. "Get off your knees or I will arrest you all for sedition and heresy!"

"Do you think we went too far?" Hanne whispered, sliding her hand into Nina's and giving it a squeeze.

"Not far enough," murmured Nina.

Because the performance and even the wave had only been a distraction. The play had been staged by the Hringsa network. The wave had arrived courtesy of a Tidemaker undercover in one of the harbor boats. But now as Jarl Brum and his men rampaged through the crowd, the honeywater vendor, who had slipped into an alley when the play began, gave a quick wave of his hands, parting the clouds.

Sunlight poured from the sky onto the butcher shop that had been raided a few nights before. The wall looked blank at first, but then the vendor uncorked the bottle Nina had slipped into his cart. He gusted a cloud of ammonia at the paint and a message appeared, as if by magic, scrawled across the storefront: *Linholmenn fe Djel ner werre peje.*

The Children of Djel are among you.

It was a cheap party trick, one she and the other orphans had used to send each other secret messages. But as Nina had learned not so long ago in Ketterdam, a good con was really about spectacle. All around her she could see the people of Djerholm gaping at the message emblazoned on the storefront, pointing to the sea that had now calmed, to the clouds that were rolling back into place as the honeywater vendor casually wiped his hands and returned to his stall.

Would it matter? Nina didn't know, but little miracles like these had been happening all over Fjerda. In Hjar, a damaged fishing boat had been about to sink when the bay froze solid and the sailors were able to walk safely back to shore, their catch intact. The next morning, a mural of Sankt Vladimir's sacred lighthouse had appeared on the church wall.

In Felsted, an apple orchard had burst into full fruit despite the cold weather, as if Sankt Feliks had laid a warming hand upon the trees. The branches had been found festooned with ash boughs—a symbol of the blessing of Djel.

Half the town of Kjerek had fallen ill with firepox, a near-certain death sentence. Except the morning after a farmer witnessed a vision of Sankta Anastasia hovering above the town well with a wreath of ash leaves in her hair, the townspeople had woken free from sickness, their skin clear of sores, their fevers gone.

Miracle after miracle created by the Hringsa and Second Army spies. Tidemakers had frozen the bay, but they'd also created the storm to wreck the fishing boat. Squallers had brought on the early frost in Felsted, but Sun Soldiers had made the trees bloom. And while Hringsa agents hadn't created the firepox, they had made sure Grisha Corporalki had been there to heal the victims. As for the vision of Anastasia, it was amazing what a little theatrical lighting and a red wig could do.

Then there was the strange blight that had struck north of Djerholm. Nina didn't know where that had come from, a natural phenomenon or the work of some rogue Hringsa operative. But she did know there'd been murmurs it was the work of the Starless Saint, retribution for the religious raids and arrests by Brum's men.

At first Nina had doubted that their miracles were making any difference at all, had feared that their efforts amounted to little more than childish pranks that would lead to nothing. But the fact that Brum had been devoting more and more resources to attempting to root out worship of the Saints gave her hope.

Brum stomped back to them, his face a mask of rage. It was hard to take him too seriously when he was soaked to the bone and it looked like a fish might wriggle out from one of his boots. Still Nina kept her head down, her eyes averted, and her face expressionless. Brum was dangerous now, a mine waiting to detonate. It was one thing to be hated or confronted, quite another to be laughed at. But that was what Nina wanted, for Fjerda to stop seeing Brum and his *drüskelle* as men to be feared and to acknowledge them for what they were: scared bullies worthy of scorn, not adulation.

"I'll see my family back to the Ice Court," he muttered to his soldiers. "Get names. All of the performers, everyone who was in the marketplace."

"But the crowd—"

Brum's blue eyes narrowed. "*Names*. This stinks of the Hringsa. If there are Grisha in my streets, in my capital, I will find out."

There are Grisha in your house, Nina thought gleefully.

"Don't get cocky," murmured Hanne.

"Too late."

They climbed into the roomy coach. The king and queen had gifted Brum one of the noisy new vehicles that didn't require horses, but Ylva preferred a coach that didn't belch black smoke and wasn't likely to break down on the steep climb to the Ice Court.

"Jarl," Ylva attempted once they were ensconced in the velvet seats. "What is the harm? The more you react to these theatrics, the more emboldened they will be."

Nina expected Brum to explode, but he was silent for a long time, staring out the window at the gray sea below.

When he spoke again, his voice was measured, his anger leashed. "I should have held my temper." He reached out and clasped Ylva's hand.

Nina saw the effect that small gesture had on Hanne, the troubled, guilty look that clouded her eyes. It was easy for Nina to hate Brum, to see him as nothing but a villain who needed to be destroyed. But he was Hanne's father, and in moments like these, when he was kind, when he was reasonable and gentle, he seemed less like a monster than a man doing his best for his country.

"But this is not a matter of a few people making trouble in the marketplace," Brum continued wearily. "If the people begin to see our enemies as Saints—"

"There are Fjerdan Saints," offered Hanne, almost hopefully.

"But they are not Grisha."

Nina bit her tongue. Maybe they were and maybe they weren't. Sënj Egmond, the great architect, was said to have prayed to Djel to buttress the Ice Court against the storm. But there were other stories that claimed he'd prayed to the Saints. And there were some who believed that Egmond's miracles had nothing to do with divine intervention, that they had simply been the result of his Grisha gifts, that he had been a talented Fabrikator who could manipulate metal and stone at will.

"The Fjerdan Saints were holy men," said Brum. "They were favored by Djel, not . . . these demons. But it's more than that. Did you recognize the third Saint flouncing across that stage? That was Zoya Nazyalensky. General of the Second Army. There is nothing holy or natural about that woman."

"A woman serves as a general?" Hanne asked innocently.

"If you can call a creature like that a woman. She is everything repugnant and foul. The Grisha *are* Ravka. Fjerdans worshipping these false Saints . . . They are giving their allegiance to a foreign power, a power with whom we are about to be at war. This new religion is more of a threat than any battlefield victory could be. If we lose the people, we lose the fight before it even begins."

If I do my job right, thought Nina.

She had to hope that the common people of Fjerda didn't hate Grisha more than they loved their own sons and daughters, that most of them knew someone who had vanished—a friend, a neighbor, even a relative. A woman willing to leave livelihood and family behind for fear of having her power discovered. A boy snatched from his home in the night to face torture and death at the hands of Brum's witchhunters. Maybe with her little miracles, Nina could give Fjerda something to rally around, a reason to question the hate and fear that had been Brum's weapons for so long.

"The Apparat's presence here undermines all we've worked for," Brum went on. "How can I purge our towns and cities of foreign influence when there is a heretic at the very heart of our government? We look like the worst of hypocrites, and he has spies in every alcove."

Ylva shuddered. "He has a most unnerving way about him."

"It's all for show. The beard. The dark robes. He likes to terrify the ladies with his strange pronouncements and his skulking, but he's little more than a squawking bird. And we need him if we're to put Demidov on the throne. The priest's backing will matter to the Ravkans."

"He smells of graveyards," said Hanne.

"It's only incense." Brum drummed his fingers on the windowsill. "It's hard to tell what the man really believes. He says the Ravkan king is possessed by demons, that Vadik Demidov was anointed by the Saints themselves to rule."

"Where did Demidov come from anyway?" Nina said. "I so hope we'll get to meet him."

"We keep him safe in case any Ravkan assassins have a mind to take a shot at him."

Pity that.

"Is he really a Lantsov?" she pushed.

"He has more claim to the crown than that bastard Nikolai."

The coach jolted to a halt and they descended, but before Nina's feet had even touched the gravel path, a soldier was running up to Brum, a folded paper in hand. Nina glimpsed the royal seal—silver wax and the crowned Grimjer wolf.

Brum broke the seal and read the note, and when he looked up, his expression made Nina's stomach sink. Despite his wet clothes and the humiliation he'd suffered at the harbor, he was beaming.

"It's time," he said.

Nina saw Ylva smile ruefully. "You'll be leaving us, then. And I will wait every night with fear in my heart."

"There is nothing to fear," Brum said, tucking the paper into his coat pocket. "They cannot stand against us. Finally, our moment has come."

He was right. The Fjerdans had tanks. They had Grisha captives addicted to *parem*. Victory was assured. Especially if Ravka was stranded without allies. *I should be there. I belong in that fight.*

"Will you be traveling far?" Nina asked.

"Not at all," said Brum. "Mila, you look so frightened! Have you so little faith in me?"

Nina forced herself to smile. "No, sir. I only fear for your safety as we all do. Here," she said, "let me take your coats so everyone can get inside and be warm. You should have every moment together as a family before Commander Brum leaves."

"What a blessing you are, Mila," Ylva said fondly.

Nina took her coat, and Hanne's, and Brum's, her hand already snaking into the pocket where he'd placed the note.

War was coming.

She needed to get a message to her king.

3

NIKOLAI

NIKOLAI TRIED TO STEADY his nervous mount with a pat to the horse's withers. His groom had suggested it wasn't appropriate for a king to ride out on a horse named Punchline, but Nikolai had a soft spot for the piebald pony with crooked ears. He certainly wasn't the prettiest horse in the royal stables, but he could run for miles without tiring and he had the steady disposition of a lump of rock. Usually. Right now he could barely keep still, hooves dancing left and right as he tugged at his reins. Punchline didn't like this place. And Nikolai couldn't blame him.

"Tell me I'm not seeing what I think I'm seeing," he said, meager hope in his heart.

"What do you think you're seeing?" asked Tamar.

"Mass destruction. Certain doom."

"Not entirely certain," said Zoya.

Nikolai cut her a glance. She'd tied back her black hair with a dark blue ribbon. It was eminently practical, but it had the unfortunate effect of making him want to untie it. "Do I detect optimism in my most pessimistic general?"

"*Likely* doom," Zoya corrected, pulling gently on her white mare's reins. All the horses were nervous.

Dawn crept over Yaryenosh, bathing the town's rooftops and streets in rosy light. In the pastures beyond, Nikolai could see a herd of ponies, their winter coats shaggy, stamping their hooves in the cold. It would have been a quaint scene, a dreamy landscape for some hack painter to sell off to a rich merchant with a surfeit of cash and a dearth of taste—if it hadn't been for the dead, ashy soil that stained the countryside like a blot of spilled ink. The blight stretched from the paddocks of the horse farm in the distance all the way to the edges of the town below.

"Two miles?" Nikolai speculated, trying to determine the extent of the damage.

"At least," said Tolya, peering through a folding long glass. "Maybe three."

"Twice the size of the incident near Balakirev."

"It's getting worse," said Tamar.

"We can't say that yet," protested Tolya. Like his sister, he wore an olive drab uniform, his huge bronze arms exposed to display his sun tattoos, despite the winter chill. "It's not necessarily a pattern."

Tamar snorted. "This is Ravka. It's always getting worse."

"It's a pattern." Zoya's blue eyes scanned the horizon. "But is it *his* pattern?"

"Is it even possible?" Tolya asked. "We've had him locked in the sun cell since he . . . returned."

Returned. There was something quaint about the word. As if the Darkling had simply been vacationing on the Wandering Isle, sketching ruined castles, sampling the local stews. Not brought back to life by an ancient ritual orchestrated by a bloodthirsty Saint with a penchant for bees.

"I try not to underestimate our illustrious prisoner," said Nikolai. "And as for what's possible . . ." Well, the word had lost its meaning. He had met Saints, witnessed their destruction, nearly died himself, and become host to a demon. He'd seen a man long dead resurrected, and he was fairly sure the spirit of an ancient dragon was lurking inside the woman next to him. If *possible* was a river, it had long since leapt its banks and become a flood.

"Look," said Tolya. "Smoke."

"And riders," added Tamar. "Seems like trouble."

At the fringes of town near where the blight had struck, Nikolai could see a gathering of men on horseback. Angry voices carried on the wind.

"Those are Suli wagons," said Zoya, the words hard and clipped.

A shot rang out.

They all shared the briefest glance, and then they were charging down the hill to the valley below.

Two groups of people stood in the shade of a large cedar tree, mere footsteps from where the blight had bled all life from the land. They were on the edge of a Suli encampment, and Nikolai saw the way the wagons had been arranged not merely for convenience but for defense. There was no child in sight. They'd been ready for a possible attack. Maybe because they always had to be ready. The old laws restricting Suli land ownership and travel had been abolished even before his father's time, but prejudice was harder to wipe from the books. And it was always worse when times got hard. The mob—there was no other word for it, their rifles and fevered eyes made that clear—confronting the Suli was testimony to that.

"Stand down!" Nikolai shouted as they galloped nearer. But only a couple of people turned toward him.

Tolya charged ahead and drove his massive warhorse between the two groups. "Lay down your arms in the name of the king!" he bellowed. He looked like a warrior Saint come to life from the pages of a book.

"Very impressive," said Nikolai.

"Show-off," said Tamar.

"Don't be petty. Being the size of an oak should have some benefits."

Both the townspeople and the Suli took a step back, mouths agape at the sight of a giant, uniformed Shu man with tattooed arms in their midst. Nikolai recognized Kyril Mirov, the local governor. He'd made good money trading salt cod and producing the new transport vehicles rapidly replacing carriages and carts. He had no noble blood in him, but plenty of ambition. He wanted to be taken seriously as a leader, and that meant he felt he had something to prove. Always worrisome.

Nikolai took the opportunity Tolya had given him. "Good morning," he said happily. "Are we all gathering for an early breakfast?"

The townspeople fell into deep bows. The Suli did not. They recognized no king.

"Your Highness," said Mirov. He was a lean man with jowls like melted wax. "I had no idea you were in the area. I would have ridden out to greet you."

"What's happening here?" Nikolai said calmly, keeping accusation from his voice.

"Look what they did to our fields!" cried one of Mirov's men. "What they did to the town! Ten houses vanished like smoke. Two families gone, and Gavosh the weaver as well."

Vanished like smoke. They'd had the same reports from other parts of Ravka: a blight that struck out of nowhere, a tide of shadow that enveloped towns, farmland, ports, each thing it touched dissolving into nothing with no more ceremony than a candle guttering out. In its wake, the blight left fields and forests leached of all life. *Kilyklava*, he'd heard it called—vampire, after a creature from myth.

"That doesn't explain why your guns are drawn," Nikolai said mildly. "Something terrible has happened here. But it's not the work of the Suli."

"Their camp was untouched," said Mirov, and Nikolai didn't like the measured sound of his voice. It was one thing to calm a snapping dog, another to try to reason with a man who had dug himself a tidy trench and fortified it. "This . . . thing, this horror struck just days after they arrived on our land."

"*Your* land," said a Suli man standing at the center of the group. "There were Suli in every country this side of the True Sea before they even had names."

"And what did you build here?" asked a butcher in a dirty apron. "Nothing. These are our homes, our businesses, our pastures and livestock."

"They're a cursed people," said Mirov as if citing a fact—last year's rainfall, the price of wheat. "Everyone knows it."

"I hate to be left out of a party," said Nikolai, "but I know no such thing, and this blight has struck elsewhere. It is a natural phenomenon, one my Materialki are studying and will find a solution to." A heady combination of lies and optimism, but a bit of exaggeration never hurt anyone.

"They're trespassing on Count Nerenski's land."

Nikolai let the mantle of Lantsov authority fall over him. "I am Ravka's king. The count holds these lands at my discretion. I say these people are welcome here and under my protection."

32

"So says the bastard king," grumbled the butcher.

A hush fell.

Zoya clenched her fists and thunder rolled over the fields.

But Nikolai held up a hand. This was not a war they would win with force.

"Could you repeat that?" he asked.

The butcher's cheeks were red, his brow furrowed. The man might well keel over from heart failure if his ignorance didn't kill him first. "I said you are a bastard and not fit to sit that fancy horse."

"Did you hear that, Punchline? He called you fancy." Nikolai turned his attention back to the butcher. "You say I am a bastard. Why? Because our enemies do?"

An uncomfortable murmur passed through the crowd. A shuffling of feet. But no one spoke. *Good.*

"Do you call Fjerda your master now?" His voice rang out over the gathered townspeople, the Suli. "Will you learn to speak their tongue? Will you bow to their pureblood king and queen when their tanks roll over Ravka's borders?"

"No!" cried Mirov. He spat on the ground. "Never!"

One down.

"Fjerda has loaded your guns with lies about my parentage. They hope you will turn your weapons on me, on your countrymen who stand at our borders even now, ready to defend this land. They hope you will do the bloody work of war for them."

Of course, Nikolai was the liar here. But kings did what they wished; bastards did what they must.

"I'm no traitor," snarled the butcher.

"You sure sound like one," said Mirov.

The butcher thrust his chest out. "I fought for the Eighteenth Regiment and so will my son."

"I bet you had quite a few Fjerdans running," said Nikolai.

"Damn right I did," said the butcher.

But the man behind him was less convinced. "I don't want my children fighting in another war. Put them witches out front."

Now Zoya let lightning crackle through the air around them. "The Grisha will lead the charge and I will take the first bullet if I have to."

Mirov's men took a step back.

"I should thank you," Nikolai said with a smile. "When Zoya takes it into her head to be heroic, she can be quite frightening."

"I'll say," squeaked the butcher.

"People died here," said Mirov, trying to regain some authority. "Someone has to answer for—"

"Who answers for the drought?" asked Zoya. Her voice cut through the air like a well-honed blade. "For earthquakes? For hurricanes? Is this who we are? Creatures who weep at the first sign of trouble? Or are we Ravkan—practical, modern, no longer prisoners of superstition?"

Some of the townspeople looked resentful, but others appeared downright chastised. In another life Zoya would have made a terrifying governess—straight-backed, sour-faced, and perfectly capable of making every man present wet his trousers in fear. But a Suli woman was staring at Zoya, her expression speculative, and his general, who could usually be counted upon to meet any insolent look with a glare powerful enough to scorch forests, was either oblivious or deliberately ignoring her.

"*Khaj pa ve*," the woman said. "*Khaj pa ve*."

Though Nikolai was curious, he had more pressing matters to attend to. "I know it is little comfort, but we should discuss what aid the crown can offer in recompense for your lost land and homes. I will—"

"I'll speak to the governor," Zoya said briskly.

Nikolai had intended to talk with Mirov himself, since the man's interest in status might make him susceptible to attention from royalty. But Zoya was already directing her mount his way.

"Be charming," he warned her under his breath.

She flashed him a warm smile and a wink. "I will."

"That was very convincing."

The smile vanished in an instant. "I've had to watch you smarm all over Ravka for years. I've learned a few tricks."

"I don't smarm."

"Occasionally you smarm," said Tolya.

"Yes," conceded Nikolai. "But it's endearing."

He watched Zoya slide down from her horse and lead Mirov away. The man looked nearly slack-jawed, a frequent side effect of Zoya's beauty and general air of murderousness. Perhaps there were some things more intoxicating than status for Mirov after all.

But Zoya hadn't been pressing an advantage with Mirov. She was running away. She hadn't wanted that Suli woman to confront her, and that wasn't like his general. At least, it hadn't been. Since she'd lost Juris, since their battle on the Fold, Zoya had changed. It was like he was viewing her from a distance, like she'd taken a step away from everyone and everything. And yet she was sharp as always, armor firmly in place, a woman who moved through the world with precision and grace, and little time for mercy.

He turned his attention to the Suli. "For your safety, it might be best if you moved on tonight."

Their leader bristled. "Whatever this horror is, we had nothing to do with it."

"I know that, but when night falls, cooler heads may not prevail."

"Is this what protection from Ravka's king looks like? A command to scurry into the shadows?"

"It's not an order, it's a suggestion. I can station armed men here to defend your camp, but I don't think you'd welcome their presence."

"You would be right."

Nikolai didn't want to leave these people with no place to shelter. "If you'd like, I can send word to Countess Gretsina to open her fields to you."

"She would welcome Suli on her lands?"

"She will or she won't get any of the new threshers we're distributing to farms."

"This king deals in both bullets and blackmail."

"This king rules men, not Saints. Sometimes more than prayer is required."

The man released a huff of laughter. "On that we can agree."

"Tell me," said Nikolai to the woman beside the Suli leader, attempting to keep his voice casual. "You said something to General Nazyalensky."

"*Nazyalensky*," she said with a laugh.

Nikolai's brows rose. "Yes. What did you say to her?"

"*Yej menina enu jebra zheji, yepa* Korol Rezni."

The Suli man laughed. "She said her words were for the general and not for you, King of—"

"I understood that part just fine," said Nikolai. *Korol Rezni.* King of Scars. Of the many things he'd been called, it certainly wasn't among the worst, but at the sound of those words, the demon in him stirred. *Easy now, we've reached an understanding, you and I.* Though the demon wasn't much for logic.

Over the next hour, Nikolai and Tamar interviewed the Suli who were willing to describe the blight to them, then reconvened with Tolya and Zoya.

"Well?" he asked, as they rode back to the hilltop.

"Same as near Balakirev," said Tolya. "A blot of shadow rolling over the countryside, like night coming on too quickly. Everything the shadow touches succumbs to blight—livestock, property, even people dissolve into smoke, leaving behind nothing but barren earth."

"Pilgrims came through only a day ago," said Zoya. "Followers of the Starless One. They claim this is punishment for the reign of a faithless king."

"How unfair. I have plenty of faith," Nikolai objected.

Tolya raised a brow. "In what?"

"Good engineering and better whiskey. Did Mirov and his friends break bread with the pilgrims and give them a fair hearing for their treason?"

"No," Zoya said with some satisfaction. "Enough of them remember the war and the Darkling's destruction of Novokribirsk. They chased those black-clad fanatics out of town."

"They do love a mob in Yaryenosh. What did that woman say to you?"

"No idea," said Zoya. "I don't speak Suli."

Tamar peered at her. "You *looked* like you understood her. You looked like you couldn't wait to be out of her sight."

So Nikolai hadn't been the only one to notice.

"Don't be ridiculous," Zoya said. "There was work to be done."

Tolya bobbed his head at Nikolai. "The Suli aren't fond of you, are they?"

"I'm not sure they have reason to be," said Nikolai. "They shouldn't have to live in fear within our borders. I haven't worked hard enough to secure their safety." Another item to add to his list of failures. Since taking the throne, he'd contended with too many enemies on the field—the Darkling, the Fjerdans, the Shu, *jurda parem*, the damned demon living inside him.

"We all live in fear." Zoya nudged her horse into a gallop.

"I guess that's one way to change the subject," said Tolya.

They followed in her wake, and as they crested the hill, Tamar looked back at the wound the blight had left on the fields. "The Starless are right about one thing. There's a connection to the Darkling."

"I'm afraid so," said Nikolai. "We've all seen the sands of the Fold. Dead and gray. Just like the areas struck by this blight. I thought that when the Shadow Fold collapsed and the darkness was dispelled, the land it covered might heal itself."

"But nothing has ever grown there," said Tolya. "It's cursed land."

For once, Nikolai couldn't brush away that word as mere superstition. The Tula Valley had been the site of some of the holiest land in Ravka, where Sankt Feliks had supposedly cultivated his orchard— or the thorn wood, depending on which story you believed. It was also the location of the first *obisbaya*, a ritual meant to separate beast from man. But the Darkling had tainted all that. His attempt to create his own amplifiers and his use of *merzost* to do it had made a mockery of his power, twisting it into a dark territory crowded with monsters. Sometimes Nikolai wondered if they'd ever be free of that legacy.

Not if you don't face your part in it. It was time they acknowledged the ugly truth of what this blight meant.

"There's no other explanation," he said. "The Fold is expanding. And we caused it."

"You don't know that—" Tamar began.

"We do," said Zoya. Her voice was cold.

Nikolai remembered the earthquakes that had been felt throughout Ravka and beyond when the boundaries of the Fold had ruptured. Elizaveta had been defeated. Three Saints, Grisha of infinite power, had died violently. Nikolai's attempt to endure the *obisbaya* and rid himself of his demon had failed. The Darkling's power lived on inside him, and now the man himself walked the earth once more. Of course there were bound to be consequences.

"We'll take soil samples," he continued. "But we know what's happening here."

"Fine. You're to blame," said Tamar. "How do we stop it?"

"Kill the Darkling," said Zoya.

Tolya rolled his eyes. "That's your answer to everything."

Zoya shrugged. "How do we know if we don't try?"

"And what about the demon trapped inside the king?" asked Tamar.

Zoya scowled. "Details."

"We could attempt the *obisbaya* again," Tolya suggested. "I found a new text that—"

"It nearly killed him last time," Zoya snapped.

"Details," said Nikolai. "We'll have to consider it."

"After the wedding," said Zoya.

"Yes," said Nikolai, trying to summon some enthusiasm. "After the wedding."

With her eyes on the horizon, Zoya said, "Please tell me you've made progress with Princess Ehri."

"Contemplating jabbing a thorn through my heart again is easier than wooing a princess."

"It certainly requires more finesse," Zoya said. "Which you have in abundance."

"That doesn't quite sound like a compliment."

"It isn't. You have more charm than sense. But while that makes you irritating, it should also be of use in delicate matters of diplomacy."

"Honestly, I've barely had a chance to speak with her." He'd meant to invite her to his Saint's day feast, but somehow he'd never gotten around to it. Nikolai knew he should talk to her. He *must* if he had any hope of seeing his plans for the future come to fruition. But he'd been avoiding spending time with the princess since that disastrous night when Isaak had died and the woman everyone had believed to be Ehri was revealed as an assassin. Since then, the real Princess Ehri had been sequestered in luxurious quarters that were still very much a prison. Her Tavgharad guards had been kept in the most hospitable part of the dungeons beneath the old stables, and the assassin—the girl who had driven a knife into Isaak's heart, thinking she was killing a king—was under lock and key, still healing from her wounds. As for Nikolai's other prisoner? Well, he had a very unique cell of his own.

"Ehri is softening," Nikolai continued. "But she's stubborn."

"A good trait for a queen," said Zoya.

"Do you think so?"

Nikolai watched Zoya's face. He couldn't help watching. Her glance at him was so swift he might have imagined it, a flash of blue, the sky glimpsed through trees. And the meaning of that glance? Something. Nothing. He'd have more luck trying to tell his fortune in the clouds.

Zoya kept her reins in one hand as she adjusted her gloves. "In less than a month, Queen Makhi will arrive, expecting a grand celebration. Without the presumed bride's cooperation, you're going to find yourself in the middle of an international incident."

"He may well anyway," said Tamar.

"Yes, but if the wedding doesn't happen, Nikolai won't have to worry about the Fjerdans or the Shu or the Fold."

"I won't?"

"No, because Genya will have murdered you. Do you have any idea how much work she's put into planning this grand event?"

Nikolai sighed. "It will happen. I've already had a new suit made."

"A suit," Zoya said, casting her eyes heavenward. "You'll be very well-dressed at your funeral. Talk to Ehri. *Charm* her."

She was right, and that vexed him more than anything. He was grateful to see a rider approaching from camp, though the messenger's grim expression instantly set Nikolai's heart racing. No one ever rode that fast when the news was good.

"What is it?" Nikolai asked as the rider drew alongside them.

"A flyer arrived from Os Alta, Your Majesty," the messenger said on a gasp. "We've had a message from the Termite." He handed Nikolai a sealed missive.

He saw Zoya lean forward in her saddle and knew she wanted to snatch the paper right out of his hands. Nina Zenik's code name was Termite.

Nikolai's eyes scanned the page. He had hoped they'd have more time. But Nina had at least given them a fighting chance.

"We need to get back to camp. Ride ahead and have them ready two of our flyers," Nikolai told the messenger, who vanished in a cloud of dust.

"This is it, isn't it?" asked Zoya.

"Fjerda is on the march. Tamar, you'll need to get word to David and our Fabrikators, and I'll send a flyer to our contacts in the west as well."

"The missiles aren't usable yet," said Tamar.

"No," said Nikolai. "But the Fjerdans aren't going to wait." He turned to Zoya. "Hiram Schenck is in Os Kervo. You know what to do. We have only one chance to get this right."

"Are we ready?" Tolya asked.

"Hardly," said Tamar. "But we'll give them hell anyway."

The demon in Nikolai roused at the thought. War was like fire—sudden, hungry, and easiest to stop before it had taken hold. He would do all he could to contain this blaze. He feared for his country and for himself. He'd be a fool not to. But some part of him, maybe the privateer, maybe the demon, maybe the prince who had clawed his way to the throne, was itching for a fight.

"Think of it as throwing a party," he said, giving his reins a snap. "When the guests show up, you find out who your real friends are."

4

NINA

NINA WOKE TO HANNE at her bedside, shaking her
arm. Her heart pounded in her chest and she realized her sheets were
soaked with sweat. Had she been talking in her sleep? She'd been
dreaming of the ice, of Matthias' wolf. Trassel had been eating from
her hand, but when she looked closer, she saw that his white muzzle
was covered in blood and that he was feasting on a corpse.

"Someone's here," Hanne said. "Someone from the convent."

Nina sat up, the night air cooling the perspiration on her body.
She was instantly awake, and now the thunder in her heart had nothing to do with a muzzy dream. Hanne had been a student at the
convent in Gäfvalle, where she and Nina had uncovered Brum's horrific scheme involving the Springmaidens and a nearby military fort.
They'd put a stop to it and rescued the Grisha they could, and Nina
had sent the Wellmother to her death with no regrets.

"Who is it?" she whispered, wrapping herself in a high-necked wool robe and cinching it tight. She pushed her feet into her slippers. At least the floors of the White Island were heated.

"I don't know. My mother sent for both of us."

"Sweet Djel, put a robe on. Aren't you freezing?" Hanne was dressed in nothing but her cotton nightgown, the light of the oil lamp in her hand gleaming off the ruddy stubble on her shorn head.

"I'm too terrified to be cold," said Hanne, and they bustled through the dressing room that connected Nina's smaller chamber to Hanne's bedroom.

The fort at Gäfvalle had been destroyed in an explosion Nina's team had set, and in the chaos that followed, Hanne and Nina had been able to plead innocence in the whole affair. Jarl Brum had no idea who Nina really was or that she had been responsible for destroying his laboratory and his program of torture. He had welcomed Mila Jandersdat into his household believing, quite accurately, that she had helped his daughter save his life. Of course, he didn't know that if she'd had her way, Nina would have put an end to him once and for all.

At the time, Hanne and Nina had believed they'd gotten away with all of it. Maybe they hadn't. When the dust had cleared, maybe someone from the convent had put together some part of their ruse. Maybe the Springmaidens had found the *drüskelle* uniform Hanne had stolen. Maybe someone had seen Hanne and Nina dragging Jarl Brum's unconscious body out of the wagon.

"Here," Nina said, holding out Hanne's robe so that she could shrug into it. In the Fjerdan way, it was made of plain slate-gray wool but lined with luscious fur, as if anything that might hint at luxury or comfort should be hidden.

"What do we do?" Hanne asked. She was shivering.

Nina turned her around and tied the sash on her robe. "We let them do the talking."

"You don't have to play lady's maid to me," said Hanne. "Not when we're in private."

"I don't mind." Hanne's eyes looked like molten copper in this light. Nina made herself focus on tying the sash into a neat bow. "We present the picture of innocence and virtue, find out what they know, deny everything. If it comes down to it, I was the ruthless spy who entangled you in my web."

"You need to stop reading novels."

"Or you need to read more of them. Your hands are ice cold."

"All of me is cold."

"That's the fear." Nina cupped Hanne's hands, rubbing heat into them. "Use your power to slow your pulse a bit, ease your breathing."

"Hanne?" Ylva's voice came from down the hall.

"Coming, Mama! Just getting dressed!" She lowered her voice. "Nina, I made my own choices. I'm not letting you take the fall for me."

"And I'm not letting you get hurt because you got wrapped up in my trickery."

"Why must you be so stubborn?"

Because Nina could be reckless and foolish and sometimes that meant the wrong people got hurt. Hanne had been hurt enough in her life.

"Let's not be so bleak," Nina said, avoiding the question. "Maybe the Springmaiden came to give us a nice present."

"Of course," said Hanne. "Why didn't I think of that? I hope it's a pony."

The walk down the narrow hall felt like a march to the gallows. Nina carefully adjusted a pin in her hair. In Fjerda, unmarried women didn't appear in public without their hair bound in braids. All the propriety had given Nina a permanent headache. But her role as Mila Jandersdat had put her at the heart of the Ice Court, the perfect base from which to stage her miracles.

Hanne had seemed less sure after their stunt in the marketplace.

"Is it worth it?" Hanne had asked her that night in the privacy of their rooms. "There will be consequences for those townspeople. My father won't stand for this kind of heresy. He'll take more drastic measures and innocent people will pay the price."

"Innocent people are already paying the price," Nina had reminded her. "They're just not Fjerdans."

"Be careful, Nina," Hanne had said as she'd climbed beneath the covers. "Don't become what my father claims you are."

Nina knew she was right. Zoya had scolded her for recklessness too. The problem was that she knew what they were doing was working. Yes, there were plenty of fanatics like Brum who would always hate Grisha—and plenty of people happy to go along with them. But the cult of the Sun Saint had found followers years ago when Alina Starkov had risen to destroy the Shadow Fold and been martyred in the process. That was a miracle Brum couldn't deny. Then there were the miracles reported from all over Ravka just in the past year—weeping statues, bridges made of bones. On both sides of the border, there were whispers that an age of Saints was beginning. The movement had been building for a long while, and Nina just needed to keep nudging it along.

Besides, if she hadn't been here at the Ice Court, Ravka would have no knowledge of the invasion the Fjerdans were planning.

But at what cost?

She suspected she was about to find out.

The central room of their dwelling on the White Island was a grand affair—soaring walls of white marble, a vaulted ceiling, and a great stone hearth built to look as if it were framed by the twisting branches of Djel's sacred ash. All of it a testimony to Commander Jarl Brum's standing—something he'd had to fight to regain after the Ice Court had been breached and he'd been humiliated by a certain Grisha on the docks.

Now Brum was dressed in his uniform and had his traveling coat slung over his arm. He'd been preparing to journey to the front. His face was unreadable. Hanne's mother looked vaguely worried, but that was almost always the case. A fire crackled in the hearth.

A woman of middle age with dark brown hair in elaborate braids sat erect in one of the cream velvet chairs by the fire, a cup of tea perched on her knee. But this was no Springmaiden. She wore the dark blue pinafore and capelet reserved for the Wellmother, the highest-ranking sister at the convent. Her face was unfamiliar to Nina, and a brief glance confirmed that Hanne didn't know her either. Hanne had lived at the convent for years, but this woman clearly hadn't trained as a novice there. So who was she and what was she doing at the Ice Court?

Nina and Hanne curtsied deeply.

Brum gestured toward the woman. "Enke Bergstrin has assumed the management of the convent at Gäfvalle since the unfortunate disappearance of the previous Wellmother."

"Was she never found?" Nina asked, her tone as blameless as a babe's first coo. It was good strategy to put Brum on the defensive if he was questioning what had taken place at the convent. Besides, she enjoyed watching him squirm.

Brum shifted his weight, eyes darting briefly to his wife. "It's believed she may have been in the fort when the explosions occurred. The convent was taking in laundry for the soldiers."

In fact, that task had been mere cover for their real business: tending to the pregnant Grisha addicted to *jurda parem* on Brum's orders.

"But why would the Wellmother go there herself?" Nina pressed. "Why not send a novice or one of the Springmaidens?"

Brum brushed a speck of lint from his coat. "A reasonable question. It may be she had other business there or had simply gone to supervise the sisters."

Or maybe she got dragged into the next world by my undead minions. Who can say?

"What an inquisitive girl you are," said the new Wellmother. Her eyes were gray-blue, her brow stern, her mouth hard. Did all Wellmothers emerge from the womb scowling? Or did they just start looking vexed as soon as they took the job?

"Forgive me," Nina said, with another demure curtsy. "I was not educated at the convent, and I'm afraid my manners show the truth of it."

"You've done nothing wrong, Mila," said Ylva. "We're all curious."

"Regardless of what became of the previous Wellmother," Brum pushed on, "Enke Bergstrin has taken on her position and is attempting to set the convent to rights after the tragedies at Gäfvalle."

"But what is this about, Papa?" asked Hanne.

"I don't know," Brum said, his voice sharp. "The Wellmother has declined to share that without your presence."

The Wellmother set down her tea. "In the wake of the destruction of the fort and the rise of irreligious elements in Gäfvalle, the convent has had to take a sterner hand with our students and extend them less privacy."

Irreligious elements. Nina savored the words. Gäfvalle had been the first step, the first miracle she'd staged, when Leoni and Adrik had saved the village from poison unleashed from the factory. It had been irresponsible, utterly imprudent—and it had worked like a charm.

She had learned the practice of deception from Kaz Brekker himself, and there was no greater teacher. Two Grisha—a Fabrikator and an Etherealnik—had saved those villagers. A miracle? No, just good people trained to use their gifts, willing to expose themselves to persecution and worse for the sake of saving a town. Two people who were now worshipped as Saints in the dark corners and candlelit kitchens of Gäfvalle. Sankt Adrik the Uneven and Sankta Leoni of the Waters.

"What does this have to do with our daughter?" demanded Brum.

"In the course of searching the convent we came across all manner of contraband, including painted icons and heathen prayer books."

"Surely they are just young," said Ylva. "I rebelled too when I was that age. It was how I ended up married to a *drüskelle*."

Nina felt an unexpected pang at the warm look Brum and his wife shared. Ylva was Hedjut, considered one of the divine people of the north, from the lost coastline near Kenst Hjerte, the Broken Heart. Had she been like Hanne in her youth—driven by stubborn spirit? Full of love for the land and the open sky? Had Jarl Brum, the military boy from the capital, seemed mysterious and alien? Nina had assumed that Brum had always been a monster, but maybe he'd grown into one.

"We cannot think that way," said Brum. "These influences must be rooted out before they take hold or all of Fjerda will lose its way."

The Wellmother nodded. "I couldn't agree more, Commander Brum. That is why I'm here."

Ylva sat forward, her face stricken. "Are you saying these items were found in Hanne's quarters?"

"We found men's riding clothes stashed beneath the slate tiles in the chapel. Also, prayer beads and an icon of Sankta Vasilka."

Sankta Vasilka. Patron saint of unwed women. She was a Ravkan Saint, said to have become the first firebird.

"That cannot be," said Brum, stepping in front of Hanne as if to protect her. "Hanne has had her wilder moments. But she would never give herself over to the worship of abomination."

"Never," whispered Hanne fervently, and no one could doubt the look of sincerity on her face.

Nina tried not to smile. Hanne would never worship a Grisha because she damn well was one, a Healer forced to hide her powers but who still found ways to use them to help people.

The Wellmother's lips pursed. "Then perhaps you think I traveled all this way to tell fanciful tales."

The room was silent except for the crackle of the fire. Nina could feel the fear radiating off Ylva, the anger that came from Brum—and the uncertainty in both of them too. They knew Hanne had been disobedient in the past. But how far had she gone? Nina wasn't sure herself.

Hanne took a deep breath. "The riding clothes were mine."

Damn it, Hanne. What had Nina said? Deny everything.

"Oh Hanne," Ylva cried, pressing her fingertips to her temples.

Brum's face flushed red.

But Hanne stepped forward, her chin held high, radiant with the pride and rigid will she'd inherited from her father. "I'm not ashamed." The sound of her voice was pure and certain. Her eyes met Nina's, glanced away again. "I didn't know who I was then or what I wanted. Now I know where I want to be. Here with you."

Ylva stood and took Hanne's hand. "And the icons? The prayer beads?"

"I don't know anything about them," Hanne said without hesitation.

"Were they found with Hanne's riding clothes?" Nina asked, taking a chance.

"No," the Wellmother admitted. "They were not."

Ylva drew Hanne close. "I'm proud of your honesty."

"Wellmother," said Brum, his voice icy, "you may have the ear of Djel, but so do the *drüskelle*. You will think more carefully the next time you come to my home to accuse my daughter."

The Wellmother rose. She looked indomitable, not remotely chastened by Brum's words. "I serve the spiritual well-being of this country," she said. "The Apparat, a heathen priest, is beneath this roof. I have heard tales of heathen worship in this very town. I will not be swayed in my mission. Still," she said, and smoothed the woolen skirts of her pinafore, "I am glad Hanne has finally found her way. I will hear her confession before I go."

Hanne curtsied, head bowed, the very picture of obedience. "Yes, Wellmother."

"And I will hear Mila Jandersdat's as well."

Nina couldn't hide her surprise. "But I was only a guest of the convent. I was never a novitiate."

"And do you not have a soul, Mila Jandersdat?"

More of a soul than you, you pinch-faced prune pit. But Nina couldn't protest further, not in front of the Brums. Besides, she was nearly giddy with relief. They hadn't been found out. And while the idea of Hanne being accused of false worship was no small thing, it was nothing compared to what the Wellmother might have said. So if Madame Prune Pit wanted her to make up a few good sins, she'd be happy to entertain her for a quarter of an hour.

"I'll go first," she said to Hanne, and cheerfully followed the Wellmother into the small receiving room that had been selected for her confessional.

It was narrow, with space for little more than a writing desk and a small sofa. The Wellmother took a seat at the desk and lit an oil lamp.

"The water hears and understands," she murmured.

"The ice does not forgive," Nina said in traditional reply.

"Close the door."

Nina did as she was bid and smiled warmly, showing she was eager to please.

The Wellmother turned, her eyes the cold color of slate. "Hello, Nina."

5
ZOYA

IN A HIGH TOWER of Os Kervo's city hall, Zoya paced the flagstone floor. Hiram Schenck was late, and she had no doubt the insult was deliberate. Once the Kerch government had acquired the secrets of the *izmars'ya*, Nikolai's deadly ships that could travel undetected beneath the surface of the sea, Ravka had lost all their leverage with the little island nation and the Merchant Council who ruled it. Schenck just wanted to make sure she knew it.

She needed to stay calm, be a diplomat, not a soldier. It was that or tear Schenck's tufty ginger head from his body.

Through the window, she glimpsed waves crashing against the base of the city's famous lighthouse. It was said Sankt Vladimir the Foolish had held the ocean at bay while the stones were laid for the sea wall and the great lighthouse. Zoya had a suspicion he'd been nothing more than a powerful Tidemaker. *Not that powerful*, she considered. He'd drowned in the bay for his troubles.

She shouldn't be here. She should be at the front, on the ground with her Squallers. With her king.

"We can't risk Fjerda finding out what we're up to," Nikolai had said. "You need to meet with Schenck."

"And if the Fjerdans attack from the sea?"

"They won't break Sturmhond's blockade."

He'd sounded certain, but Nikolai had a talent for sounding sure of himself. Sturmhond, the legendary privateer—and the Ravkan king's alter ego—had sent a fleet of ships to guard Ravka's coastline. In theory, the king and the Triumvirate were meant to leave that job to the Ravkan navy. But the navy was too closely tied to West Ravka and their interests for Nikolai's comfort. They couldn't be trusted, not when the stakes were so high.

At least Nina's message had arrived in time for them to prepare. At least Nina was still alive.

"Order her home," Zoya had urged, determined to keep the pleading from her voice.

But the king had refused. "We need her there."

It was true, and she hated it.

Let the Fjerdans come by sea, Zoya thought, *let Jarl Brum and the rest of his bloody witchhunters come to us on the waves. My Squallers and I will give them a warm welcome.*

She rested her head against the cool stone of the window casement. Some part of her had been glad to leave the king. To avoid Tamar's knowing gaze. She could still hear the Suli woman's voice, still see her standing fearless beneath the cedar tree. *Khaj pa ve. We see you.* Zoya was a warrior, a general, a Grisha who wore the scales of a dragon around her wrists. So why did those words fill her with so much fear?

She consulted the timepiece she wore on a jeweled fob, clipped to the sash of her *kefta*. It was a gift from the king, the silver lid shaped like a dragon curled around a quince. When she flipped it open, the abalone face caught the light, shimmering with faint rainbows. The silver hands ticked away.

"He's late," she bit out.

"Perhaps he got lost," offered Count Kirigin nervously. He was always nervous around her. It was tiresome. But he was very wealthy, and his interminably jolly mood made him a perfect foil. When Kirigin was in the room, it was impossible to take anything too seriously. Besides, his father had been a war profiteer, which made him a villain in Ravka but quite popular among the noblemen of West Ravka who had enriched themselves with the help of the elder Kirigin. "My watch says he's still got two minutes until he's strictly considered late."

"Our king needs every minute."

Kirigin's cheeks flushed. He tapped his fingers on the table. "Yes. Yes, of course."

Zoya turned back toward the window.

She *felt* his shame, his eagerness, his longing. They came on like a sudden storm, a gust that swept her off solid ground and into free fall. One moment she was standing, sure-footed in a sunlit room in Os Kervo, looking out at the sea. The next she was gazing at a beautiful girl before her, raven-haired, her blue eyes distant. She reached out to touch the girl's smooth cheek.

"Zoya?"

Zoya slammed back into her own consciousness just in time to smack Kirigin's hand away. "I did not give you leave to touch me."

"My apologies," he said, cradling his hand as if she'd broken one of his fingers. "You just looked so . . . lost."

And she had been lost. She glanced down at the shimmering

black fetters on her wrists. They looked like shackles but they felt natural, as if they'd always been meant to lie cool against her skin. *Power.* The hunger for it like a heartbeat, steady and unrelenting. It was the temptation of all Grisha, and the acquisition of an amplifier only made it worse. *Open the door, Zoya.*

She could never be sure if it was her own voice or Juris' that spoke in her head. She only knew that his presence within her was real. No figment of her imagination could be so irritating. Sometimes, beneath Juris, she could sense another mind, another presence that was not human, had never been human, something ancient—and then the world would shift. She would hear a servant whispering gossip in the kitchens, smell apple blossoms in the orchard at Yelinka—nearly fifteen miles away. All that she could bear, but the emotions, this sudden drop into someone else's pain or joy . . . It was too much.

Or maybe you're losing your mind, she considered. It was possible. After what she'd seen on the Fold, what she'd done—murdered a Saint bent on destruction, driven a blade into the heart of a dragon, into the heart of a friend. She had saved Nikolai's life. She had saved Ravka from Elizaveta. But she hadn't stopped the Darkling from returning, had she? And now she couldn't help but wonder if there was any chance she could save her country from war.

"I was lost in thought," Zoya said, shaking out the sleeves of her blue *kefta*. "That's all."

"Ah," said Kirigin. But he didn't look convinced.

"You never served, did you?"

"No indeed," said the count, seating himself at the end of a long rectangular table engraved with the West Ravkan crest—two eagles bracketing a lighthouse. He was wearing a custard-yellow coat and a coral waistcoat that, in combination with his pallid skin and bright red hair, made him look like an exotic bird seeking a perch. "My father sent me away to Novyi Zem during the civil war." He cleared his throat. "Zoya—" She flashed him a look and he hastily corrected himself. "General Nazyalensky, I wonder if you might consider a visit to my holdings near Caryeva."

"We are at war, Kirigin."

"But after the war. In the summer, perhaps. We could go for the races."

"Are you so sure there will be an after?"

Kirigin looked startled. "The king is a brilliant tactician."

"We don't have the numbers. If he fails to stop the Fjerdans at Nezkii, this war will be over before it begins. And to win, we need reinforcements."

"And we will have them!" Kirigin declared. Zoya envied his optimism. "One day there will be peace again. Even in a time of war, we might slip away for a moment. For a quiet dinner, a chance to talk, to get to know each other. Now that the king is to be married—"

"The king's plans are none of your concern."

"Certainly, but I thought that now you might be free to—"

Zoya turned on him. She felt current crackle through her, felt the wind lift her hair. "Be free to what, exactly?"

Kirigin held up his hands as if he could ward her off. "I simply meant—"

She knew what he meant. Rumors had surrounded her and Nikolai for months, rumors she had encouraged to hide the secret of the demon that lived inside him and what it took to keep the monster under control. So why did it make her so angry to hear these words now?

She took a slow breath. "Kirigin, you are a charming, handsome, very . . . amiable man."

"I . . . am?" he said, then added with more surety, "I am."

"Yes, you are. But we are not suited in temperament."

"I think if you just—"

"No *just*." She took another breath and forced herself to rein in her tone. She sat down at the table. Kirigin had been a loyal friend to the king and had put himself at considerable risk over the last few years by letting his home be used as a base for their weapons development. He wasn't a bad sort. She could try and be *pleasant*. "I think I know the way you see this playing out."

Kirigin flushed even redder. "I highly doubt that."

Zoya suspected it involved bodies entwined and possibly him playing her a song on the lute, but she would spare them both that particular image.

"You will invite me to a fine dinner. We'll both drink too much wine. You'll get me to talk about myself, the pressures of my position, the sadness of my past. Perhaps I'll shed a tear or two. You'll listen sensitively and astutely and somehow discover my secret self. Something like that?"

"Well, not precisely. But . . . yes!" He leaned forward. "I want to know the true you, Zoya."

She reached out and took his hand. It was clammy with sweat.

"Count Kirigin. Emil. There is no secret self. I'm not going to reveal another me to you. I'm not going to be tamed by you. I am the king's general. I am the commander of the Second Army, and right now my people are facing down the enemy without me there."

"But if you would only—"

Zoya dropped his hand and slumped back in her chair. So much for pleasant. "War or not, if I ever hear another amorous word or invitation leave your mouth, I will knock you unconscious and let a street urchin steal your boots, understood?"

"My boots?"

Hiram Schenck breezed through the doors without knocking, his cheeks florid and what looked like hard-boiled egg crumbled over the lapels of his staid black merchant's suit. His pride struck Zoya like a blow, his confidence bright and buoying.

"Good morning," he declared, clapping his hands together. "By Ghezen's hand, this room is frigid."

"You're late."

"Am I? Duke Radimov serves a very fine lunch. A most excellent host indeed. Your king might take a page from his book."

Radimov and the other West Ravkans were entertaining Kerch's dignitaries in style. There had been rumblings of secession ever since the Fold had been destroyed and Ravka had been reunified. The west resented being saddled with the east's debts, and the threat of war with Fjerda had unraveled much of the diplomatic work Nikolai had done to woo them to his side. They didn't want to send their children to the front, and they didn't want their taxes going to a war they doubted the king could win.

"While you dine, Ravkan soldiers may be marching to their deaths."

Schenck patted his stomach, as if his digestion was essential to the war efforts. "Most distressing, of course."

Diplomacy, she reminded herself. *Pleasant.* Zoya met Kirigin's eye and gestured for him to pour the wine, an extraordinary vintage that had come straight from Kirigin's legendary cellars, one that was almost impossible to get in Schenck's home country.

"Join us for a glass, won't you?" said Kirigin. "This is a Caryevan wine, aged in clay."

"Is it really?" Schenck's eyes lit and he seated himself at the table. The Kerch Merchant Council preached restraint and economy, but Schenck had a clear taste for luxury. Zoya waited for him to drink and endured the nearly obscene look of pleasure that overtook the merchant's face. "Exceptional!" he declared.

"Isn't it?" said Kirigin. "I have several casks of it if you'd like me to send one your way. I'll have to get one of my servants to deliver it by hand, otherwise the travel will ruin it."

Zoya was grateful for the count's merry aptitude for small talk. It gave her a moment to gather her wits and resist the urge to slap the glass from Schenck's hand. If Ravka needed her to be gracious, she would damn well be gracious.

"I've heard tell Novyi Zem's sea routes have been all but obliterated," Zoya said, "their shipping interrupted, their ability to defend their ships undone."

"Yes, terrible. I hear their vessels have been reduced to little more than sticks upon the waves, nothing found but splinters. No survivors." Schenck was struggling to keep his face solemn, his glee straining his voice like an eager dog on a leash. "Pirates, you know."

"Of course." But these tragedies had not been the work of pirates. They had been the work of the Kerch, using Ravkan technology the Merchant Council had demanded for the courtesy of extending Ravka's loans. It allowed them to attack Zemeni ships without risk or concern for discovery, never emerging from beneath the waves to reveal themselves or become targets.

"The Zemeni economy must be suffering," Zoya noted. "I imagine the price of *jurda* and sugar must be at an all-time high."

At this, Schenck frowned. "No, not yet. The Zemeni have shown no signs of financial strain, and every attempt to raise the price of *jurda* has been met with resistance by our customers abroad. It's simply a matter of time before they capitulate."

"To pirates?"

Schenck fiddled with a button on his waistcoat. "Yes. Exactly. To pirates."

"You continue to trade *jurda* with Fjerda and the Shu Han," Zoya said. "Even though you know that *jurda* is being converted to *parem* and used to torture and enslave Grisha."

"We know no such thing. Idle speculation, colorful tales. The Kerch have always maintained a policy of neutrality. We cannot allow ourselves to be drawn into the squabbles of other nations. We trade with all, fair coin for fair purchase. The deal is the deal."

Zoya knew he was not just talking about the trade of *jurda*. He was making his country's stance clear.

"You won't come to Ravka's aid."

"I'm afraid that is impossible. But please know our thoughts are with you."

Zoya slanted him a glance. To a certain extent, she knew that was true. The Kerch didn't like war because it tended to disrupt shipping routes, and peaceful, prosperous countries made for better trade partners. But the Kerch could just as easily make their profits in weapons and ammunition, in the selling of steel and gunpowder, lead and aluminum.

"If Fjerda invades Ravka, are you sure the Shu will be able to keep them in check?" Zoya asked. The Shu had a massive land army, but no one knew the true extent of Fjerda's military might. Kerch might be next on their list of acquisitions.

Schenck just smiled. "Perhaps the wolves will have a few less teeth after a prolonged fight with their neighbor."

"So you're hoping we'll weaken Fjerda. You just aren't willing to help us do it. There are ships from the Kerch navy anchored off the northern coast. We have a flyer. There's time to send a message."

"We *could* rally our ships. If the Kerch had sent me here to offer aid to Ravka, that's precisely what we would do."

"But they didn't."

"No."

61

"They sent you to waste our time and keep me from where I belong."

"While I appreciate the wine and your charming company, I'm afraid I see no point to this meeting. You have nothing to bargain with, Miss—"

"General."

"General Nazyalensky," he said, like an uncle indulging his most precocious niece. "We have everything we want."

"Do you?"

Schenck's brow creased. "What does that mean?"

This was Zoya's last gamble, her last opportunity to salvage this parlay.

"Our king has a gift for making the impossible possible, for building extraordinary machines that can conquer new frontiers. He has assembled some of the greatest scientific minds among Grisha and otkazat'sya. Are you sure you want to be on the opposing side of that?"

"We choose no sides, Miss Nazyalensky. I thought I made that clear. And we do not bargain against the future. Ravka may have a gift for inventions we have not yet seen, but Fjerda has a gift for brutality the world well knows."

Zoya watched him for a long moment. "You were willing to wed your daughter to Nikolai Lantsov. You know he is a good man." Simple words, but Zoya was too aware of how rare they were.

"My dear," said Schenck, finishing his glass of wine and pushing back from the table. "Perhaps the Shu have lower standards, but I sought to wed my daughter to a king, not a bastard."

"Meaning what?" Zoya retorted, feeling her composure fray. Was this wart of a man brazen enough to question Nikolai's parentage openly? If that was the case, they were worse off than even she had thought.

But all Schenck did was smile slyly. "Only whispers. Only rumors."

"Be careful whispers don't become talk. It's a good way to lose a tongue."

Schenck's eyes widened. "Are you threatening a delegate of the Kerch government?"

"I only threaten gossipmongers and cowards."

Schenck's eyes bugged out even farther. Zoya wondered if they would bolt from his skull.

"I am due for a meeting," he said, rising and striding toward the door. "And I believe you are due on the losing side of a battlefield."

Zoya dug her nails into her palms. She could almost hear Nikolai in her head, counseling caution. All Saints, how did he meet with these spineless, self-satisfied toads without committing murder once a day?

But she managed. Only after Schenck was gone did she release a gust of air, hurling that fine bottle of Caryevan wine into the wall with a gratifying *smash*.

"Schenck never meant to offer us any help, did he?" asked Kirigin.

"Of course not. Schenck's only purpose was to humble us further."

Her king would face the Fjerdans and there would be no help from Hiram Schenck and his ilk. Nikolai had known the endeavor was futile but he had sent her nonetheless. *Do this gallows deed for me, Zoya*, he'd said. And of course, she had.

"Should we send a message to King Nikolai?" Kirigin asked.

"We'll deliver it ourselves," said Zoya. There might still be time to meet the Fjerdan tanks and guns beside her soldiers. She strode outside, where a servant was waiting. "Go, get our pilot to ready the flyer."

"Our bags?" Kirigin asked, hurrying after her down the hall.

"Forget the bags."

They rounded a corner and headed down a flight of stairs, through the courtyard, and out onto the docks where they'd landed their sea flyer. Zoya was not made for diplomacy, for closed rooms and polite talk. She was made for battle. As for Schenck and Duke Radimov and every other traitor who sided against Ravka, there would be time to deal with them after Nikolai found a way to win this war. *We are the dragon and we bide our time.*

"I . . . I have never been in the air," Kirigin said as they approached the docks where the flyer was moored. She should probably leave him here. He didn't belong anywhere near combat. But she also didn't want him under the influence of West Ravka's nobility.

"You'll be fine. And if you're not, just vomit over the side and not into your lap. Or mine."

"Is there any hope?" Kirigin asked. "For Ravka?"

She didn't reply. She'd been told there was always hope, but she was too old and too wise for fairy tales.

Zoya sensed movement before she actually saw it.

She whirled and glimpsed light glinting off the blade of a knife. The man was lunging at her from the shadows. She threw up her hands and a blast of wind hurled him backward into the wall. He struck with a bone-breaking crunch, dead before he hit the ground.

Too easy. A decoy—

Kirigin sprang forward, knocking the second assassin to the ground. The count drew his pistol to fire.

"No!" Zoya shouted, using another hard gust of wind to redirect the bullet. It pinged harmlessly off the hull of a nearby ship.

She leapt onto the assassin, pressing his chest into the deck with her knees, and closed her fist, squeezing the breath from his lungs. He clawed at his throat, face turning red, eyes bulging and watering.

She opened her fingers, letting air flood into his lungs, and he gasped like a fish freed of a hook.

"Speak," she demanded. "Who sent you?"

"A new age...is coming," he rasped. "The false Saints...will be...purged."

He looked and sounded Ravkan. Again she sucked the air from his lungs, then let it return in the barest trickle.

"False Saints?" said Kirigin, clutching his bloody arm.

"Who sent you?" she demanded.

"Your power...is unnatural and you will...be punished, Sankta Zoya." He spat the last two words like a curse.

Zoya hauled back and punched him in the jaw. His head drooped.

"Couldn't you have choked him unconscious?" asked Kirigin.

"I felt like hitting someone."

"Ah. I see. I'm glad it was him. But what did he mean by 'Sankta Zoya'?"

"As far as I know, I've worked no miracles nor claimed to." Zoya's eyes narrowed. She knew exactly who to blame for this. "Damn Nina Zenik."

6

NIKOLAI

"BLESS NINA ZENIK," Nikolai murmured as he walked the line of silent Ravkan troops camouflaged with mud and scrub. In the near dark before dawn, he'd taken his flyer up with Adrik—one of Zoya's most skilled Squallers—on board to dampen the sound of the engine. Fjerda thought they had the element of surprise, and Nikolai wanted to keep it that way.

But he had to wonder if his enemy needed it. From his vantage in the skies, he'd watched the line of tanks rolling toward Ravka in the gray dawn light. He supposed he should be praying, but he'd never been much for religion—not when he had science and a pair of well-made revolvers to cling to. Right now, though, he hoped that each Ravkan Saint, Kaelish sprite, and all-powerful deity was looking down with some fondness in their hearts for his country, because he needed every bit of help he could get against these odds.

"At least I only have one arm to lose," Adrik said glumly. For all his Grisha talent, he had to be the most depressing person Nikolai had ever encountered. He had sandy hair and a boyish freckled face, and he was the human equivalent of a head cold. Nikolai had no idea what Leoni saw in him. That woman was a delight and a hell of a Fabrikator too.

"Cheer up, Adrik," Nikolai had called back from the cockpit. "We may all be dead soon, and then it will be up to your disembodied spirit to make gloomy prognostications."

To avoid giving away their location, they'd set down on a makeshift airstrip two miles south of camp and ridden the rest of the way to join the Ravkan forces.

"How many?" asked Tolya as he approached and handed Nikolai a rifle, another slung over his enormous shoulders. They'd already had reports from their scouts, but Tolya still had hope. The same hope Nikolai had let himself entertain before his own eyes had been cruel enough to dash it.

"Too many," he said. "I was hoping it was a trick of the light." The ranks of Fjerdan war machines were far larger than their intelligence had suggested.

Tamar and Nadia greeted them silently, Nadia giving her brother a nod of acknowledgment. She and Adrik were both Squallers, both green-eyed and wiry. But Nadia was an optimist, and Adrik was a member of the doomsayers club—the one they didn't allow at meetings because he brought the mood down.

Nikolai checked the sight on his repeating rifle. It was the right weapon for when they needed to engage, but the revolvers at his hips gave him more comfort.

Fjerda and Ravka had been at odds for hundreds of years, sometimes meeting in outright conflict, sometimes skirmishing when treaties were in place. But this was the war Fjerda meant to win. They knew

Ravka was outnumbered and without reinforcements. They intended to tear through the northern border in surprise attacks at Nezkii and Ulensk. After swift victories, they would push south to the capital, where Nikolai's meager army would be forced to retreat and make some kind of heroic stand.

Nikolai looked out over the field. The land north of Nezkii was little more than a shallow, muddy basin, a sad stretch of nothing stuck in a state between swamp and pasture, impossible to farm and bearing a strong odor of sulfur. It was known as the Pisspot, and it was not the stuff of which glorious battle songs were written. It offered little cover and miserable soil for his foot soldiers, who were already up to their ankles in the muck. But he doubted it would stop Fjerdan tanks.

Nikolai's commanders had erected wooden platforms and towers to get a better view of the battlefield—all of it camouflaged behind the straggly scrub and low, twisted trees the Pisspot was known for.

The sun was barely visible in the east. From the north, Nikolai heard a sputtering sound like some great beast clearing its throat—Fjerda's war machines firing their angry engines to life. Black smoke rose on the horizon, an orchard of columns, a promise of the invasion to come.

The tanks sounded like thunder rolling over the horizon, but they looked like monsters that had crawled out of the mud, their gray hides glinting dully, their giant treads eating up earth. It was a disheartening sight, but if not for Nina, their blessed termite eating at the heart of Fjerda's government, Ravka never would have seen them coming at all.

Nina's note had given them the two points on the border where their enemies planned to launch their surprise invasion. Ravka had barely had time to mobilize their forces and put up some kind of defense.

Nikolai could have chosen to meet the enemy in the field, banners up, troops in plain sight. A show of force. It would have been the honorable thing, the brave thing. But Nikolai figured his soldiers were more interested in surviving than looking noble before the Fjerdans shot them full of holes, and he felt the same.

"Do you think they know?" Tolya asked, peering through binoculars that looked like a child's toy in his huge hands.

Tamar shook her head. "If they did, they'd be staying very, very still."

Boom. The first explosion echoed over the basin, seeming to shake the mud they stood in.

A silent signal moved down the ranks: *Hold your position.*

Another explosion ruptured the air around them. Then another. Another.

But those weren't the sounds of tank guns firing. They were mines.

The first Fjerdan tank burst into flames. The second capsized, rolling onto its side, its huge treads whirring helplessly. *Boom.* Another exploded in a plume of fire as its driver and crew tried to escape.

Fjerda had assumed their tanks would roll through the basin, that their attack would be quick and decisive, that Ravka would have no chance to mount any real opposition. They would occupy key northern cities and drive the front south as Nikolai's troops scrambled to meet them in the field.

They would have done just that—if not for Nina Zenik's warning. Hours before dawn, Fjerdan bombs had begun to fall on Ravkan military targets, places where they believed Ravkan flyers were grounded, a munitions factory, a shipyard. There had been nothing Nikolai could do about the shipyard; there simply wasn't time. But everywhere else, flyers and airships and personnel had been moved to new locations.

And while the Fjerdans were unleashing their bombs, Nikolai's special soldiers, his Nolniki—Grisha and First Army troops working together—had crept through the darkness of Nezkii and Ulensk, planting anti-tank mines under cover of night, an ugly surprise for an enemy who had believed it would face no resistance. The mines had been carefully mapped. One day Nikolai hoped they could call the Fjerdans friends, and he didn't want to render all their borderlands useless.

The battlefield was a grim site: smoke and mud, Fjerdan tanks reduced to hunks of still-burning metal. But the mines had slowed the enemy, not stopped them. The tanks that survived the explosions charged ahead.

"Masks on!" He heard the call go down the line from his First Army captains and Second Army commanders. They had every reason to believe those tanks wouldn't just be firing mortars but shells full of *jurda parem*, the gas that could kill ordinary men and instantly addict Grisha. "Prepare to engage!"

Nikolai looked to the skies. High above, Ravka's flyers patrolled the clouds, making sure the Fjerdans couldn't bomb their forces from the air and taking any opportunity to strafe the Fjerdan lines. Ravka's flyers were lighter, more agile. If only they had the money for more machines.

"Hold the line!" Adrik shouted. "Let them come to us."

"For Ravka!" Nikolai yelled.

"For the double eagle!" came the reply, soldiers' voices raised in solidarity.

Fjerdan troops armed with repeating rifles followed behind the tanks that had made it through the minefield, cutting a swath through the smoke and haze. They were met by Ravkan soldiers fighting side by side with Grisha.

Nikolai knew a king did not belong on the front lines, but he also knew he couldn't hang back and let others wage this war. His officers were mostly former infantry, grunts who had risen through the ranks and earned the respect of their men. There were the aristocrats too, but Nikolai didn't trust them in precarious positions. Old men like Duke Keramsov had fought in long-ago wars and could have provided valuable experience, but most had refused the call. Their fighting days were over. They'd built their homes and now they wanted to rest in their beds, tell stories of old victories, and complain about their aches and pains.

"On my command," he said.

"This is a terrible idea," moped Adrik.

"I have a surplus of bad ideas," said Nikolai. "I have to spend them somewhere."

Tamar touched her hands to her axes. When her bullets were spent, those would have to suffice. She signaled to her Heartrenders. Nadia signaled to her Squallers.

"Forward!" Nikolai shouted.

Then they were moving ahead, plunging into the fray. The Squallers drove back the Fjerdan tanks as the Heartrenders gave them cover. A squad of Inferni used the burning remnants of the tanks to create a wall of flame, another barrier the Fjerdan troops would have to breach.

All of the Ravkan forces wore gas masks specially crafted by Fabrikators to prevent the inhalation of *jurda parem*. The drug had changed everything, made the Grisha vulnerable in ways they had never been, but they refused to wear those masks as emblems of weakness or fragility. They'd painted them with fangs and curling tongues, gaping mouths. They looked like gargoyles descending onto the field in their combat *kefta*.

Nikolai stayed low, the rattle of gunfire filling his ears. He squeezed off a shot, another, saw bodies fall. The demon in him sensed the chaos and leaned toward it, hungry for violence. But even if the *obisbaya* hadn't purged Nikolai of the thing, it had given him better control. He needed cool strategy now, not a monster with a taste for blood.

Tolya's hands shot out, his fists closing, and Fjerdan soldiers dropped, their hearts bursting in their chests.

Nikolai almost let himself hope. If tanks and infantry were all the fight Fjerda had to offer, Ravka might stand a chance. But as soon as he saw the hulking machine lumbering onto the field, he knew Fjerda had more horrors in store. This wasn't a tank. It was a transport. Its huge treads kicked up dirt and mud, the roar of its engine shaking the air as it disgorged smoke into the gray sky. A mine went off beneath one of its huge treads, but the thing just kept coming.

Nikolai looked to the west. Had Zoya succeeded on her mission? Would rescue come?

This is the crossroads. This day would decide if Ravka had a chance or if Fjerda would blow through the border like a cold northern wind. If they failed this test, their enemy would know just how precarious Ravka's position was, just how strapped for cash, just how weakened. A victory, even a wobbly one, would buy his country some desperately needed time. But that would require reinforcements.

"They're not coming," said Tolya.

"They'll come," said Nikolai. *They have to.*

"We gave them everything they needed. Why would they?"

"Because an agreement must mean something, otherwise what are we all doing here?"

A high metal shriek sounded as the transport drew to a halt and its gigantic metal doors opened like the jaws of an ancient monster.

The dust cleared and a line of soldiers advanced from inside the transport. But they wore no uniforms, only ragged clothes, some of them barefoot. Nikolai knew instantly what they were—Grisha, addicted to *parem*. Their bodies were emaciated and their heads hung like wilted flowers on narrow stalks. But none of that would matter once they were dosed with the drug. He saw the cloud of orange gas puff toward them from spigots somewhere inside the transport. Instantly, they snapped to attention.

This was the moment Nikolai had been dreading, one he had hoped he could prevent.

Three of the dosed Grisha charged forward.

"Get down!" Nikolai yelled. The land before the enemy Grisha rose up in a rippling wave, mines exploded, tanks overturned. Ravkan soldiers were thrown over and buried beneath mountains of mud and rock.

"Squallers!" Nadia called to her troops, and she and Adrik were back on their feet, combining their strength to push rubble and earth aside, freeing their compatriots.

Then Nadia stumbled.

"Amelia!" she cried. The wind she'd summoned faltered. She was staring at one of the dosed Grisha, a slender girl with chestnut hair, dressed in little more than a faded smock, her sticklike legs jammed into heavy boots.

"Saints," Tamar said on a breath. "She's a Fabrikator. She vanished from a mission near Chernast."

Nikolai remembered. Nadia had worked side by side with her in the labs before her capture.

Tamar seized Nadia by the shoulder, pulling her back. "You can't help her now."

"I have to try!"

But Tamar didn't let go. "She's as good as dead. I'll put an axe in her heart before I let you fall into this trap."

Amelia and the other dosed Fabrikators raised their hands, about to cause another earthquake.

"I have a clear shot," said Tolya, his rifle raised.

"Hold," said Nikolai. Again he looked to the west, hoping— because hope was all they had left.

"Take the damned shot!" Adrik said.

Nadia struck him with a gust of air. "They can't make us kill our friends, our own kind! We're doing the Fjerdans' work for them."

"Those aren't our friends," Adrik snapped. "They're ghosts, sent back from the next life, haunted and hopeless and looking for blood."

Nikolai signaled for the second wave of fighters to engage as their flyers tried to get close enough to the Fjerdan lines to fire on the transport without being blown from the sky themselves.

And then he heard it, a sound that echoed with a steady *whump whump whump* like a beating heart, too even and unyielding to be thunder.

Every head turned to the west, to the skies, where three vast airships—larger than anything Nikolai had ever seen airborne— emerged from the clouds. Their hulls weren't emblazoned with Kerch's flying fish. They bore the orange stars of the Zemeni naval flag.

"They came," said Nikolai. "I think you owe me an apology."

Tolya grunted. "Just admit you weren't sure either."

"I was hopeful. That's not the same as unsure."

Nikolai had known Zoya's diplomatic mission to speak to the Kerch had been doomed from the start, as had she. The Kerch had always been led by one goal alone: profit, and they would remain neutral. But Ravka had needed to maintain the pretense of asking— quite desperately—for aid. They had needed Fjerda's and Kerch's spies to believe they were without allies.

Months before, Nikolai had given the Kerch exactly what they'd demanded: plans for how to build and arm *izmars'ya*, underwater ships that could be used to disrupt Zemeni trade routes and blow up Zemeni ships. And the Kerch had gone about doing just that. But what the Kerch didn't know was that those ships they'd so successfully destroyed had been empty of men and cargo. They were phantom ships, decoys sent out to sea to give the Kerch the illusion of success, while the Zemeni had moved their trade routes up into the clouds with Ravkan airship technology.

The Kerch could have the ocean. The Zemeni would take the sky. Ravka had kept its word and delivered exactly what the Kerch wanted, but not what they needed. That was a lesson Nikolai had learned from his demon.

"The Kerch are going to be furious when they find out," said Tamar.

"Making people happy isn't the province of kings," Nikolai noted. "Perhaps if I'd been born a baker or a puppeteer."

As they watched, doors at the base of the airships opened and a froth of fine powder gusted downward in a gray-green cloud.

"Squallers!" Nadia bellowed, her face beaming now, her cheeks wet with tears, as Ravkan flyers in the air and Grisha soldiers on the ground directed the powdery antidote onto the regiment of addicted Grisha.

The antidote drifted down onto them like a fine coating of frost and Nikolai saw them turn their palms up, confused. Then they tilted their heads to the sky, breathing deeply. They were like children seeing snow for the first time. They opened their mouths, held out their tongues. He saw them turn to one another as if waking from a nightmare.

"To us!" commanded Tamar as she and Tolya advanced, laying down cover for the Grisha prisoners with their rifles.

Arm in arm, the sickly Grisha stumbled toward the Ravkan lines, toward home and freedom.

The Fjerdan officers called for their soldiers to open fire on the deserting Grisha, but Nikolai's flyers were ready. They strafed the Fjerdan lines, forcing them to take cover.

Ravkan Grisha and soldiers moved forward to guide their weakened friends. Now they really did look like ghosts, strange spirits coated in silvery powder.

"Your Majesty?" Amelia said in confusion as Nikolai slung her arm around his shoulders. Her lashes were dusty with antidote, her pupils dilated.

Around them, Nikolai saw the Fjerdan ranks breaking in the tumult the Zemeni arrival had caused. The skies were thick with Ravkan and Zemeni flyers. Fjerda had lost their Grisha assassins, and half their tanks lay in smoldering pieces.

Nikolai and the others plunged back through the field, taking the Grisha prisoners with them. He handed Amelia off to a Healer, and then he was commandeering a horse and shouting to Tolya, "Come on!"

He wanted to see this from the air. When they reached the runway, they leapt into his flyer. It roared to life and they soared skyward.

The view from above was both heartening and terrible. The Fjerdan lines had broken and they were in retreat, but brief as the battle had been—barely a battle, a skirmish, really—the damage was shocking. The muddy basin below had been carved up by Grisha Fabrikators, the landscape pocked with deep wounds and furrows.

The dead lay scattered in the mud: Fjerdan soldiers, Ravkan soldiers, Grisha in their bright *kefta*, the frail bodies of the sickly prisoners who hadn't made it off the field.

It was just a taste of what was coming.

"This is going to be a different kind of war, isn't it?" Tolya asked quietly.

"If we don't stop it," said Nikolai as they watched the Fjerdans fall back.

This tiny victory wouldn't solve the problem of his parentage or fill their coffers or swell the ranks of their army, but at least the Fjerdans would have to recalibrate. Ravka couldn't afford to rig the entire northern border with mines. But Fjerda had no way of knowing that, so they would have to waste valuable time sweeping potential incursion points. They could no longer rely on *parem* as a weapon against Ravka's Grisha. And more importantly, the Zemeni had shown that Ravka was not alone. The Fjerdans had wanted to play quick and dirty. This day had shown them what this fight would really look like. *See what your country thinks of war now that your soldiers will have to bleed too.*

Nikolai let his flyer coast gently into the landing bay at the base of the largest airship, bringing it to an abrupt stop that taxed the little craft's brakes.

Kalem Kerko was there to greet him and Tolya. He wore blue fatigues, his hair in short twists.

"Your Highness," he said with a sharp bow.

Nikolai clapped Kerko on the back. "Let's not stand on ceremony." He had trained with Kerko's family when he was learning the work of gunsmiths, and he was not remotely surprised to see the ways in which the Zemeni had improved upon Ravkan airships. "You just saved our asses."

"You gave us the skies," said Kerko. "We can at least help you keep this miserable country. Will you pursue the Fjerdans? They're in retreat."

"We can't afford to. Not yet. But you've granted us valuable time."

"We'll travel with you to Poliznaya."

"The stockpile of antidote?" Nikolai asked.

Kerko gestured to a wall of what looked like grain sacks. "You can say that you hoped there would be more. I won't be offended. Your soldier's face shows the truth of it."

"Tolya always looks that way. Except when he's reciting verse, and no one wants that." Nikolai tallied the sacks of antidote and sighed. "But yes, we hoped there would be more."

"*Parem* is fairly easy to manufacture if someone manages the formula. But the antidote?" Kerko shrugged. "It requires too much raw *jurda*. Perhaps your Fabrikators can find a new way to process the plant."

The formula had been the work of David Kostyk, Ravka's most talented Materialnik, working with Kuwei Yul-Bo, the son of the very man who had invented *parem*. But the idea had come from the source of *jurda*, Novyi Zem, and a young boy who had grown up on a farm there. He'd told Kuwei that during the harvest, mothers would put balm from the stalks of the *jurda* plant on babies' lips and eyelids to prevent the pollen from affecting them.

"It takes a tremendous amount of the crop to create the antidote," said Kerko. "Worse, the harvesting of the stalks ruins the fields. If we keep pushing, our farmers will revolt. And there's something else. One of our suppliers reported a bizarre occurrence in his fields, a blight that seemed to come from nowhere. It turned two of his pastures to barren wasteland, and the livestock grazing there vanished like—"

"Smoke," finished Nikolai. So the vampire had sunk its teeth into Novyi Zem.

"Then you know of this plague? It's the second event of this kind our country has seen in two months. Are you witnessing its like in Ravka?"

"Yes," Nikolai admitted. "There was an occurrence near Sikursk and another south of Os Kervo. We're running experiments on the soil. We'll let you know what we discover."

But Nikolai knew what they would find: death. Nothing would grow in that soil again. And if this blight kept spreading, who knew where it might strike next or if it could be stopped? Even the thought of it was enough to rile the demon inside him, as if it recognized the power that had created it in the source of this destruction.

"Is it connected to the Fold?" asked Kerko.

Tolya looked surprised. "You've been there?"

"After the unification. I wanted to see it for myself. A cursed place."

That word again: *cursed.*

"There's a connection," said Nikolai. "We just don't know what it is yet." That much was true. And Nikolai wasn't prepared to tell Kerko that the Darkling had returned. "I'll escort you to Poliznaya. We can store the antidote on base."

"There will be retribution from the Kerch," warned Kerko as they walked back to the flyer. "For all of us. They'll find a way."

"We know," said Tolya solemnly. "And we know the risk you've taken by coming to our aid."

Kerko grinned. "They were willing to attack our ships and our sailors without ever raising the flag of war. The Kerch have never been friends to the Zemeni, and it's best they know we're not without friends either."

They shook hands, and Nikolai and Tolya climbed back into the flyer.

"Nikolai," said Kerko. "End this war and end it quickly. Show that Magnus Opjer is a liar and banish the Lantsov pretender. You must prove you're not a bastard and that you're fit to sit that throne."

Well, thought Nikolai as the engine of his flyer rumbled to life and they shot into the brilliant blue sky. *One out of two isn't bad.*

7
NINA

HELLO, NINA.

Nina was a trained covert operative. She'd made her way in the brothels of Ketterdam and run with the most dangerous thugs and thieves of the Barrel. She'd faced killers of every variety, and occasionally she chatted with the dead. But when the Wellmother spoke those words, Nina felt her heart plunge right out of her chest and slide all the way to her fur-lined slippers.

She only smiled.

"Mila," she corrected gently. A misheard name, an innocent mistake.

The Wellmother lifted her hand and a gust of wind made the lamplight flicker, glinting off the twinkle in her eyes.

"You're Grisha," whispered Nina in shock. A Squaller.

"Foxes go to ground in the winter," said the Wellmother in Ravkan.

"But they don't fear the cold," Nina replied.

She sat down on the sofa with a heavy thump. Her knees felt weak, and she was embarrassed to find tears in her eyes. She hadn't spoken her language in so long.

"Our good king sends his thanks and his regards. He's grateful for the intelligence you sent. It saved many Ravkan lives. And many Fjerdan lives too."

Nina wanted to weep with gratitude. She'd had contact with messengers and members of the Hringsa, but to talk to one of her people? She hadn't realized the weight she'd been carrying with her.

"Are you really from the convent?"

"Yes," the woman said. "When the previous Wellmother disappeared, Tamar Kir-Bataar took the opportunity to install one of her spies there. I was undercover at a convent in the Elbjen before that."

"How long have you been living this way? As a Fjerdan?"

"Thirteen years. Through wars and kings and coups."

Thirteen years. Nina couldn't fathom it. "Do you never . . . do you miss home?" She felt like a child asking.

"Every day. But I have a cause, just as you do. Your campaign of propaganda has been a bold one. I've seen the results myself. The girls under my care share stories of the Saints by moonlight."

"And they're punished for it?"

"Oh yes," she said with a laugh. "The more we forbid talk of the Saints, the more fervent and determined they become."

"Then I'm not in trouble?" She'd been following no order when she'd come to the Ice Court with Hanne and started staging miracles. After the stunt she'd pulled in Gäfvalle, she could have been dragged back to Ravka and court-martialed.

"General Nazyalensky said you would ask that and she said you absolutely are."

Nina had to restrain a laugh. "How is she?"

"Terrifyingly competent."

"And Adrik? Leoni?"

"Now that they're Saints, they're not fit for espionage work, but Adrik is commanding a team of Squallers and Leoni is working with David Kostyk's Fabrikators. She did essential work on the antidote to *jurda parem*."

"So," said Nina, "they're both stationed at the Little Palace."

A slight smile touched the Wellmother's lips. "I hear they're often in each other's company. But I didn't come to share gossip or offer comfort. The king has a mission for you."

Nina felt a spike of exhilaration. She'd defied direct orders from Adrik to come to the Ice Court, to put herself in the position to help Grisha and help Ravka. She'd done what she could with her phony miracles; she'd eavesdropped and used every wile in her possession to gather information, passing along coded letters full of whatever she'd managed to glean about troop movements and weapons development. But Brum's disclosure of the places Fjerda had intended to launch their invasion had been mere luck, not true spy work.

"Listen closely," the Wellmother said. "We don't have much time."

"She wants you to do what?" Hanne whispered, her copper eyes wide, when she returned to the rooms they shared and Nina described her mission. "And who did I just give my confession to?"

"A Grisha spy. What did you tell her?"

"I made up something about too many sweets and swearing on Djel's holy days."

Nina laughed. "Perfect."

"Not perfect," Hanne said with a wince. "What if I'd told her something personal about . . . something."

"Like what?"

"Nothing," said Hanne, her cheeks flushing. "What does she want you to do?"

The Wellmother's orders had been simple, but Nina had no idea how she was going to pull them off.

"Find out where the letters from Tatiana Lantsov are being kept."

"That part isn't so bad."

"And get close to the Lantsov pretender," Nina said. "Discover who he really is and if there's a way to discredit him."

Hanne bit her lip. They'd settled on her bed with hot tea and a tin of biscuits. "Couldn't we just . . . well, couldn't you just eliminate him?"

Nina laughed. "Easy now. I'm the ruthless assassin and you're the voice of reason, remember?"

"I think I'm being eminently reasonable. Is the Ravkan king really a bastard?"

"I don't know," Nina said slowly. "But if the Fjerdans prove he is, I'm not certain he'll be able to keep the Ravkan throne." In times of trouble, people tended to cling to tradition and superstition. Grisha cared less about royal blood, but even Nina had been raised to believe the Lantsovs had been divinely chosen to lead Ravka.

"And Vadik Demidov?" Hanne asked. "The pretender?"

"His death won't buy back Nikolai's legitimacy. But if he's shown to be a liar, it will cast doubt on the entire endeavor and everything the Fjerdan government has claimed. Only . . . how are we supposed to do that?"

Brum had close contact with Fjerda's royal family and presumably Demidov, but Nina and Hanne had only ever seen them from afar. The Brums dined occasionally with high-ranking soldiers and military officials, and Ylva sometimes went to play cards with the aristocratic women of the court. But that was a far cry from meeting people who could be mined for information on the Lantsov pretender.

Hanne stood and slowly paced the room. Nina loved who Hanne became when they were alone together. Around her parents, there was a tension in her, a hesitation, as if she was second-guessing every movement, every word. But when the door was closed and it was just the two of them, Hanne became the girl Nina had met in the woods, her gait loose and long, her shoulders freed from their rigid posture. Now Hanne's even white teeth worried her lower lip, and Nina found herself studying the movement like a piece of fine art.

Then Hanne seemed to reach some kind of decision. She strode to the door and opened it.

"What are you doing?" Nina asked.

"I have an idea."

"I can see that, but—"

"Mama?" Hanne called down the hall.

Ylva appeared a moment later. She'd taken her braids down and her hair hung in thick, ruddy brown waves, but it was clear she'd still been awake, probably discussing the Wellmother's visit with her husband.

"What is it, Hanne? Why are you two still up?"

Hanne gestured for her mother to enter, and Ylva sat down on the edge of the bed.

"The Wellmother got me thinking."

Nina's brows rose. *Oh, did she now?*

"I want to enter *Jerjanik*."

"What?" Ylva and Nina said in unison.

Jerjanik meant Heartwood, and it coincided with the winter festival of Vinetkälla, which had just begun. The name was a reference to Djel's sacred ash. But it really referred to the tradition of eligible young women being presented at court with the goal of making a marriage. The idea of Hanne participating was brilliant. It would throw them both into a six-week whirlwind of social events at court and potentially put her in the path of the very people who could lead them to Vadik Demidov. But Nina had thought . . . She didn't know what she'd thought. All she knew was the idea of Hanne being courted by a roomful of Fjerdan men made her want to kick something.

"Hanne," Ylva said cautiously. "This is not something to be entered into lightly. You will be expected to wed at the end of Heartwood. You've never wanted such a thing before. Why now?"

"I have to start thinking about the future. The Wellmother's visit . . . It reminded me of my wild ways. I want to show you and Papa that I'm beyond that now."

"You needn't prove yourself to us, Hanne."

"I thought you wanted me to join the court? To find a husband?"

Ylva hesitated. "Please don't do this to make us happy. I couldn't bear to think of you miserable."

Hanne sat down next to her mother. "What other options are open to me, Mama? I won't go back to the convent."

"I have a little money set aside. You could go north to the Hedjut. We still have relatives there. I know you're not happy cooped up at the Ice Court."

"Papa would never forgive you, and I won't see you punished for my sake." Hanne took a deep breath. "I want this. I want a life we can all be part of."

"I want that too," said Ylva. Her voice was barely a whisper as she hugged her daughter.

"Good," said Hanne. "Then it's decided."

Nina still didn't know what to think.

"Hanne," she said after Ylva had gone, "the ritual of Heartwood is binding. If you're offered a reasonable proposal, they're going to make you choose a husband."

"Who says I'll get any reasonable proposals at all?" Hanne said, wriggling beneath the covers.

A proposal would have to come from a man of equal social standing who could adequately provide for Hanne and who had the approval of her father.

"And what if you do?" Nina asked. Hanne didn't want that life. Or Nina didn't think she did. Maybe Nina just didn't want it for her.

"I don't know exactly," Hanne said. "But if we're going to help your king and stop a war, this is how we do it."

The preparations began the next morning in a whirl of fittings and lessons. Nina still wasn't sure this was the right choice, but if she was honest with herself, the chaos of readying for Heartwood was shockingly, horrifyingly . . . fun. She was distressed at how easy it was to get lost in the business of new gowns for Hanne, new shoes, dancing lessons, and discussions of the people they would meet at Maidenswalk, the first event of *Jerjanik*, where all the hopeful young ladies would be presented to the royal family.

Some part of Nina had missed frivolity. There had been too much sadness in the last two years—her struggle to free herself from addiction, losing Matthias, the long, lonely months in Ravka trying to cope with her grief, and then the constant fear of living among her enemies. Sometimes she wondered if she'd made a mistake leaving her friends in Ketterdam. She missed Inej's stillness, the knowledge that she could say anything to her without fear of recrimination. She missed Jesper's laughing ways and Wylan's sweetness. She even missed Kaz's ruthlessness. Saints, it would have been a relief to hand over this whole mess to the bastard of the Barrel. He'd have sussed out Vadik Demidov's origins, raided the Fjerdan treasury, and placed himself on the throne in the time it took Nina to braid her hair. On second thought, probably best Kaz wasn't here.

"You're enjoying this, aren't you?" Hanne asked, as she sat at their shared dressing table while Nina applied sweet almond oil to curl the short strands of her hair, red and gold and brown. A color she could never quite name.

"If I am?"

"I guess I'm jealous. I wish I could."

Nina tried to meet her eyes in the mirror, but Hanne kept her gaze trained on the array of powders and potions on the table. "This was your idea, remember?"

"Yes, but I forgot how much I hate all of it."

"What's to hate?" Nina asked. "Silk, velvet, jewels."

"Easy for you to say. I feel even more *wrong* than usual."

Nina couldn't believe what she was hearing. She wiped her hands clean of oil and sat down on the bench. "You're not an awkward little girl anymore, Hanne. Why can't you see how gorgeous you are?"

Hanne picked up one of the little jars of shimmer. "You don't understand."

"No, I don't." Nina plucked the jar from her fingers and turned Hanne toward her. "Close your eyes." Hanne obeyed and Nina dotted the cream onto her lids, then her cheekbones. It had a subtle, pearlescent sheen that made it look like Hanne had been dusted in sunlight.

"Do you know the only time I felt beautiful?" Hanne asked, her eyes still closed.

"When?"

"When I tailored myself to look like a soldier. When we cut off all my hair."

Nina exchanged the shimmer for a pot of rose balm. "But you didn't look like *you*."

Hanne's eyes opened. "But I did. For the first time. The only time."

Nina dipped her thumb into the pot of balm and dabbed it onto Hanne's lower lip, spreading it in a slow sweep across the soft cushion of her mouth.

"I can grow my hair, you know," Hanne said, and moved her hand over one side of her scalp. Sure enough, a reddish-brown curl twined over Hanne's ear.

Nina stared. "That's powerful tailoring, Hanne."

"I've been practicing." She drew a small scissors from a drawer and snipped away the curl. "But I like it the way it is."

"Then leave it." Nina took the scissors from her hand, brushed her thumb over Hanne's knuckles. "In trousers. In gowns. With your hair shorn or in braids or down your back. You have never not been beautiful."

"Do you mean that?"

"I do."

"I've never seen your real face," Hanne said, eyes scanning Nina's features. "Do you miss it?"

Nina wasn't sure how to answer. For a long while she'd startled every time she glimpsed herself in the mirror, when she caught sight of the pale blue eyes, the silky fall of straight blond hair. But the longer she played Mila, the easier it became, and sometimes that scared her. *Who will I be when I return to Ravka? Who am I now?*

"I'm beginning to forget what I looked like," she said. "But trust me, I was gorgeous."

Hanne took her hand. "You still are."

The door flew open and Ylva bustled in, trailed by maids, their arms full of dresses.

Hanne and Nina leapt up from the bench, watching the maids heap piles of silk and tulle onto the bed.

"Oh, Mila, you've worked wonders!" Ylva said when she saw Hanne's gilded cheeks. "She looks like a princess."

Hanne smiled, but Nina saw the way her fists clenched. *What have we gotten ourselves into?* Heartwood might give them everything they wanted—access to Vadik Demidov, a chance to locate Queen Tatiana's love letters. But what had seemed like a straight path felt more like a maze. Nina picked up the amber curl Hanne had dropped onto the dressing table and slipped it into her pocket. *Whatever happens, I'll find a way out,* she vowed. *For both of us.*

Maidenswalk took place in the grand ballroom in the royal palace, just a short walk from their rooms on the White Island. Nina had been here before in a different disguise, dressed as a member of the notorious Menagerie. That had been during Hringkälla, a raucous party full of indulgence. This afternoon was a more staid affair. Noble families packed the alcoves. A long, pale gray carpet stretched the length of the room, pausing at a giant fountain in the shape of two dancing wolves, and then rolling on to the dais where the royal family sat. Gathered there, the Grimjers looked like a beautiful collection of dolls—all blond, blue-eyed, and sylphlike. They liked to claim Hedjut blood, and the evidence could be seen in the tawny warmth of the king's complexion and the younger son's thick curls. The little boy was tugging on his mother's elegant hand as she laughed at his antics. He was sturdy and rosy-cheeked. The same could not be said for the crown prince. Prince Rasmus, lanky and sallow, looked almost green against the alabaster throne he sat beside his father.

Through a tall, peaked window, Nina could just see the gleam of the moat that surrounded the White Island, covered in a thin

skin of frost. The moat itself was ringed by a circle of buildings—
the embassy sector, the prison sector, and the *drüskelle* sector—all
of them protected by the Ice Court's supposedly impenetrable wall.
It was said the capital had been built to symbolize the rings of Djel's
sacred ash, but Nina preferred to think of it the way Kaz had: the
rings of a target.

The young women participating in Heartwood gathered with
their parents in the back of the ballroom.

"They're all staring at me," said Hanne. "I'm too old for this."

"No, you are not," said Nina. It was true that most of the girls
seemed to be a few years younger, and they were all shorter.

"I look like a giant."

"You look like the warrior queen Jamelja come down from the
ice. And all these little girls with their simpers and blond curls look
like undercooked puddings."

Ylva laughed. "That's unkind, Mila."

"You're right," said Nina, then added beneath her breath, "But it's
also accurate."

"Hanne?" A pretty girl in pale pink wearing enormous diamonds
approached them. "I don't know if you remember me. I was at the
convent two years ago."

"Bryna! Of course I remember, but I thought . . . What are you
doing here?"

"Trying to catch a husband. I've been traveling with my family
since I left the convent, so I'm a bit late to all of this."

Ylva smiled. "Then you can be late together. We'll leave you now,
but we'll be waiting for you after the processional."

Nina gave Hanne a wink, and then she and Ylva went to join
Brum, where he stood with a general and an older *drüskelle* named
Redvin, who had trained with Brum in their youth. He was a spite-
ful, humorless stick of a man, and his constant demeanor of bitter

resignation entertained Nina to no end. She delighted in being as ridiculous as possible around him.

"Isn't it all glorious, Redvin?" she exclaimed breathlessly.

"If you say so."

"Don't they all look just splendid?"

"I hadn't noticed."

He looked like he wanted to hurl himself over a cliff rather than spend another minute with her. A girl had to take her pleasures where she could.

Brum handed Nina a glass of sickly sweet punch. If he was troubled by the Fjerdan defeats at Nezkii and Ulensk, he hid it well. *It would have been nice to string up the fox on our first hunt,* he had said when he returned from the front. *But now we know what the Ravkan forces can do. They won't be ready for us next time.*

Nina had smiled and nodded and thought to herself, *We'll see.*

"Is it hard to watch another woman swathed in silks and made the center of attention?" he asked, his voice low and uncomfortably intimate.

"Not when it's Hanne." That had come out with an edge on it, and she felt Brum stiffen beside her. Nina bit her tongue. Some days meekness was harder than others. "She is a good soul and deserves every indulgence. These luxuries are not meant for such as me."

Brum relaxed. "You deal unfairly with yourself. You would look most fetching in ivory silk."

Nina wished she could blush on command. She had to settle for a maidenly giggle and staring down at the toes of her shoes. "The fashions of the court are far more suited to Hanne's figure."

Nina expected Brum to wave away her talk of fashion, but instead the glint in his eye was calculating. "You are not wrong. Hanne has flourished under your tutelage. I never believed she could make much of a match, but you've changed all of that."

Nina's gut twisted. Maybe she *was* jealous. The idea of Hanne being paired off with some nobleman or military commander tied her stomach in knots. But what if Hanne could be happy here, happy with her family, with a husband to love her? What if she could finally find the acceptance she'd sought for so long? Besides, it wasn't as if she and Nina were going to have a future together, since Nina had every intention of murdering her father.

"You look so fierce," Brum said with a laugh. "Where do your thoughts carry you?"

To your prolonged humiliation and early death. "I hope she finds someone worthy of her. I only want the best for Hanne."

"As do we both. And we shall have some new dresses cut for you as well."

"Oh no, that isn't necessary!"

"It is what I wish. Would you deny me?"

I would push you into the sea and do a jig as you drowned. But Nina turned her eyes up to him, wide and thrilled, a young woman flustered and overwhelmed by a great man's attention. "Never," she said on a breath.

Brum's eyes strayed slowly over her face, her neck, and lower. "Fashion may favor a trimmer figure, but men do not care for fashion."

Nina wanted to crawl right out of her skin, but she knew this game now. Brum wasn't interested in beauty or desire. All he cared about was power. It excited him to think of her as prey, pinned by his gaze as a wolf might trap a lesser creature with its paw. It pleased him to think of offering Mila gifts she could never afford, of making her grateful.

So she would let him. Whatever it took to find Vadik Demidov, to help the Grisha, to free her country. A reckoning was coming. She was not going to forgive Brum for his crimes even as he sought to commit new ones. Whatever she might feel for Hanne, she intended to see Brum dead, and she doubted Hanne would be able to forgive her for that. The divide was too great. The Shu had a saying, one she'd always liked: *Yuyeh sesh.* Despise your heart. She would do what had to be done.

"You are too good to me," she simpered. "I am not deserving."

"Let me be the judge of that."

"They're beginning!" said Ylva giddily, oblivious to the overtures her husband was making mere feet from her. Or was she? Maybe she was glad to have Brum's attention elsewhere. Or maybe she'd overlooked the man's flaws for so long that it had become a well-worn habit.

Nina was glad for the interruption. It gave her a chance to assess the crowd in the ballroom as one by one the girls approached the fountain at the center of the room, where they were met by the crown prince. Prince Rasmus was of average height for a Fjerdan, but eerily gaunt, his face a portrait in angles, the cheekbones high and sharp. He had only just turned eighteen, but his slight build and the tentative way he moved gave him the look of someone much younger, a sapling that wasn't quite used to the weight of its branches. His hair was long and golden.

"Is the prince ill?" Nina asked quietly.

"Every day of his life," Brum said with contempt.

Redvin shook his grizzled head. "The Grimjers are a warrior's line. Only Djel knows how they shat out a weakling like that."

"Don't say that, Redvin," said Ylva. "He endured a terrible illness when he was a child. It was a blessing he survived."

Brum's expression was unforgiving. "It would have been a greater mercy if he'd perished."

"Would you follow that boy into battle?" Redvin asked.

"We may have to," said Brum. "When the old king passes."

But Nina didn't miss the look that Brum exchanged with his fellow *drüskelle*. Would Brum consider colluding against the prince?

Nina tried not to look too interested and kept her attention on the processional of young women. Once each girl reached the fountain, she curtsied to the royal family observing from the dais beyond, and then curtsied again to the prince. Prince Rasmus took a pewter cup from a tray held by a servant beside him, dipped it into the fountain, and offered it to the girl, who drank deeply of Djel's waters before returning the cup, curtsying once more, then backing down the aisle the way she'd come—careful never to turn her back on the Grimjer royals—where she was greeted by family and friends.

It was an odd little ritual, meant to mark Djel's blessing over the season of balls and dances to come. But Nina's focus was only partially devoted to the monotonous parade. The rest was given over to the crowd. It didn't take her long to spot the man she knew must be Vadik Demidov. He stood close to the dais in a position of privilege, and Nina felt a shock of rage when she saw he wore a sash of pale blue and gold emblazoned with the Ravkan double eagle. *The Little Lantsov.* He bore a striking resemblance to the portraits she'd seen in the halls of the Grand Palace. Maybe too close a resemblance. Had they found a Grisha Tailor to make him look like Nikolai's father? And if so, who was he really? Nina was going to have to get close enough to him to find out.

Her gaze moved on and met another pair of eyes staring directly at her—their irises so dark they seemed almost black. A chill spread over Nina's body. She forced herself to ignore the Apparat's piercing stare, to keep her attention roving over the crowd, an interested bystander and nothing more. But she felt as if a cold hand had closed over her heart. She knew the priest had come to the Fjerdan court, that he had forged an alliance to back Vadik Demidov, but she hadn't expected to see him here. *There's no way for him to recognize you*, she told herself. And yet his gaze had certainly felt knowing. She had to hope his interest was only in Brum's household.

Ylva's slender fingers dug into Nina's arm. "It's time!" she whispered excitedly. Hanne was next to make the walk down the aisle. "Her dress is perfect."

It was—a high-necked gown of copper beads and long strings of rosy river pearls that ideally suited Hanne's coloring. Hanne's shorn head was shocking, but they'd chosen not to hide it with a scarf or headdress. Between the decadent gown and the austere beauty of Hanne's features, the effect was striking. She looked like a statue cast in molten metal.

As Hanne waited for the previous girl to finish her return, her eyes flickered around the room in panic. Nina wasn't sure if Hanne could actually see her in the crowd, but she concentrated on her friend, sending every bit of strength her way.

The smallest smile touched Hanne's full lips, and she glided forward.

"*Ulfleden*," Ylva said. "Do you know what that means?"

"Is it Hedjut?" Nina asked. She'd never learned the dialect.

Ylva nodded. "It means 'wolf-blooded.' It's a compliment among the Hedjut, but not so much here. When a child is odd or behaves strangely, they say 'her place is with the wolves.' It's a kind way of saying she doesn't belong."

Nina wasn't sure how kind it was, though it made a sort of sense for Hanne, who would always be happiest beneath a wide sky.

"But Hanne has found her place here now," said Brum proudly, watching her measured steps along the gray carpet.

When she reached the fountain, Prince Rasmus handed her the pewter cup and smiled. Hanne took it; she drank. The prince coughed, hiding his face in his sleeve—and kept coughing.

The queen shot up from her throne, already shouting for help.

The prince crumpled. Guards were moving toward him. There was blood on the prince's lips; a fine spray of it spattered over Hanne's beaded gown. She had him in her arms, and her knees buckled as they fell to the floor together.

8
NIKOLAI

ONCE THE ANTIDOTE HAD been delivered to Poliznaya, Nikolai and the others said goodbye to the Zemeni forces and began the ride to Os Alta. Adrik and Nadia would remain at Nezkii for a time.

"To enjoy the scenery," Adrik had said, gesturing at the muddy, miserable landscape.

But Nikolai wanted a chance to think and their flyers needed repairs, so he, Tamar, and Tolya would ride. Messages were waiting for him on base at Poliznaya, confirming what his early scouts had reported: With the help of the Zemeni, General Raevsky had routed Fjerda at Ulensk. Ravka's northern shipyards and bases had taken the brunt of the damage from Fjerda's bombings. Thankfully, Fjerdan flyers were too heavy and too fuel-hungry to venture farther south, so many of Ravka's potential military targets remained out of range.

Victory at Nezkii and Ulensk had bought them a chance, time to get their missiles working, build up their fleet of flyers, and most importantly, deal with the Shu. The upcoming nuptials would help to stave off Queen Makhi, and maybe, if he could finesse this elaborate bit of diplomacy, make them allies. The price would be steep, but for Ravka, he would pay it.

Nikolai was dictating a reply to General Raevsky, and trying to ignore the noise of Tolya and Tamar sparring outside the stables, when he sensed her. What they had endured on the Fold had connected them in some way, and he knew he would see Zoya when he turned—yet the sight of her struck like a sudden change in the weather. A drop in temperature, the crackle of electricity in the air, the feeling of a storm coming on. The wind lifted her black hair, the blue silk of her *kefta* whipping around her frame.

"Your heart is in your eyes, Your Highness," murmured Tamar, wiping the sweat from her brow.

Tolya poked his twin in the arm with a sparring sword. "Tamar knows because that's the way she looks at her wife."

"I am free to look at my wife any which way I please."

"But Zoya is *not* Nikolai's wife."

"I'm standing right here," said Nikolai. "And there is nothing in my eyes except the never-ending dust you two kick up."

He was glad to see his general. There was nothing out of the ordinary about that. Her presence brought a perfectly understandable relief, a feeling of calm that came with knowing that whatever the problem was, they would best it, that if one of them faltered, the other would be there to drag them along. That comfort was not something he could afford to get used to or rely on, but he would enjoy it while he might. If only she weren't wearing that damned blue ribbon again.

"I hear someone tried to kill you," Tamar called as Zoya drew near.

"Neither the first nor the last," Zoya said. "One of the assassins is still alive. I've had him sent along to Os Alta for questioning."

"He's one of the Apparat's?"

"That's my guess. I hear we won."

"I'd call it a draw," said Tolya.

Nikolai signaled for another horse to be brought around. He knew the mare Zoya preferred, a swift-hooved creature named Serebrine. "The Fjerdans are not currently marching toward our capital," he said. "I'll call it a victory."

"Then enjoy it," Tolya said, climbing atop his huge gelding.

"People only say that when they know it won't last."

"Of course it won't last," said Zoya. "What does?"

"True love?" suggested Tamar.

"Great art?" said Tolya.

"A proper grudge," replied Zoya.

"We've bought time," admitted Nikolai. "Not peace." They had to neutralize Queen Makhi before Fjerda chose to act again. And Fjerda would, Nikolai had no doubt of that.

When Zoya had mounted, they joined their armed escort and rode out of the gates. For a while, they took to the roads in silence, not speaking, only the sound of the wind and their horses' hooves to keep them company. They slowed when they reached a creek to let their mounts drink and stretch their legs. Then it was back onto the road at a trot. They were all eager to reach the capital.

"We have an advantage and we should press it," said Zoya when she couldn't contain herself anymore. Nikolai had known this was coming. "Fjerda didn't expect us to push back so hard. We should keep up the pressure while their forces are scrambling."

"Are you so eager to see good men die?"

"If it will save the children of those men and countless others, I'll lead the charge."

"Give me a chance to build this peace," said Nikolai. "I have a gift for folly—let me indulge it. We have daily sorties flying along the border and we've bolstered our forces there. This invasion was meant to be the tip of the arrow for Fjerda. Now that arrow is broken and they'll have to rethink their approach."

Fjerda had two great advantages: the size of their army and the speed at which they were able to turn out tanks. Nikolai could admit the tanks were well built too. They had a bad tendency to explode due to the fuel they used, but they were sturdier and faster than those his engineers had managed, even with Grisha Fabrikators in the lab.

"David's mines will only buy us so much time," said Tamar. "Once they've figured out how to track the metals, they'll be sweeping the border."

"It's a long border," noted Tolya.

"True," said Nikolai. "And it has more gaps than my aunt Ludmilla's teeth."

Zoya shot him a dubious glance. "Did you actually *have* an aunt Ludmilla?"

"I did indeed. Hideous woman. Prone to stern lectures and handing out black licorice as a treat." He shuddered. "May the Saints watch over her."

"The point is we only have a short amount of time," said Tolya.

Tamar clicked her tongue. "Hopefully enough time to forge this alliance with the Shu."

Nikolai didn't like to think of everything that might go wrong in the meantime. "Let us all pray to our Saints and the spirits of our bilious aunts."

"If we could get more flyers in the air, none of it would matter," said Tamar.

But like everything, that took money. They also had a shortage of trained pilots.

Zoya scowled. "None of it *will* matter if we have to fight a war on two fronts. We need a treaty with the Shu."

"The wheels are already in motion," said Tamar. "But if Princess Ehri isn't willing—"

"She'll be willing," Nikolai promised with more surety than he felt.

"The Fjerdans could rally more quickly than we think," said Tamar. "And West Ravka could still move to secede."

She wasn't wrong. But maybe their successes on the border would help West Ravka remember that there was no east or west, only one country—a country with friends and resources.

Tolya looped his reins over the horn of his saddle so that he could tie back his black hair. "If the Fjerdans do make a rash move, will the Kerch back them?"

They all looked to Zoya.

"I think the Merchant Council will be divided," she said at last. "Hiram Schenck was feeling very smug about Kerch's neutrality, and they've always preferred covert operations to outright war. But when the full breadth of our betrayal regarding the Zemeni becomes clear—"

"'Betrayal' seems an unfair word," said Nikolai.

"Double cross?" suggested Tolya. "Deception?"

"I didn't *lie* to the Kerch. They wanted technology that would give them dominion over the seas. They said nothing about the air. And honestly, taking two elements for yourself seems a bit greedy."

Zoya's brows rose. "You forget that in Kerch greed is a virtue."

They emerged over a crest and the famous double walls of Os Alta came into view. It was called the Dream City, and when its white spires were seen from this distance, away from the clamor of the lower town and the pretense of the upper town, one could almost believe it.

Tamar stood up in her stirrups, stretching her back. "The Kerch may offer to support Vadik Demidov behind the scenes."

"The Little Lantsov," murmured Zoya.

"Is he short?" asked Nikolai.

Tamar laughed. "No one has thought to ask. But he *is* young. Just turned twenty."

There was only one real question for Nikolai to ask. "And is he actually a Lantsov?"

"My sources can't confirm or deny," Tamar said. She had built up Ravka's intelligence network, recruiting spies who wished to defect, training soldiers and Grisha who could be tailored to take on covert missions, but there were still plenty of holes in their information gathering. "I'm hoping the Termite will have better luck."

Nikolai saw the way Zoya's lips flattened at that. She had never quite forgiven him for letting Nina remain at the Ice Court, but she couldn't argue with the value of the intelligence their spy had delivered.

They passed through the gates and began the slow climb up the hill through the market and on to the bridge that would take them to the fine houses and parks of the upper town. People waved at Nikolai and his guards, shouted "Victory for Ravka!" News of their wins at Nezkii and Ulensk had begun to trickle in. *This is only the start*, he wanted to warn the hopeful people crowding the streets and leaning out of their windows. But all he did was smile and return their greetings.

"Most of the Lantsov line was wiped out the night of my ill-fated birthday party," Nikolai said as he waved. He didn't like to think of the night when the Darkling had attacked the capital. He'd disliked his brother Vasily, but he hadn't been prepared to watch him die. "Still, there must be obscure cousins."

"And is Demidov one of them?" asked Tolya.

Tamar shrugged. "He claims he's from the household of Duke Limlov."

"I remember visiting there as a child," said Nikolai.

"Was there a boy named Vadik?" Zoya asked.

"Yes. He was a little shit who liked to taunt the cat."

Tamar snorted. "It seems he's taken to hunting bigger game."

Maybe this boy was a Lantsov. Maybe he was the valet's son. He might have a claim to the throne or he might just be a pawn. Why should a name give him some right to rule Ravka? And yet, it did. The same was true of Nikolai. He wasn't a king because he could build ships or win battles. He was a king because of his supposed Lantsov blood. His mother had been a Fjerdan princess, a younger daughter sent far from home to forge an alliance with Ravka that no one intended to adhere to. And Nikolai's true father? Well, if his mother was to be believed, he was a Fjerdan shipping magnate of common blood named Magnus Opjer—the same man who had recently provided Nikolai's enemies with his mother's love letters. It was bad enough Opjer cared nothing for the bastard son he'd sired, but to add insult to injury by trying to deny him a perfectly good throne? It spoke of a fundamental lack of manners.

Nikolai had sent his parents into exile in Kerch's Southern Colonies during the civil war. It hadn't been an easy decision. But his father hadn't been a popular king and the army had begun to desert rather than follow him. When the extent of his crimes against Genya Safin had been revealed, Nikolai had given his father a choice: face trial for rape or relinquish his crown and go into permanent exile. It was not how Nikolai had wanted to become king, and he supposed he would never know if it was the right choice.

They passed over the bridge and onto the Gersky Prospect, where couples strolled in the park and nannies pushed children in prams. This place couldn't have seemed farther from the muddy battlefield they'd left behind. And yet, if they'd failed at Nezkii or Ulensk, Fjerdan tanks would be rolling toward these grand thoroughfares and green parks right now.

The palace gates emblazoned with the gold double eagle opened to them, and only when they clanged shut did Nikolai let himself breathe a sigh of relief. There were times when he'd resented these manicured grounds, the many-tiered wedding cake of terraces and gilding that was the Grand Palace. He'd been embarrassed by its excesses and exhausted by its demands. But the last time he'd ridden out, it had been no sure thing he would return. He was grateful to be alive, grateful his most trusted friends were safe, grateful for the cold winter air and the crunch of gravel beneath his horse's hooves.

When they reached the palace steps, a group of servants approached to take their horses. "Rostik," he said, greeting the groom. "How are my favorite members of the royal household?"

The groom smiled. "Avetoy was favoring one of his back legs last week, but we got him healed up right. Did Punchline do his best for you?"

Nikolai gave the horse a fond pat. "I think he's rather majestic in this light."

He heard a loud pop, like a cork being loosed from a bottle, then another. A shout from somewhere inside the palace.

"Gunshots!" said Tamar.

Nikolai shoved the groom behind him and drew one of his revolvers.

"Stay down," he told Rostik.

Tolya and Tamar moved to flank him, and Zoya's arms were already raised in combat stance. The royal guards arrayed themselves at the base of the stairs.

"Nikolai," said Tolya, "we need to get you out of here. There are flyers moored at the lake."

But Nikolai had no intention of running. "Someone is in my house, Tolya. They're shooting at my people."

"Your Highness—"

"All Saints," Zoya gasped.

The Tavgharad flooded onto the steps, fanning out in a fighting formation.

There were eleven of them, all women, wearing black uniforms marked by carnelian falcons. Two of them had taken rifles from palace guards, but even unarmed, they were some of the deadliest soldiers in the world.

"Ehri, what are you doing?" Nikolai asked carefully.

Princess Ehri Kir-Taban stood at the center of their formation in a green velvet gown and coat—traveling clothes. This was not another assassination attempt. It was something else entirely.

Ehri's pointed chin lifted high. "Nikolai Lantsov, we will be your captives no longer."

"So the courtship is going well?" Zoya muttered.

"I see," said Nikolai slowly. "Where is it you plan to go?"

"Home," she declared.

"And how did your friends get free?"

"I . . ." Her voice wavered. "I struck a guard. I don't think I killed him. The rest was easy."

That was Nikolai's fault. He'd kept the Tavgharad behind bars in the palace dungeon, but he'd given Ehri free use of the upper floors of the palace, the gardens. He hadn't wanted her to feel like a prisoner. Now, he suspected at least two of his guards were dead, and he didn't want to see more violence done this day.

Nikolai holstered his weapon and stepped forward, hands raised.

"Please," he said. "Be reasonable, Princess. You cannot hope to escape. There are too many miles between you and the Sikurzoi."

"You will provide us transport. You cannot harm us without incurring the wrath of my sister and all of Shu Han. The wedding you desire is a sham and a travesty."

"I can't argue with that," Nikolai admitted. "But have I been cruel to you? Treated you unfairly?"

"I . . . No."

A look passed from one member of the Tavgharad to the next. Inside him the demon snarled. Something was wrong. He was missing something right in front of him.

The Tavgharad guard with the rifle set down her weapon, but it was hardly a gesture of peace. Her expression looked carved from stone.

"What is that smell?" said Zoya.

"I don't smell anything," said Tolya.

Zoya fluttered her fingers and a bare breeze wafted toward them from the steps.

"Accelerant," said Tamar, edging closer to the stairs. "Their clothes are soaked."

Understanding and terror struck Nikolai. They couldn't mean to . . .

"Set us free!" demanded Ehri. "Queen Makhi will never stand for—"

"Ehri, move away from them," he said, watching one of the Tavgharad reach into her pocket. "This is not an escape. This is—"

"I will never—"

107

"Ehri!"

But it was too late. The Tavgharad guard who had put down her rifle shouted something in Shu. Nikolai glimpsed the match in her hand.

One by one, the Tavgharad burst into flame, each of them a torch engulfed in golden fire. All of it too fast, a slide of keys on the piano, a sudden doomed flourish.

"No!" Nikolai cried, rushing forward. He saw Ehri's shocked face, the flames racing up her skirts as she screamed.

Zoya acted in an instant, a rush of cold wind extinguishing the fire in a single icy blast. It wasn't enough. Whatever the Tavgharad had doused themselves with had worked too well. Ehri was on the ground, screaming. The others were silent heaps of charred flesh and ash. His servants were crying out in terror and the palace guards stood frozen in disbelief.

Nikolai's hands and forearms were badly burned where he'd tried to grab Ehri, his clothing clinging to his smoking flesh. But it was nothing compared to what had happened to the princess. Her skin was scorched black, and where the top layer of flesh was burned away, her limbs were red and wet. Nikolai could feel the heat radiating from her body. She was shaking, her screams stuttering as she convulsed, her body going into shock.

"Tamar, drop her pulse and put her into a coma," Nikolai commanded. "Tolya, get a Healer."

Ehri's screams went silent as Tamar knelt and did her work.

"Why would they do this?" Zoya said, her face stricken as she took in the sudden carnage, the burned piles of blood and bone that had been women mere moments before.

Tamar's hands were trembling as she monitored Ehri's pulse. "We gave her too much freedom. We should have kept her in the dungeons, sent the Tavgharad to the brig at Poliznaya."

"She didn't know," said Nikolai, looking down at Ehri's ruined flesh, the hitching rise and fall of her chest. They had to get her to the infirmary. "She didn't know. I saw it on her face. The accelerant was only on the hem of her robes."

"Where did they even get it?" asked Zoya.

Nikolai shook his head. "From the kitchens when they escaped? It's possible they made it themselves."

Tamar rose as Tolya returned with a stretcher borne by two Corporalki in their red *kefta*. Their faces showed their dismay, but if anyone could heal Ehri, the Grisha could.

Nikolai stood on the steps, surrounded by death, watching Ehri and her keepers disappear in the direction of the Little Palace.

"Why?" Zoya said again.

"Because they are Tavgharad," Tamar replied. "Because they serve their queen unto death. And Ehri is no queen."

9

ZOYA

ZOYA HOVERED BY THE WINDOW in Nikolai's bedroom, watching the winter wind play over the palace grounds, as it made the bare branches rattle and sigh as if resigned to the dark days to come. The gardens looked bleak at this time of year, before snow fell to soften them. Ehri had been taken to the Little Palace, where she would be seen to by the same Grisha Healers who had brought her double, Mayu Kir-Kaat, back from the brink of death only weeks before.

Behind her, she heard Nikolai draw a swift breath. He was lying atop his covers as a Healer tended to his burns. She'd seen to his hands first, where the worst of the damage had been, but the rest would take far longer.

Zoya went to his side. "Can't you give him something more for the pain?"

"I gave him the strongest draught I could," said the Healer. "Anything else he won't wake up from. I could put him into a coma, but—"

"No," Nikolai said, his eyes fluttering open. "I hate that feeling."

Zoya knew why. When he'd been fighting the demon, she'd used a powerful sleeping tonic to knock him out every night for months. He'd said it felt like dying.

The Healer filled a bowl with some sharp-smelling solution. "It would be easier to put him under. I can't have him moving around while I work."

Zoya sat down beside Nikolai on the bed, trying not to jostle him.

"You must be still," she murmured.

"Don't go."

He shut his eyes and gripped her hand in his. Zoya knew the Healer had noticed it, knew he would probably gossip about it later. But she could weather the gossip. Saints knew she'd endured worse. And maybe she needed to feel his hand in hers after the shock of what they'd witnessed. She couldn't stop seeing those women burn.

"You shouldn't be here for this," said the Healer. "It's an ugly process."

"I'm not going anywhere."

The Healer flinched and Zoya wondered if the dragon had emerged, shining silver in her eyes. Let him gossip about that too.

Nikolai clung to her hand as the Healer stripped the ruined flesh from his arm. Only then could it be replaced with healthy skin. It seemed to take hours, first one arm, then the other. Whenever Zoya left the king's side—to fetch a cool cloth for his head, to turn up the lanterns so that the Healer had better light—Nikolai would open his eyes and mutter, "Where is my general?"

"I'm here," she repeated, again and again.

Once the Healer had dealt with the singed flesh of his arms, no hair remained on them, but the scars on his hands—the veins of shadow the Darkling had left—were still visible.

"He'll need to rest," said the Healer, rising and stretching when the work was done. "But the damage was fairly superficial."

"And Princess Ehri?" Zoya asked.

"I don't know. Her burns were much more severe."

Once the Healer was gone, Zoya waited for Nikolai's breathing to turn deep and even. Dusk had fallen. Outside the lanterns in the garden were being lit, a string of stars strewn across the grounds. She had missed this room, who Nikolai became in this room, the man who for a moment might let the mantle of king fall away, who trusted her enough to close his eyes and fall into dreams as she stood watch. She needed to get back to the Little Palace, check on Princess Ehri, talk to Tamar, forge a plan. But this might be the last time she saw him this way.

At last she rose and turned down the lights.

"Don't go," he said, still half asleep.

"I have to bathe. I smell like a forest fire."

"You smell like wildflowers. You always do. What can I say to make you stay?" His words trailed off into a drowsy mumble as he fell back asleep.

Tell me it's more than war and worry that makes you speak those words. Tell me what they would mean if you weren't a king and I weren't a soldier. But she didn't want to hear any of that, not really. Sweet words and grand declarations were for other people, other lives.

She brushed the hair back from his face, placed a kiss on his forehead. "I would stay forever if I could," she whispered. He wouldn't remember anyway.

Hours later, Zoya's sitting room was crowded with people. She hadn't invited anyone; they'd simply gathered there, settling in front of the fire with cups of sweetened tea. Saints, she was glad of it. Usually, she valued her privacy, but tonight she needed company.

Despite the bath she'd taken, she felt like she could smell death clinging to her, in her hair, in her clothes. She had curled up beside Genya on the couch next to the fire. Its cushions were embroidered in pewter silk, and usually she was fussy about people putting their feet up on it, but right now she couldn't have cared less. She took a long sip from her mug of warmed wine. Tea was not enough for her tonight.

David and Nadia sat at the round table at the room's center. He'd set out neat little stacks of papers in what was no doubt an important order, and he was buried in a long row of calculations. Occasionally, he would hand a paper to Nadia, who was working on her own set of numbers, her feet resting in Tamar's lap. Tolya sat on the rug beside the tiled grate, gazing into the fire. It might have been a cozy scene, but the horror of what had happened that morning hung heavy in the air.

Genya studied her designs for the wedding gown, traditional gold and paired with a jeweled kokoshnik. She held up a sketch. "Too much?"

Zoya touched her fingers to the gown's delicately drawn hem. "For the royal chapel? No. The more sparkle the better." It was a gloomy place.

"I know," Genya said. She adjusted the patch over her missing eye. "If only we could hold the ceremony in the gardens."

"In the middle of winter?" said Nikolai, strolling into the sitting room and heading straight for the wine on the side table. It was as if he'd never been hurt, never been helpless. He had bathed, dressed in fresh clothes. The man seemed to gleam with confidence. "Do you want our guests to freeze to death?"

"That's one way to win a war," mused Genya.

"You shouldn't have wine," said Zoya. "The Healer's draught isn't out of your system yet."

Nikolai wrinkled his nose. "Then I suppose I'll drink tea like an old woman."

"There's nothing wrong with tea," objected Tolya.

"Far be it from me to argue with a man as big as a boulder." Nikolai poured himself a cup of tea and glanced at the papers laid out on the table. "Are those the new calculations for our launch system?" David nodded without looking up. "And how are they coming along?"

"They aren't."

"No?"

"I keep getting interrupted," David said pointedly.

"Splendid. Good to know I've done my part."

Nikolai sank into a large chair by the fire. Zoya could tell he was trying to summon the spirit to rib David or maybe even to celebrate the advantage their new rockets might grant them against the Fjerdans. But even Nikolai's relentless optimism was no match for what they'd seen on the palace steps.

At last he set his cup down on his knee and said, "Help me understand what happened this morning."

Tamar and Tolya exchanged a glance.

"This was a message from Queen Makhi," said Tamar.

"So she does *not* approve of the wedding? She might have simply sent her regrets."

"She rolled the dice," Tamar said. "And she almost won. If she had killed Ehri, she would have had cause for war, and she would have tied up the loose ends of her assassination scheme."

"We're going to have a hell of a time explaining what happened here as it is," said Zoya. "How do we account for the death of eleven high-ranking prisoners in our care?"

"Ehri saw what happened," said Tolya quietly. "It will be up to her to tell the truth. All of it."

"All of it," Tamar repeated.

Nadia laid her pen on the table and took her wife's hand. "Do you think Queen Makhi will actually come to the wedding?"

"She will," said Tamar. "But I wouldn't put it past her to use the occasion to stage some kind of attack. She's a wily tactician."

"A good queen," said Zoya.

"Yes," Tamar conceded. "Or an effective one. Her mother created a policy of outlawing experimentation on Grisha and had begun to allow them certain rights in exchange for military or governmental service."

"Like in Ravka," Nikolai said.

Tolya nodded. "Grisha still couldn't own property or hold any kind of political office, but they were worthwhile reforms."

"We've never been seen as unnatural there," said Tamar. "Just dangerous. But not everyone approved. Some Shu didn't like the idea of Grisha passing as ordinary people."

"And Makhi didn't like her mother's policies?" Nikolai asked.

Now Tamar frowned. She picked up Nadia's cup and her own and paced to the side table to refill them. "Even before she was crowned, Makhi had her own ideas about how to strengthen Shu Han. When *jurda parem* was discovered, it presented her with a choice: She could have attempted to keep the secret by destroying Bo Yul-Bayur's work. Instead Makhi chose to start up the old laboratories and make use of *parem* as a weapon."

"That's what led to the *khergud*," Tolya said, his voice desolate, a man surveying the wreck, pointing to a yawning black hole in the hull. *This is where it all went wrong.*

The *khergud* were Shu Han's deadliest soldiers, though the government had never acknowledged them in any official way. They were tailored by Grisha under the influence of *parem*, their senses heightened, their bones reinforced and altered. Some could even fly. Zoya shivered, remembering being yanked off her feet, the grip of the *khergud* soldier's arms around her like steel bands.

Tamar placed the full cups on the table but did not sit. She ran Nikolai's spy networks. She knew, better than any of them, what was happening to Grisha under Makhi's stewardship.

"The creation of the *khergud* . . ." She hesitated. "It's a process of trial and error. The Grisha they bring to the labs are referred to as volunteers, but . . ."

"We know better," Tolya growled.

"We do," said Tamar. "The choices the Grisha are presented with are impossible ones. The power the Taban government wields is too absolute."

"So it's not a choice at all," said Genya.

Tolya shrugged. "It's the same way the Darkling built the Second Army."

Zoya bristled at that. "The Second Army was a refuge."

"Maybe for some," said Tolya. "The Darkling took Grisha from their parents when they were only children. They were taught to forget the places they came from, the people they knew. They served the crown or their families suffered. What kind of choice is that?"

"But no one experimented on us," said Zoya. *And some of us were perfectly happy to forget our parents.*

"No," said Tolya, resting his huge hands on his knees. "They just turned you into soldiers and sent you out to fight their wars."

"He's not wrong," said Genya, looking down at her wine. "Don't you ever think about what life you might have led if you hadn't come to the Little Palace?"

Zoya leaned her head back against the silk of the couch. Yes, she wondered. As a little girl, the thought had haunted her dreams and hounded her into waking. She would close her eyes and find herself walking down the aisle. She would see her aunt bleeding on the floor. And always, her mother was there, coaxing Zoya forward, reminding her not to trip on the hem of her little golden wedding dress, as Zoya's father sat silent in the pews. He'd hung his head, Zoya remembered. But he hadn't said a word to save her. Only Liliyana had dared to speak. And Liliyana was long dead. Murdered by the Fold and the Darkling's ambition.

"Yes," said Zoya. "I think about it."

Tamar ran a hand through her short hair. "Our father promised our mother that we would have a choice. So when she died, he took us to Novyi Zem."

Would that have been the better thing? Should Liliyana have put her on a ship to cross the True Sea instead of bringing her to the palace gates to join the Grisha? Nikolai had abolished the practice of separating Grisha from their parents. There was no mandatory draft to pull children from their homes. But for the Grisha who had no homes, who had never felt safe in the places they should feel safe, the Little Palace would always be a refuge, somewhere to run to. Zoya had to preserve that sanctuary, no matter what the Fjerdans or the Shu or the Kerch threw at them. And maybe, somewhere on the other side of this long fight, there was a future where Grisha wouldn't have to fear or be feared, where "soldier" would just be one of a thousand possible paths.

She stood and shook out her cuffs. She wanted to sit by the fire, argue with Tolya, look at Genya's sketches, watch Nikolai frown into his tea. And that was exactly why she had to leave. There could be no rest. Not until her country and her people were safe.

"Your Majesty?" she said. "We've put this off long enough."

Nikolai got to his feet. "At least I don't have to drink any more tea."

"Do you want company?" Genya asked.

Zoya did. She wanted an entire army at her back. But she saw the way Genya clutched the papers in her hands, the way David's gaze snapped to his wife, the desire to protect her the one thing that could draw him from his work.

"When you're ready," Zoya said quietly. "And not before." She cracked her knuckles. "Besides," she drawled as she sailed from the room, "that dress needs a proper train. Let's not have the Shu queen thinking we're peasants."

"That was good of you," Nikolai said as they crossed the palace grounds to the old zoo. A full moon was rising.

Zoya ignored the compliment. "Why can't it be as simple as war? One enemy facing another in honest combat? No, now we have some kind of monstrous blight to face."

"Ravka likes to keep things interesting," said Nikolai. "Don't you enjoy a challenge?"

"I enjoy a nap," said Zoya. "I can't remember the last time I was allowed to sleep in."

"None of that. A full night's sleep might put you in a good mood, and I need you at your most disgruntled."

"Keep spewing inanities and you may see me at my worst."

"All Saints, are you saying I haven't seen you at your worst?"

Zoya tossed her hair. "If you had, you'd be under the covers, gibbering prayers."

"A unique way of getting me into bed, but who am I to question your methods?"

Zoya rolled her eyes, but she was grateful for the distraction of this easy back-and-forth. This was safe, simple, nothing like the quiet of his bedchamber, his hand tight in hers. And what would she do when Nikolai was married and propriety rose like a wall between them?

She straightened her spine and tightened the ribbon in her hair. She would get by just fine, as she always had. She was a military commander, not a simpering girl who wilted from a lack of attention.

The old zoo was located in the wooded area on the eastern end of the palace grounds. It had been abandoned generations ago, but somehow it still smelled of the animals that had been caged there. Zoya had seen the weathered illustrations: a leopard in a jeweled collar, a lemur wearing a velvet waistcoat and performing tricks, a white bear imported from Tsibeya that had mauled three different keepers before escaping. It had never been caught, and Zoya hoped it had somehow found its way home.

The zoo was built in the shape of a large circle, the old cages facing outward and overgrown with brambles. At the center was a high tower that had once housed an aviary at the top. Now it was home to a different animal.

As Zoya climbed the stairs behind Nikolai, she felt the ancient intelligence inside her rouse—thinking, calculating. It always seemed to come alive with her anger or her fear.

The Fold is expanding. Nikolai had said the words so easily, as if remarking upon the weather. *I hear there will be rain tomorrow.*

The calla lilies are in bloom again.

The world is being devoured by nothingness and we have to find a way to stop it. More tea?

But that was always the way. The world might crumble, but Nikolai Lantsov would be holding up the ceiling with one hand and plucking a speck of dirt from his lapel with the other when it all went to ruin.

He and Zoya had built this prison carefully, leaving only the skeleton of the aviary. Its walls were now made entirely of glass, letting light in throughout the day. At night, Sun Soldiers, heirs to Alina Starkov's power, many of whom had fought against the Darkling on the Fold, kept the light alive. They had all been sworn to secrecy, and Zoya hoped that vow would hold. The Darkling had emerged into this new life without his powers—or so it seemed. They were taking no chances.

When the door opened, their prisoner rose from where he'd been sitting on the floor, moving with a kind of grace Yuri Vedenen had never possessed. Yuri, a young monk who had preached the gospel of the Starless Saint, had led the cult dedicated to worship of the Darkling. They believed the Starless One had been martyred on the Fold and that he would return. And to Zoya's great surprise, Yuri and the rest of the addlepated zealots clad in black and chanting for a dead dictator had been right: The Darkling had been resurrected. His power had poured into Yuri's own body and now . . . now Zoya wasn't sure who or what this man was. His face was narrow, his pale skin smooth, his eyes gray beneath dark brows. His long black hair almost brushed his collarbones. He wore dark trousers and nothing else, his chest and feet bare. Vain as always.

"A royal visit." The Darkling sketched a short bow. "I'm honored."

"Put on a shirt," said Zoya.

"My apologies. It gets quite warm in here with the relentless sunlight." He shrugged into the rough-spun shirt Yuri had worn beneath his monk's robes. "I'd invite you to sit, but . . ." He gestured to the empty room.

There was no furniture. He had no books to occupy him. He was let into the neighboring cell only to wash and relieve himself. Another two heavily padlocked doors stood between that cell and the stairs.

The Darkling's new residence was empty, but there was quite a view. Through the glass walls, Zoya could see the palace grounds, the rooftops and gardens of the upper town, lights from the boats drifting on the river that ringed it, and the lower town below. Os Alta. This had been her home since she was only nine years old, but she'd rarely had the chance to see it from this angle. She felt a rush of dizziness, and then she was remembering. Of course. She knew this city, the countryside that surrounded it. She had flown over it before.

No. Not her. The dragon. It had a name, one known only to itself and long ago to the others of its kind, but she couldn't quite remember what it was. It was right on the tip of her tongue. Infuriating.

"I am eager for company," said the Darkling.

Zoya felt a sudden rush of his resentment, his rage at this captivity—the Darkling's anger. The dragon's presence in her head had left her vulnerable. She drew in a breath, grounding herself, here, in this strange glass cell, the stone floor beneath her boots. *What might you learn*—Juris' voice, or was it her own?—*what might you know, if only you would open the door?*

Another breath. *I am Zoya Nazyalensky and I am getting truly sick of the cocktail party in my head, you old lizard.* She could have sworn she heard Juris chuckle in reply.

Nikolai leaned against the wall. "I'm sorry we don't visit more often. There's a war on and, well, no one likes you."

The Darkling touched a hand to his chest. "You wound me."

"All in due time," said Zoya.

The Darkling raised a brow. A faint smile touched his lips—there in that expression, there was the man she remembered. "She's afraid of me, you know."

"I'm not."

"She doesn't know what I may do. Or what I can do."

Nikolai gestured to one of the Sun Soldiers for chairs to be brought in. "Maybe she's afraid of being spoken of as if she's not standing right in front of you."

They all sat. The Darkling somehow managed to make his rickety old chair look like a throne. "I knew that you would come."

"I hate to be predictable." Nikolai turned to Zoya. "Maybe we should go? Keep him on his toes?"

"He knows we won't. He knows we need something."

"I've felt it," said the Darkling. "The blight coming on. The Fold is expanding. And you feel it too, don't you, Lantsov? It's the power that resides in my bones, the power still seeping black in your blood."

A shadow passed over Nikolai's face. "The power that created the Fold in the first place."

"I'm told some people consider it a miracle."

Zoya pursed her lips. "Don't let it go to your head. There are miracles everywhere these days."

The Darkling tilted his head to the side, watching them both. The weight of his gaze made Zoya want to leap through one of the glass walls, but she refused to show it. "I've had a lot of time to think in this place, to look back on a long life. I made countless mistakes, but always I found a new path, a new chance to work toward my goal."

Nikolai nodded. "Until that little bump in the road when you died."

Now the Darkling's expression soured. "When I look back on where things went wrong, where my plans all unraveled, I can trace the moment of disaster to the trust I placed in a pirate named Sturmhond."

"Privateer," said Nikolai. "And I wouldn't know, but if the privateer you've hired is entirely trustworthy, he's probably not much of a privateer."

Zoya couldn't just brush past with a joke. "*That's* the moment? Not in manipulating a young girl and trying to steal her power, or destroying half a city of innocent people, or decimating the Grisha, or blinding your own mother? None of those moments feel like an opportunity for self-examination?"

The Darkling merely shrugged, his hands spread as if indicating he had no more tricks to play. "You list off atrocities as though I'm meant to feel shame for them. And perhaps I would, were there not a hundred that preceded those crimes, and another hundred before those. Human life is worth preserving. But human lives? They come and go like so much chaff, never tipping the scales."

"What a remarkable calculation," said Nikolai. "And a convenient one for a mass murderer."

"Zoya understands. The dragon knows how small human lives are, how wearying. They are fireflies. Sparks that dwindle in the night, while we burn on and on."

There were not enough deep breaths in the world to keep a leash on Zoya's anger. How did Nikolai maintain that air of glib composure? And why did they bother trying to prick the Darkling's conscience? Her aunt, her friends, the people he had sworn to protect meant nothing in the long expanse of his life.

She leaned forward. "You are stolen fire and stolen time. Don't look to me for support." She turned to Nikolai. "Why are we here? Being around him makes me want to break things. Let's take him to the Fold and kill him. Maybe that will set things right."

"It won't work," said the Darkling. "The demon lives on in your king. You'd have to kill him too."

"Don't give her ideas," said Nikolai.

"The only way to heal the rupture in the Fold is to finish what you started and perform the *obisbaya*."

Tolya had made the same suggestion. The Ritual of the Burning Thorn. They had been lured into attempting it by Elizaveta, who had only wished to use the opportunity to kill Nikolai and resurrect the Darkling. If they wanted to attempt it again, this would be the time, when the Darkling was still powerless, and the Fjerdans were licking their wounds. But the risk was simply too great. And even if they were willing to take it, they didn't have the means.

"We have no thorn wood," said Zoya. "It crumbled to ash when the Saints died and the boundaries of the Fold fell."

"But we might acquire one," said the Darkling.

"I see. From whom?"

"Monks."

She threw up her hands. "Why is it always monks?"

"There was fruit taken from the thorn wood when it was still young. Its seeds were preserved by the Order of Sankt Feliks."

"And where are they?"

Now the Darkling looked less certain. "I don't know exactly. I've never had need of them. But I can tell you how to find them."

"I smell a bargain in the works," Nikolai said, rubbing his hands together. "What will this knowledge cost us?"

The Darkling's eyes glittered, gray quartz beneath a false sun. "Bring me Alina Starkov and I'll tell you what you need to know."

All the humor left Nikolai's face. "What do you want with Alina?"

"A chance to apologize. A chance to see what became of the girl who drove a knife into my heart."

Zoya shook her head. "I don't believe a word that leaves your mouth."

The Darkling shrugged. "I might not either. But you know my terms."

"And if we don't agree to them?" she asked.

"Then the Fold will keep expanding and swallow the world.

The young king will fall and I will sing myself to sleep in my prison cell."

Zoya stood. "I don't like any of this. He's up to something. And even if we find the monastery and the seeds, what would we do with them? We would need an extraordinarily powerful Fabrikator to bring forth the thorn wood the way that Elizaveta did."

The Darkling smiled. "Does this mean you have not mastered all Juris set out to teach you?"

Zoya felt the dam containing her rage give way. She lunged toward the Darkling as Nikolai seized her arms to hold her back. "You do not speak his name. Say his name again and I'll cut the tongue from your mouth and wear it as a brooch."

"Don't," Nikolai said, his grip strong, his voice low. "He's not worth your anger."

The Darkling watched her as he had when she was a pupil, as if there was something only he could see inside her. As if it amused him. "They all die, Zoya. They all will. Everyone you love."

"Is that right?" said Nikolai. "How tragic. Can you be still, Zoya?"

Zoya shook Nikolai off. "For now."

"How she struggles," the Darkling said, his voice thick with mirth. "Like an insect pinned by her own power."

"Poetic," said Nikolai. "You have something in your beard."

To Zoya's confusion, the Darkling raised his hand to his smooth chin, then dropped it as if he'd been burned. His gaze lit with something very like hate.

Now it was Nikolai who was smiling. "That's what I thought," said the king. "Yuri Vedenen is still there, somewhere inside you. Is that why your powers haven't returned?"

The Darkling watched the king with narrowed eyes. "Such a clever fellow."

"That's why you want us to raise the thorn wood and perform the *obisbaya*. You could care less what damage the Fold does. You want to purge yourself of Yuri and become host to my demon. You want a way back to your power."

"I've told you what I want. Bring me Alina Starkov. That is the bargain."

"No," said Zoya.

The Darkling turned his back on them and looked out over the lights glittering in the city spread below. "Then I can live as a weakling and you can watch the world die."

10
NINA

NINA WAS AT HANNE'S SIDE in seconds. The prince's eyes were bulging, his whole body convulsing as his slender chest heaved. Worse was the sound that came from him, a deep, painful rattle. Nina saw Hanne's hand reach out, even as she sank to her knees beside them. It rested on his chest—as if she couldn't help herself—and almost instantly the prince's coughing eased.

"Take my hand," Nina whispered furiously. "Pray. *Loudly.*"

She seized the prince's bony fingers so that they formed a circle of three and chanted with Hanne in staccato Fjerdan, a prayer to Djel, the Wellspring. *"As the waters scour the riverbed, let them cleanse me too. As the waters scour the riverbed, let them cleanse me too."*

Prince Rasmus stared at them. His coughing ceased and his breaths came in great gasps, as Hanne's healing gift soothed his inflamed lungs and opened the airways.

Bare seconds later the royal guards surrounded them, pulling Hanne and Nina away as the king and queen rushed toward them.

"No!" Rasmus gasped. His voice was weak, thready. He was starting to cough again. "Bring her back. Bring them back."

But the crowd was already surging around them and Rasmus was rushed through a pair of doors behind the royal dais, leaving the ball-room awash in shocked and baffled whispers.

Brum was suddenly next to Hanne and Nina, herding them away, as Ylva and Redvin helped to keep the curious crowd at bay. Flanked by *drüskelle*, they were ushered down a corridor, and then through the twisting passages that led back to their chambers.

"Prince Rasmus—" Hanne began, but Brum silenced her with a look.

"The servants," he said quietly as they made their way to the room Brum used as his office. It was all dark wood and white stone, and through the frost-lined windows, Nina could see it had begun to snow.

Ylva vanished, then returned with a bowl of warm water and two soft cloths that she handed to Nina and Hanne. Nina hadn't real-ized the prince's blood was on her too. She wiped her face and hands clean.

She made her eyes wide, forced her lip to tremble, but every part of her was watchful, alert, ready to move into fight mode if Hanne had to be protected. There was a graveyard on the White Island, bodies she could call to her service as soldiers. What had Brum seen? What did he know?

Hanne looked terrified. She'd used her power in front of the entire Fjerdan court, healing the prince without thinking of it. Nina's mind reeled at the risk of it, the carelessness. And yet, even in her fear and anger, Nina knew Hanne couldn't help it. She couldn't watch someone suffer and not act. It was her nature to try to fix things, when all Nina did was destroy. Had any of the onlookers realized what she'd done? Had Brum? He was a trained witchhunter. Here, away from the pomp and drama of the court, Nina's ruse of prayer felt impossibly flimsy.

"What happened?" Ylva asked, a desperate, frightened edge to her voice.

Brum's face was grim. "The prince is very ill."

"But not like that!" cried Ylva. "He collapsed!"

"Why do you think they keep him away from the public?"

"He . . . he has never been one for social occasions, but . . ."

"Because the king and queen have coddled him. They let him appear in public only for short times and in highly controlled situations like the start of Heartwood today."

"What do you suppose brought this fit on?" asked Redvin, taking a swig of something from a flask.

Brum shrugged. "Too much noise. Too much heat. Who knows?"

"His weakness is appalling," said Redvin.

"He's a child," protested Ylva.

Brum sneered. "He's eighteen years old. You forget because he is so far from what a man should be."

At that, Hanne's gaze hardened. "He cannot help what he is, how he was born."

"Maybe not," said Brum. "But has he pushed himself? Challenged himself? I've done my best to help him, to be a mentor and a guide. He is the heir to the throne, but if the extent of his infirmity became common knowledge, do you really think Fjerda would accept him as their king?"

Again, Nina wondered what game Brum was playing. She had no doubt he believed all this nonsense he was spewing about manhood and Fjerdan strength. It was also clear he had no respect for the prince. But was there more?

In the week since Fjerda's defeat at Nezkii and Ulensk, Brum had done his best to hide his frustration. The failed invasion meant that Fjerda had to at least entertain the possibility of diplomacy over war. But if the prince died or was incapacitated, Fjerda would have only the old king and the younger prince to rule. It might be a perfect opportunity for someone to step in and take the reins for a grateful royal family. And once that was done, just who would convince Brum to hand them back? He had the respect and support of the military. He knew the workings of the court inside and out. Nina felt dread like a yoke around her neck. Fjerda's policies had grown only more brutal under Brum's influence. What would it mean for her country and for her people if there was no check on his power?

Ylva shook her head. "Why did you never tell me the prince's case was so dire?"

"Our position at court and my position with the military are closely tied to the favor of the royal family. After the prison break and the destruction of the treasury . . . I've had to fight for our place here, and I could not risk indiscretion. The Grimjers will do everything they can to minimize this incident and to discredit those who witnessed it most closely."

"I had his blood on me," said Hanne. "He's dying."

Nina wanted to kick her. They needed to stay quiet until they knew what Brum had seen or what he thought he'd seen. And yet she was starting to think they'd gotten away with Hanne's breach. Maybe Brum had been too focused on the prince's public display of weakness to understand what had really happened.

"Probably," said Brum. "But he's doing the throne the discourtesy of dying slowly. The royal family will want to silence Hanne. Young women gossip."

"Not Hanne!" cried Ylva.

"But how are they to know that? She has no reputation at court. She's been gone so long, few could speak to her character."

"Surely you can protect her?"

"I don't know."

Ylva moaned. "Tell me they won't harm her."

"No, but they might send her away."

"Exile?" Ylva threw her arms around her daughter. "I won't allow it. We waited too long to have her back with us. I won't let her be taken from me again."

Nina watched Hanne's mother cling to her daughter in fright and didn't know what to do. She could feel danger speeding toward them. She was good at anticipating threats, she'd had to be, but this one had seemed to come from nowhere in the fragile body of a boy.

A knock sounded at the door. It was a young man in a *drüskelle* uniform. Nina recognized him from the prince's retinue in the ballroom.

"Joran." Brum waved him in. "Joran is bodyguard to the prince."

"Is he all right?" asked Hanne.

Joran nodded. His training was too good for him to twist his hands together or fidget, but Nina could see he was nervous. "Sir," he said, then hesitated. "Commander Brum, the royal family has ordered the presence of your daughter and her maid."

A soft sob escaped Ylva. But Brum simply nodded. "I see. Then we must go."

Joran cleared his throat. "They were specific in their invitation. Only the girls are wanted."

"Djel, what is this?" Ylva said, tears streaming down her cheeks now. "We can't let this happen. Hanne cannot face them alone."

"I'm not alone," said Hanne. She was trembling slightly, but she rose. "I have Mila."

"Change your dress," said Brum.

She glanced down at the bloodstains. "Of course. I'll need a moment."

Ylva grabbed Hanne's arm. "No. *No.* Jarl, you cannot let her do this."

"She must." He laid his hand on Hanne's shoulder. "You are my daughter and you will not hang your head."

Hanne lifted her chin. "Never."

The look in Brum's eyes might have been pride.

Hanne and Nina hurried to their rooms to change their clothes.

As soon as they shut the door, Hanne blurted, "I didn't mean to."

"I know, I know," Nina said, already choosing a new gown for Hanne, chaste ivory wool, with none of the glamour of the sparkling amber thing she'd gotten to wear for such a brief time. She selected a similarly drab brown gown for herself.

"Do you think the prince knows?"

"No. Maybe. I don't know. He was in no condition to think straight."

"My father—I thought he saw."

"I know."

Nina couldn't believe that Hanne had healed the prince before Brum's very eyes without his knowledge. But people saw what they wanted to see. Brum would never believe his daughter had been born an abomination.

Hanne pulled on the gown. She was shaking. "Nina, if they test me . . ."

There were Grisha amplifiers kept as prisoners at the Ice Court, people gifted with the ability to call forth another Grisha's power.

"There are ways around that," said Nina. She'd learned them from the Dregs. Jesper Fahey had covered his arms in paraffin so that he could play in high-stakes card games where Grisha—able to manipulate everything from a shuffle to a man's mood—were not welcome.

But there might not be time to deploy those techniques. Nina didn't know if she could protect Hanne. They were trapped on the White Island in the middle of the Ice Court, and if Hanne was revealed to be a Grisha, there would be no path open to escape. "If they find you out, they'll put you in prison to face trial. That will give me time."

"Time for what?"

"To make a plan. To break you out."

"How?"

"I learned from the best in Ketterdam. I'll find a way." She held Hanne's gaze. "Never doubt it."

Joran was waiting when they emerged. He led them out of their chambers and back to the palace through a series of confusing passages. Nina didn't think she'd be able to make her way back. Maybe that was the point.

"The prince is well?" Nina asked.

Joran said nothing. His shoulders were rigid. Nina knew the *drüskelle*, especially those still in training, were fastidious about maintaining protocol, but this one seemed even more tautly wound. He was tall, even by Fjerdan standards, but he couldn't be more than sixteen or seventeen—still a boy, made even more boyish by the fact that he wasn't permitted to grow any kind of beard.

"How long have you been the prince's bodyguard?" she asked.

"Nearly two years," he said curtly.

Nina and Hanne exchanged a glance. They weren't going to get much out of him. Nina reached for Hanne's hand; her fingers were cold.

They arrived at a door flanked by royal guards and were escorted into a sitting room layered in cream and gold cushions. Its vast windows looked out over the gleaming expanse of the Ice Bridge, which linked the White Island to the outer ring of the Ice Court, and they could see soft flurries of snow gusting past the glass in the gray afternoon light. Nina had assumed they'd be brought before some kind of royal tribunal, but other than the servants in their royal livery, the only other person in the room was Prince Rasmus, propped on a sofa embroidered with gold brocade.

"It's not much of a view, is it?" said the prince. He was pale and fragile as an eggshell, nearly the same shade as the heap of white pillows upon which he was settled. There was a blanket over his legs, and a cup of tea in his hands.

When Hanne said nothing, Nina murmured, "I was just thinking it was very grand."

"Only if you never want to see more of the world. Sit."

They lowered themselves onto two plush chairs that had been designed to ensure that no one would ever be seated higher than the crown prince.

"Leave us," the prince instructed the servants with a wave of his hand. Joran closed the door behind them and stood at attention, his gaze fixed on nothing at all. "I trust Joran with my life. I have to. We have no secrets from each other." Nina noted the slight clenching of Joran's jaw. *Interesting.* Maybe some secrets after all.

"Joran is two years younger than I am, barely sixteen, but he is taller and stronger than I'll ever be. He can carry me up a flight of stairs as if I weighed no more than kindling. And to my great shame, he's had to do so more than once." Joran's face remained inscrutable. "He never shows emotion. It's quite comforting. I've had more than my share of pity." He studied Hanne. "You look nothing like your father."

"No," said Hanne, a slight tremor to her voice. "I take after my mother's people."

"I don't seem to take after anyone," said the prince. "Unless there was a goblin somewhere in the Grimjer line." He leaned forward and patted Hanne's hand, then Nina's. "It's all right. I'm not going to let them exile you. Go ahead and pour yourselves tea."

Hanne still looked terrified, and Nina felt only wary as she served first Hanne then herself. It was hard to indulge in much relief after everything Brum had said.

"Nothing will happen to you!" the prince said. "I forbade it." He leaned closer and dropped his voice. "I threw quite the fit. There are benefits to being able to turn blue."

"But . . . but why, Your Highness?" Hanne asked.

It was a reasonable question but a perilous one. Did he know Hanne was Grisha? Was he playing with them?

The prince leaned back on his cushions, his air of mischief vanishing. "I've been sick my whole life. Since I was a child. I can't remember a time I wasn't an object of scorn or worry. I'm often not sure which is worse. Other people shy away from my weakness. You . . . you drew closer."

"Sickness is sickness," said Hanne. "It's not something to fear."

"You had my blood on your hands. On your skirts. Did they tell you to change?" Hanne nodded. "You weren't afraid?"

"That's mugwort in your cup, isn't it?"

The prince glanced down at the cup, which now sat cooling on the table beside him. "It is."

"I was educated at a convent in Gäfvalle, but I was most interested in herb lore, in healing."

"The Springmaidens taught you? That doesn't seem like a subject the Wellmother would encourage."

"Well," Hanne said carefully, "I may have taken it upon myself to learn."

The prince laughed and then began to cough. Nina saw Hanne's fingertips flex slightly. She shook her head. *No, this is not a good idea.*

But Hanne couldn't see suffering and not respond.

The prince's cough ceased and he took a long, shuddering breath.

"The convent at Gäfvalle," he continued, "as if nothing had

135

happened. "I thought that was where they sent difficult girls to beat the spirit out of them and make them ready to be good wives."

"It is."

"But your spirit is still intact?" said the prince, studying Hanne closely.

"I hope so."

"And you have no husband."

"I don't."

"Is that why you came back to the Ice Court? Put on that fanciful gown?"

"Yes."

"And instead you got a lapful of wheezing prince."

Nina nearly choked on her tea.

"It's all right to laugh," said the prince. "I won't have you beheaded." He cocked his head to one side. "Your hair is shorn. That's a sign of devotion to Djel, is it not?"

"It is."

"And you both prayed over me." His eyes fastened on Nina. "You took my hand. People have been executed for daring to touch the hand of a prince."

"It was not I," said Nina piously. "It was the spirit of Djel that moved through me."

"So, you are true believers?"

"Are you not?" asked Nina.

"It's hard to believe in a god that would deny me breath."

Hanne and Nina stayed silent. That was blasphemy, pure and simple, and not something either of them were free to remark upon. Who reigned in this room? Djel or the prince?

At last, Rasmus said, "Healing and herbs are not the province of most noblewomen."

Hanne shrugged. "I am not like most noblewomen."

The prince took in Hanne's set shoulders, the stubborn line of her jaw. "I see that. If devotion to Djel will make me as sturdy as the two of you, perhaps I'll take up prayer after all." He smoothed the blankets over his waist. "You will come to see me again soon. I find your presence . . . comforting."

Because Hanne is healing you as we speak.

"Go," he said with a wave of his hand. "Joran will see you back to your rooms. Give my regards to your father."

There was no mistaking the sour edge to his voice. So Brum's disdain had not gone unnoticed.

Hanne and Nina rose, curtsied, backed out of the room.

"You were healing him," Nina whispered in accusation.

"The spirit of Djel moved you?" Hanne said beneath her breath. "You're shameless."

Joran led them out the doors, but before they could go more than a few paces down the hall, they were stopped by two royal guards.

"Mila Jandersdat," one said. "You will come with us."

"But why?" exclaimed Hanne.

Nina knew they would get no answer. It was not for commoners to question the royal guard.

She grabbed Hanne in a quick hug. "I'll be back before you know it."

As they led her down the corridor, she glanced over her shoulder and saw Hanne watching, fear in her eyes. *I'll come back to you*, she promised. She could only hope that was true.

❦

The corridor changed as Nina followed the guards, and she realized she was in a part of the palace she'd never seen before. The stone here seemed older, its color closer to ivory than white, and when she looked up, she saw that the walls had been carved into ridges so that it felt like they were passing through the rib cage of some great beast, a tunnel of bones.

This place had been built to intimidate, but the ancient architects of the Ice Court had chosen the wrong motif. *Death is my gift*, Nina thought, *and I do not fear the lost.* She always made sure to have two thin spikes of bone tucked into her sleeves to use as darts if she needed to. Her buttons were bone too. And then, of course, there were the dead. Kings and queens and favored retainers had been buried on the White Island since before the Ice Court had been built around it, and Nina could hear their whispers. An army awaiting her command.

The guards stopped in front of two tall, narrow doors that reached almost all the way to the ceiling. They were emblazoned with the Grimjer wolf rampant, a globe beneath its paw and a crown hovering above its pointed ears. The doors opened and Nina found herself in a long room lined by columns carved to look like birch trees. The whole place glowed blue as if it really had been hewn from ice, and Nina felt like she was entering a frozen forest.

The old audience room, she realized as they walked toward a high-backed throne of alabaster so elaborately carved it looked like sheets of lace. Queen Agathe sat upon it in the same white gown she'd worn at the processional earlier. Her back was straight, her sleek hair the color of pearl, and she wore a circlet of opals on her head.

Nina knew better than to speak first. She curtsied deeply and kept her eyes on the floor, waiting, her mind reeling. Why had she been brought here? What could the Grimjer queen want from her?

A moment later, she heard the doors close with an echoing thud and realized that she had been left alone with Queen Agathe.

"You prayed over my son today."

Nina nodded, keeping her eyes averted. "I did, Your Majesty."

"I know Hanne Brum, of course. But I did not know the girl who knelt beside my son and dared to take his hand, who spoke the words of Djel to ease his suffering. So I asked my advisers who you are." Queen Agathe paused. "And it seems no one knows."

"Because I am no one, Your Majesty."

"Mila Jandersdat. Widow of a dead merchant who traded fish and frozen goods." She said the words as if she thought disdain could cure them of their meaning. "A young woman of humble beginnings who has wormed her way into the house of Jarl Brum."

"I have been very fortunate, Your Majesty."

Nina's cover was designed to withstand scrutiny. There really had been a Mila Jandersdat from a little town on the northern coast. Her husband really had been lost at sea. But when Mila had run off to Novyi Zem to begin a new life with a handsome farmer, her identity had been pilfered by the Hringsa for Nina's use.

"I have sent my men to inquire about this Mila Jandersdat, to ask what she looks like, to discover if we have a spy in our midst."

Nina let her head snap up at this, her expression shocked. "A spy, Your Majesty?"

The queen's lips thinned. "A talented actress."

"Your men will find I am just who I say I am. I have no reason to lie." Nina had been tailored to look like Mila. It would do for a description. But if the queen's investigators brought back any of Mila's friends or neighbors to confirm her identity, that would be another thing entirely.

The queen studied Nina for a long moment. "My eldest son was not supposed to survive childhood. Did you know that, Mila Jandersdat? I miscarried three times before I bore him. It was a miracle when he took his first breath, when he lived through his first night, his first year. I prayed for him each morning and each evening, and I have done so ever since." The queen tapped her fingers on the arm of her throne. "Perhaps I won't wait for my inquisitors to return.

My son is vulnerable. You saw that well enough today, and I do not take any threat to him or my family lightly. It might be easier just to send you packing."

So why haven't you? Nina waited.

"But I think that might cause him some distress, and . . . and I want to know what happened today."

Now Nina understood. Brum hadn't questioned the prince's quick recovery, not even Prince Rasmus himself had. But the queen had a mother's care, a mother's fear—a mother's hope.

She'd chosen to interrogate Mila Jandersdat, not Hanne Brum, because she knew Mila was defenseless, without name or status. If Mila wanted the queen's favor, if she wanted to stay at the Ice Court, and if she knew something about Hanne or what had happened, Mila was more likely to talk.

And Nina intended to do just that.

When she had first heard the voices of the dead, she had shrunk from them, tried to ignore them. She'd been too deep in her grief, too desperate to keep hold of her tie to Matthias. Death had still been the enemy, the monster that could strike without warning and take all you held dear. She hadn't wanted to make peace with it. She couldn't. Until she'd laid Matthias to rest. Even now her heart rebelled at the thought that there was no loophole, no secret spell to return him to her, to give her back the love she'd lost. No, she hadn't made peace with death, but they'd come to an understanding.

Speak. Nina reached out with her power, feeling the cold river of mortality that ran through everyone and everything, letting it carry her to the sacred burial ground that lay in the shadow of the Elderclock only a few hundred yards away. *Who will speak the name of Agathe Grimjer, queen of Fjerda?*

The voice that answered was loud and clear, a strong soul, recently gone. It had a great deal to say.

"Six miscarriages," Nina said.

"*What?*" The word fell like a stone in the old throne room.

"You miscarried six times before you gave birth to Rasmus. Not three."

"Who told you that?" The queen's voice was harsh, her cool demeanor shaken.

Linor Rundholm, the queen's best friend and lady-in-waiting, dead and buried on the White Island.

"You had given up on praying," said Nina, letting her eyes close, swaying as if she was in a trance. "So you had a Grisha Healer brought from the dungeons to see you through your pregnancy."

"That is a lie."

But it wasn't. Linor had whispered it all. The queen had resorted to what was considered witchcraft.

"You think your boy is cursed." She opened her eyes and stared directly at the queen. "But he is not."

Queen Agathe's slender fingers gripped the arms of her throne like white claws. "If what you were saying were true, then I would have committed heresy. My son would have been born with the demon's mark upon him, forsaken by Djel. There would be no hope for him, no matter how many prayers I said."

Nina almost felt sorry for this woman, a helpless mother wanting only to give birth to a healthy child. But once Rasmus had been born and weaned, she'd sent the Grisha Healer who had helped her to her death. She couldn't risk anyone learning of what she'd done. Only Linor knew, her dear friend, a friend so beloved the queen had refused to let her travel with her husband to the front. *I need you with me*, Agathe had said, and a queen's need was as good as a command. Linor's husband had died on the field of battle and Linor had remained year after year on the White Island, her grief turning bitter as she tended to a selfish queen and her sickly son.

"When I was a little girl," said Nina, "I fell into a river. It was the dead of winter. I should have frozen. I should have drowned. But when my parents found me lying on the banks nearly two miles from where I'd fallen in, I was warm and safe, my cheeks pink and my heartbeat even. I was blessed by Djel. I was touched by his far-seeing. Ever since then, I have known things I have no right to know. And I know this: Your son is not cursed."

"Then why does he suffer?" Her voice was pleading, all dignity lost to desperation.

A good question. But Nina was ready. As a Grisha, she'd learned to use the dead as her informants and her weapons. As a spy, she'd learned to do the same with the living. Sometimes all they needed was the right nudge. She spoke the words she knew the queen would want to hear, not because of what the dead had whispered, but because of the need she'd felt when Matthias died, the terrible longing to believe there was a reason for her pain.

"There is a purpose to all of it," she said, a promise, a prediction. "And to your suffering as well. Djel spoke through the waters today. Your son will heal and grow strong and he will find greatness."

The queen drew in a long, trembling breath. Nina knew she was struggling to keep tears at bay. "Leave me," she said, her voice quaking.

Nina curtsied and backed from the room. Before the doors closed, she heard a sound like wailing, as the queen went to her knees, her head in her hands.

11
ZOYA

NIKOLAI AND ZOYA WERE SILENT as they descended the stairs, the gloom heavy after the unnatural brightness of the Darkling's prison.

Outside, a full moon hung low on the horizon, its light staining the night blue. The white gravel of the path back to the Grand Palace shone bright as spilled stars. They didn't speak until they were in Nikolai's sitting room, the door safely closed behind them.

"He's fun," said Nikolai, pouring a glass of brandy. "I forgot how fun he is."

She took the glass he offered. "It has to be Alina's choice."

"You know what she'll decide when she understands the stakes."

Zoya took a long sip and crossed the room to the hearth. She set the glass on the mantel. The heat from the fireplace felt like comfort, and the beast within her seemed to sigh with pleasure. "She shouldn't have to be the hero again."

"He wants a conversation, not a rematch."

"You're sure of that?"

"You're wearing the watch I gave you."

Zoya looked down at the little silver dragon. "You should have given me a raise instead."

"We can't afford it."

"Then you should give me a shiny medal. Or a nice estate."

"When the war is over, you shall have your pick of them."

Zoya took another sip of her brandy. "I choose the dacha in Udova."

"That's my ancestral home!"

"Are you taking back your offer?"

"Absolutely not. It's too hot in the summer and hell to heat in the winter. Why do you want it?"

"I like the view."

"There's nothing to see from that dacha except a broken-down mill and a muddy little town."

"I know," she said. She could have stopped at that. Maybe she should have. Instead, she continued, "I grew up there."

Nikolai did his best to hide his surprise, but Zoya knew him too well. She never spoke of her childhood.

"Oh?" he said too casually. "Do you have family there?"

"I don't know," she admitted. "I haven't spoken to my parents since they tried to sell me off to a rich nobleman when I was nine years old." She'd never told anyone about what had happened that day. She'd let her life, her family, and her losses stay in the past. But lately it felt hard not to be known, like keeping herself together was all the more difficult without someone to see who she truly was.

Nikolai set down his glass. "That isn't—that's not . . . The laws prohibit—"

"Who enforces the laws?" Zoya asked softly. "Rich men. Rich men who do what they wish. Power doesn't make a man wise."

"I'm proof enough of that."

"You're occasionally a useless podge. But you're a good man, Nikolai. And a good king. I will not serve another."

"I don't like that word."

"Serve? It's an honest word. You are the king I've chosen." She took another sip of her drink and turned to face the fire. It was easier to speak her worry to the flames. "The last time we attempted the *obisbaya*, you almost died. You can't render yourself defenseless like that again. For Ravka's sake."

"The Darkling will be vulnerable too. And this is the time to attempt it. We don't know when or if his powers may return, and I have no intention of letting him banish Yuri."

"You mean to drive the Darkling out instead."

"He's the invader. The little monk is still in there. You saw that."

Zoya watched the flames snap and spark. "You must not underestimate him." The way so many had. The way she had.

"Zoya."

"What?"

"Zoya, look at me."

Zoya turned and gasped. She raised her hands to fight, her glass slipping from her fingers and shattering on the floor.

Nikolai stood beside the table.

And the demon stood beside him. It seemed to hover there, a blot of darkness in the shape of her king, its black wings curling at the edges like smoke.

"It's . . . How?"

"The monster is me and I am the monster. If the Darkling is right and this isn't all some ruse, the *obisbaya* may be the secret to unraveling the Fold once and for all. The demon may go out of me and into the darkness forever."

The demon hissed and Zoya flinched back, her foot nearly landing in the fire.

"But he is *my* demon, not the Darkling's," Nikolai said. He held his hand out to her, scarred beneath the gloves he wore. "Don't be afraid."

She felt the need in him as palpably as if he'd spoken. *Don't turn away from me. Anyone but you.* Was that the dragon's eye opening inside her? Or did she just recognize her own want? There was no one else she would trust to see her at her weakest, her most fearful. Her most monstrous.

Zoya met Nikolai's gaze. "You can control it?"

"I can."

She took a step forward, then another, forcing herself to cross the room until she was standing before both of them. Her mind screamed at her to run from the wrongness of what she was seeing, this creature made of nothing beside her king.

"Maybe the *obisbaya* will work," said Nikolai, his hazel eyes steady. "But what if it doesn't? What if I told you the demon will always be with me? That there will always be a part of me tied to the Darkling, to this shadow power? Would I still be your king? Or would you fear me? Would you come to despise me as you despise him?"

She didn't know how to answer that. She had always assumed that somehow, eventually, they would find a way to rid Nikolai of this creature. Maybe she *wanted* to attempt the *obisbaya* again, despite the terrible risk to his life. Not for the sake of destroying the Fold, but because she hated that any part of the Darkling resided within the king.

The shadow thing raised its hand and Zoya clenched her fists, determined to stand her ground. The edges of its form were blurred like thick fog. Its long fingers ended in claws.

It reached for her and Zoya willed herself not to recoil. It brushed its knuckles across the skin of her cheek, and she drew in a sharp breath. Its touch was cold. It was solid. It had form.

Power. The ancient thing inside her recognized this darkness, the very substance of the universe. It was Nikolai and it was not.

"You would still be my king," she said, as the demon stroked its fingers down her cheek to her throat. "I know who you are."

Was it the monster touching her or was it her king? Was there a difference anymore? The fire crackled in the stillness of the room, the silence of the palace surrounding them, the heavy blanket of night.

The demon closed its talons over the ribbon in her hair and tugged. It slid loose, fluttering to the floor. Slowly, it withdrew its hand. Did she imagine its regret?

The thing melted back into Nikolai's body, as if his shadow had come to meet him.

Zoya released an unsteady breath. "I think I may need another drink." Nikolai offered her his glass and she tossed back the remaining brandy. He was watching her closely. She saw him flex the fingers of his hand, as if it really had been him touching her. "How long have you been able to . . . do that?"

"Since the Fold."

"Another," Zoya said, holding out the glass. He poured. She downed it. "And you really think that it's worth attempting to find these monks so we can raise the thorn wood?"

"I do."

"I don't know," said Zoya. "This stunt to see Alina. It feels like he's stalling. Or he has some other plan."

"I'm sure he does. But we need to find a way to stop the spread of this blight. If the Fjerdans weren't breathing down our necks, if the wedding weren't right around the corner, we might try to master this phenomenon without him. We'd let loose David and every scholar we have on this problem. But David's mind must remain on the work of winning the war. We need the Darkling now, just as I knew we would."

"Alina gave up her power to defeat him. She'll probably want to murder both of us for managing to bring him back."

Nikolai gave a rueful laugh. "The worst part is I don't think she would have fallen for his scheme. She would have taken one look at Elizaveta and turned right back around. Orphans, you know. Very wily."

Zoya contemplated another glass of brandy, but she didn't want to make herself ill. "We can't bring her here, not with all the guests arriving. And there's no way I'm letting him near Keramzin."

"We'll need a secure location. Isolated. And plenty of Sun Soldiers on hand."

"Not good enough. If Alina agrees, I'll take him to see her myself. I'll find whatever we need to raise the thorn wood."

Nikolai paused with his hand on the bottle. "The wedding is in less than two weeks. I . . . I need you here."

Zoya studied her empty glass, turning it clockwise, counterclockwise. "It would be better if I wasn't here. The rumors about us . . . No doubt Queen Makhi has heard them. My presence would only complicate things." That was some part of the truth. "Besides, do you trust anyone else to travel with him? To contain him if things go wrong?"

"I could go with you. At least part of the way."

"No. We need a king, not an adventurer. Your work is here. With Princess Ehri. Talk to her. Build the bond between you. We need her trust."

"You say that as if earning her trust will be easy."

"Her injuries could be a boon. Sit by her side dutifully. Read her stories, or have Tolya pick some poetry."

Nikolai shook his head. "All Saints, you're callous. She was almost burned alive."

"I know. But I'm also right. The Darkling knew how to use the people around him."

"And are we to behave as he did?"

Zoya's laugh sounded brittle to her ears. "A king with a demon inside him. A monk with the Darkling inside him. A general with a dragon inside her. We're all monsters now, Nikolai." She pushed her glass aside. It was time to say good night. She moved toward the door.

"Zoya," Nikolai said. "War can make it hard to remember who you are. Let's not forget the human parts of ourselves."

Did she want to forget? What a gift that would be. To never feel as humans did, to never grieve again. Then it wouldn't be so hard to leave this room. To shut the door on what might have been.

To say goodbye.

Early the next morning, Zoya sat down with Tamar to plan which Sun Soldiers would travel with her and to find the right location for this misbegotten meeting. They considered a decommissioned military base and a vineyard that had been struck by the blight. But the base was next to a town, and Zoya was wary of putting the Darkling near anything resembling the Fold. It might be an unreasonable fear, but she didn't want to risk the possibility that those dead sands might somehow trigger his powers. Eventually they decided on an abandoned sanatorium between Kribirsk and Balakirev. It was only a day's travel from Keramzin—assuming Alina was willing to help them.

As Zoya rolled up the map, Tamar placed a hand on her shoulder. "This is the right thing."

"It feels like a mistake."

"He can be bested, Zoya."

If that was the case, Zoya had yet to see the evidence. Even death hadn't beaten the Darkling. "Maybe."

"We have to make a move. Last night I had word that the blight struck near Shura. It covered ten square miles."

"*Ten?*" So it was getting worse.

"We're out of time," said Tamar.

Zoya rubbed a hand over her face. Just how many wars could they fight at once?

"You won't be here for the wedding," Tamar said, her lips curved in a sad half smile. "Everything will be different when you return."

Zoya didn't want to think about that. "Promise me you'll be careful," she said briskly. "There's no way to predict what Makhi might do. Or Princess Ehri, for that matter."

"It's a gamble," Tamar said, then grinned and flicked her thumbs over her axe handles. "But I'm ready for a good fight."

"I hope it doesn't come to that."

Tamar shrugged. "I can keep hope in my heart and a blade in my hand."

There was more Zoya wanted to say, but it all amounted to the same impossible thing: *Be safe.*

Zoya sent scouts to patrol the area around the sanatorium and make sure they'd have a clear place for their airship to land. The other preparations would have to wait. She needed to talk to Genya and David.

She found them in the Materialki workshops. When the Triumvirate had rebuilt the Little Palace after the Darkling's attack, they'd expanded these chambers to reflect the Fabrikators' greater role in the war effort. David had his own workroom and three assistants to help interpret and execute his plans. He split his time between here and the secret laboratory at Kirigin's estate, and Genya often shared this space, tailoring spies, helping people to remove scars, and concocting poisons and tonics when called for.

Now Zoya found her curled up on a settee beside David's desk, the light from his lamp making a circle around them. Her boots were off and she had tied her bright auburn hair into a knot. She had a half-eaten apple in one hand and a book on her lap, the sun emblazoned on her eye patch glinting. She looked like a beautiful, rakish pirate who had wandered off the pages of a storybook, a bit of sparkling chaos in David's carefully ordered world.

"What are you reading?" Zoya asked as she sat down by Genya's stockinged feet.

"It's a Kerch book on the detection of poisons. I had to send away for a Ravkan translation."

"Useful?"

"We'll see. The case studies are wonderfully gory. The rest is mostly moralizing about the perfidy of women and the dangers of the modern age, but it's giving me some ideas."

"For poisons?"

"And medicines. They're one and the same. The only difference is the dose." Genya frowned. "Something's wrong, isn't it?"

"The Darkling wants to see Alina."

Genya set aside her apple. "Are we meeting his demands now?"

"He claims he knows how to stop the Fold from expanding further."

"Do we believe him?"

"I don't know. He says we need to restage the *obisbaya*."

Genya's look of worry made perfect sense to Zoya. "The ritual that almost killed Nikolai."

"The very one. But to do it, we need to bring back the ancient thorn wood. Or so he says. What do you think, David?"

"Hmm?"

Genya shut her book with a snap. "Zoya would like to know if our greatest enemy should be allowed to try to kill the king again in order to possibly return stability to the Fold. Will it work?"

David put down his pen, picked it up again. His fingers were ink-stained. "Possibly." He thought for a moment. "The Fold was created through failed experiments in resurrection, attempts to raise animals from the dead as Morozova did and make them into amplifiers. He managed it with the stag and the sea whip."

And then with his own child. Alina had told them all the story, the truth behind the ancient legend. Ilya Morozova, the Bonesmith, had intended that the third amplifier would be the firebird. Instead it had been his daughter, a girl he had raised from the dead and imbued with power. That power had passed down through her descendants to a tracker—Alina's tracker, Malyen Oretsev—who had himself died and been brought back to life on the sands of the Fold.

"You remember Yuri?" she asked. "The Darkling wants to use the ritual to drive whatever remains of the little monk out of his body and absorb the king's demon. He thinks it will allow him to reclaim his power." A kind of shadow shell game. Zoya hated even thinking about it.

Genya's fists bunched, crushing the fabric of her *kefta*. "And we're going to let him?"

Zoya hesitated. She wanted to reach out to Genya, rest a comforting arm around her. Instead she said, "You know I would never let that happen. Nikolai believes he can prevent it."

"It's too great a risk to take. And will any of this really stop the Fold from spreading?"

David had been staring into space, tapping his fingers against his lips. His mouth was smudged with blue ink. "It *would* be a kind of return to the order of things, but . . ."

"But?" pressed Genya.

"It's hard to know. I've been reading through the research that Tolya and Yuri did. It's mostly religion, fanciful Saints' tales and very little science. But there's a pattern there, something I can't quite make out."

"What kind of pattern?" Zoya asked.

"The Small Science has always been about keeping power in check and maintaining the Grisha bond to the making at the heart of the world. The Fold was a violation of that, a tear in the fabric of the universe. That rupture has never actually been healed, and I don't know if the *obisbaya* will be enough. But those old stories of the Saints and the origins of Grisha power are all bound up together."

Zoya folded her arms. "So what I'm hearing from the greatest mind in the Second Army is, 'I guess it's worth a try'?"

David considered. "Yes."

Zoya didn't know why she bothered searching for certainty anymore. "If the Darkling's information is good, we'll need a powerful Fabrikator to help us raise the thorn wood once we have the seeds."

"I can attempt it," he said. "But it's not my particular talent. We should consider Leoni Hilli."

Zoya knew David didn't traffic in false humility. If he said Leoni was the better choice, he meant it. It was strange to realize that, excluding the king, she trusted no one in the world as much as the people in this room. It was Alina who had thrust them together, chosen each of them to represent their Grisha Orders—Materialki, Etherealki, and Corporalki. She had charged them to rebuild the Second Army, to gather the wreckage the Darkling had left in his wake and forge something strong and enduring from the scraps. And somehow, together, they had done it.

At the time, she had cursed Alina's name. She hadn't wanted to work with Genya or David. But her ambition—and her certainty that she was the best person for the job—hadn't allowed her to reject the opportunity. She'd believed she deserved the position and that over time she would bend Genya and David to her will or force them to relinquish their influence. Instead she'd come to value their opinions and rely on their judgment. Again and again, she'd found herself grateful that she wasn't alone in this.

"What are you scowling at, Zoya?" Genya asked, a smile quirking her mouth.

"Was I?" She supposed she was scowling at herself. It was embarrassing to realize how wrong she'd been.

Genya drew a handkerchief from her pocket, leaned over the back of the settee, and dabbed at David's lips. "My love, there's ink all over your face."

"Does it matter?"

"The correct response is, 'Beautiful wife, won't you kiss it away?'"

"Spontaneity." David nodded thoughtfully and drew out a journal to make note of this latest instruction. "I'll be ready next time."

"It's technically later. Let's try again."

How comfortable they were together. How easy. Zoya ignored the pang of jealousy she felt. Some people were built for love and some were built for war. One did not lend itself to the other.

"I'll write to Alina," Genya said. "The news should come from me. But . . . does that mean you won't be here for the wedding?"

"I'm sorry," Zoya said, though that was not entirely true. She wanted to be there for Genya, but she had spent her life standing on the outside of moments, unsure of where she belonged. She was at her best with a mission to accomplish, not in a chapel festooned with roses and echoing with declarations of love.

"I forgive you," said Genya. "Mostly. And people should be staring at the bride, not the gorgeous General Nazyalensky. Just take care of our girl. I hate the thought of the Darkling being near Alina again."

"I don't like it either."

"I hoped we wouldn't have to tell her he's returned."

"That we could put him in the ground and she'd never have to find out?"

Genya scoffed. "I would never bury that man. Who knows what might spring up from the soil?"

"He doesn't have to survive this trip," Zoya mused. "Accidents happen."

"Would you be killing him for you or for me?"

"I don't honestly know anymore."

Genya gave a little shiver. "I'm glad he'll be gone from this place. Even for a short while. I hate having him in our home."

Our home. Was that what this place was? Was that what they had made it?

"He should have a trial," said David.

Genya wrinkled her nose. "Or maybe he should be burned on the pyre as the Fjerdans do and scattered at sea. Am I a monster for saying so?"

"No," said Zoya. "As the king likes to remind me, we're human. Do you . . . I look back and I hate knowing how easy I was to manipulate."

"Hungry for love and full of pride?"

Zoya squirmed. "Was I that obvious?"

Genya looped her arm through Zoya's and leaned her head against her shoulder. Zoya tried not to stiffen. She wasn't good at this kind of closeness, but some childish part of her craved it, remembered how easy it had felt to laugh with her aunt, how glad she'd been when Lada had climbed into her lap to demand a story. She'd pretended to resent it, but she'd felt like she belonged with them.

"We were *all* that way. He took us from our families when we were so young."

"I don't regret that," Zoya said. "I hate him for many things, but not for teaching me to fight."

Genya looked up at her. "Just remember, Zoya, he wasn't teaching you to fight for yourself but in his service. He had only punishment for those who dared to speak against him."

He was the reason for Genya's scars, for all the pain she'd endured.

No, that wasn't true. Zoya had known what Genya was forced to suffer when they were just girls. Everyone had. But the other Grisha hadn't comforted her or cared for her. They'd mocked her, sneered at her, excluded her from their meals and the circle of their friendship. They'd left her unforgivably alone. Zoya had been the worst of them. The Darkling wasn't the only one who owed penance.

But I can change that now, Zoya vowed. *I can make sure he never returns here.*

She let herself rest her cheek against the silky top of Genya's head and made them both a promise: Wherever this adventure led, the Darkling wasn't coming back from it.

12
NIKOLAI

ZOYA HADN'T WAITED TO SAY goodbye. Alina had been contacted and—thanks to her generosity or an unhealthy taste for martyrdom—had agreed to the meeting. Zoya had arranged the mission with predictably ruthless efficiency, and a week later, she was gone. Before dawn, without fanfare or parting words. Nikolai was both stung and grateful. She was right. The gossip around them had become a liability, and they had enough of those already. Zoya was his general and he her king. Best for everyone to remember it. And now he could visit the Little Palace without having to worry about bumping into her and enduring her acid tongue.

Excellent, he told himself as he made the walk from the Grand Palace. *So why do I feel like I've had my guts gently gnawed on by a volcra?*

He passed through the wooded tunnel that he now recognized as quince and headed down past the lake, where he could see two of his new flyers bobbing gently in the water, gray morning light glinting off their hulls. They were extraordinary machines, but Ravka simply didn't have the money to produce them in any real quantity. Yet. Perhaps an infusion of Shu gold would do the trick.

Tamar's spies had brought them news of the Fjerdan prince's public collapse, and it didn't bode well for Ravka. They'd renewed diplomatic talks, but Nikolai knew Fjerda was holding separate conversations with West Ravka and trying to encourage them to secede. Jarl Brum had been steering his country's strategic choices for years, and a weakened Prince Rasmus would only embolden him.

The infirmary was located in the Corporalki wing of the Little Palace, behind the imposing red-lacquered doors. There were private rooms for patients who needed extensive care and quiet, and one of them had been set aside for Princess Ehri Kir-Taban. The hallway was heavily protected by both Grisha and palace guards.

Ehri lay in a narrow bed. She wore a green silk dressing gown embroidered with pale yellow flowers. Her skin was a raw pink, shiny and taut. The fire had scorched the hair from her head, which was wrapped in soft white linen. She had no eyebrows or lashes. Genya had explained that it would still take several days to bring Ehri's flesh and hair back to full health, but they had reversed the worst of the damage. It was a miracle she had survived—a miracle wrought by Grisha Healers, who had restored her body and kept her pain in check as they did it.

Nikolai sat down beside the bed. Ehri said nothing. She rolled her head to the side, turning her gaze to the gardens and away from him. A single tear slipped down her pink cheek. Nikolai drew a handkerchief from his pocket and dabbed it away.

"I would prefer that you left," she said.

That was what she'd said every time he'd summoned the will

to speak to her since her true identity had been discovered. But he couldn't put this off any longer.

"We should talk," he said. "I've brought novels and summer cherries by way of a bribe."

"Summer cherries. In the dead of winter."

"It is never winter in the Grisha greenhouses."

She closed her eyes. "I'm grotesque."

"You are pink and rather hairless. Like a baby, and people love babies." Actually, she looked more like the hairless cat his aunt Ludmilla had favored more than any of her children, but that seemed an impolitic thing to say to a lady.

Ehri did not wish to be charmed. "Must you make a joke of everything?"

"I must. By royal mandate and the curse of my own disposition. I find life quite unbearable without laughter."

She returned to studying the gardens.

"Do you like the view?" he asked.

"This palace is nothing compared to the grandeur of Ahmrat Jen."

"I imagine not. Ravka has never been able to match Shu Han for monuments or scenery. I'm told the architect Toh Yul-Gham took one look at the Grand Palace and declared it an affront to the eyes of god."

The corner of Ehri's lips tugged up in the barest smile. "Are you a student of architecture?"

"No. I just like to build things. Contraptions, gadgets, flying machines."

"Weapons of war."

"That has been a necessity, not a calling."

Ehri shook her head and another tear escaped. Nikolai offered her the handkerchief. "Keep it," he said. "It's got the Lantsov crest embroidered on it. You can blow your nose into it and take revenge upon your captors."

Ehri pressed it to her eyes. "Why? Why would the Tavgharad do such a thing? Shenye guarded my cradle while I slept as an infant. Tahyen taught me to climb trees. I don't understand it."

"What happened before we arrived that afternoon?"

"Nothing! Your guards brought me a letter from my sister. A reply to the wedding invitation you insisted on sending. She asked that I inform the Tavgharad of the wedding, and I brought it to them. They . . . they told me the message was a code. That it was time to escape."

"But there was another command in your sister's letter."

"I read it myself!" Ehri cried. "There was no such thing!"

"What else could make the Tavgharad take such an action?"

Ehri turned her head away again.

Nikolai hadn't really expected her to believe him. The princess had never been willing to accept that she was not meant to survive her trip to Os Alta, that her older sister had been planning her death all along. Even after what she had suffered, maybe because of what she had suffered, she couldn't stand the thought. The physical pain was bad enough, but another betrayal from her sister was too much to accept.

The proper thing was to give her space, a chance to heal. But he'd squandered the time required to be a sensitive suitor. And now he needed someone else to make his argument for him.

"A moment please," he said, and headed into the hall.

He returned pushing a wheeled chair.

"Mayu!" Ehri exclaimed.

Nikolai had deliberately kept them separated in the weeks since Mayu Kir-Kaat's attempt to assassinate him. Until last night, there had been no little chats with Mayu or attempts to win her to his side. It had been impossible for him to feel sympathy for the girl who had killed Isaak. His own guilt was too overwhelming. Commanding armies had meant sending countless men to their deaths. Being a king meant knowing there would be more. But Isaak had died pretending to be Nikolai, wearing Nikolai's face, protecting Nikolai's crown.

"They said you were near death!" said the princess.

"No," Mayu whispered. She had been kept under restraint, and the Grisha Healers had not allowed her to return to full health. She was simply too much of a threat. Mayu Kir-Kaat had tried to kill the king, and the women of the Tavgharad were some of the best-trained soldiers in the world.

"Last night, I showed Mayu the letter your sister sent," said Nikolai.

"It's just a letter! An answer to an invitation!"

Nikolai settled back into his chair and gestured for Mayu to speak.

"I recognized the poem she quoted."

"'Let them be as deer freed from the hunt,'" said Ehri. "I remember one of my tutors taught it."

"It's from 'The Song of the Stag' by Ni Yul-Mahn," said Mayu. "Do you remember how it ends?"

"I don't recall. I've never had a taste for the new poets."

A sad smile touched Mayu's lips, and Nikolai wondered if she was thinking of Isaak, who had consumed poetry the way other men drank wine.

"It tells the story of a royal hunt," she said. "A herd of deer are pursued through the woods and countryside by a relentless pack of hounds. Rather than let themselves be slaughtered by the pack, the deer hurl themselves off a cliffside."

Ehri's brow furrowed. "The Tavgharad killed themselves . . . because of a poem?"

"Because of a queen's command."

"And they tried to kill you too," said Nikolai.

"Why?" Ehri said. She opened her mouth, closed it, trying to find some argument to make, some logic. In the end the same word escaped her. "Why?"

Nikolai sighed. He could say that Queen Makhi was ruthless, but she wasn't any more ruthless than she'd had to be. "Because when I sent that invitation, I forced her hand. Queen Makhi doesn't want us to marry. She doesn't want a Ravkan-Shu alliance. Ask yourself this: If Mayu was sent to impersonate you, to murder me and herself, then why put you in harm's way at all? Why not let you rest comfortably at home while Mayu Kir-Kaat did the dirty work?"

"I was meant to be here to help Mayu, to answer questions, coach her through matters only royalty could understand. Then when it was . . . over, I would return home."

"Did your sister's ministers know about the plot to assassinate me?" How coolly he spoke of his own death. He really was getting good at this. *Is it the demon?* he wondered. The constant proximity to the darkness of the void? Or was he just getting reckless?

Ehri made nervous folds in the sheets with her pink fingertips. "I . . . assume they did."

He looked to Mayu, who shrugged and said, "It was not for me to ask."

"My sister told me to keep silent," Ehri said slowly, smoothing out the folds she'd just made. "She said . . . she said the people would not approve of her . . . of our plot."

Nikolai had to respect that she didn't try to lay full blame for the assassination attempt at her sister's door.

"I should think not," he said. "The people love you. They wouldn't want you in danger." He sat forward and clasped his hands. "She was *counting* on their love for you. If you had perished with the Tavgharad the other day, I would have no way to prove that they had died by their own hand or that you had been their victim. When your death became known, the Shu people would have risen up, demanding action, and Queen Makhi would have what she wants: an excuse for war."

"The queen doesn't know I'm alive, does she?" asked Mayu as realization struck.

"No, indeed."

Mayu looked at Ehri. "We are the last witnesses. Only we know of the plot she formulated against the king. We have both been her pawns."

Nikolai stood and began wheeling Mayu's chair back toward the hall. But before they reached the door, Ehri said, "Mayu Kir-Kaat." She was sitting up, her frame silhouetted against the glass, her back erect, her bearing every inch the princess. "I am sorry for what my sister asked of you . . . and for what I asked of you."

Mayu looked up, startled. For a long moment they stared at each other, princess and commoner. Mayu bobbed her head. Nikolai didn't know if it was a thank-you or just an acknowledgment.

"Why did you bring us together?" Mayu asked as he wheeled her down the corridor, past the guards.

"I like to keep all of my potential assassins in one room." It wasn't much of an answer. He knew he was taking a chance in allowing these women to speak, to find common ground. They had both been part of the plot to kill him. They were both responsible for Isaak's death. They were both bound to the Shu throne through ties of tradition and blood. But Mayu's voice meant more than Nikolai's ever could. He decided to opt for the truth. "I'm not sure why. My gut told me it was right you should talk. I suppose I'm hoping you'll help me keep my crown and keep our countries from going to war."

They entered Mayu's room. It had no windows, no view of the gardens. It was more like a prison cell.

"If Queen Makhi wants war, then that is what the Tavgharad want."

"Are you so sure you're still Tavgharad?" he asked.

That arrow struck its mark. Mayu looked at her lap and said, "You're nothing like Isaak. If any of us had so much as glimpsed you before, we never would have been fooled by a pretender."

"And if it had been me you met, your plot would have ended before it began. I never would have been deceived by a bodyguard in fancy gowns."

"You're so sure?"

"Yes," he said simply. "But Isaak was trained to be a soldier, not a king."

When Mayu looked up, her golden eyes were full of rage. "You are a glib, vain fool. You are everything Isaak was not."

Nikolai held her gaze. "I would argue we were both fools."

"He was a better man than you'll ever be."

"On that we can agree." Nikolai sat down on the edge of her bed. "You fell in love with him."

Mayu looked away. She was a soldier. She would not weep, but her voice was ragged when she spoke. "I thought I loved a king. I thought it could never be."

"One of those things was true." Did it help to know how much she regretted Isaak's loss? That they both grieved for the sacrifice he'd made? Even if it did, he couldn't spare her now. "Mayu, my spies have found word of your brother."

Mayu covered her face with her hands. Nikolai remembered what Tolya and Tamar had told him about the *kebben*, about the bond between twins. He'd understood what this information would mean to her.

"He's alive," Nikolai said.

"I know. I would know if he was dead. I would feel it. Have they hurt him?"

"He's a part of the *khergud* program."

"Queen Makhi swore she would free him." Mayu released a bitter laugh. "But why would she keep her word? I failed. The king lives."

"Thank you for that." Nikolai watched her carefully. "You're thinking of taking your own life."

Her expression showed the truth of it. "I am a prisoner in a foreign country. Your Grisha keep my body weak. My brother is having his soul tortured out of him and I can do nothing to stop it." She cast her eyes up to the ceiling. "And I murdered an innocent man, a good man, for nothing. I am not Tavgharad. I am not a princess. I am not anyone."

"You are Reyem Yul-Kaat's sister, and he still lives."

"But as what? The *khergud* . . . The things they endure, they lose their humanity."

Nikolai thought of the demon lurking inside him, the power of it. "Maybe the gift of being human is that we do not give up—even when all hope is lost."

"Then maybe I'm the one who isn't human anymore." A grim thought, but her look was speculative when she asked, "Will you force Princess Ehri to wed you?"

"I don't think I'll have to."

Mayu shook her head in disbelief. And perhaps in grief for the humble boy she'd met in a king's clothes. "You're that charming?"

"I have a gift for persuasion. I once talked a tree out of its leaves."

"Nonsense."

"Well, it was autumn. I can't take full credit."

"More foolishness. You think to persuade Ehri and me to turn against Queen Makhi."

"I think the queen has made the argument for me. She nearly cost both of you your lives."

"Tell me you would have spared my life or even Isaak's, if your nation's future hung in the balance."

There was no room for lies now. "I can't."

"Tell me you wouldn't sacrifice my life and Princess Ehri's to save your crown."

Nikolai rose. "I can't do that either. But before I put anyone to death and we all go merrily to the next world, I'd ask you to stay alive and try to entertain a bit of hope."

"Hope for what?"

"That there is never only one answer to a question. You're alive today, Mayu Kir-Kaat, and I'd prefer you kept it that way. And Isaak, that brave, besotted martyr, would want the same."

She closed her eyes. "Though I put a knife in his heart?"

"I think so. Love is not known for making men reasonable. I think that's one of the few things Isaak and I had in common—an inability to stop loving whom we should not. Give me a chance to show you what might be."

He'd spoken almost those same words to Zoya. *Give me a chance. Give me time.* Every day he prayed he might find a way to keep his country from destruction, to make peace a possibility. But he couldn't do it alone.

He strode to the door. "I will tell my Healers to restore your strength."

"You . . . you will?" She didn't believe him.

"Friend or foe, Ravka will have you at your best, Mayu Kir-Kaat. I've never been one to shy away from a challenge."

Nikolai had planned to ride to Lazlayon to meet with David and the other Fabrikators, but he needed to clear his head, and the sky was the best place to do it. Instead of returning to the Grand Palace, he walked down to the lake. He released the tethers that bound his favorite flyer to the dock and slipped into the cockpit of the *Sparrowhawk*, engaging the propellers. He pulled on his goggles, and in moments, the flyer was bouncing over the water of the lake like a skipping stone, then rising into the air.

The demon liked to fly. Nikolai could feel it turn its face to the wind, longing to be free to ride the clouds. He soared past the walls of Os Alta, and northeast, sailing over miles of farmland. Up here, the world felt wide and he felt less like a king than the privateer he'd once been. *We need a king, not an adventurer.* A shame.

He'd had to be a king when he spoke to Ehri and Mayu. He had needed to seem confident and assured, just human enough. But being around them, talking about Isaak, had left him shaken. Nikolai had been the one to bring Isaak to the palace and make him one of his guards. They were the same age and yet, how little of the world had Isaak had a chance to see? He would never be at home with his sisters again, his mother. He would never translate another poem or greet another day. Nikolai knew guilt would only cloud his judgment, slow him down, keep him from making the difficult choices he would need to make in the days to come. It wasn't useful, but he couldn't shrug it off like some kind of mood. Isaak had trusted him, and that trust had gotten him killed.

Too quickly, he saw the glittering rooftops of the Gilded Bog, Count Kirigin's estate and pleasure gardens, the secret home of Ravka's weapons development base. He cut his engines and let the *Sparrowhawk* glide gently down through the cloud cover, the rumble of the flyer replaced by the rush of the air, the heavy silence of the sky. He thought he heard a low whistle from somewhere below. His mind understood what it was a bare second too late.

Boom.

Something struck the *Sparrowhawk*'s right wing. It caught fire instantly, smoke billowing from the little craft.

All Saints. He'd been fired upon.

No, that wasn't quite right. David and his team thought he was arriving on horseback, and they were in the middle of weapons testing. Nikolai had essentially flown his plane into a missile. He really was a fool. *Glad I got to see the rockets working before I die in a fiery blaze.*

Nikolai strummed the engine to life again, trying to right the little flyer, but he was already going into a spin, hurtling toward the ground at terrifying speed.

The demon tore at his mind, wild and thrashing within him, screaming to be free.

But Nikolai would not give up control. *If this is the end, then you die with me.* Maybe this was the way he would liberate his country from the Fold. Zoya would be free to kill the Darkling after all.

Think.

Nikolai had lost track of where the ground was. The noise from the engine rattled his skull. The controls in his hands were useless. *This is it*, he thought, desperately trying to pull back on the throttle.

The demon shrieked, but Nikolai would not release it. *I will die a king.*

He was yanked backward against the seat. His stomach lurched. It felt as if a huge hand had seized the flyer and thrust it upward.

A moment later the craft was gently set upon the mist-shrouded waters of the Gilded Bog. Nikolai heard shouting, and then he was being pulled from the cockpit.

"I'm fine," he said. Though he had cracked his skull against the seat at some point. He touched the back of his head. He was bleeding. And there was a very good chance he might vomit. "I'm fine."

"David," said Genya. "You almost killed the king."

"He wasn't supposed to be there!"

"It was my fault," said Nikolai. He took a woozy step on the dock, then another, trying to get his bearings. "I'm fine," he repeated.

Nadia and Adrik must have summoned wind to stop his descent. David, Genya, and Leoni were staring at him, along with a group of First Army engineers. A weapons test, just as he'd thought. He only wished he'd thought it sooner rather than later. "It was good practice," he said, trying to ignore the throbbing in his skull. "In case I'm ever shot down."

"If you're ever shot down, there won't be Squallers there to save you," Adrik said. "Why didn't you eject?"

"He wasn't wearing a parachute," Genya said, glowering at him.

"I didn't think I would need one," Nikolai protested. "This wasn't supposed to be a dogfight. More importantly, does this mean the rockets work?"

"Absolutely not," said David.

"Sort of," said Leoni.

"Show me," said Nikolai.

Genya planted her hands on her hips. "You will sit yourself down and let me make sure you don't have a concussion. Then you will have a cup of tea. And then, if I'm feeling generous, you can talk to David about things that explode."

"You do realize I'm the king?"

"Do *you*?"

Nikolai looked to David for help, but David just shrugged. "I don't argue with my wife when she's right."

"Oh, fine," said Nikolai. "But I want a cookie with my tea."

They descended to the laboratories in the clanking brass elevator. The dark rooms and narrow hallways didn't make for the most healing atmosphere, but they did guarantee privacy. He was grateful for a few minutes to gather his thoughts. He'd been fired at plenty of times, shot more than once, turned into a shadow creature, and stabbed with a letter opener by an otherwise lovely young lady who

169

had been insulted by his attempt at a romantic sonnet. But really, how many things rhymed with "tremulous nests"? He was also fairly sure his older brother had tried to poison him when he was twelve. But this was the closest he'd ever come to dying. The demon was still writhing inside him. It had felt the nearness of death too, and it had been trapped, powerless as they plummeted toward the earth.

What would have happened if Nikolai had let the demon break free? Would it have helped him? Could he have controlled it? It was too steep a wager.

They settled around a table in one of the blueprint rooms as Genya tended to the back of Nikolai's head and David brewed tea.

"Why is my lead scientist fussing with a kettle?" Nikolai asked.

"Because he doesn't like the way anyone else makes it," said Adrik, pulling a tin of chocolate biscuits from a drawer and setting it on the table.

"I wrote out instructions," David said, brushing the messy brown hair from his eyes. He looked even paler in the dim light of the lab. As much as Nikolai appreciated David's work ethic, the Fabrikator could use a holiday.

"My love," Genya said gently. "It doesn't take seventeen steps to brew tea."

"It does if you do it properly."

"Talk to me about my rockets," said Nikolai.

Nadia set down a tray of mismatched cups and saucers, most of them chipped, though the pattern of golden hummingbirds was exquisite. Nikolai suspected they were the castoffs from Count Kirigin's collection, victims of his often rowdy guests.

David and Nadia looked to Genya, who gave a gracious nod. "You may proceed."

"Well," said David, "a rocket can be very simple."

"Like a cup of tea?" asked Leoni innocently.

"A bit," said David, oblivious to the glint in her eye. "Any child can build one with a little sugar and some potassium nitrate."

Genya cast Nikolai a suspicious glance. "Why do I think you did just that?"

"Of course I did. If one can, one ought to. You know the skylight in the western ballroom?"

"Yes."

"It wasn't always there."

"You put a hole in the ceiling?"

"A small one."

"Those frescoes are hundreds of years old!" she cried.

"Sometimes one must break with tradition. Quite literally. Now would someone please distract Genya?"

Nadia sat up a bit straighter. "There are three challenges to a rocket. Launching it without blowing it up. Arming it without blowing it up. And aiming it without blowing it up."

Nikolai nodded. "I detect a theme."

"We seem to be able to manage two out of the three, but never all three at once," said Leoni, her sunny smile bright against her brown skin. Somehow she still managed to make it seem like she was delivering good news.

If they could master the rockets, Nikolai knew it would change everything. Ravka and Fjerda were nearly evenly matched in the air. But Fjerda had what could be a decisive advantage on the ground. The rockets would allow Nikolai to keep Ravka's troops well away from the front lines, and they'd have a real answer to the might of Fjerda's tanks. It would become a game of range.

"Just how big can these rockets get?" asked Nikolai.

"Big enough to level an entire factory," said David. "Or half a city block."

The room was suddenly very quiet, the reality of what they were discussing settling around them, making the air feel thick with the consequences of what they would decide here. *Give me a chance to show you what might be*, Nikolai had told Zoya. He'd meant peace. He'd meant compromise. Not this.

"At what distance?" Nikolai asked.

"I don't really know," said David. "The issue is weight. Steel is too heavy. Aluminum may be too. They're fine for testing, but if we're serious about using these rockets, we need a lighter metal."

"Like what?"

"Titanium is lighter but more durable," said Leoni. "And it doesn't degrade."

"It's also rarer," said Nadia, tucking a loose strand of her blond hair back into a twist. "We don't have much of a stockpile."

"*Are* we seriously considering this?" Genya said softly.

"I'll give you the rockets we've been working on," said David. "But even if we can source more titanium, I won't build them bigger."

"May I ask why?" said Nikolai, though he thought he knew.

"I won't make a city killer."

"And if it's the threat we need?"

"If we build one," said David, "it won't stop with us. It never does."

David was one of the most talented Fabrikators and thinkers of his time, maybe of any time. But his gifts had always been turned to waging war. That was the nature of being Ravkan. It had been for hundreds of years.

And David was right. Only a short time ago, they'd all been fighting with sabers and muskets, then the repeating rifle had come along and made swords all but useless. What they were talking about would be a frightening escalation, and once Ravka mastered targeted rockets, Fjerda would as well.

"We have to decide what kind of war we want to wage," David said.

"I'm not sure we get to make that choice," Nikolai replied. "We can't ignore what will happen if Fjerda masters this technology first. And even if they don't, they're going to be ready the next time we meet."

David was silent for a long moment. "The things the Darkling asked me to do . . . I did them mindlessly, thoughtlessly. I helped put the collar around Alina's neck. I created the *lumiya* that allowed him to enter the Fold without her power. Without my help, he never could have . . . I won't be responsible for this too."

Nikolai turned his attention to Genya. "And do you agree with this?"

"No," said Genya, taking David's hand. "But I was the Darkling's weapon too. I know what that feels like, and this is David's choice to make."

"We don't have enough titanium for a city killer," said Leoni, eager to make peace. "Maybe it doesn't matter."

"It matters," said Adrik. "There's no point to fighting a war if you don't intend to win it."

"There's more," said Nikolai. "There are rumors the Fjerdan crown prince may not survive the winter."

Genya shook her head. "I didn't realize his condition was so severe."

"No one did. I suspect his family has worked hard to keep it a secret, something with which I can certainly sympathize. It's possible that our alliance with the Shu will give them pause—assuming we're successful in forging it. But we need to accept that the prince may die and the Grimjers may have no choice but to wage war."

Leoni rubbed her thumb over the chip in her saucer, using her power to slowly repair it. "I don't understand. If Rasmus dies, his father will still rule. His younger brother will become heir."

"Heir to nothing," said Adrik. "Fjerdans don't think of the royal family the way that the Shu do, or even the way Ravkans do. They follow the will of Djel, and *strength* is the way Djel shows favor. The Fjerdan dynasties that have reigned have always taken their place by force. The Grimjers will need to prove they still deserve the throne."

"Perhaps I should try to take that crown instead," suggested Nikolai.

Adrik sniffed. "Do you even speak Fjerdan?"

"I do. So badly a nice man named Knut once offered me a sizable ruby to stop."

"So now the Grimjers have a young, weak, sickly prince poised to succeed an elderly king?" asked Nadia.

"Yes," said Nikolai. "The royal family is vulnerable and they know it. If they opt for peace, they risk looking weak. If they opt for war, they will be determined to win at any cost, and Jarl Brum will be there to goad them on."

"We have the Zemeni," said Leoni, hopeful as always.

"And the Kerch won't ally with Fjerda outright," Genya added. "Not at the risk of their precious neutrality."

"But they may be angry enough to secretly lend Fjerda aid," said Adrik.

"What about the Apparat?" Genya asked, turning her cup in its saucer.

Nikolai shook his head. "The man has changed sides so many times, I wonder if even he knows where his loyalties lie."

"He always goes to the side he believes will win," said David. "It's what he did in the civil war."

"That explains why he's in Fjerda," Adrik said gloomily.

"Unfortunately," Nikolai admitted, "Adrik is right. Fjerda has the advantage and if they march, it will mean an end to a free Ravka." Demidov would take the throne. Grisha would be rounded up for trial. His people would be subjects of a puppet king committed to serving Fjerda's interests. And his country? It would become a staging ground for the inevitable fight between Fjerda and Shu Han. "My desire to be beloved conflicts mightily with our need to win this war. I've become an accountant, tallying lives to be taken, lives to be spared."

"The choices we're making are awful ones," said Genya.

"But we must make them just the same. I hope diplomacy may still win this fight. I hope we can offer Fjerda a peace that they will take. I hope we'll never need to unleash the terrors we seek to build."

"And what happens when we're out of hope?" asked David.

"We end where we always end," said Nikolai. "With war."

13
NINA

THE ROYAL GUARDS ESCORTED Nina back to the Brums' quarters. With every step, she wondered if an order would ring out down the corridors for her to be clapped in chains and thrown into a jail cell, then burned as a witch for good measure. Her whole body was slicked in cold sweat and her heart was pounding.

But no alarm came. Once Nina had understood the Grimjer queen's longing, her fear for her son, she hadn't hesitated to play on it. It was cruel, but if she could guide the queen's faith in Djel, that meant she might open the door for the Saints, possibly even Grisha. Nina's life and her country's future were at stake, and she would use whatever weapon she could fashion to win this fight.

All of the Brums were waiting in their grand parlor, a fire roaring in the hearth. A tray with a cold supper of cured meats and pickled vegetables had been laid out along with barley water and a bottle of *brännvin*, but it didn't look as if anyone had done more than pick at it. Nina went straight to Hanne and practically fell into her arms.

For once she didn't have to pretend weakness or worry. She had taken a huge leap with the queen, made another reckless move, but maybe, maybe it would pay off.

"What happened?" said Hanne. "What did she say?"

"Very little." Nina tried to pull herself back together as Ylva settled her onto the sofa and poured her a glass of water. She had been too busy recovering from her audience with Queen Agathe to come up with a proper lie to tell. "I scarcely know what to think."

At least that much was true.

"What did she ask you?" Brum queried. He was watching Nina very closely, and everything in his stance spoke caution. He had invited a near stranger into his home and today, both his daughter and this stranger had put his political career at risk.

"She's concerned for her son," said Nina. "I was never blessed with children, but I do understand. She is sending investigators to my old village to confirm that I am who I say."

Hanne drew in a breath at this, her face turning ashen.

"And what will they find?" asked Brum.

"Jarl!" exclaimed Ylva. "How can you ask that?"

"It's better that we know now so that we can better protect ourselves."

Nina took Ylva's hand. "Please," she said, forcing admiration into her voice. "Do not quarrel. Of course your husband would want to protect his family. It is his duty and his honor to do so. I can't tell you how often I wish my husband were still here to look after me." She let her exhaustion pour into her voice, making it quiver. "Commander Brum, I can only assure you that the queen's men will find no reason to doubt me or my sad history."

Brum seemed to thaw a bit. "It is a dangerous time. For all of us."

"But maybe that will change," said Ylva. "Through their kindness and piety, Hanne and Mila earned Prince Rasmus' true regard today. He wishes to see them again. That favor can only be a good thing."

"I'm not so sure," muttered Brum, pouring himself a tiny glass of *brännvin*. "The prince is capricious. His health has made him unpredictable and secretive."

Hanne bristled at this. "He is in pain, Papa. Perhaps that's why he isn't always in good temper."

"Perhaps." Brum sat. He was choosing his words carefully. "He's not fond of my advice. It's possible he may take it out on you."

"If that's the case, there's nothing we can do about it." Hanne's tone was matter-of-fact. "He is the crown prince. If he wishes to string me up by my toes, he may do it. If his mother the queen wishes to send Mila out into the snow barefoot, then she may do that too. But for now, all he has done is command us to join him for lunch, and I hardly see how we can refuse him."

Ylva was smiling. "She's right, you know. We've raised a very sensible daughter."

Brum's expression remained unyielding. "Just be on your guard, Hanne. And you too, Mila. The Ice Court is a sorry place for soft hearts."

Niweh sesh, Nina thought as she and Hanne said their good nights. *I have no heart.*

~ ❧ ~

Two days later, Hanne put on one of her new gowns of sea-foam silk and Nina dressed in more modest rose wool. They'd been too deluged with invitations since Maidenswalk to do much more than try to keep up, but now Nina fastened a necklace of blue topaz around Hanne's neck and said, "Your father was right."

Hanne laughed. "Words I never expected to hear from your lips."

"This *is* a dangerous time. You were healing the prince when we spoke to him the other day. You can't keep doing that."

"Why not? If I can offer some small comfort, I should." She hesitated. "We can't just abandon him. I know what it's like not to measure up to what Fjerdans idealize. That's a hurt that never goes away. And he has thousands of people staring at him, judging him. What if we could help him heal, help him become a better prince and someday a better king?"

Now, that was interesting. A tonic to Brum's warmongering, someone who might guide Fjerda in the direction of peace. All of Nina's instincts told her this could be worth the risk, a perfect complement to her gamble with the Grimjer queen. It just felt different when Hanne was taking the risk too.

"If he were to find out what you are—"

Hanne picked up her wrap. "How would he find out? I am the daughter of Fjerda's most notorious witchhunter. I attended the Gäfvalle convent under the watchful eye of the Wellmother—"

"May she rest in misery."

"As Djel commands it," Hanne said with theatrical primness. "I healed the crown prince before the entire royal court and no one has discovered what I am. Besides, isn't this what you wanted? A chance to get close to people who might know something about Vadik Demidov?"

"Not *this* close. A nice count. Maybe a duke. Not a *prince*."

Hanne grinned. "Why settle?"

Her eyes were sparkling, her cheeks were flushed. She looked happier than Nina had seen her in weeks.

All Saints, it's because she's helping someone. Grisha always looked and felt healthier when they used their power. But this was something more.

"You are too good, Hanne. You get the chance to help some spoiled royal whelp and you light up like you've just seen a three-foot-tall stack of waffles."

"I've never actually had a waffle."

Nina clutched at her heart. "Yet another thing this cursed country has to account for." She paused, then fluffed a bit of pale green lace that had gotten caught on Hanne's neckline. "Just . . . be careful. And don't get carried away."

"I won't," said Hanne, rising in a cloud of rustling silk. She glanced over her shoulder. "Anyway, that's *your* job."

———— ❦ ————

This time, they were brought to a larger, circular receiving room, ringed by columns, a fountain at its center—three stone sylphs holding a pitcher aloft in their slender arms. There was some kind of party or salon going on, and murmured conversation filled the echoing space.

"What exactly do we do here?" whispered Hanne.

"I think we find something to drink and try to look like we belong?"

"Have I mentioned that I loathe parties?"

Nina looped her arm through Hanne's. "Have I mentioned that I love them?"

They made their way through the crush of people toward a table covered in glasses of something pink and sparkling. Could it possibly be—

"The look on your face," Hanne said with a laugh. "It's lemonade, not champagne."

Nina tried to hide her disappointment. She should know better by now. If Fjerda could have made fun a punishable offense, they would have. Then she spotted a pale blue sash and a muddy-blond head moving through the crowd.

She didn't let her gaze linger, but that was most definitely Vadik Demidov, surrounded by a cluster of noblemen—and trailed by the Apparat.

"Let's try to get closer," she whispered.

Before they could even take a step in Demidov's direction, Joran had swooped down upon them. He looked like a rotten tooth in his black uniform, completely out of place in this confectionery of pastel silk and chiffon. "Prince Rasmus commands your presence."

"Of course," said Hanne. There was no other reply to a prince. They were led to an alcove nearly hidden from the room by silvery potted trees and thick cream curtains. It was the perfect place to spy without concern for being spied upon.

Prince Rasmus sat on a cushioned chair that was something between a throne and a settee. He was not reclining in comfort as he had been last time, and the effort of remaining upright and hiding his fatigue was costing him. He looked pale, and Nina could see the rapid rise and fall of his chest. This was what Brum had meant. The royal family knew the prince had to appear in public—particularly after the disaster at Maidenswalk—but they had tried to place him away from the bustle so that he wouldn't be overtaxed.

Nina and Hanne curtsied.

"Go on," the prince said with a disinterested wave of his hand. He was far more out of sorts than he'd seemed the other day.

They entered and sat themselves on low tuffets.

"You both need to work on your curtsies," he observed with displeasure.

But Hanne only smiled. "I fear mine will get no better with practice. I've never been known for my grace."

181

That wasn't true at all. Hanne was graceful running or on horseback. The artifice of court didn't suit her. And as for Nina, she could manage an exquisite curtsy, but Mila Jandersdat, widow of a man who traded frozen fish, certainly could not.

Rasmus' eyes roved over Nina now. "Your mistress wears silk but dresses her maid in wool. That speaks of a petty and jealous disposition."

He really was in a foul temper. Nina saw Hanne's fingers flex slightly and gave her a warning glance—not too much, not too soon.

"Wool suits me very well," said Nina. "I wouldn't know what to do in silks or satin." A profound lie. She could think of nothing better than sliding about naked on satin sheets. Matthias would have been scandalized. And what would Hanne think? The thought popped into her head unbidden, followed by a wave of guilt.

"I find most women learn to love luxury quickly enough," the prince said. "I see no jewels at Mila's neck nor on her ears. Your father should remedy that, Hanne. He doesn't want to look like a miser."

Hanne inclined her head, then looked up at the prince from beneath her lashes. "I should tell you that I'll pass along your advice, but I have no intention of doing so."

Rasmus huffed a breath. "You are brash to admit you would deny a prince." Hanne's fingers shifted again, and the prince gave a deep sigh of what might have been relief. "All the same, I can't blame you. Your father can be quite terrifying." He glanced at Joran, who stood at attention beside him. "Of course, Joran isn't afraid, is he? Answer, Joran."

"I have only respect for Commander Brum."

It was hard to believe the guard was just sixteen, especially beside the prince.

"Joran is always appropriate. Minding me is a great honor. Or so they say. But I know better. It was some kind of punishment. Joran ran afoul of the good Commander Brum, and now he must play nanny to a weakling prince."

"You are not so weak as all that," said Hanne.

The prince took another long breath. He'd lost some of the rigid set of his shoulders, and the sheen of sweat was gone from his forehead.

"Some days I feel all right," he said. "Some days I don't feel weak at all." He gave a little laugh. "And today I actually find I have some appetite. Joran, have food brought to us."

But the servants had already heard and were scurrying to obey.

"We saw that Vadik Demidov is here," Nina ventured.

"Oh yes," said Rasmus. "The Little Lantsov never misses a party."

"And is he really of royal blood?"

"That's the topic of conversation at every dinner party from here to the Elbjen. Why are you so interested?"

Hanne laughed easily. "Mila is obsessed with Vadik Demidov."

"Sweet Djel, why? He's a boring lump of country bumpkin."

"But it's such a marvelous story," said Nina. "A boy of royal blood plucked from obscurity."

"I suppose it does have the ring of a fairy tale to it. But it's not as if he was found herding goats somewhere."

"Where *was* he found?"

"I don't really know. Shivering in some obscure dacha he couldn't afford to heat. Or at least I think that's the story."

"You aren't curious?" Nina pushed.

The servants returned and set a spread of smoked eel and herring before them.

"Why should I be?"

Nina felt her temper rising. "He will be a king, will he not?"

"So will I, assuming I live."

An awkward silence fell.

"I . . . I'm in a mood today," said Rasmus. It wasn't an apology, but it was as close as a future king might come. "My parents felt it was essential that I appear in public quickly after what happened at the start of Heartwood."

"They should have let you rest," said Hanne.

"No, I was feeling quite well after that. But events like these . . . It's hard for me to be in a room full of people I know wish me dead."

"Your Highness!" Hanne exclaimed in horror.

Nina glanced at Joran, but the guard's face remained impassive. "That can't be true," she said.

"I know the way people talk about me. I know they wish I hadn't been born at all and that my little brother could be the one to inherit."

Hanne's face was fierce. "Well then, you must stay alive to spite them."

The prince looked surprised but pleased. "You have a lively spirit, Hanne Brum."

"One must to survive."

"That's true," he said thoughtfully. "That's very true."

"Have you traveled to Ravka?" Nina asked, hoping to steer the conversation back to Demidov.

"Never," he said. "I'll admit I'm intrigued. I've heard the Ravkan women are very beautiful."

"Oh, they are," said Hanne.

"You've been there?"

"Once, near the border."

The prince shifted slightly, as if trying out the new comfort he felt. "If you're so interested in Demidov, I'll introduce you."

"Oh, would you?" Nina said breathlessly. "What a thrill."

The prince's eyebrows twitched, and Nina could tell he thought Mila Jandersdat was a trifling ninny. All for the best. *No one takes care to guard against a dull blade.*

He gave a brief command to a servant and a moment later, Demidov was sauntering through the room toward them, the Apparat drifting in his wake. Just her luck. Nina wanted to stay as far from the priest as possible.

"Taking his time," grumbled Prince Rasmus. "I vouch if your father snapped his fingers, the Little Lantsov would come running."

Nina wondered. How much of Fjerda's policy was Brum dictating and how much did the prince resent it? She and Hanne rose to greet Demidov, who gave the prince a brief nod.

"Prince Rasmus, how can I be of service?"

The prince's brow arched. "You can begin with a bow, Demidov. You're not a king yet."

Demidov's cheeks flushed. His resemblance to Ravka's exiled king was uncanny. "My most sincere apologies, Your Highness." He bowed deeply, almost comically. "I have no wish to offend, only to offer gratitude for all your family has done for me and for my country."

Nina had a profound urge to kick him in the teeth, but she beamed happily, as if she could imagine no greater joy than meeting this pretender.

Rasmus propped his head on his hand, weary as a student about to endure an hours-long lecture. "May I introduce you to Hanne Brum, daughter of Jarl Brum?"

Hanne curtsied. "It is an honor."

"Ah," said Demidov, bowing over Hanne's hand and pressing a kiss to her knuckles. "The honor is mine. Your father is a great man."

"I'll tell him you said so."

"I hope it isn't rude, but . . . I must inquire about your extraordinary haircut. Is it the new fashion?"

Hanne touched her hand to the short stubble of her hair. "No. I shaved my head to show fealty to Djel."

"Hanne and her companion are very devout," said Prince Rasmus.

"*I should have known it had something to do with their barbarian religion,*" the Apparat murmured in Ravkan.

"*She looks like more of a soldier than her father's silken-haired troops,*" Demidov replied, his smile still in place.

Nina narrowed her eyes. His Ravkan was impeccable, but that wasn't necessarily meaningful.

"If you will allow me," Hanne ventured, "may I introduce my companion, Mila Jandersdat."

Demidov smiled, but no warmth reached his eyes. "Charmed."

He clearly found conversation with a mere servant beneath him but was attempting to hide it. Nina took her chance, ignoring the Apparat's piercing stare.

"What a great delight to meet you, Your Majesty!" she gushed, giving him the honorific that Prince Rasmus would not. A little flattery never hurt. "Prince Rasmus told us you grew up in the country. How lovely that must have been."

"I have always preferred the country to the city," Demidov said unconvincingly. "The fresh air and . . . such. But I will be glad to be in Os Alta again."

"Was it a very beautiful house?" Hanne inquired.

"One of those lovely dachas in the lake district I've seen illustrated?" said Nina. "They have the most extraordinary views."

"Just as you say. It had a rustic elegance one cannot find in the halls of grand palaces."

Demidov's eyes darted left, then right. He licked his lips. He was

lying, but not about growing up in a dacha. He had that very particular embarrassment of genteel poverty. Exactly as a poor Lantsov
relation might. Nina's heart sank.

"But you will grow used to the luxuries of Os Alta," said the
Apparat in heavily accented Fjerdan. "Just as you will grow to be a
fair and pious king."

"And a biddable one," Prince Rasmus said beneath his breath.
Nina saw a muscle in Demidov's jaw twitch. "Is there any wine to
be had, Joran? Or maybe you'd like some of that filthy kvas Ravkans
love so much?"

Demidov opened his mouth, but the Apparat spoke first. "Our
king follows in the path of the Saints. He does not partake of spirits."

Prince Rasmus gestured to the servant who had scurried forward
to pour. "Isn't Sankt Emerens the patron saint of brewers?"

"You are familiar with the Saints?" the Apparat asked with some
surprise.

"I've had plenty of opportunity for reading. I always liked that
wonderfully bloody book, the one with all the illustrations of mar-
tyrdoms. Better than stories of witches and merfolk."

"They are meant for education, not entertainment," the Apparat
said stiffly.

"Besides, there's a new Saint every week now," Rasmus continued, clearly enjoying baiting the priest. "Sankta Zoya, Sankta Alina,
the Starless One."

"Heresy," the Apparat snarled. "The followers of the so-called
Starless Saint are nothing but a cult of fools dedicated to destabilizing
Ravka."

"I hear their membership grows daily."

Demidov laid a comforting hand on the priest's sleeve. "My first
act when we return to Ravka will be to root out the members of this
Starless cult and stop their heresy from infecting our country."

"Then let us all pray to Djel that you're back in your homeland soon," Prince Rasmus said.

A frown pinched Demidov's brow. He knew he'd been insulted, he just wasn't sure how.

The Apparat turned to Demidov. "Let us walk, Your Majesty," he said indignantly.

But Demidov knew they couldn't simply turn their backs on a prince. "With your permission?"

Prince Rasmus waved them off, and Demidov departed with the priest.

"I don't think they like you," said Hanne.

"Should I be worried?" Prince Rasmus asked cheerily.

Nina thought so. Demidov had none of Nikolai's charm, but he'd been both pleasant and diplomatic. And unless he was an extraordinary actor, she didn't think he was lying about his Lantsov blood. He was certainly Ravkan. She'd seen his reaction when Rasmus had suggested Demidov would rule as a Fjerdan puppet. *He didn't like that at all.* He had a nobleman's pride. But was it Lantsov pride?

Nina turned to Prince Rasmus and bit her lip. "Do you really believe Ravka has a bastard sitting the throne?" she asked in scandalized tones.

"You saw Demidov. He's said to be the spitting image of the deposed king. If that's true, I'm not surprised his wife strayed."

Nina decided to try a different approach. "Perhaps she was wise to. I've heard Nikolai Lantsov is quite the leader, beloved by rich and poor alike."

"Oh yes," said Hanne, catching on. "He fought in the wars himself. As infantry, not an officer! And word has it he's also an engineer—"

"He's a coarse fool without a drop of Lantsov blood in him," Rasmus snapped.

"Hard to prove, though," said Nina.

"But we have his whore mother's letters."

"Are they locked up in some magical vault?" said Hanne.

"Or maybe in the prison sector," added Nina. Now, that would be glorious. Nina knew the plan of the prison inside and out.

The prince shook his head "The prison had a security breach a while back, though no one likes to talk about it. No, your dear papa has taken on the duty of guarding Queen Tatiana's letters. Of course no one else would be trusted with the task."

Could they possibly be under the very roof Nina slept beneath? "Then—"

"They've been neatly tucked away in the *drüskelle* sector. I haven't gotten so much as a peek at them. I hear they're very racy. Maybe Joran will sneak a look and memorize some juicy passages for us."

The *drüskelle* sector. The most secure, unbreachable part of the Ice Court, crowded with witchhunters and wolves trained to hunt Grisha.

Nina sighed and reached for a piece of rye toast. Since she seemed to be headed for utter calamity, she might as well enjoy the food.

Hanne didn't even wait for them to be behind closed doors before she whispered furiously, "I know what you're going to do. You cannot break into the *drüskelle* sector."

Nina kept a smile on her face as they headed into the little conservatory in the Brum family quarters. "I can. And you have to help me."

"Then let me go with you."

"Absolutely not. I only need you to draw me a plan, talk me through the security protocols. Your father must have brought you there."

"Women aren't permitted in that sector of the Ice Court, not inside the buildings."

"Hanne," Nina said disbelievingly. "Not even when you were a child?"

"If you're caught there—"

"I won't be. This is my chance to help stop a war. If Fjerda doesn't have those letters, the case for deposing King Nikolai will crumble."

"You think that's enough to stop my father?"

"No," Nina admitted. "But it will mean greater support for Nikolai from Ravka's nobility. It will be one less thing for him to overcome."

"Even if I drew you a plan, how would you get inside? The only entrance to the *drüskelle* sector is through the gate in the ringwall, and they added additional security after the prison break two years ago."

Hanne had a point. Nina would have to leave the Ice Court entirely and then reenter through the heavily armed gate that led to the kennels and the witchhunters' training rooms and quarters.

"You're telling me your father leaves the Ice Court every time he needs to see his troops? That doesn't make any sense."

"There's another way, but it means crossing the moat. It's only ever used at Hringkälla initiation and during emergencies. Someone on the inside would have to let you in. Not even I know how it's done."

The secret path. Matthias and Kaz had used it during the Ice Court heist, but it left anyone trying to cross the ice moat badly exposed. Nina looked out at the buildings of the White Island, the glowing face of the Elderclock.

"Then I'll have to go out before I can get back in. On the day of the royal hunt." That would give Nina two days to make this work. A plan had already started to take shape in her mind. She'd need to signal the Hringsa and request a bottle of scent from the gardener.

Hanne groaned. "I was hoping we could make an excuse to get out of that."

"I thought you'd leap at the chance to ride again."

"Sidesaddle? In pursuit of some poor stag no one intends to eat so some podge can put his antlers on a wall?"

"We can talk the prince into giving the meat to the poor. And think of sidesaddle as . . . a challenge?"

Hanne cut her a withering glance. The parties and balls and constant social interaction of Heartwood had exhausted her, but they just made Nina feel more alive. She liked dressing up with Hanne, she liked the whirl of people, and she finally felt like she was positioned to garner the intelligence she needed.

The prince's favor would ensure that they were invited to all the best parties, and she'd been able to eavesdrop on Brum's conversation with Redvin for most of the previous night as they dined on smoked eel and braised leeks and discussed plans for some new weapon. Being Mila Jandersdat had made her nearly invisible—a young widow of no consequence, not very bright or well informed, happy to shadow her mistress—to everyone but the queen. Queen Agathe watched Nina from every corner of every ballroom. She had been pious before, visiting the Chapel of the Wellspring each morning and night to pray to Djel for her son's health. But since Rasmus had begun to improve, she'd become even more devout. A good first step.

"We don't have to go *on* the hunt," said Nina. "We just need to get outside and then talk your father into taking us into the *drüskelle* sector."

"He won't do it! Women aren't permitted there."

"Not even to see the kennels?"

Hanne hesitated. "I know he's brought my mother to see the wolves."

"And you've been inside."

"I told you, it was years ago."

"You liked going with him, didn't you?" A little Grisha girl who didn't even know what she was, following her father the witchhunter to work.

"I liked any chance to be with him. He was . . . he was fun."

"Jarl Brum?"

"When I was very little. And then . . . he didn't change exactly. He'd always been stern, but . . . Have you ever seen a petrified forest? The trees are still trees, but they don't bend to the wind. They have no leaves to rustle. He was the mighty Commander Brum, unyielding, the ruthless witchhunter, Fjerda's scythe. The more he sopped up their praise, the less like my father he became."

It's Fjerda, Nina thought, not for the first time. She had no mercy for Jarl Brum, no matter who he'd been as a young father. But she understood that all of this hadn't begun with him and it wouldn't end with him either. Fjerda with its hard ways and its old hatreds filled men with shame and anger. It made the weak weaker and the strong cruel.

"Can you draw me a plan of the *drüskelle* buildings?"

Hanne huffed a breath. "This may be the worst idea you've ever had."

"Maybe so, but can you draw me a plan?"

"Yes, but *you'll* still have to get us past the gate."

"Don't you worry, Hanne Brum. I have a gift for getting past Fjerdan defenses."

14
ZOYA

"WHERE IS SHE?"

They'd traveled via airship to a field just a few miles from the sanatorium, the Sun Soldiers bending light around the craft to keep them camouflaged. It was a trick David had devised and Alina had pioneered to evade the Darkling's forces during the civil war. Zoya remembered that terrifying flight from the Spinning Wheel, summoning wind to keep them aloft for hour after hour as they tried to put some distance between themselves and their pursuers. That was the same day Adrik had lost his arm to the Darkling's shadow soldiers.

She watched the Darkling now, seated across from her in the coach. His hands and feet were shackled and four Sun Soldiers rode alongside. The rest of their unit had gone ahead to prepare the sanatorium and set up security.

The Darkling had been kept blindfolded in the airship, and the coach's windows were covered by shades that blocked the view but let in the afternoon light. The less he knew about where they were going, the better. Despite the chains that bound him, it was disconcerting to share such close quarters, the shadows creeping in around them.

He has no power, she had to keep reminding herself. And she knew he was just as uneasy as she was. The expression on his face when the airship had taken off would give her joy for the rest of her life.

"Where is she?" he repeated, his gray quartz eyes glinting in the gloom. "You might as well tell me now."

"How is it you don't know?" asked Zoya. "Your dear Sankta Elizaveta was nearly omniscient."

The Darkling studied the closed shade as if there was a view to behold. "She wouldn't tell me."

Zoya didn't bother to stifle her pleasure. "A jealous Saint. Who knew? I'll tell you about the meeting after you tell me about the thorn wood. Is this monastery you spoke of real?"

"It is."

"But there's some kind of catch, isn't there?"

"It's possible that it's located in the Sikurzoi."

The mountains that ran along the Ravkan border with Shu Han. The lower hills were crawling with patrols of Shu soldiers, and the rocky terrain beyond would be hard to traverse. But Tamar would find a way to get them where they needed to be. "An inconvenient obstacle, but hardly an insurmountable one."

"It's also possible the path to this particular monastery was blocked by a landslide nearly three hundred years ago, and only the monks know the way through."

"Then we'll simply go over it."

"It's also possible no one has spoken to or heard from these monks for another three hundred years before that."

"Saints' blood," she swore. "You have no idea if these monks have thorn-wood seeds."

"I know they *had* them."

"You don't even know if they really exist!"

"Perhaps it's a matter of faith. Are you thinking of killing me, Zoya?"

"Yes."

"Your king wouldn't be pleased."

"I'm not going to do it," she lied. "I just enjoy thinking about it. It's soothing, like humming myself a little melody. Besides, death is too good for you."

"Is it?" He sounded almost curious. "What would make my atonement complete? An eternity of torture?"

"It would be a start. Though letting you live a long life without your power isn't a bad beginning either."

Now his face went cold. "Make no mistake, Zoya Nazyalensky. I did not live a hundred lives, die, and return to this earth, to live as an ordinary man. I will find a path back to my power. One way or another, I'll cast out the remainders of Yuri's soul. But the *obisbaya* is your king's only chance to be free of his demon and for the world to be free of the Fold." He leaned back against the seat. "I hear tell there was an attempt on your life."

Damn it. Which guards had been talking? What had he overheard?

"The more powerful you become, the more enemies you acquire," he said. "And the Apparat is not a good enemy to have."

"How do you know the Apparat was behind the attack?" They'd gotten little information from the assassin, but he was definitely one of the Apparat's Priestguard. Zoya suspected the Apparat cared less about people calling her a Saint—though that was disconcerting enough—and more about eliminating her to weaken Ravka's forces. His zealot followers had been happy to make the attempt.

A smug smile touched the Darkling's mouth. "After hundreds of years, one becomes a very good guesser. The Apparat wants Saints he can control. A weak girl, or better yet a dead one. This assassination was meant to be your martyrdom."

"I'm no Saint. I'm a soldier."

He tried to spread his hands, the chains at his wrists clanking. "And yet, do we not make miracles?"

"Yuri really is still in there, prattling on, isn't he?" This journey already felt interminable. "I'm not in the business of miracles. I practice the Small Science."

"You know as well as I that the line between Saint and Grisha was once blurred. It was a time of miracles. Maybe that time has come again."

Zoya wanted nothing to do with it. "And when one of the Apparat's assassins slips through my guard or a Fjerdan bullet lodges in my heart, will I be resurrected like Grigori? Like Elizaveta? Like you?"

"Are you so very sure you can be killed at all?"

"What are you talking about?"

"The power that I possess, that Elizaveta and Grigori and Juris possessed, that now crackles through your veins, is not so easily wiped from the world. You can strike a bird from the sky. It's far harder to vanquish the sky itself. Only our own power can destroy us, and even then it's not a sure thing."

"And your mother?"

The Darkling's gaze slid back to the covered window. "Let us not speak of the past."

She had been Zoya's teacher, feared and beloved, powerful beyond measure. "I watched her throw herself from a mountaintop. She sacrificed herself to stop you. Was that *her* martyrdom?"

The Darkling said nothing. Zoya couldn't stop herself.

"Grigori was eaten by a bear. Elizaveta was drawn and quartered. Still they returned. There are stories whispered in the Elbjen mountains of the Dark Mother. She crowds in when the nights grow long. She steals the heat from kitchen fires."

"Liar."

"Maybe. We all have stories to tell."

Zoya pulled up the shade, then lowered her window, inhaling the cold winter air.

The woods were thick with snow, the branches of the birch trees glittering with frost.

She felt something in her stir, as if waking, as if whatever was inside her had also lifted its head to breathe deeply of the pines. These woods should have felt barren, maybe even sinister with their long shadows, but instead . . .

"Do you feel it?" the Darkling asked. "The world is more alive here."

"Be silent."

She didn't want to share this with him. It was winter but she could still hear birdsong, the rustle of small creatures in the brush. She saw the tracks of a hare through the white drifts of snow.

She reached over and raised the shade on the Darkling's side. From this vantage, they could see a low hill and the abandoned sanatorium.

"What is that place?" the Darkling asked.

"It was a duke's dacha long ago. The hill was covered in his vineyards. Then it became a quarantine house during an outbreak of the wasting plague. They dug up the vines to bury the bodies. When the quarantine ended, the duke was dead and no one wanted the property. They said it was cursed. It seemed just the right spot for this wretched endeavor."

The sanatorium was miles from any real village or town and had long been rumored to be haunted. They wouldn't have to worry about unwanted visitors.

As they watched, a coach pulled up and three figures emerged—a man, a young boy accompanied by an orange cat that bolted for the trees, and a small, slender woman, her hair long and white as the first snowfall. She tilted her face up to the sky, as if letting the winter light pour through her. Alina Starkov, the Sun Saint.

Is she afraid? Zoya wondered. *Eager? Angry?* She felt the dragon stir as if called. *No.* She didn't want to feel what Alina was feeling. Her own emotions were enough of a burden. Mal placed a shawl around Alina's shoulders, wrapping his arms around her as they looked out over the old vineyard.

"Charming."

Zoya studied the Darkling's face. "You can sneer, but I see your hunger."

"For the life of an otkazat'sya?"

"For a life of the kind you and I have never known and will never know—quiet, peace, the surety of love."

"There is nothing sure about love. Do you think love will protect you when the Fjerdans come to capture the Stormwitch?"

She didn't. But maybe she wanted to believe there was more to life than fear and being feared.

She yanked down the shade and tapped the roof. The coach traveled on, up the cramped cart track in slow switchbacks. At last, they rattled to a stop.

"Stay here," she said, hooking his shackles to the seat.

She descended from the coach, closing the door behind her. Mal and Alina stood on the sanatorium's stairs, but when Alina saw Zoya, she smiled and raced down the steps with arms open. Zoya blinked away an embarrassing prickle of tears. She hadn't known how Alina might greet her, given the circumstances. She let herself be hugged. As always, Ravka's Saint smelled of paint and pine.

"Is he in there?" Alina asked.

"He is."

"You bring me the worst gifts."

The tabby had returned from its sojourn and was twining through Misha's legs. It padded over to Zoya. "Hello, Oncat," she murmured, hefting the cat into her arms and feeling the comforting rumble of its purr.

Misha said nothing, just watched, his young face tense. He was only eleven years old, but he'd seen tragedy enough for ten lifetimes.

"Are you ready?" she asked Alina.

"Not at all. Couldn't we have met someplace slightly less . . . nightmare-inducing?"

"Believe me, I'd rather be in a plush hotel in Os Kervo sipping a glass of wine."

"It's not so bad," said Mal. "We don't get out much."

"Just for the occasional hunting trip?" asked Zoya.

Noblemen loved to hunt on the lands around Keramzin, and in the company of two humble peasants, they often drank and gossiped and talked matters of state. Alina and Mal had turned the orphanage into a way station for intelligence gathering.

The Sun Soldiers had fanned out to surround the sanatorium and create a perimeter. Now a young soldier with sun tattoos on both of her forearms emerged from the building.

She bowed to Zoya but paid little attention to the girl with the shawl tucked around her head. As far as these soldiers and everyone in Ravka knew, Alina Starkov had died on the Shadow Fold.

"There's water damage throughout, so we've placed chairs in the entry."

Zoya set down Oncat. "There's hot tea?"

The soldier nodded. Alina cut Zoya a glance, and she shrugged. If they had to endure the Darkling, they could at least be civilized about it.

"Keep eyes on the door," Zoya commanded. "If you hear anything out of the ordinary—anything at all—do not wait for my orders."

"I've guarded him in the sun cell," the tattooed soldier said. "He seems harmless enough."

"I didn't ask for an assessment of the threat," Zoya bit out. "Stay alert, and respond with deadly force. If he gets free, we won't have a second shot at him, understood?"

The soldier nodded, and Zoya dismissed her with a disgusted flick of her hand.

"Still making friends?" Alina said with a laugh.

"These children are going to get themselves and us killed."

Mal smiled. "Are you nervous, Zoya?"

"Don't be absurd."

He turned to Alina. "She's nervous."

"You're not?" asked Alina.

"Oh, I'm terrified, but I didn't expect Zoya to be."

Alina yanked her shawl tighter. "Let's get this over with."

Zoya strode to the coach and ducked inside. She unhooked the Darkling's shackles from the seat and drew the blindfold back over his eyes.

"Is that strictly necessary?"

"Probably not," she admitted. "Behave yourself."

Flanked by Sun Soldiers, she led him across the yard and up the stairs.

"Wipe your feet," Alina said.

He stilled at the sound of her voice, then obeyed.

Zoya met her eyes and Alina winked. Any little victory.

It was colder inside than out, the sanatorium's battered marble floors and broken windows providing little insulation. The entry had once been a grand receiving room, with double staircases that led to the east and west wings. But now one of those staircases had buckled from rot. A shattered chandelier lay on its side in the corner, beside heaps of dust and glass the Sun Soldiers had swept up. Old medical equipment was propped against the walls—the twisted frame of a cot, a rusty metal tub, what might have been leather straps for restraining patients.

Zoya stifled a shudder. That cozy hotel was sounding better and better. A table had been set with a samovar and glasses at the center of the room. Four chairs surrounded it. Zoya hadn't known Misha was coming.

Two Sun Soldiers led the Darkling to a chair, his shackles jangling. They had no idea they were in Alina Starkov's presence, that their power had come from her loss.

Zoya gestured for them to take up positions at the base of the steps. She didn't want anyone to overhear their conversation. There were already soldiers posted outside every exit point, and high above, she heard the distant but comforting sound of engines. She had requisitioned two of Nikolai's armed flyers to patrol the skies.

When they were alone, Alina sat and said, "Misha, will you pour the tea?"

"For him too?" Misha asked.

"Yes."

The boy complied, setting the glasses in their little metal frames neatly on the table.

"I'll get my own," said Zoya. She was particular about sugar, and she needed a moment to take in this peculiar scene. It was strange that after so much pain and sacrifice, they should all meet again in this abandoned place.

The room fell silent. Oncat meowed plaintively.

"Where do we start?" Mal asked.

"You do the honors," said Alina.

Mal crossed the room and yanked the blindfold away. The Darkling didn't blink, didn't reorient himself, merely looked around the room as if assessing a property he might like to purchase.

"You didn't bring me to Keramzin," he said.

Alina went very still. They all did. Zoya knew the shock of this. The Darkling's face was different—the sharp bones were there, the glimmering gray eyes, but its shape was slightly altered, the scars once given to him by the volcra gone. His voice, though—that cool glass voice of command—was the same.

"No," said Alina. "I didn't want you in my home."

"But I've been there before."

Alina's face hardened. "I remember."

"Do you remember me?" asked Misha. He was too young to hide his hatred with polite talk.

The Darkling raised a brow. "Should I?"

"I took care of your mother," said Misha. "But my mother was murdered by your monsters."

"As was mine. In the end."

"They say you're a Saint now," Misha spat.

"And what do you say, boy?"

"I say they should let me kill you myself."

"Many have tried before. Do you think you could manage it?"

Mal laid a hand on Misha's shoulder. "Leave it be, Misha. Threatening him only makes him feel important."

"What do we call you now?" asked Alina. "What does anyone call you?"

"I've had a thousand names. You'd think it wouldn't matter. But Yuri doesn't suit me at all." He peered at her. "You look different."

"I'm happy. You never really saw me that way."

"Living in obscurity."

"In peace. We chose the life we wanted."

"Is it the life you'd have chosen if you hadn't sacrificed your power?"

"I didn't *sacrifice* my power. It was taken from me because I fell prey to the same greed that drove you. I paid the price for tampering with *merzost*. Just as you once did."

"And does that make your grief any less?"

"No. But every child I help heals something inside me, every chance I have to tend to someone left in the wake of your wars. And maybe when our country is free, then that wound will close."

"I doubt it. You might have ruled a nation."

"It's amazing," said Mal, settling in a chair and stretching out his legs. "You died." He turned his gaze on Alina. "And you pretended to die. But you both picked up right where you left off. Same argument, different day."

Alina jabbed him in the thigh. "It's very rude to make accurate observations."

The Darkling's gray eyes studied Mal with more interest than he'd ever shown before.

"I understand we're blood related."

Mal shrugged. "We all have relatives we don't like."

"Do you, orphan?"

Mal's laugh was real and surprisingly warm. "He says it like it's an insult. You're rusty, old man."

"Alina's blade wrapped in my shadows and your blood." The Darkling's voice was thoughtful, like he was remembering a favorite recipe. "That was how you almost ended me. Barely more than children and you came closer to killing me than anyone had before."

"Not close enough," Misha growled.

"You dragged us out to this miserable place," said Alina. "What is it you want now?"

"What I have always wanted, to make a safe place for the Grisha."

"Do you think you could manage it?" she asked, echoing the Darkling's taunt to Misha. "It's not like you didn't get a fair try before. Hundreds of tries."

"If not me, then who?"

"Nikolai Lantsov. Zoya Nazyalensky."

"Two monsters, more unnatural than anything either Morozova or I ever created."

Zoya's brows rose at that. Being called a monster by a monster somehow felt like a badge of honor.

"I'm pretty sure I'm talking to a dead man," said Alina. "So maybe this isn't the time to throw stones."

The Darkling's shackles clinked. "They are children, barely able to understand themselves or this world. I am——"

"Yes, we know, eternal. But right now, you're a man without a scrap of power sitting in a house full of ghosts. Zoya has been fighting for years to keep the Grisha safe. She rebuilt the Second Army from the tatters you left behind. Nikolai has unified the First and Second Armies in a way never seen in Ravka's history. And what about the innovations of Genya Safin and David Kostyk?"

Zoya stirred her tea, afraid to show how much Alina's words meant to her. After the war, she had begun her journey as a member of Alina's chosen Triumvirate, unplagued by hesitation. She'd thought she was born to lead. But through time, and trial, and failure, doubt had crept in.

The Darkling looked only bemused. "If Ravka is so strong, why is Fjerda attacking? Why are the wolves at the door once more? Do you really believe these cubs can lead a nation?"

"Safety for the Grisha. A united Ravka. What if *they* are the ones to give this dream to us? Why does it have to be you? Why do *you* have to be the savior?"

"I am the man best suited to the job."

But there was something in the Darkling's voice that made Zoya wonder if he was quite as sure as he had been before he'd taken tea with a Saint.

The Darkling's shoulders lifted. "It has always been easier to see me as the villain, I know. But for a moment, can you imagine that I have only ever tried to do what is best for my country and my people?"

"I can," said Alina. "Of course I can."

"Don't say that!" Misha cried, his face flushed. "He never cared about any of us!"

"Tell me you regret some of it," Alina said softly. "Any of it." Her voice was gentle, coaxing. Hopeful. Zoya knew that hope. When you'd followed someone, believed in someone, you didn't want to think you'd been a fool. "It's not too late for you."

"I didn't come here to speak lies," said the Darkling.

Alina blew out a disgusted breath, but Zoya could only shake her head.

"Do you really believe this is the life you were meant for?"

the Darkling asked. "Powerless and pathetic? Wiping the noses of children who will forget you? Telling them bedtime stories that will never come true?"

But this time Alina smiled. She reached for Mal's hand. "I am not powerless. Those stories tell us the only people who matter are kings and queens. They're wrong."

The Darkling sat forward, but suddenly Zoya wasn't looking at the Darkling at all. It was Yuri's bony, desperate face that stared out at her, Yuri's frightened voice that shouted, "He's going to—"

The Darkling seemed to be falling forward onto his knees. He reached out and seized Alina's and Mal's clasped hands. The samovar clanged to the floor.

Zoya stood, knocking her chair backward, but it was already too late.

"No!" Alina shouted. Oncat hissed.

Shadows flooded the room. Zoya couldn't see, couldn't fight. She was lost in the dark.

15
NIKOLAI

THE MORNING OF THE WEDDING, Nikolai dressed with care. *Zoya should be here*, he thought as he pinned a sprig of blue hyacinth to his lapel. This was a momentous day, a turning point for Ravka, the culmination of careful planning and a potential diplomatic disaster. But what possible good could come from Zoya being with him today? She would see him in his fancy new clothes?

It still didn't sit right. They had traveled together for months, endured hardships, witnessed miracles. She had become his closest confidante and most trusted adviser. And he'd sent her away. *Not just away, you podge.* He'd sent her on an impossible quest with their most deadly enemy. Well, one of them. Truth be told, it was hard to keep track of who was deadliest these days—the Fjerdans with their war machines and Grisha prisoners, the Kerch with their unparalleled navy and bottomless coffers, the blight slowly devouring the world, the Shu who were currently arriving at their door.

Nikolai's flyers had been tracking Queen Makhi's airship from a distance, and he'd received word when the party arrived. They'd docked at Poliznaya, where they'd unloaded horses, carriages, and a large retinue of servants, including twelve Tavgharad in black uniforms. General Pensky had greeted them in full military dress, and his soldiers had escorted them on to Os Alta. Nikolai had made sure that the crowds assembled in the streets were watched over by First Army soldiers and Grisha Heartrenders, prepared to drop the pulses of anyone who wanted to make trouble. Though they hadn't been at war with the Shu in several years, there was still plenty of anti-Shu sentiment, and he didn't want this day to be more fraught than it had to be.

Tolya knocked at the door to Nikolai's dressing room and leaned in. "They're at the gates. You're making ships again. That nervous?"

Nikolai looked down at the little wire boat in his hand. It was an old habit from childhood, fashioning bits and pieces into the shapes of animals or objects.

"You're not worried about this whole madcap endeavor?" Nikolai asked.

"I am," Tolya said grimly. "But this is the right choice. I know it."

"Saints, are you wearing a *kefta*?"

Tolya and Tamar usually favored the olive drab of First Army soldiers. They had rejected the trappings of the Second Army from their earliest days at the Little Palace. But now here Tolya was, filling the doorway in Heartrender red, his sleeves heavily embroidered in black and his long hair bound tightly at the nape of his neck.

"Today we stand with Ravka's Grisha," said Tolya.

Zoya was going to be very sorry she missed this.

Nikolai took a last glance in the mirror, his medals affixed to the pale blue sash across his chest. He touched his fingers to the blue velvet ribbon tucked into his pocket.

"Let's go," he said. "The sooner we start this day, the sooner it will be over."

"It's almost as if you don't like weddings," Tolya said as they made their way out of the palace.

"I'm very fond of weddings, particularly the part where I can start drinking. I'm amazed they had a *kefta* in your size."

"The Fabrikators made it for me. They had to sew two together."

They descended the steps, where the royal guard had already positioned themselves in front of the remaining members of the Grisha Triumvirate. The white stone stairs had been scrubbed clean of any sign of the violence that had been done there only a short time ago, and every balustrade and balcony had been festooned with clouds of hortensia in the pale blue and green of Ravka and the Shu Han. If only it were so easy to bring two countries together.

"Tolya!" Genya exclaimed as they joined her and David on the steps. "Red suits you."

"Don't get used to it," Tolya grumbled, but he couldn't stop from preening like a heavily muscled peacock at the compliment.

Genya wore a *kefta* of shimmering gold, her red hair braided with slender strands of river pearls, and David's hair had been properly cut for once.

"You both look splendid," said Nikolai.

David took his wife's hand in his and pressed a kiss to her knuckles. Genya's cheeks flushed pink with pleasure. Nikolai knew David's gesture had been learned. The Fabrikator wasn't given to spontaneous demonstrations of affection, but they made his wife happy, and he loved to see his wife happy. Then David reached out and rubbed a piece of her silky red hair between his fingers. Genya blushed even more deeply.

"What are you doing?" she whispered.

"Studying something beautiful," he said without the faintest hint of flattery, as if he truly were trying to find the formula for the woman before him.

"Stop making moon eyes at each other," Nikolai said, not meaning a word of it. They deserved to be happy. Lucky bastards.

A rider appeared on the main drive to tell them the Shu had reached the double-eagle gates, and a plume of dust from the road announced their presence a moment later.

The Shu carriages were of exquisite make, the black lacquer shimmering green in the sunlight like a beetle's back, their doors bearing the two crossed keys of the Shu flag emblazoned in gold.

The Tavgharad rode in processional beside the carriages, their horses as black as their uniforms and their caps set at a sharp angle on their heads. On these very steps, their sisters had died mere weeks before. By order of their queen. And Nikolai knew that these women would set themselves alight just as fast should Makhi command it.

The lead coach rolled to a stop and Queen Makhi emerged. She was tall and lean, and though there was some resemblance to Princess Ehri, Makhi looked like an artist's illustration of a queen come to life—her toffee-brown eyes luminous, bronze skin without flaw, black hair falling in lustrous waves to her waist. She wore silks of leaf green, a pattern of silver falcons taking flight from the hem, and a crown of massive green stones that would have put the Lantsov emerald to shame. She was quickly flanked by two ministers in dark green.

The Taban queens didn't take husbands but had multiple male consorts, so no man could claim any child as his nor make any bid for the throne. Makhi would never wed, but her sisters would. For alliance.

Nikolai bowed deeply. "Queen Makhi, we welcome you to the Grand Palace and hope you will find it to your liking."

The queen glanced around, the faintest sneer on her lips. This was her first opportunity to insult his country.

"The celestial throne of the Shu and wearer of the Taban crown greets you. We are most grateful for your hospitality." At least they were beginning well.

Nikolai offered her his arm. "It would be my honor to escort you to the royal chapel. Or perhaps your party would like a chance to rest themselves and have some refreshment?"

The queen glanced at her ministers, who remained stone-faced. She gave a brief sigh and slid her hand into the crook of Nikolai's elbow. "Best this distasteful business was done quickly."

Nikolai led her down the path, and in a great wave of velvet, silk, and sparkling gems, their party processed toward the royal chapel, which lay almost exactly halfway between the Grand Palace and the Little Palace.

"The chapel is said to have been built on the site of Ravka's first altar," said Nikolai. "Where the first Lantsov king was crowned."

"Fascinating," she said, then added beneath her breath, "Are these niceties strictly necessary?"

"No, but I find they help ease the way when meeting with a woman who tried to engineer my death and the overthrow of my rule."

Makhi's hand tensed slightly against his arm. "Where is my sister? I would speak to her before the ceremony."

No doubt, but there would be none of that. Nikolai ignored her.

The chapel had been carefully restored after the Darkling's attack, and Fabrikator craft had ensured that its dark beams and golden dome had been made even lovelier than what had come before. The whole place smelled of wood polish and sweet incense. Its pews were packed with guests in their finest: Ravkan nobility in fashionably cut coats and gowns, Grisha in their jewel-hued *kefta*.

"Who will perform this travesty of a ceremony?" Makhi asked, peering down the aisle at the gilded altarpiece of thirteen Saints. "I hear your priest is occupied elsewhere. To imagine my sister will marry a bastard."

It seemed Makhi's supply of civility was expended. "I didn't think the Taban queens gave much care to whether a child was born out of wedlock."

Makhi's brown eyes flashed. "Did you read that in a book? Marriage is a pretense. But bloodline is everything."

"Thank you for explaining the distinction. Vladim Ozwal will perform the ceremony."

The young priest already stood at the altar, wearing a long brown cassock emblazoned with a golden sun. He was one of the Soldat Sol who had abandoned their service to the Apparat to follow Alina Starkov. He had fought beside the Sun Saint on the Fold and had received her powers, and if Zoya's story was true, he bore the handprint of the Sun Summoner as a brand upon his chest. When the Apparat had slithered off to Fjerda, Ravka's priests had scrambled to appoint a new head of the church who would serve as spiritual counselor to the king. There had been older, more experienced candidates, many of whom were little more than the Apparat's cronies. But in the end, the new guard had won out and Ozwal had been chosen. Apparently, it was hard to argue with a man who bore the fingerprints of the Sun Summoner seared into his own flesh.

"I can barely see," said Queen Makhi. "We should be at the front of the chapel."

"Not just yet," said Nikolai. "Ravkan tradition."

Adrik and Nadia rose and faced the guests, side by side in their blue *kefta*, their cuffs embroidered in Squaller silver, Adrik's bronze arm polished to a high shine. They began to sing in close harmony. It

212

was an old Ravkan folk song about the first firebird and the sorcerer who had tried to capture her.

David and Genya had already begun their slow walk down the aisle. Genya had chosen an extraordinarily long train.

"Who are these people?" Makhi asked. "Where is my sister?"

"They are two members of the Grisha Triumvirate, David Kostyk and Genya Safin."

"I know who they are. What are they doing here? I will march to the front of this chapel and stop this whole proceeding if—"

Nikolai rested a hand on Makhi's silk sleeve, then removed it at her glare.

"Do not *think* to lay a hand on this, the most holy body of Queen Makhi Kir-Taban."

"My apologies. Truly. But I do think it would be best not to make a scene."

"Do you think I care about creating a spectacle?"

"No, but you should. I don't think you want all these people to know where your sister is."

Makhi tilted her head back, looking down her nose at Nikolai. He felt less victorious than wary. This queen was ruthless and brilliant and very dangerous when cornered. But corner her he must.

"David and Genya were wed with little pomp on a rather hasty trip to Ketterdam," Nikolai said. "They never had a chance to exchange their vows in Ravka."

But they were speaking them now.

"Here, witnessed by our Saints and our friends," Genya said, "I speak words of both love and duty. It is not a chore but an honor to swear faith to you, to promise love to you, to offer my hand and my heart to you in this life and the next." They were the traditional Ravkan words, spoken at the weddings of nobleman and peasant alike.

The Grisha vows were very different.

"We are soldiers," David recited, low and shaky. He was unused to speaking in front of a crowd. "I will march with you in times of war. I will rest with you in times of peace. I will forever be the weapon in your hand, the fighter at your side, the friend who awaits your return." His voice grew stronger and louder with every word. "I have seen your face in the making at the heart of the world and there is no one more beloved, Genya Safin, brave and unbreakable." The vow rang through the chapel. Genya's face was shining, as if those words had kindled some secret light.

Tolya, towering over the bride and groom, set a thorn-wood crown upon David's head and then one upon Genya's, as Vladim said the blessings. Nikolai would have liked to be a part of the ceremony, to stand with his friends in this moment of happiness when there was so much uncertainty before them. But this wedding had been constructed for the benefit of Queen Makhi, and there was no way he was leaving her side.

"You will answer my questions," Makhi hissed. "We were brought here for *your* wedding to my accursed sister."

"I don't recall the invitation saying any such thing."

Queen Makhi's cheeks were red with indignation. "A *royal* wedding. It said a royal wedding."

"And here we are in the royal chapel."

"Where is Princess Ehri? Is she imprisoned? Has the wedding already taken place?"

"Now what good would a quiet ceremony do me? And who would marvel at my glorious new suit?"

"Where is my sister?" she whispered furiously.

Vladim was finishing the ceremony. David leaned forward to kiss Genya. He smiled, taking that same auburn strand of hair between his fingers. The guests burst into applause.

Now it was Nikolai's turn to speak.

"She is home, Your Highness. In Ahmrat Jen. In Shu Han."

Makhi blinked slowly. "Home," she repeated. "In Shu Han."

"Yes," said Nikolai. "She and a regiment of Grisha guards and First Army soldiers departed via airship two days ago along with Tamar Kir-Bataar."

"Tamar Kir-Bataar is a mongrel and a traitor."

"Mongrels and bastards make fine companions. She is also one of my most trusted advisers and friends, so I will respectfully ask you to watch your tongue. Princess Ehri will have landed and spoken to your other ministers by now."

"My . . . my ministers? Are you mad?"

"She will tell them of the plot you hatched to assassinate me and have her killed for the sake of invading Ravka and starting a war with Fjerda—a war your subjects would never want without good reason, like the slaying of Princess Ehri Kir-Taban, beloved of the people. It must be galling to know how much your younger sister is adored."

Makhi laughed, and Nikolai had to admire her poise. "You expect Ehri to make this case? Shy, retiring, sweet-natured Ehri? She will crumple under questioning. She is no politician, no ruler, and there is no way she can persuade—"

"She is in the company of Mayu Kir-Kaat."

Queen Makhi was too practiced a politician to show her distress. Her eyes widened only slightly.

"Yes," said Nikolai. "Your assassin lives. Mayu Kir-Kaat will corroborate Ehri's story and explain the instructions you sent to your Tavgharad."

"It was a line of poetry."

"Even if your ministers do not know their verses, I imagine your court is full of learned men and women who will understand its meaning, just as your guards did, just as Mayu did."

215

Makhi sniffed. "Let them make their case. Let them shout it to the heavens. I am the queen, and that cannot be changed or altered. Only a Taban queen can name a Taban queen."

Nikolai almost felt bad for the blow he was about to deal. But this was for Ravka. And for Isaak too.

"Very true. But I believe your grandmother still lives, tending to her rosebushes at the Palace of the Thousand Stars. I've always wanted to see it for myself. She is still very much a Taban queen and can take her crown back with a single command."

A second loud cheer went up from the crowd, and David and Genya began their trip down the aisle in a shower of quince blossoms, Tolya trailing behind them with a huge grin on his face and Genya's train in his hands.

Nikolai applauded heartily, then watched as Tolya's golden eyes met Queen Makhi's furious gaze. The giant's grin faded. He had given up his twin to thwart Makhi, and he did not look ready to forgive the sacrifice. As the wedding party passed, he whispered something in Shu that made Makhi practically snarl.

She regained her composure as they exited the chapel behind the happy couple. Surrounded once more by their guards and trailed by the bewildered Shu ministers, Nikolai and Makhi passed back into the woods on the path that would lead them to the Grand Palace. Nikolai paused there, beneath the trees. The sky was a hard gray. It looked like it might snow.

"What is it you want?" the queen inquired. "My sister has never sought the crown, and she is incapable of ruling."

"I want a treaty, sealing the peace between Shu Han and Ravka and agreeing to the current border at Dva Stolba. Any act of war against Ravka will be considered an act of war against the Shu as well. And you will guarantee the rights of all Grisha."

"The rights of . . . ?"

Zoya and Tamar had worked to fashion the wording of the treaty themselves.

"You will close your secret bases where Grisha are being drugged to death in order to create *khergud* soldiers. You will stop the conscription of innocent people into these programs. You will guarantee the rights of Grisha among your citizens."

"The *khergud* are a myth, anti-Shu propaganda. If—"

"We are not negotiating, Your Highness."

"I could kill you where you stand. Your guards are no match for my Tavgharad."

"Are you so sure?" said Tolya, coming up behind them. "My father once trained the Tavgharad. He taught me too."

"It would certainly make for a lively reception," said Nikolai.

Queen Makhi's lips curled into a sneer. "I know well who your father was, Tolya Yul-Bataar. It seems treason is thick in your blood."

Tolya's voice was forged steel, the edge honed by years of anger. "Mayu Kir-Kaat and her brother will be brought back together. You will never separate *kebben* again."

"You dare to command a Taban queen?"

"I have no queen, no king, and no country," said Tolya. "I have only ever had what I believe."

"Queen Makhi," said Nikolai quietly, "please understand, I know that you will use all of your considerable cunning to maneuver back into power as soon as you return. But the intelligence Tamar's sources have gathered, Mayu's testimony, and Princess Ehri's damnable popularity will not be easily denied. It isn't Ravka's place to decide who should rule Shu Han, and you said yourself that Ehri doesn't want the crown. But if you don't abide by the terms of our treaty, she'll have the support she needs to take it."

"There will be a civil war."

"I know what that can do to a country, but you have the power to

217

prevent it. Sign the treaty. Close the laboratories. It's that simple. I will not have my Grisha hunted any longer, and we will be amicable neighbors if not friends."

"Ehri would be a better puppet queen for Ravka than I."

"She would. But I have no wish to be a puppeteer. It's hard enough to rule one country, and a strong Shu Han allied with Ravka is the best possible deterrent to Fjerda's ambitions."

"I will consider it."

"That's not agreement," said Tolya.

"It's a beginning," said Nikolai. "Dine with us. Do us that honor. Then we'll have a look at the treaty."

Makhi sniffed. "I hope your chef is more skilled than your architects."

"And I hope you enjoy aspic."

Nikolai's gaze met Tolya's as they followed Makhi back toward the palace. Tolya had risked his sister's life to make this mission happen. Nadia had given up her wife's presence in a time of war. Tamar, Mayu, and Ehri had all put their lives on the line for the opportunity to finally fashion an alliance with the Shu and change the world forever for Grisha. It was a wild leap, an audacious one, but they had agreed they were willing to take the risk for a chance at a different future.

"I don't know when I may see my sister again," said Tolya as they walked to dinner. "It's a strange feeling."

"There's no one else I would have trusted with such a challenge. But I feel her absence too. Now tell me what you whispered to Queen Makhi in the chapel."

"You should learn to speak Shu."

"I was thinking of taking up Suli."

Suddenly, the demon inside Nikolai howled, rearing up like a feral beast, struggling to break free. Nikolai caught a glimpse of an empty foyer, an overturned samovar, a woman's stunned face—Alina. It all vanished in a wash of darkness. Nikolai forced himself to breathe and yanked hard on the leash that had bound him and the demon since the *obisbaya*. He felt his feet in his boots, saw the branches overhead, heard the comforting murmur of chatter from the wedding guests.

"What's wrong?" said Tolya, placing a steadying hand at Nikolai's elbow.

"I'm not sure." Nikolai took another breath, feeling the demon snap and screech at the end of its tether. All he needed was for the monster to escape in front of half of Ravka's nobility and the Shu. "Have we had any word from Zoya?"

"Not yet."

Was what he'd seen real or imagined? Was Zoya in trouble? "They should be done at the sanatorium by now. Let's send riders to intercept and lend support. Just in case."

"In case of what?"

"Bandits. Brigands. A bad case of hay fever." *In case I sent my general into some kind of ambush.* "But what did you say to the queen?"

"It's a line from 'The Song of the Stag' by Ni Yul-Mahn."

Now Nikolai understood the queen's reaction. "The poem Makhi used to order the deaths of Ehri and her Tavgharad?"

"That's right," said Tolya. His eyes gleamed like coins in the last of the afternoon sun. "'Let the hounds give chase. I do not fear death, because I command it.'"

16
NINA

TWO DAYS AFTER THE SALON where they'd met
Demidov, Nina and Hanne dressed for the royal hunt, Hanne in dark
green wool lined in golden fur, and Nina in slate gray. But they made
sure to leave their heavy coats at home.

They took the long way to the glass bridge so that Nina could
pass through the gardens, skirting the colonnade where Djel's sacred
ash had once stood, now replaced by a stone copy, its white branches
spread over the courtyard in a wide canopy. They would never bloom.

"Enke Jandersdat," the gardener said when he caught sight of her.
"I have that distillation of roses you asked for."

"How kind you are!" Nina exclaimed, taking the tiny bottle from
him, along with a second, smaller vial tucked behind it. She slid both
into her pocket.

The gardener smiled and returned to trimming the hedges, a tattoo of a thorn-wood tree barely visible on his left wrist, a secret emblem of Sankt Feliks.

A groom was waiting outside the ringwall with two horses. Nina and Hanne were both uncomfortable riding sidesaddle, but Hanne was too good an athlete to be thwarted. Besides, they weren't really meant to ride, just journey out to the royal camp to join Prince Rasmus and Joran in the tents erected for the hunt.

The main tent was as big as a cathedral, draped with silks and heated by coals placed in silver braziers hung from tripods. Food and drink had been laid out on long tables at one side, and on the other, noblemen chatted in comfortable chairs heaped with skins and blankets.

The prince was dressed to ride in breeches and boots, his blue velvet coat lined with fur.

"You'll join the hunt today, Your Majesty?" Hanne asked as they sat on low benches near the smoldering coals.

"I will," said Rasmus eagerly. "I'm not much of a shot, but I'll manage. This is the only event of Heartwood that everyone enjoys."

"I doubt the stag is fond of it," said Hanne.

"You don't like seeing your men go off to slay wild beasts?"

"Not for sport."

"We must take our enjoyment while we can. Soon we'll be at war, and we'll have nothing for entertainment but the killing of Ravkans."

Hanne met Nina's glance and asked, "Aren't we still in talks with Ravka?"

"Your father isn't much for talking. If he had his way, I think we'd be at war forever."

"Surely not forever," said Nina.

"What good is a military commander without a war to fight?"

Rasmus was no fool.

"But it's not up to Jarl Brum to choose for Fjerda," Nina said. "That is the role of the king. That choice is for you."

Rasmus was quiet as he looked at the horses gathering beyond the entry of the tent.

"What would you choose?" Hanne asked softly.

The prince's smile was more like a grimace. "Men like me aren't suited to war."

But that wasn't entirely true. Not anymore. Rasmus would never be tall among Fjerdans, but now that he stood straight, he could look Hanne directly in the eye. He'd lost the grim pallor that had made him resemble a corpse left out in the cold, and he was sturdy if not strong.

"There is more to life than war," offered Nina.

"Not in the Grimjer line. The Fjerdan throne belongs to those strong enough to seize it and keep it. And there's no denying the Grisha are a menace and always will be until their kind are eradicated."

"And what of the people who think the Grisha are Saints?" Joran asked, his face troubled. Nina was surprised. The bodyguard rarely joined their conversations.

Prince Rasmus waved his hand. "A passing fad. A few radicals."

We'll see about that. There was poison at the heart of Fjerda. Nina was going to change its chemistry.

She spotted Queen Agathe holding court at the far side of the tent. There was no way Nina would be allowed close enough to speak to her, but she didn't think she would have to be the one to make the approach.

She caught Hanne's eye, and Hanne said, "Mila, will you fetch us some ribbons to braid and some ash? We will make you a token to wear on the hunt, Prince Rasmus. A Grimjer wolf for one who is made for war, but chooses not to wage it."

"What an odd sentimental thing you are," Rasmus said, but he made no protest.

Nina rose and crossed slowly to the table of ribbons and ash boughs, making sure Agathe saw her.

"I wish to make a token," she heard the queen say, then, "No, I'll select the materials myself."

A moment later Queen Agathe was beside her.

"My son grows stronger every day," she whispered.

"Such is the will of Djel," said Nina. "For now."

The queen's hand stilled over a spool of red ribbon. "For now?"

"The Wellspring does not like this talk of war."

"What do you mean? Djel is a warrior. Like the water, he conquers all in his path."

"Have you said your prayers?"

"Every day!" the queen cried, her voice rising dangerously. She caught herself. "Every night," she whispered. "I have worn my dresses bare, kneeling on the floor of the chapel."

"You pray to Djel," Nina said.

"Of course."

Nina took a leap, a leap that might end with her body broken from the fall. Or her vision might take flight. "But what of his children?" she murmured, and, arms full of ribbons and ash, she hurried back to Hanne and the prince.

A horn sounded: the call to the hunt. Rasmus rose, pulling on his gloves. "You'll have no time to make me a token," he said. "The riders are ready."

"Then we can only wish you good fortune," said Nina as she and Hanne both curtsied.

Rasmus and Joran headed out of the tent, and Nina and Hanne followed to see them off. But before they'd reached the group of riders, the queen's voice rang out. "I would have you with me to watch the hunt, Rasmus."

She stood at the dais that had been erected for that purpose. Her younger son was there, along with her ladies-in-waiting.

A hush fell in the camp. Someone snickered. Brum and Redvin were with the riders. Nina could see the contempt on both of their faces.

"Yes," tittered someone under her breath. "Go sit with the children and the women."

Did the queen understand the insult she was dealing her son? *No*, thought Nina guiltily, *she's too afraid for him*. Probably because Nina had reminded her of her son's mortality.

Rasmus stood rooted to the spot, unable to deny the queen but knowing the blow his reputation would take.

"Your safety is our highest priority," said Brum, a smile playing over his lips.

Rasmus was trapped. He executed a short, sharp bow. "Of course. I'll join you momentarily, Mother."

He strode to one of the smaller tents with Joran in tow. Hesitantly, Hanne and Nina followed.

The tent was full of saddles and crops and other tack, the smell of leather sweet in the air. Rasmus stood with his back to them.

"It seems I had no reason to put my riding clothes on today," he said without looking at them. "I could have worn silk and lace like the ladies."

"We could return to the palace," suggested Hanne.

"No, we could not. My mother has requested my presence and she will have it. Besides, I can't be seen running off. Do you still think I will be the one to choose Fjerda's path?"

"It's only love that makes her act so," said Hanne. "She's afraid—"

"Hanne feels sorry for me." Prince Rasmus turned. "You do too, don't you, Mila? But Joran doesn't. Joran doesn't feel anything. Let's test it. Come here, Joran."

"Is anyone hungry?" Hanne said nervously. "Perhaps we could call for food."

"I could eat," Nina said.

Joran didn't look nervous as he approached the prince. If there was any expression on his studiously blank face, it was resignation. *Whatever this is, it's happened before*, Nina realized.

"Do you feel anything, Joran?" asked the prince.

"Yes, Your Highness."

"Like what?"

"Pride," said Joran. "Regret."

"Pain?"

"Of course."

"But you don't show it."

Before the guard could answer, the prince lifted a crop and smacked Joran hard across the face, the sound like a branch snapping on a cold morning.

Shock reverberated through Nina as if the blow had struck her own cheek.

Hanne lunged forward. "Your Highness!"

But the prince ignored her. His gaze was fixed on Joran as if the young guard was the most fascinating thing he'd ever seen. He hauled back the crop.

"Don't!" cried Nina.

The prince struck Joran again.

Joran didn't flinch, but Nina could see two angry red welts on the guard's cheek.

"Does it hurt?" the prince asked. His voice was eager, like

someone watching a friend swallow a spoonful of custard and asking, *Is it good?*

Joran held the prince's gaze. "It does."

The prince held out the crop. "Hit me, Joran."

Joran did nothing. He wouldn't fight back, wouldn't stop the prince, because it was his sacred duty to serve Rasmus, because to strike a prince was a death sentence. Rasmus had been snide, petulant, even spiteful—but this was something deep and ugly. It was Fjerda's poison in his veins.

The crop made a *whoosh* as it cut through the air again, then smacked against Joran's cheek.

"Go get your father," Nina whispered to Hanne. "Hurry."

Hanne bolted from the tent, but Rasmus didn't seem to notice.

"Hit me," the prince demanded. He giggled, a bright, happy sound. "He wants to, my god how he wants to. *Now* Joran feels something. He feels rage. Don't you, Joran?"

"No, Your Highness."

But there was anger in Joran's eyes; shame too. Prince Rasmus had made the exchange. He'd traded his humiliation for Joran's. The guard's cheek was bleeding.

Was this who the crown prince really was? She had thought he was a sickly boy with a good heart. Curse all the Saints, maybe she'd wanted to believe he was like Matthias. Another boy brutalized by Fjerda's traditions and Brum's hate. But Matthias had never been cruel. Nothing had been able to corrupt the honor in his mighty heart.

"Brum is coming," Nina said, her voice low. She couldn't afford to compromise her cover, but she couldn't let this go on. "You will not want him to find you with a crop in your hand."

Rasmus' glance was speculative, as if he was wondering what

might happen if Brum confronted him. Joran was Brum's *drüskelle*. But Rasmus was a prince.

Then it was as if a spell had broken. He shrugged and tossed the crop aside. "I'm going to join my mother. Clean yourself up," he told Joran.

He strode past Nina as if nothing had happened. "Tell Hanne I expect to see her at the ball later."

"Joran," Nina began when the prince had gone.

He had taken out a handkerchief and pressed it to his cheek. "Don't let Commander Brum see me this way," he said.

"But——"

"It will only make trouble for the commander. For everyone. I'll be fine. Please."

He remained composed, a soldier, but his blue eyes were pleading.

"All right," she said.

She turned her back on him and left the tent, scanning the crowd. She caught sight of Hanne speaking to Brum.

Nina hurried to her side and heard Brum say, "You must tell me what has upset you. I'm needed at——"

"Papa, please, if you would just come with me."

"It's fine," said Nina, smiling. "All is well." Both Hanne and Brum looked baffled. "I . . . I was feeling poorly, but now I'm right as rain."

"Is that all?" asked Brum.

"Yes, and I . . ." This wasn't the approach she'd intended to make, but there was nothing to do but forge ahead. "I had hoped you might bring your wolves out for the hunt?"

"The *isenulf*? They're not made for such silly pursuits. Perhaps if we were hunting fox."

The man really couldn't resist a jab at the Ravkan king.

"Oh, Papa," said Hanne. "Mila is so disappointed, and it's so much colder out here than we expected. Can't you have one of your soldiers take us back to the kennels?"

"Hanne, you should have dressed for the weather."

"I told you Mila needed a new cloak, didn't I?"

"I'm f-fine," Nina said, offering a brave, trembling smile as she shivered.

"Silly girls," said Brum, his gaze lingering on Nina in a way that made her stomach turn. "I'll take you back myself."

Hanne stiffened. "Won't it be perceived as an insult to the prince's hunt?"

"The prince isn't riding. Why should I?"

So he wanted to insult the crown. Seeing the prince embarrassed by his mother had emboldened him.

Nina tried to gather her focus as she and Hanne followed Brum back to the ringwall. Was Rasmus a lost cause? She'd thought healing the prince was a good thing, that a strong Rasmus might find it easier to stand against Fjerda's drive toward war. She wanted to believe that could still be the case. There had to be an alternative to Brum's violence. But she couldn't stop seeing the red marks on Joran's cheek, the ferocity in his eyes. There had been rage there, shame, and something else. Nina didn't know what.

Get your head on straight, Zenik, she told herself. She would have one opportunity to find the letters in Brum's office, and she'd need her wits about her to make the most of this chance.

It was even colder in the shadow of the ringwall, and Nina didn't have to pretend to shiver as they approached the *drüskelle* gate. She'd never stood at the base of the Ice Court walls before. She'd been brought in hooded as a prisoner once, and she'd left by an underground river—nearly drowning in the process. She looked up and saw gunmen guarding the huge portcullis gate. She could hear the wolves in their kennels, their howls rising. Maybe they were like those Shu soldiers engineered to sniff out Grisha. Maybe they knew she was coming.

You've been living beneath the roof of the country's most notorious witch-hunter for months, she reminded herself. But this felt different, as if she were willingly walking into a cell and she'd have only herself to blame when the door slammed shut behind her.

They passed beneath the colossal arch and into the courtyard lined with kennels.

"*Tigen, tigen*," Brum crooned as he approached the cages on the right, where the largest of the white wolves leapt and snapped at the air. Wolves trained to fight alongside their masters, to help them hunt down Grisha. The animals took no notice of Brum's soothing words, growling and snarling, pressing against the wire fences. "You can smell the hunt, eh, Devjer? Don't be afraid, Mila," he said with a laugh. "They can't get you."

She thought of Trassel, Matthias' wolf, with his scarred eye and huge jaws. He'd saved her life and she'd helped him find his pack.

She took a step toward the fences, then another. One of the wolves began to whine and then the animals fell silent, going to their bellies, resting their heads on their paws.

"Strange," said Brum, his brow furrowing. "I've never seen them do that before."

"They must not be used to having women here," said Hanne hurriedly, but her eyes were startled.

Do you know me? Nina wondered as the wolves whimpered softly. *Do you know Trassel watched over me? Do you know I walk with death?*

Brum knelt by the cages. "Even so——"

An alarm began to ring, a high, staccato sound that rattled the air.

229

A shout came from the guardhouse. "Commander Brum! Red protocol!"

"Where was it triggered?" demanded Brum.

"Prison sector."

Sector breach. And right on time. The night she'd hatched her plans with Hanne, she'd tossed a handful of special salts into the fire, so that they would send a burst of red smoke into the sky above the Ice Court—a signal to the Hringsa lookout posted nearby. The network hadn't been able to get a servant into Brum's quarters, but Nina was able to pass information to one of the gardeners, who had served as a messenger and informant. She needed a distraction, a big one, at just after ten bells. They'd delivered, but she couldn't be certain how much time she had.

Brum's men lined up behind him, rifles in hand, clubs and whips at the ready. "Stay here," he told Hanne. "The guards will remain posted on the ringwall."

"What's happening?" Nina cried.

"There's some kind of disturbance. Most likely it's nothing. I'll be back in no time."

Nina forced tears to fill her eyes. "You can't just leave us here!"

"Calm yourself," Brum snapped. Nina flinched and pressed her hand over her mouth, but she felt like laughing. Jarl Brum, the great protector. But he only liked his women weak and wailing when it was convenient for him. The prison sector had been breached before and Jarl Brum had been made a fool. He didn't intend to let that happen again.

"You can't leave us defenseless," Hanne said. "Give me a gun."

Brum hesitated. "Hanne——"

"You can abide by propriety or put a weapon in my hand and let me defend myself."

"Do you even know how to use a revolver?"

With a sure hand, Hanne spun the barrel to make sure it was loaded. "You taught me well."

"Years ago."

"I didn't forget."

Brum's expression was troubled, but all he said was, "Be careful." He and his men vanished through the gate.

Two guards remained on the battlements, but they had their attention turned outward, rifles raised and pointed at whoever might seek to breach the ringwall.

"Go," said Hanne. "But be quick."

Nina hurried across the courtyard past the kennels and the wolves, who stared at her silently despite the commotion. She had never regretted her heavy skirts more. *Maybe that's why Fjerdans like to keep their women swimming in wool*, she considered, slipping inside the building Hanne had marked on her map of the sector. *So they can't get away too fast.*

She tried to keep Hanne's map in her head as she sped down a long corridor. She glimpsed a huge dining room on the right, beneath a pyramid-shaped skylight. There were long mess hall tables and an immense tapestry hung on the back wall, woven in blue, red, and purple. Her footsteps faltered as her mind caught up to what she'd seen. That tapestry that covered nearly the entirety of the wall—it was made out of scraps of *kefta*. Blue for Etherealki, a smattering of purple for Materialki, and row after row of red for Corporalki, her order. The Order of the Living and the Dead. They were trophies taken from fallen Grisha. Nina felt sick. She wanted to set the damn thing on fire. Instead she pushed her anger aside and made her feet move. Vengeance would come, retribution for Brum and his minions. But not until she saw this mission through.

Up the stairs—the newel posts capped by snarling wolves—then down another gloomy hallway. She counted the doors: third on the left. This should be Jarl Brum's office. She grasped the handle of the door and jammed in the key she'd taken from Brum's key ring that morning.

Nina hurried inside. It was an elegant room, though windowless. The mantel was crowded with medals, awards, and souvenirs that made Nina's heart hurt—spent bullet cartridges, what might have been a child's jawbone, a dagger with a woman's name engraved on the handle in Ravkan: *Sofiya Baranova.*

Who were you? Nina wondered. *Did you survive?*

An old-fashioned musket hung above the hearth beside one of the whips Brum had innovated for restraining Grisha.

She made herself focus on Brum's desk. The drawers and cabinets weren't locked. They had no reason to be; this was the safest, most secure place in the Ice Court. But Nina wasn't sure where to begin searching for Queen Tatiana's letters. She combed through schedules and ship manifests, and set aside entire files of what looked like trial transcripts. There were coded messages she didn't know how to decipher, as well as detailed plans of the military base at Poliznaya and a city plan of Os Alta. There were markings on both that she couldn't make sense of. She touched her finger briefly to the squares labeled as the Little Palace, the grounds, the school. Home. *Move, Zenik.*

But the letters weren't in the desk. So where were they? She looked behind the portrait of a blond man in antiquated armor—Audun Elling, she suspected, the founder of the *drüskelle*. Then she felt along the walls, knocking softly, forcing herself to slow down, to be thorough. The Elderclock sounded the quarter chime. She'd been gone for almost fifteen minutes. How much longer did she have before Brum returned or the guards noticed Hanne was alone?

She knocked gently against the wall beside the mantel—there, a hollow *thunk*. She trailed her fingers over the panels, looking for some slot or indentation, pressing carefully. A fur hat hung from a hook at just above eye level. She pulled gently on it. The panel slid to the right. A safe. The letters had to be inside. She was definitely not a safecracker and hadn't bothered to study the art while in Ketterdam. But she'd anticipated that the letters might be locked away. She removed the bottle of scent from her coat pocket, opened it, and poured in a few drops from the second vial the gardener had handed her. *No more than three drops*, he'd whispered, *or it will eat through the walls of the safe too.* And Nina didn't want there to be any visible damage. When she was done, all that would remain was the scent of roses.

She pulled a slender rubber tube from her pocket and fitted one end over the nozzle of the bottle, then wiggled the other end through the narrow space between the door of the safe and the wall. She pumped the bulb attached to the bottle, forcing air through the tube, listening closely. A faint hissing came from behind the safe's door. Whatever treasures lay inside were slowly disintegrating.

A sudden sound made her go still. She waited.

It came again—a low moan. *Oh Saints, what now?* Was a *drüskelle* dozing in the room next door? Or was something worse waiting? Had Brum brought Grisha here to torture and interrogate?

She yanked out the tube and returned the whole contraption to her pocket. Time to get out of here.

She should run down the stairs, back to the courtyard, back to Hanne. But hadn't Hanne said it was her job to get carried away?

Nina drew a bone dart into her hand, feeling it vibrate there, waiting only for her command to find a target. Slowly, she opened the door.

It *was* a cell. Not one of the new modern enclosures built to contain and control Grisha, but a cell for an ordinary man. Except the man gripping the iron bars didn't look ordinary. He looked like King Nikolai.

His hair was golden, though streaked with gray, his beard unkempt. His fine clothes were rumpled and stained. He'd been gagged and chained to the cell bars to give him a limited range of movement. There was nothing in the tiny cell but a cot and a chamber pot.

Nina stared at him, and the man looked back at her with frantic eyes. She knew who this was.

"Magnus Opjer?" she whispered.

He gave a single nod. Magnus Opjer. The Fjerdan shipping magnate who was supposedly Nikolai's true father. Jarl Brum had him locked away in a cell. Did Prince Rasmus know? Did anyone but the *drüskelle* know?

She pulled the gag from the prisoner's mouth.

"Please," Opjer said, his voice ragged. "Please help me."

Nina's mind was whirring. "Why are they keeping you here?"

"They kidnapped me from my home. I'm their insurance. They need me to authenticate the letters."

The letters from Queen Tatiana throwing King Nikolai's parentage into doubt.

"But why would they keep you prisoner?"

"Because I wouldn't speak publicly against my son or Tatiana. I wouldn't vouch for the letters. Please, whoever you are, you must free me!"

My son. So Nikolai Lantsov really was a bastard. Nina Zenik realized she didn't care.

The Elderclock chimed the half hour. She had to get out of here. But how was she supposed to take Magnus Opjer with her? She had nowhere to hide him, no plan to get a fugitive out of the Ice Court.

You could kill him. The thought came to her with cold clarity. There was no mistaking Opjer's resemblance to Nikolai. This was the true father of the Ravkan king. And that meant he was a threat to her country's future. She needed to think.

"I have no way to get you out."

Opjer clenched the bars. "Who are you? Why have you come here if not to rescue me?"

Yet another reason to kill him. He had seen her. He could tell the *driiskelle*, could easily describe her. He grabbed her sleeve with his bony fingers. They hadn't been feeding him well.

"Please," he begged. "I never meant to hurt my son. I would never speak against him."

Nina knew he was desperate, but his words had the ring of truth. "I believe you. And I'm going to help you get out of here. But you need to give me time to plan."

"There isn't time, they—"

"I'll return as soon as I can. I promise."

"No," he said, and it was not the refusal of a weakened prisoner. It was a word of command. In it she heard the echo of a king. "You don't understand. I must get a message to—"

Nina yanked his gag back into place. She needed to get to the courtyard. "I'll return," she vowed.

Opjer seized the bars, grunting as he attempted to shout around his gag.

She closed the door and hurried down the hall, trying not to think of the terror in his eyes.

17

ZOYA

"SOLDIERS!" ZOYA SHOUTED into the darkness.

"Where is he?" Misha cried.

Zoya heard footsteps, the door opening. She whirled and saw the Darkling silhouetted in the day's sunlight, the snowy hill behind him, the Sun Soldiers running toward him.

She threw her hands forward, unleashing a gust of wind that knocked him down the stairs. The Sun Soldiers blasted him with light, but he was already on his feet, darkness surging from his body like water overflowing a dam.

Zoya summoned the storm, the clouds rolling in on a crash of thunder. Lightning spiked through the sky, bright daggers in her hands. But the bolts never reached the Darkling.

In a shower of sparks, the lightning broke against two writhing heaps of shadow—the *nichevo'ya*, shadow soldiers summoned from nothing in violation of all the rules of Grisha power. *Merzost.* Abomination.

"Thank you for bringing me here, Zoya," the Darkling said as his winged soldiers took shape and lifted him from the ground. "My resurrection is complete."

It had all been a ruse. His apology. His desire to see Alina. Even his wish to reenact the *obisbaya.* Were the monks and their thornwood seeds a lie too? Just another fairy tale he'd concocted to feed to them like bedtime stories? He was right. They *were* children, grasping for understanding, stumbling along, learning to walk as the Darkling sprinted ahead of them. They had been fools to think they could predict or control him. He had never intended to drive Yuri out. He needed Alina and Mal: the Sun Summoner who had slain him, and the amplifier who carried the blood of his ancestors. He'd felt no guilt, no shame. She'd been so wrong about what he wanted here.

"Signal the flyers!" she shouted to the Sun Soldiers, then turned her wrath on him. If only she'd had time to master the gifts Juris had granted her. "You have nowhere to go. The king's soldiers will hunt you to the ends of the earth and so will I."

Gunshots shattered the air as the flyers overhead opened fire on the Darkling from above. One found its target, and the Darkling gave a yelp of rage and pain. *He can still bleed.*

But the *nichevo'ya* swarmed around him in a mass of wings and writhing bodies, absorbing bullets as if they were nothing at all.

Two of the shadow soldiers surged skyward, and a moment later the flyers were plummeting toward the earth.

Zoya screamed, hurling her power in a wave of wind to break their fall.

Not one more, she vowed. She would not lose a single soldier more to this man.

"I have bested many kings and survived many foes greater than you," said the Darkling. The shadows leapt and dove around him as he rose into the sky. "And now I will become what the people most desire. A savior. When I am done, they will know what a Saint can do."

Darkness swirled around him, as if the shadows were glad in their dancing, returned to their beloved keeper. The Sun Soldiers pushed against the darkness with their light. But Zoya saw his hands in motion—the Darkling was going to use the Cut. He would kill them all.

We are the dragon. Juris' consciousness tugged at hers, pulling her toward something more, even as her own heart refused it. *No.* She couldn't. She wouldn't.

She threw her arms out in a circle of wind that flattened the trees and threw the Sun Soldiers off their feet but away from harm. *Not one more.* She drew a bolt of pure crackling lightning from the sky, a spear of fire to end the Darkling as they should have ended him years ago.

But darkness enveloped her, and in the next minute, when the shadows cleared, he was gone.

Alina stood at the top of the sanatorium steps, her face ghostly in the gray light. Her right hand was bleeding. Misha was screaming, his anguish like the cry of something born wild as Mal held him back. Oncat looked on, unmoved, tail twitching, as if there was nothing a cat hadn't seen.

"Let him go," Alina said softly.

Misha shot down the stairs, angry tears spilling from his eyes, and stumbled into the woods in the direction the Darkling had gone. Mal's hand was bleeding too.

The Sun Soldiers slowly climbed to their feet. They looked dazed, frightened.

"You're all right?" Zoya asked.

They nodded.

"No broken bones?"

They shook their heads.

"Then prepare the coach. I need to get back to the airship. We'll get messages to the nearest base to send sorties out to track him."

"You won't find him," said Alina. "Not until he wants you to. He has the shadows for refuge."

"I can damn well try," Zoya said. "We have to get you out of here. We can evacuate you to—"

Alina shook her head. "We're going back to Keramzin."

"He'll find you. Don't underestimate him." Zoya knew she sounded angry, even cold. But she didn't know how else to hold back the flood of fear and helplessness threatening to overtake her. She'd let him get away and now she didn't know what he might do, who he might hurt. *She'd* let this happen.

"I know what the Darkling is," said Alina. "I know how he treats his enemies."

"We both do," said Mal, taking a handkerchief from his pocket to bind Alina's hand. "We're not letting him chase us from our home."

"You don't understand." He was going to kill them. He was going to kill all of them and Zoya would be powerless to stop it. "We can find someplace to hide the orphans for a while. We can—"

Alina rested her hands on Zoya's shoulders. "Zoya. Stop."

"We're not going to uproot the children," Mal said. "They've already been through enough."

"Then I'll send a contingent of First Army soldiers and Summoners to you."

Mal blew out a breath. "You can't afford to waste soldiers, and they'd be no good against him anyway. All they'll do is terrify the children."

"Better that they're scared and safe."

"There is no safe," Alina said, her voice steady. "There never has been. Not in my lifetime. But I meant what I said. You and Nikolai are the ones who can change that."

"How did he do it? What happened in there?"

"He drove this through our hands." Mal uncurled his fingers. In his palm lay a long, bloody thorn.

A piece of the thorn wood. The Darkling must have hidden it somewhere in Yuri's clothing. He'd kept it with him since the failed *obisbaya* and their battle on the Fold, waiting for his moment.

"He needed our blood," said Alina.

The Sun Saint and the tracker—Morozova's other descendant. The two people who had almost ended his life. *Only our own power can destroy us, and even then it's not a sure thing.* He'd been taunting them the whole time, begging them to guess at his plan. *I understand we're blood related.*

Panic reared up in Zoya, a clawing, panting thing. "I let him go. I failed all of us."

"Not yet," said Mal. "Unless, of course, you're giving up."

Alina smiled and gave her a little shake. "I didn't put you in charge because you run from a fight."

Zoya broke away and pressed her palms against her eyes. "How can you be so damn calm?"

Alina laughed. "I don't feel calm at all."

"Definitely still terrified," said Mal.

"Did he seem different to you?" Alina asked.

Mal shrugged. "He seemed about the same. Gloomy and insufferable."

"What was the boy's name? The monk?"

"Yuri Vedenen," Zoya said. "I never would have guessed that skinny little runt could cause so much trouble."

"I bet you said the same thing about me once."

Zoya scowled. "You'd win that bet."

"Genya's letter said you thought Yuri was still inside him. I think you're right. The Darkling seemed different, off-kilter."

Mal's brows rose. "Has he ever been on-kilter?"

"Not exactly," conceded Alina. "Eternity will do that to a person."

She rested her bandaged hand on Zoya's cheek and Zoya stilled, feeling suddenly like she was with her aunt again, in that kitchen in Novokribirsk. *I could stay here,* Zoya had said. *I could stay with you and never go back.* Her aunt had only smoothed Zoya's hair and said, *Not my brave girl. There are some hearts that beat stronger than others.*

"Zoya," Alina said, drawing her back to the present, to her fear, to this wretched place. "You are not alone in this. And he can be beaten."

"He is immortal."

"Then why did he flinch when you brought down the storm?"

"It did nothing!"

"He sees something in you that frightens him. He always has. Why do you think he worked so hard to make us doubt ourselves? He was afraid of what we might become."

We are the dragon. We do not lie down to die. Some tiny fraction of the fear in her receded.

"Zoya, you know we're here if you need us."

"But your power—"

"I can still pick up a rifle. I was a soldier before I was a Saint."

I like this one. She's unafraid. Juris' whisper, an echo of Zoya's own grudging thoughts about the orphan girl she'd once resented and despised. The dragon's laugh rumbled through her. *Loss has made her bold. If only I could say the same of you.*

Zoya sighed. "That's all well and good," she said. "But how am I going to tell the king?"

18
NIKOLAI

THE DINNER WAS LONG but merry, and Nikolai's chef outdid himself by serving at least seven different foods in jelly. Makhi and her retainers left when the dancing began—and once the treaty was signed. Whether she would keep to the agreement they'd made was in Tamar's, Ehri's, and Mayu's hands now.

"You're welcome to stay," Nikolai said as the queen's horses and carriage were brought around to take them out to the airfield.

"I've performed as much as I'm able this night," Makhi replied. "I even managed to hold down that hideous meal. Now I need to see just how much damage my sister has done."

Before Makhi climbed into her carriage, she gestured to Nikolai, clearly wishing to speak away from her ministers.

"Something happened in Ahmrat Jen. Some kind of blight. There were similar incidents near Bhez Ju and Paar."

"They call it *Kilyklava*, the vampire. The same thing has happened in Ravka."

"I know. But I have to wonder if those occurrences were simply cover for the deployment of some new Ravkan weapon."

"This isn't a weapon," said Nikolai. "Not one any of us know how to wield. The blight has struck in the Wandering Isle, Fjerda, and Novyi Zem."

She paused, taking that in. "The shadows, the dead soil that follows in the wake of this blight. All of it is reminiscent of the Fold."

"It is."

"There is talk of the return of the Darkling, the Starless One."

"I've heard the same talk."

"And what will you do if he *has* found a way to return?"

If only Nikolai knew. But he doubted *strap him to a big thornbush and try to send him to hell once and for all* would incite much confidence.

"First I need to best the wolf at my door. Then we'll see what nightmares lurk in the dark."

"You will share any intelligence you gather."

"I will."

"And if you find out who's responsible . . ." Her words broke apart, and Nikolai understood that it had not just been land lost in this blight. For the queen, this was very personal. "I will be the one to punish him."

But who was the villain? The Darkling had created the Fold, but Nikolai and Zoya and Yuri had all played a part in bringing him back. What had Zoya said? *We're all monsters now.*

Nikolai could only offer a half-truth. "If that becomes clear, vengeance will be yours to take."

"I look forward to it." Makhi stepped into the coach. "You may be surprised at how long I can hold a grudge."

"A pity you didn't meet General Nazyalensky. I think you two would have found plenty to talk about."

The carriage door closed, and in a cloud of dust and hoofbeats, the Shu retinue was gone.

Nikolai returned to the ballroom, where the musicians had struck up a lively tune. Queen Makhi had stayed at the wedding only as a show of strength, so she wouldn't be seen running off after the treaty was signed.

It felt strange to drink and dine and toast without Tamar there, knowing she was in danger, that if this all went wrong, she might never return to Ravka. Nadia had wished David and Genya well, then retired early, too worried about the woman she loved to enjoy the party. Tolya said he had made his peace with being separated from his twin, but Nikolai could see the melancholy on his face. Despite his intimidating size, Tolya was the shyer of the twins, the killer who should have been a scholar, if fate had ordered their lives differently.

"Where did David go?" he asked as Genya, smiling and rosy-cheeked from dancing, threw herself down in a chair and drank deeply from her wineglass. She seemed to glow in her golden gown, her eyepatch embroidered with rubies.

"We were in the middle of a dance when he muttered something about nose cones and vanished. It was very romantic."

"David danced?"

"I know! He whispered the count beneath his breath and stepped on my toes more than the floor." Her grin could have lit the entire ballroom. "I've never had more fun. And to think I had a queen at my wedding."

"And a king," Nikolai said with false indignation.

She waved him off. "You're old news. Her gown was just divine."

"I'm fairly sure she wanted to murder us all."

"That's just what weddings are like. When can we hope to hear from Tamar?"

"We received word of their arrival and their meeting with Makhi's ministers. Beyond that . . ."

Who knew what lay ahead of them? A hope for alliance. A chance at peace.

By midnight, the party had begun to wind down, noblemen stumbling blearily to their carriages, Grisha meandering back to the Little Palace, singing and laughing. The candles were extinguished and Nikolai retired to his quarters to look over the correspondence that had arrived with that afternoon's messenger. He would have liked nothing better than to go to bed and call the day a success, but his plans had only just begun to come together, and there was still so much to do.

The sitting room felt empty and too silent. He was used to spending this time with Zoya, talking through the day's events. When there were two of them to face their battles, it didn't feel so overwhelming, and tonight that feeling was worse than usual. It wasn't just that they'd thrust themselves into the unknown with this false wedding and their play to win the Shu to their side. The demon had almost broken free today. Nikolai had nearly lost control, and he still wasn't sure what had caused it or if it might happen again. He'd managed to leash the cursed thing, but he'd felt like he'd had one hand on the reins all night. He was almost afraid to fall asleep. Maybe it was safer not to.

He rang for tea. He'd spend the night working.

It was Tolya who brought the tray. He'd abandoned his red *kefta* and changed back into his olive drab uniform. "I can't sleep."

"We could play cards," suggested Nikolai.

"I've been working on a new poem—"

"Or we could shoot ourselves out of a cannon."

Tolya's glower was ferocious. "A bit of culture wouldn't hurt you."

"I have no objection to culture. I'll have you know I've fallen asleep at some of the very best ballets. Pour a cup for yourself." As Tolya poured, Nikolai asked, "Tolya, Tamar found the girl of her dreams. How is it you're still alone?"

Tolya shrugged his huge shoulders. "I have my faith, my books. I've never wanted more."

"Were you in love with Alina?"

Tolya finished pouring before he said, "Were you?"

"I cared about her. I still do. I think I could have loved her, in time."

Tolya took a sip of his tea. "I know she was only a girl to you, but to me she is a Saint. That's a different kind of love."

A loud bell began to ring from somewhere in the distance.

"What is that?" asked Tolya, his brow creasing.

Nikolai was already on his feet. "The alarm bells in the lower town." He hadn't heard them since his doomed birthday party, when most of the Lantsov line had been slaughtered. "Get—"

He heard a distant drone—engines in the sky. *All the Saints, it can't be . . .*

Then a *whoosh*, like the loud, excited roar of a crowd.

Boom. The first bomb struck. The room shook, and Nikolai and Tolya were nearly thrown from their feet. Then another *boom* and another.

Nikolai threw the door open. Half the hallway had caved in, leaving it blocked by a slump of rubble. The air was full of plaster dust. Nikolai could only pray that no guards or servants had been trapped already.

He sprinted down the hall, Tolya beside him, and grabbed the first guard he could find, a young captain named Yarik. He was covered in dust and bleeding from where he'd been struck by something, but he had his rifle in hand and his eyes were clear.

"Your Highness," he shouted. "We have to get you to the tunnels."

"Gather everyone you can. Clear the palace and get them underground."

"But—"

Boom.

"The roof may come down," said Nikolai. "Move!"

The very earth was shaking. It felt as if the world was coming apart.

"Mobilize the Grisha to the town," Nikolai said as he and Tolya ran toward the Little Palace. "They'll need Healers and Squallers to help move the debris. Signal Lazlayon and get our flyers in the air."

"Where are you going?" said Tolya.

Nikolai was already racing toward the lake. "Up."

His boots pounded the dock. He leapt into the cockpit of the *Peregrine*. It wasn't quite as agile as the *Sparrowhawk* but carried heavier guns. It was fast and lethal and it felt like an animal coming to life around him.

The flyer surged forward on the water, and then Nikolai was rising into the moonlight, searching the sky. The demon inside him shrieked in anticipation.

Fjerdan bombers were built of heavy steel. They carried major firepower but were slow to maneuver. They shouldn't have been able to haul their payloads so far from home; they were too heavy, too fuel-hungry. *A game of range.* And Fjerda had just made a move that would change that game forever. David's missiles could not remain a hypothetical any longer.

Nikolai had never dreamed the Fjerdans would attack a civilian target or risk harming the Shu queen. Had they known she would depart early or simply gotten lucky? Or had Queen Makhi known when the bombs would fall all along?

He couldn't be sure, and he couldn't consider the implications now.

Far below, he saw fires burning in the lower and upper towns. He didn't know how much damage the Grand Palace had sustained, but two of the Little Palace domes had crumpled and one wing was engulfed in flame. At least they hadn't managed to strike the dormitories. No one would be in the classrooms or workshops this late at night. He could see a smoldering crater at the lakeshore, mere feet from where Grisha children trained and slept. They'd been aiming for the school.

Nikolai peered into the night. Fjerda painted its flyers dark gray for stealth. They were almost impossible to see, and hard to hear over the roar of the *Peregrine*.

So he cut the engine. He let his flyer's wings catch the air and he listened. *There.* To his left, thirty degrees. He waited for the clouds to part and sure enough, he saw a shape moving, lighter than the night around it. He sent the engine rumbling to life and pushed the plane into a dive, firing.

The Fjerdan bomber burst into flame.

The rattle of gunfire filled his ears and he banked hard right, chased by another bomber. He needed better visibility. The clouds gave cover, but they were his enemy too. Bullets pinged off the side of the *Peregrine*. He couldn't tell how much damage he'd sustained. He remembered the feeling of plummeting toward the earth when David's rocket had hit. There would be no Squallers on hand to save him now. He should land and take stock.

No. He wasn't setting down, not when the people below, *his* people, were still vulnerable.

The clouds were heavy, he couldn't see. But the demon inside him could. It was made of night. It wanted to fly.

Nikolai hesitated. He'd never attempted something like this. He didn't know what might happen. What would it mean to give up control? Would he ever regain it? *And while you debate, your people suffer.*

Go, he told the demon inside him. *It's time to hunt.*

The sensation of releasing the monster was always a strange one—a breath snatched from his lungs, the feeling of rising up to pierce the surface of a lake. Then he was in two places at once. He was himself, a king taking a risk he shouldn't, a privateer making a gamble he must, a pilot with his hands gripping the *Peregrine*'s controls—and he was the demon, racing through the air, a part of the dark, his wings spreading.

His monster senses caught the roar of the engine, the smell of fuel. He spotted prey and dove.

He seized the . . . his demon mind did not have words. It only knew the satisfaction of steel giving way beneath its talons, the screech of metal, the terror of the man it tore from the cockpit and slashed into with its claws. Blood poured over the demon's mouth—his mouth—hot and salty with iron.

Then he was airborne again, leaping from the plummeting bomber, seeking another quarry. The demon was in control. It sensed the presence of the next bomber before Nikolai saw it. Was this the last?

Hungry for destruction, the demon hurtled toward it through the night and slammed into the Fjerdan bomber, its talons tearing into steel.

No. Nikolai willed it to pull back. *I want them to know. I want them to live in fear.* The demon climbed onto the front of the plane and slammed its clawed hand through the cockpit glass. The Fjerdan pilot screamed, and Nikolai was looking directly into his eyes. *Let them understand what they're fighting now. Let them know what's waiting next time they invade Ravka's skies.*

He saw the demon reflected in his enemy's eyes.

I am the monster and the monster is me.

The demon opened its fanged mouth, but it was Nikolai's rage that rang out in its roar—for what had been done to his people, his home. The Fjerdan pilot babbled and wept and the demon scented urine in the air.

Go home and tell them what you've seen, Nikolai thought as the demon soared through the night. *Make them believe you. Tell them the demon king rules Ravka now and vengeance is coming.*

Nikolai drew the demon back, and to his surprise, the thing didn't fight. The shadow disappeared inside him, but it felt different now. He could sense its satisfaction; its thirst for blood and violence had been met. Its heart beat in time with his. It was frightening and yet, the satisfaction was his as well. He was meant to be the wise king, the good king, but right now, he didn't know how to be wise or good, only angry, the wound inside him burning like the city below. The demon's presence made it easier to bear.

As the *Peregrine* descended, he tried to count the plumes of smoke rising from Os Alta. Only daylight would reveal the true extent of the destruction and the lives lost.

He set the plane down on the lake and let it coast to shore. Without the thunder of the engine in his ears, there were only the sounds of fear in the night—the ringing of alarm bells, the shouts of men as they attempted to put out fires and pull friends from the rubble. They would need his help.

Nikolai stripped off his jacket and broke into a run. He would gather Squallers, Sun Soldiers. They could aid with the search for survivors. He knew his flyers would already have departed from the Gilded Bog and Poliznaya to patrol the skies for more signs of the enemy. He would have to issue blackout warnings. They were in place at the shipyards and bases that could be considered military targets. But now every Ravkan town and village would have to snuff out their lanterns and find their way in the dark.

As Nikolai approached the Little Palace, he saw the Fabrikator workshops and Corporalki laboratories had been completely obliterated, but whatever research they'd lost could be excavated or replicated. He spotted Tolya's massive frame in the crowd. He was about to call out to him when he registered the tears in Tolya's eyes, his hand pressed to his mouth.

There were Squallers trying to clear the rubble. And Genya was with them. She was on her knees in her golden wedding gown.

He muttered something about nose cones and then vanished.

Dread crept into Nikolai's heart.

"Genya?" He went to his knees beside her.

She clutched his sleeve. For a moment, she didn't seem to recognize him. Her red hair was thick with dust, her face streaked with tears.

"I can't find him," she said, her voice lost, bewildered. "I can't find David."

THE
MAKING
AT THE HEART
OF THE
WORLD

19
MAYU

MAYU WAITED. She was good at it. She'd had to be. A soldier's job was to fight; a guard's job was to remain watchful.

"There's an art to it," her old commander had said. "Your human
mind may wander, but the falcon's eye remains keen."

She peered out the window of the airship. She couldn't see much
in the dark, and she didn't know where Tamar and the princess had
gone. They hadn't seen fit to tell her the whole of their plan—
another reminder that, though she'd played the part of royalty, she
was no more than a bodyguard, valued as much for her loyalty and
her willingness to obey as her talent with a sword or a pistol.

Why the detour? she wondered. What if Queen Makhi made it back
to the capital before them? But she'd always followed instructions,
abided by the rules, so she sat, and she waited.

"A teacher's pet," her brother Reyem had called her, and he was right. She loved praise, had thrived on any little bit of it. Because she'd always known Reyem was the better fighter.

It wasn't just that he was stronger and faster, but his instincts were more alive.

"She can't hear it," their mother had said, watching Reyem and Mayu spar as children. It was meant to just be a play fight, meaningless, but Mayu knew her parents were watching and the knowledge made her clumsy. "See how Reyem doesn't hesitate. Mayu is thinking; Reyem is listening. He hears the music of the fight."

I can listen too, she'd vowed to herself. But try as she might, she heard nothing, only her own thoughts, constant and noisy, seeking understanding.

Mayu was no different now, her rebellious mind rattling with possible outcomes when it should remain quiet and ordered. She wished she had a watch or some way of telling the time.

They had left Ravka two days before the wedding, the moment Tamar had received word from her spies that Queen Makhi's airship had left the capital. Their transport was a Shu cargo vessel that had been intercepted by Ravkan forces months ago and redeployed with a new crew.

She'd thought they would go straight to the palace in Ahmrat Jen, but apparently, Tamar and the princess had other plans. They'd set down in the dark, her only clue to their location the heavy scent of roses in the air, and Mayu had sat in silence, watching Tamar and Ehri disembark, accompanied by several Grisha: Heartrenders, Squallers, Inferni. Ten soldiers of the Second Army. King Nikolai could not have liked giving them up. And for what? So that Princess Ehri could be well guarded on some sentimental trip through a botanical garden?

Sure enough, Ehri returned with her arms full of roses the bright orange of coral. Mayu kept her face blank, hiding her contempt. She knew Ehri was an emotional creature, but surely the princess didn't think a few pretty flowers would sway Makhi's ministers? If only Tamar and Ehri would tell her what they'd planned.

They didn't trust her. Why should they? Queen Makhi, whom Mayu was supposed to serve above all others, had tried to kill Princess Ehri twice. Mayu herself had tried to kill Tamar's king— even if it hadn't actually been King Nikolai. She was here because they needed her testimony, but she wasn't a part of this, not really.

Over the course of the journey, Mayu had listened to Tamar and Ehri talk and scheme, unwinding the different threads of their mission, then binding them up again, a bit cleaner, a bit tighter than they had been before. She knew she was only glimpsing a fraction of their plans, and she said little because she had little to say. She had never needed to take much interest in politics, and she wasn't meant to eavesdrop on the conversations of her betters.

But everything had changed now, and if she was going to survive, if she was going to find a way to save her twin, she had to learn. It wasn't easy. The way Ehri and Tamar spoke of the players in the Taban court made her feel like she was looking through a foggy lens focusing, then blurring, then focusing again, as it showed her a picture she'd never quite been able to see before.

"We will have no luck with Minister Yerwei," Ehri said. "He's the wiliest of Makhi's advisers and her most valued confidant."

"Was he close to your mother as well?" Tamar asked, though Mayu had the sense she already knew the answer to this question, that she was testing Princess Ehri.

"Oh yes. He was smart, very ambitious. He comes from a long line of doctors who serve the Taban queens."

"Doctors," said Tamar flatly.

Ehri nodded. "You've guessed rightly. Those same doctors who began the attempts to root out and harness Grisha power." Ehri must have seen the way Tamar's jaw set. "I know how it sounds and you're not wrong, but it began innocently enough."

"I find that hard to believe."

Ehri spread her hands wide, the gesture graceful. She wore a green velvet traveling dress with a high neck and tiny buttons that ran all the way from her wrists to her elbow. The Grisha Healers and Genya Safin had done their job well. Her body was fully healed, her hair regrown. She would never be a great beauty like Makhi, but she had an easy elegance that made her look completely out of place in the hold of this airship, with its heaps of coiled rope and the crates of weapons Tamar's crew had stockpiled. Mayu resisted the urge to stretch her legs, test the muscles in her arms. The king had been as good as his word and she'd had her strength restored. There wasn't so much as a scar on her chest to mark the place where she'd tried to plunge the knife into her heart.

"They began with autopsies performed on the dead," said Ehri. "Attempts to study the organs and brains of Grisha, to see if there were biological differences between them and ordinary people."

"And when you couldn't find any differences, you thought, why not take a closer look at the living?"

"You say 'you' as if these were my practices. I have played no part in my sister's government."

Tamar folded her arms. "Is that your idea of an excuse? Turning away from atrocity isn't something to be proud of."

Queen Makhi would have struck Tamar where she sat for such insolence—regardless of those silver axes slung at her hips like sickle moons. But Ehri looked only thoughtful. She didn't have a queen's pride.

"It was an ugly practice," she admitted. "My mother put an end to those experiments for a reason."

"Then where did the *khergud* come from?" asked Mayu, unable to hold her tongue any longer. It felt strange to speak this way to a Taban princess, and yet Ehri didn't look scandalized or offended.

"I don't know. I had never heard of them until a few weeks ago."

"How can that be?" Mayu couldn't keep the resentment from her voice. "You are a princess."

"*You* were a princess for a time," said Ehri gently. "Did you find much meaning in it?"

Mayu had no reply to that, but it did nothing to quell her anger. Nikolai, Makhi, all the kings and queens and generals made their grand decisions, decided who should live, who should die, who should suffer. She had never cared, not really. She'd been happy to follow, happy to have found her place in the world. Until she'd lost Reyem and then Isaak.

Tamar unsheathed one of her axes, letting it spin in her palm. "The *khergud* hunted Grisha indentures in Ketterdam. They've attacked behind Ravka's own borders. You're saying you didn't know about them?"

"No," said Ehri. "And I doubt most Shu did."

"And Makhi's advisers?"

"That I can't be certain of."

That was part of the problem. There was too much Ehri didn't know. Just how was she supposed to give Queen Makhi any kind of a fight?

"Your sister is a bold one," Tamar said, as if she'd read Mayu's thoughts. "She had to have started up the labs before your mother's death, before she was made queen."

Ehri frowned. "There was an incident . . . a scientist tried to defect to Kerch. He was captured by Fjerdans. I know there was an investigation. But my mother was already in poor health and couldn't pursue it. She died not long after."

"Interesting timing," said Tamar, and returned the axe to its holster.

Mayu met her gaze. Was she implying Makhi had played some role in her mother's death?

The web was too tangled, full of too many threads and too many spiders. She and her brother were bound to be trapped and eaten.

Mayu had cheated death once. She was meant to die by her own hand, the same night she had killed Isaak. His blood had still been on the knife blade when she'd driven it into her heart. Or that was what she'd intended. She'd missed the mark. An accident? Or in those vital seconds had her desire to live won out over her desire to free her brother and serve her queen?

If she'd managed her own death, would Queen Makhi have honored their bargain? Mayu didn't think so. And she didn't really believe she'd ever see Reyem again.

Mayu's parents had encouraged her competition with her twin, thinking it was all a game, all in good fun.

"Who will run up the hill to fetch water?"

"I will!" they would each cry.

"Who will land three strikes without getting hit?"

"I will!" they would shout.

But it was always Reyem who *did*. He was never smug about it. He would ruffle her hair and say, "Next time you'll get me. Let's go see if we can steal some green melon."

Mayu had almost wished he would be cruel, because then maybe she could hate him. But he was her best friend and her favorite companion. When they were running through the woods, she didn't care that he was faster. When they were roaming through the muddy creek looking for tadpoles, she was the sharp-eyed one who somehow knew where to look. She could celebrate his victories and his gifts because they were *kebben*. And she knew he shared in her failures because he was her twin. She would have happily shared in his losses—if he'd ever had one.

They'd been together in the marketplace when they'd spotted the poster advertising the arrival of the Royal Creance, who was coming to their city to find girls to train to join the Tavgharad. WHO WILL DARE TO SHOW HER SKILLS? the sign asked in tall red letters.

I will, thought Mayu. They only wanted girls. It was something Reyem couldn't try. She'd gone down to the pasture outside the academy and filled out the forms and joined the other hopefuls. She'd run and sparred and crawled on her belly, all the time chanting to herself, *I will. I will. I will.*

And she had. She'd been chosen to travel to Ahmrat Jen and train.

Her mother's worry at the news had been like a slap to the face.

"She isn't ready! She isn't good enough!"

Her father had been more reasonable. "They wouldn't have chosen her if she didn't have a chance."

"They chose her because she is obedient, not skilled. What will become of her when she fails at her training?"

"She'll come home," Mayu's father said.

"In shame? She's not strong enough to survive such failure."

But they were wrong about that. Mayu had been failing her whole life. Her constant competition with Reyem had prepared her well for the trial she was about to endure. The other Eyases selected to train as Tavgharad had all been the very best of the best in the towns and villages they came from. They took their first losses hard.

Not Mayu. She loved training. She loved the exhaustion that silenced her thoughts, the routine that gave order to her world. She loved being out of Reyem's shadow. In his absence, in the fatigue of fighting, running, learning to disassemble and reassemble guns, climb walls and scamper along rooftops, her mind finally quieted. And in that silence she heard the music of combat at last. Becoming

Tavgharad meant she had joined a dance that had begun centuries ago. The first Taban queen had traveled with an elite bodyguard of women and a fleet of trained falcons. She had trusted her guards and her raptors and no one else. Those guards had gone on to train other women, and their symbol had become the carnelian falcon. This was the tradition Mayu had become a part of, and she carried new pride with her every day to the temple fields, where they ran drills in the blazing sun or the pouring rain.

That pride carried her home for the spring festivals. She missed Reyem more than she had ever believed possible. Her envy had been eaten away by achievement, and now she could feel the hollow in her heart left by her twin's absence. At the first glimpse of him, she'd broken into a run, grateful for her brother, grateful for her commanders and the queen who had finally freed her from jealousy.

Mayu and Reyem had sat together, decorating custard cakes, surrounded by clusters of anemones arranged in their mother's white stone bowls, and she'd told her brother all about the palace, the temple fields, her instructors.

"I'll be given my post when I return," she'd told him. "I won't be home again for a very long time."

"Good," Reyem said with a laugh. "Mother and Father can go back to fussing over me."

"Does it bother you?"

Reyem wiped powdered sugar from his fingers. He had joined a military unit and was faring well, though he had yet to distinguish himself. "I know you deserve it. You worked hard for so long while I grew lazy on compliments. But . . . I think I may be jealous."

Mayu grinned. "Reyem, I cannot pity you. If you would try, if you would be willing to fail, you would learn. It's good to do things you're not good at."

Forever after, Mayu would curse those words. Because Reyem

had started trying and he'd begun to succeed. She hadn't understood how well until her father showed up at the Tavgharad barracks.

"Your brother has gone missing," he'd said. He looked frail, his skin nearly gray from worry and the hardships of travel. "They say he deserted and that he may be dead."

Mayu had known that couldn't be. "Reyem would never do such a thing. And I would know if . . . if he were gone."

It had taken months, but Mayu had pieced together rumor and fact and finally discovered that her brother—her twin who had been happy to avoid notice in his regiment until she'd goaded him—had displayed such gifts as a soldier that he'd been drafted into the Iron Heart program. The *khergud* were half myth among the Tavgharad. No one could confirm that they really existed, and yet the stories of their abilities were legendary—as were the horrific tales of what they endured in the conversion and what they lost when it was complete. She had set out to find him, to free him, when she'd been called before Queen Makhi.

Mayu thought her investigation had been discovered, that she would be banished or put to death.

Instead the queen had said, "You're from Nehlu, one of the larger towns. Is that why you have no country accent?"

"My mother was a teacher, Your Majesty," Mayu had said. "She wanted us to have every advantage as we tried to make our way in the world."

"There is little call for elocution in the Tavgharad. Your fists speak for you. Did she teach you a passable curtsy?"

She had not, but Mayu could learn. That was her gift. She could always learn. The queen had offered her an opportunity to save her brother.

Or so Mayu had believed at the time.

Now, sitting in the cargo hold, she heard the Ravkan king's voice in her head: *You are Reyem Yul-Kaat's sister, and he still lives.* If there was any chance her brother might still be saved, she had to take it.

"Where are we?" she asked as the airship began to descend a second time. "This isn't the palace."

"The temple fields outside Ahmrat Jen," said Tamar. She turned to Ehri and the remaining Grisha guards. "This place is too conspicuous by half. Stay alert."

She wasn't wrong. The darkness provided cover, but Mayu's instincts told her they were badly exposed. Maybe instead of finding her brother, she'd only succeed in getting herself killed.

"Here," Tamar said, handing Mayu a sword belt and a curved blade.

"Where did you get this?" she asked, and fastened it around her waist. The talon sword was the traditional weapon of the Tavgharad, often worn with a pistol, but they weren't easy to come by, and none of the Tavgharad had been permitted to bring them to Ravka.

"My father," said Tamar. "It was a gift from one of his students long ago. I'll be expecting it back. Let's go."

"Why this place?" Mayu asked as they walked down the long gangway to the fields where Mayu had once trained to become Tavgharad. Though she couldn't see them, Mayu knew some of Tamar's Grisha were stationed around the temple.

"We can't just go marching up to the palace gates," said Tamar. "My spies have made contact with Ministers Nagh and Zihun. We'll meet them in the Temple of Neyar. My scouts recommended a barn farther afield, but the princess insisted on the temple."

"The ministers will be skeptical," Ehri said. "We need the temple to give our words weight."

Neyar. One of the Six Soldiers, the sacred protectors of Shu Han. Mayu knew this temple. She'd been reminded of it when she'd seen the six-sided hall at the Little Palace. It was built as a hexagon, the six entries guarded by slender garnet columns, the statue of Neyar holding her famous sword, Neshyenyer, beneath a roof open to the sky. This was where Mayu had taken her oath when she'd been inducted into the Tavghai ad. And this was where she would break it and betray a queen.

They approached through the eastern entry. The ministers were waiting with guards in tow.

"You vowed to come alone," said Tamar.

Minister Nagh recoiled. "What is this treachery?" he demanded. "You bring Ravka's trained attack dog beneath the roof of one of our temples?"

Everyone in the Shu government knew of the *kebben* who served first the Sun Saint and then a Ravkan king. Tamar's tattoos, her axes, her short hair, all made her instantly recognizable.

"She is the enemy," said Minister Zihun, and punctuated the statement by spitting at the floor near Tamar's boots.

Tamar didn't react, but her golden eyes narrowed, and Mayu wondered at the arrogance of these politicians. Tamar was not someone she would seek to provoke, and Ehri seemed to agree.

"Friends," Ehri said sweetly, shyly, "I do not believe you think Tamar Kir-Bataar is a threat. If you did, you would never speak to her thus. Not when you know she is a Heartrender. Not when she wears those silver axes as another woman might wear jewels. She has put her life at risk to save mine. I hope you will hear me out."

"To save your *life?*" Zihun sputtered. "What is the meaning of all of this, Princess? The queen was supposed to be attending your wedding this very day. Have we sent her into a trap? You must explain yourself."

"The trap is of the queen's own making," said Tamar.

"You dare—"

Ehri stepped forward. "I will explain. If you will only give me the chance. That is why Tamar escorted me here."

We're lost, Mayu thought. Ehri had none of Makhi's authority, none of her mighty presence.

Minister Nagh sniffed. "And what does the traitor get from this?"

"A chance to see two windbags in a temple," Tamar muttered.

"What was that?" the minister snapped.

Tamar plastered a smile over her face. "I said, a chance to see peace thrive."

"Please," said Ehri. "As a Taban princess, I ask you to hear me."

The ministers exchanged a glance and gave the barest nod. They couldn't very well deny her, but they didn't intend to be won over.

"Gentle friends," the princess began, using the formal address, "my story is a sad one, but I hope you will hear me."

Ehri didn't speak like a politician. She told her tale in the cadence of the great poets. It was like listening to someone play music, as if she had her hands on the *khatuur* at this very moment and was plucking out a melancholy song, each verse revealing a new tragedy: a cunning plot to kill a king, a failed assassination, a sister's betrayal. No, Ehri didn't have Makhi's fire. There was a sweetness in her, a softness that Mayu had never liked. But now she couldn't help but think of the legendary generals who feigned a weakened flank to lure their enemy closer. Mayu watched as the ministers' expressions shifted from rigid suspicion to stunned disbelief to outrage and then to fear. Because if Ehri's story was true, they had no choice but to challenge Makhi.

Mayu felt an ache in her throat. Her own story was woven in with Ehri's words, a silent counterpoint, a harmony that would go unheard. What it had meant to wear another woman's clothes, another woman's crown, to believe she had fallen in love with a king,

266

to be forced to choose between the funny, gentle boy she'd known she could never have and the brother Queen Makhi had stolen away from her.

It was Isaak's story too. A boy who had given up his heart to an impostor, who had given up his life for his king. Mayu had no right to grieve for him. She'd chosen Reyem. She'd driven a knife into Isaak's heart. Sometimes she wished her aim had been better and she'd died that day too. But then who would remain to fight for Reyem? She had to find her brother, or it was all for nothing.

Mayu gave her testimony when Ehri called upon her to do so. Her words felt shapeless in her mouth, blunt soldier's talk after Ehri's eloquence. Still, it was no small thing for a Tavgharad guard to speak against her queen. Then Tamar showed them the note Makhi had sent, and Mayu told them of the coded message within it.

The ministers stepped aside to consult with each other as Mayu and Tamar and the princess waited. What the ministers did next would tell them everything they needed to know.

Minister Nagh and Minister Zihun turned slowly. They bowed their heads and knelt before the princess. "We have failed you. We should have protected you from your sister's deceptions."

"But I must beg *your* forgiveness," said Ehri. "I have put you at risk by sharing this information with you. We are all in danger now."

"You can set this right," said Tamar. "Queen Makhi may be returning to the capital even now. Bring Ehri to the palace and place her under your protection."

"We can," said Zihun as they rose. "Of course we can. We only beg that you will show us mercy when you are queen."

"I do not want the crown," said Ehri. "Only justice and peace."

I should be relieved at that, thought Mayu. She'd always considered the princess useless, a woman who could barely fight, who liked to sip tea and play her songs and who dreamed of an ordinary life.

She'd thought Ehri's charm and gentle ways were liabilities. Now she wondered. Had the princess always been a diplomat, wielding the careful ways of court and etiquette as her weapons while Makhi chose the cudgels of might and cunning? Which type of leader did Shu Han need?

But the next step would require more than fine speeches. In many ways, the palace was the most perilous place for them to be. They would be surrounded by guards, Tavgharad, Makhi's spies. But it was also where they had to make their stand. They couldn't simply meet with ministers. There had to be a public reckoning, and Princess Ehri would only be safe when everyone knew she was back on Shu soil and Makhi couldn't pursue action against her in secret.

"You should come to the palace by night," said Minister Nagh. "Under cover of darkness."

"Yes," agreed Ehri. "We will join you at the garden door in two hours."

The ministers departed with many pledges of loyalty. But Tamar and Ehri made no move to follow.

"We're not going tonight, are we?" Mayu asked.

Ehri shook her head. "We can't arrive at the palace skulking around in the dark like criminals."

"You don't believe the ministers will help us?"

Tamar gave a small shrug. "Zihun and Nagh seem honest and righteous enough, but we need better protection than the promises of politicians."

That Mayu could agree with. She was tired of placing her faith in the honor of kings and queens and commanders. "And if Makhi is waiting when we arrive?"

Tamar flashed a wicked grin. "We're counting on it."

Dawn came and went and they remained inside, as they waited for the crowds to enter the morning market that surrounded the temple fields. The Shu airship and the Grisha had long since departed.

Ehri changed into fresh silks, and when she returned, Tamar brought her a package wrapped in linen.

"You have it," Ehri said with obvious relief.

Tamar unwrapped the package.

"A *khatuur*?" Mayu asked incredulously. "I was hoping for a weapon."

"It *is* a weapon," said Ehri. "Beauty of all kinds is a weapon."

Tamar huffed a laugh. "You sound like Zoya."

Ehri clearly didn't appreciate the comparison. "She's all bluster, like my sister. No, the *khatuur* is much more than that."

"Are you ready?" Tamar asked. "Once we begin this, there will be no turning back."

Ehri rested her fingers on the strings of the *khatuur*. For a moment, she said nothing, tuning the instrument, guiding the notes to arrange themselves in the air, then letting them fade.

"I have never been so frightened," she said. "I thought I could imagine this all as a performance, but it's not, is it?"

"No," said Tamar. "It's very real."

Mayu wanted to scream. They were really going to *walk* to the palace, out in the open, in the bright light of day. How could Tamar let the princess do something this foolish? They were never going to make it to the palace. Queen Makhi would simply send an assassin to pick them off before they ever set foot in the city proper. But Mayu was a soldier, and a soldier had to follow.

"I've never wanted to be the hero in any story," Ehri said, gazing down at the softly curved neck of the *khatuur*. "I only wanted to sing their tales. A hero would think of the possibility of war, the lives that hung in the balance, the women who burned at a callous queen's order. But I find it is my own life that worries me the most."

Tamar tapped her axes. "That only means you're a survivor, Princess. And that's nothing to be ashamed of."

Ehri put her fingers to the strings. "Very well. Let's begin."

She descended the temple steps into the morning market. Instantly the shoppers left off their haggling to marvel at the sight of Ehri Kir-Taban, Daughter of Heaven, returned to them. Mayu knew this was not the first time the princess had played at the temple fields, but she was meant to be off in Ravka, courting and marrying a Ravkan king.

The princess glided through the marketplace in her leaf-green silks, her hair drawn back, a chrysanthemum tucked behind her left ear. She played her music and the people followed, pulling their children along with them, clapping and dancing. The song Ehri chose was no coincidence: "The Flower Maiden." *She is the sun, and spring-time has returned.*

As they entered the city, people emerged from their homes with bells and drums in hand to play along. They cast flowers into her path.

"They really do love her," said Tamar in wonder.

"We heard you went to meet the barbarians!" someone cried.

"We thought you were to be wife to the Scarred King!"

"But you see I am back and unwed and just happy to be among you," said Ehri, and the people cheered.

Over the bridge they paraded and Ehri struck up a new song, one triumphant and patriotic, a Shu soldiers' anthem. A fighting song.

Queen Makhi was waiting for them on the wide palace balcony that overlooked the river.

"Sister!" she called, her arms open. "How like you to arrive in such fine style."

No one who wasn't watching closely would have noticed the way the queen's teeth were bared, the way her eyes slid to Mayu and then back to Ehri.

"Are we not glad to see our sister returned?" Makhi demanded of the crowd, and the people cheered in reply. "Are we not grateful for her safety and good health? Then let this be a day of feasts and celebration!" Makhi clapped her hands and the square was flooded with royal servants handing out currant cakes and little bags of golden coins.

Mayu studied the queen's face, the brittle smile, the hands spread wide in a gesture of beneficence.

She wants to be loved, Mayu realized. *Just as I did. She can't understand why her sister is favored when she is smarter, stronger, more lovely. She will spend a lifetime trying to unravel this mystery, sure there's some secret she can uncover, offering her subjects bribes of money and sweets to show her generosity.* Queen Makhi had tried to murder Ehri, not once but twice, rather than live forever in her shadow. She might have a sister's envy, but she did not have a sister's love.

As soon as they entered the palace, they were surrounded by guards. Minister Yerwei, the queen's doctor, came forward to greet them.

"Princess Ehri, are you well? We must have you examined and prescribe the proper tonics to restore your vitality after such a long trip."

"I thank you, Minister Yerwei. But I am in good health. I have been well fed and looked after by our Ravkan friends."

"Where are the rest of your Tavgharad guard?"

"I would give my answers to my sister," Ehri said serenely.

"She will receive you in the audience chamber."

Minister Zihun cleared her throat. "I'm afraid the chamber is under repair. May I suggest the Court of the Feathered Bower?"

"But I was just in the chamber—" Yerwei protested.

"There was a flood."

"A flood?"

"A small flood by one of the fountains," added Minister Nagh. "The workers are still inside."

Mayu hid her relief. Maybe Nagh and Zihun had always planned to keep their promises to Ehri. Maybe they had been swayed by the sight of a city following her through the streets. It didn't matter. They'd done their part. Ehri and Tamar needed to speak to the queen privately, not in front of her ministers and not in a place where she could look down on them cloaked in the power of a thousand years of Taban queens.

"I see," murmured Minister Yerwei. There was nothing else for him to say.

⋙━◆━⋘

The Court of the Feathered Bower was all soft white and gold, like the glow of clouds in the hour before dusk. It suited Ehri well, softening the angles of her face. Servants brought them glass ewers of wine and water, a plate of sliced red plums. But they scattered when the doors burst open and Makhi strode in, flanked by her Tavgharad.

"You dare summon me like some kind of serving girl?"

Ehri only smiled. She rose and bowed deeply. "Forgive me if I offended, sister. The audience chamber was flooded, and it seemed best we talk in private."

"The time for that has passed," snapped Makhi. "You should have come to me with your concerns. Instead you conspired with the barbarian king. You went to my ministers with absurd tales of assassina-

272

tions and poetry and secret laboratories. We will meet in the council chamber and you will recant your testimony and throw yourself on my mercy."

"I cannot," said Ehri. "Not even you, most celestial sister, can bid me lie."

"You have no proof."

"I am the proof," said Mayu, ashamed of the way her voice trembled. "I who was asked to kill a king to save my brother."

"You have no proof of that either. All I see is a girl looking healthy when all of her Tavgharad sisters are mysteriously dead."

"We have your note," said Ehri softly. "It was meant to burn with me, was it not? I didn't quite believe it until this moment. But I can't mistake that look on your face, Makhi. I remember it from when we were children, when Mother would catch you doing something you knew you shouldn't."

Makhi's chin lifted. "What do you want?"

"Keep to the treaty you signed with Ravka and grant them monies from our treasury. Give up your dreams of war. And end the *khergud* program."

"Without admitting that any of what you've said is true, I can agree to hold to the treaty, for now. Its terms are acceptable to us."

"Then you will dismantle the laboratories."

Makhi flicked a graceful hand through the air as if swatting a bug. "Nonsense. This *khergud* program you speak of is nothing but conspiracy theory and fanciful thinking."

"I've seen the *khergud* myself," said Tamar. "I didn't imagine them."

Makhi's chin rose even higher. "I met your twin in Os Alta. He is as insolent and ill-mannered as you."

"You will take us to the labs," said Mayu. She was tired of all this back-and-forth. She wanted to see her brother.

"Do you really think to dictate terms to me in my own palace?

You have gravely overestimated the influence of Ministers Zihun and Nagh."

Ehri shook her head. "I did not think to rely on their influence."

She had been standing in front of a golden table. Now she moved behind it and bent to smell the vase of vibrant coral roses she had placed upon it. Their petals looked like they'd been dipped in gold.

The queen's face paled.

"They're lovely, no? Bright as fire, but they have very little scent. Their beauty is all on the surface. I think I prefer wild roses myself. But these are very rare."

"You took them from our grandmother's garden." Queen Makhi's voice was barely a whisper.

"They were a gift. She likes a story well told."

Now Mayu understood where the airship had landed that night, the scent of roses on the air. Tamar and Ehri had gone to Ehri's grandmother for protection. Leyti Kir-Taban, Daughter of Heaven, was still considered a Taban queen. She had given her crown to her daughter when she was ready to leave off ruling and enjoy her old age. When her daughter had died, Leyti had given Makhi, her daughter's chosen successor, her blessing. But Leyti could withdraw that blessing at any time. The roses—the flowers Mayu had so naively dismissed as mere sentiment—were bred in Leyti's garden and nowhere else.

"Our grandmother should be careful in the garden," said Makhi. "Accidents happen."

"I know," said Ehri. "That's why we left an entire cadre of Grisha guards with her along with her own Tavgharad."

"How solicitous."

"I didn't tell her everything," said Ehri. "But I certainly could. You will take us to the labs, Makhi, or our grandmother will know why."

"I'll think on it," said the queen, and without another word, she turned on her heel and departed.

"Do you think she took the bait?" Tamar asked when the queen and her guards were gone.

Ehri pulled one of the roses from its arrangement and replaced it in another spot, just so. "Yes. She can't help herself."

Mayu looked at the roses, then out the window to the sunny winter sky and the gardens beyond. She could only pray Ehri was right.

I'll find you, Reyem, she vowed silently. *I will.*

20

ZOYA

THEY STOOD ON THE SHORE of the lake at the Little Palace, watching David's body burn.

Inferni ignited the flames. Squallers protected the fire from the cold and damp. When the time came, Durasts would fashion a brick from David's ashes. That was the ritual, the proper way of caring for the dead. When there was a body. When there was time. So many had been left on battlefields, had died in prisons or laboratories far from people who might tend to them, who might speak words of love and remembrance.

Who will speak for me? Zoya wondered. Nikolai? Genya? And what would they say? *She was impossible and vain, bitter and poisonous as yewberries. She was brave.* It didn't add up to much.

Zoya watched the fire leap toward the night sky, the flames dancing as if they didn't know this was a solemn occasion, their light reflected in the water. Ordinary soldiers had gathered on the lakeshore to pay their respects alongside the Grisha, palace guards, Nolniki—those special troops who had declared themselves neither Grisha nor First Army, who had toiled together, side by side, in solidarity forged by new technology and the Small Science, working for a future born of Nikolai's vision and David's ingenuity.

Zoya knew she had to preserve that future. She had to find a way to move forward with the war effort, figure out whom to choose from among the Materialki to join the Triumvirate in David's place. She was a general. She was a soldier. That was her duty and she would fulfill it, but right now . . . Right now she couldn't think, couldn't find that solitary place inside her, that bunker that could survive any bomb blast or storm.

You cannot save them all.

Maybe Juris was eternal, maybe his dragon's eyes could perceive that one death was nothing in the great sprawl of time. But Zoya couldn't take flight with the dragon. She had never felt more mortal or more small.

"Stay with me," Genya had whispered. "Stand with me."

So Zoya was here, on this lakeside where they had all trained together, near the school where they'd sat for their lessons, Genya's arm looped through hers. Nikolai stood on Genya's other side, his arm around her shoulders, as if they could protect her from grief when they had failed to protect her from loss.

Zoya felt her friend's body, swathed in a heavy red *kefta*, beside her. There was no Grisha color of mourning. They'd had too many lives to grieve.

Genya was trembling and her weight against Zoya felt insubstantial, as if she might be carried away with the sparks from the fire. But the heft of her sorrow clung to Zoya, heavy and dense, a sodden coat, dragging her down, pulling at her limbs. She wanted to cast it off, but the dragon wouldn't allow it, wouldn't let her run from this pain.

"I can't do this," Genya whispered. Her face was swollen from crying. Her vibrant hair lay limp down her back.

"You don't have to do anything," Zoya said. "Just be here. Stay standing."

"Not even that."

"I've got you. I won't let you fall."

It felt like a lie. Zoya was breaking apart. She was shattered on the rocks. *You are strong enough to survive the fall.* Juris was wrong. But she owed Genya this and so much more.

"Nikolai," Zoya said, "I don't think she's ready to speak."

Nikolai nodded. He looked out at the crowd gathered in the dark, their faces lit by flames.

"David and I spoke in numbers," he began. "Our deepest conversations were transcribed in blueprints for some new invention. I can't pretend I understood him."

Zoya had expected to hear the tones of a king rallying his troops, but Nikolai's voice was raw and weary. He was just a man, grieving the loss of a friend.

"I wasn't smart enough to keep up with his genius," Nikolai continued. "All I could do was respect his intellect and his desire to do right with the gifts with which he was born. I relied on him to find answers I couldn't, to blaze a path when I found myself lost. David saw things no one else did. He saw through the world to the mysteries on the other side. I know that he's gone on to solve those mysteries." A faint smile touched Nikolai's lips. "I can see him in some great library, already lost in his work, head bent to some new problem, making the unknown known. When I enter the laboratory, when I wake in the night with a new idea, I will miss him . . ." His voice broke. "I miss him now. May the Saints receive him on a brighter shore."

"May the Saints receive him," the crowd murmured.

But David hadn't believed in Saints. He'd believed in the Small Science. He'd believed in a world ordered by facts and logic.

What do you believe? Zoya didn't know. She believed in Ravka, in her king, in the chance that she could be a part of something better than herself. But maybe she didn't deserve that.

All eyes had turned to Genya now. She was David's wife, his friend, his compatriot. She was expected to speak.

Genya stood straighter, lifted her chin. "I loved him," she said, her body still trembling as if it had been torn apart and hastily stitched back together. "I loved him and he loved me. When I was . . . when no one could reach me . . . he saw me. He . . ." Genya turned her head to Zoya's shoulder and sobbed. "I loved him and he loved me."

Was there any greater gift than that? Any more unlikely discovery in this world?

"I know," said Zoya. "He loved you more than anything."

The dragon's eye had opened and Zoya felt that love, the enormity of what Genya had lost. It was too much to endure knowing she could do nothing to erase that pain.

"Tell them, Zoya. I can't . . . I can't."

Genya looked frail, curled in on herself, the frond of some delicate flower hiding from winter.

What could Zoya say to her? To any of them? How could she give them hope she didn't have?

This is what love does. That had been one of her mother's favorite sayings. When the larder was bare, when her husband couldn't find work, when her hands cracked from taking in the neighbors' washing. *This is what love does.*

279

Zoya could see Sabina, her hands red from lye, her beautiful face carved with lines, as if the sculptor who had wrought her loveliness had lost control, dug too deep beneath the eyes, the corners of the mouth. *You cannot imagine how handsome he was,* Sabina would say, looking at Zoya's father, her voice bitter. *My own mother warned me I would have no life with a Suli, that she and my father would turn their backs on us. But I didn't care. I was in love. We met by moonlight. We danced to the music his brothers played. I thought love would be our armor, wings to fly with, a shield against the world.* She'd laughed, the sound like bones rattling in a fortune-teller's cup, ready to spill and show only disaster. Sabina spread her cracked hands, gesturing to their meager home, the cold stove, the piles of laundry, the earthen floor. *Here is our shield. This is what love does.* Her father had said nothing.

Zoya had seen her Suli uncles only once. They'd arrived after dark by her mother's order. Sabina had already retired to bed and told Zoya to stay with her, but as soon as her mother had nodded off to sleep, Zoya had snuck out to see the strangers with their black hair and their black eyes, their brows thick and dark like hers. They looked like her father, but they didn't. Their brown skin seemed lit from within. Their shoulders were straight and they held their heads high. Beside them, her father looked like an old man, though she knew he was the youngest brother.

"Come away with us," Uncle Dhej had said. "Now. Tonight. Before that shrew wakes."

"Don't speak of my wife that way."

"Then before your loving wife wakes to claim you. You will die here, Suhm. You're nearly dead already."

"I'm fine."

"We're not meant to live among them, locked up in their houses, wilting beneath their roofs. You were meant for the stars and open skies. You were meant for freedom."

"I have a child. I cannot just—"

"The mother is spoiled fruit and the daughter will grow up sour. I can see the sorrow hanging around her already."

"Be silent, Dhej. Zoya has a good heart and will grow up strong and beautiful. As her mother might have. In a different life. With a different husband."

"Then bring her with us. Save her from this place."

Yes. Take me away from here. Zoya had clapped her hands over her mouth as if she'd spoken the words aloud, released some kind of curse into the world. Guilt flooded her, choking her, bringing tears to her eyes. She loved her mother. She did, she did. She didn't want anything bad to happen to her. She didn't want to leave her alone to fend for herself. She'd crept back into Sabina's bed and hugged her close and cried herself to sleep. But she'd dreamed she was riding in a Suli wagon and she'd woken the next morning, confused and disoriented, still sure she could smell hay and horses, still certain she could hear the happy chatter of sisters she didn't have.

She'd never seen her uncles again.

This is what love does.

Love was the destroyer. It made mourners, widows, left misery in its wake. Grief and love were one and the same. Grief was the shadow love left when it was gone.

I've lived too long in that shadow, Zoya thought, gazing out at the lakeshore, at the soldiers huddled against the cold, waiting for someone to say something.

"Please," Genya whispered.

Zoya racked her brain for a message of hope, of strength. But all she had was the truth.

"I used to . . ." Her voice was husky with unshed tears. She hated that sound. "I used to believe there was one kind of soldier. The kind of soldier I aspired to be. Ruthless and unrelenting. I worshipped at the altar of strength—the storm, the Heartrender's blow, the Cut. When I was chosen to lead the Triumvirate, I . . ." Shame washed over her, but she made herself keep speaking. "I resented the people selected to lead alongside me. *I* was the most powerful and the most dangerous, and I thought I knew how to lead." Zoya felt memories crowd in on her, long nights arguing with Genya and David. When had they begun scheming together instead of squabbling?

"I knew nothing. David didn't set out to teach me the power of silence, but he did. Genya didn't try to convince me to be kinder, she showed me what kindness could do every day. David wasn't . . . He wasn't an easy person. He didn't tell jokes or crack smiles or try to make you comfortable. He hated small talk and he could fall so deeply into his work, he forgot to eat or sleep. The only distraction he ever had was Genya. When he looked at her, you could see that he had found his perfect equation." She shrugged, unable to make her own figures tally. "David was a different kind of soldier. His strength came from his brilliance but also from his silence, his willingness to listen, his belief that every problem had a solution. All over Os Alta today, there are funerals. People are grieving. We are facing a new and terrible challenge, a different kind of enemy and a different kind of war, but just as we grieve together, we'll face this new enemy together. We will fight just as we grieve, side by side. We'll march forward as soldiers—and aspire to be the kind of soldier that David was—not driven by revenge or rage but by a desire to know more and do better. David Kostyk returns to the making at the heart of the world. He will always be with us."

Most of the soldiers didn't know the traditional reply, but the Grisha did. "As he returns, so will we all."

There was some small comfort in those words, in that murmured reply. Could she be a soldier like David? Zoya didn't know. She was afraid of what might happen when this moment of quiet was over, when David's ashes had been gathered and interned in the white walls that circled the palace grounds. A space beside him would be left for Genya. Thousands of bodies, thousands of bricks, thousands of ghosts standing watch over generations of Grisha. For what?

The Fjerdans had shoved them all into uncharted territory. Zoya knew her rage was waiting on the other side of this sorrow, and when it was unleashed, she wasn't certain what she would do.

"I need to go to him," Genya whispered. "One last time."

She had pulled a notebook from her pocket, the pages held open. It took Zoya a moment to understand what it was. She glimpsed a few words in David's scrawl: *Ideas for compliments—hair (color, texture), smile (causes and effects), talents (tailoring, tonics, sense of style—inquire on "style"), teeth? size of feet?*

"His journal," Zoya said. Where David had written down all his little reminders for how to make Genya happy.

Genya looked out at the lake. "I need to get across."

Zoya could signal a Tidemaker, but the dragon was near and she wanted to be the one who held Genya in this moment. She lifted her arms, moving her palms slowly together. *Are we not all things? If the science is small enough.* There'd been no time to hone her gifts or shape the power Juris had granted Zoya with his life. But her Squaller talents were not so far from the abilities of a Tidemaker. *I need to give her this.* The dragon demanded it. Zoya's grieving heart required it.

Ice formed on the surface of the lake, a shimmering white path that spread with each step Genya took, leading her from the shore to David's pyre. She stood before the flames, her red hair gleaming like the feathers of a firebird. She pressed a kiss to the cover of the notebook.

"So you'll remember when I meet you in the next world," she said softly. She tossed the notebook onto the fire.

Zoya shouldn't have been able to hear the words, not at this distance. She didn't want to know this private thing, this painful thing. But she saw with the dragon's eyes, heard with its ears. For every life Zoya had grieved, the dragon had grieved a thousand.

How? How do you survive a world that keeps taking?

There was no answer from the dragon, only the crackle of flames and the cold silence of the stars, lovely, bright, and uncaring.

After the ceremony ended, Zoya intended to escort Genya back to her rooms, but Genya refused.

"I can't be alone. Are you meeting with the king?"

"I am, but——"

"I can't be alone," Genya repeated.

"Leoni and Nadia will be there."

"I know. The Fjerdans won't wait for us to mourn our dead. We'll need to select someone to represent the Materialki on the Triumvirate."

"We have time."

Genya's eyes were haunted. "Do we? I keep seeing the way he looked when they pulled him from the rubble. He was still dressed in his wedding clothes and . . . he had a pen in his hand. His fingertips . . ." Genya held up her own hand, touched her fingers to her lips. Fresh tears filled her eyes. "They were stained with ink."

Zoya hadn't been there. She had returned to Os Alta too late to help, too late to fight. "If you don't feel ready to——"

Genya wiped away her tears. "I'm a member of the Triumvirate, not just a grieving widow. I need to be there. And I can't sit alone with my thoughts."

That much Zoya understood.

Everyone gathered in her sitting room, at the table where the Darkling's *oprichniki* and then Alina's guards had once sat. The king's chambers were still intact, but the halls around them weren't yet cleared of rubble.

Tolya wrapped a shawl around Genya's shoulders and settled her by the fire while Zoya paced, unsure of what came next. Nadia and Leoni had brought a stack of files with them, most likely the work they'd been doing on the missiles. Adrik was there too. Zoya wondered if Nikolai intended to demote her and give Nadia's little brother her command. He had every right to.

"Forgive the delay," Nikolai said when he entered at last. "It's hard to keep up with correspondence since . . . Well." He poured a cup of tea and brought it to Genya, placing it on a saucer in her hands. "Are you hungry?"

She shook her head.

He moved a chair so that he could sit beside her. No one said anything for a long time.

At last, the king sighed. "I don't know where to begin."

There had been funerals held all over Os Alta in recent days, once the danger had passed and the bodies could be found, some burned, some buried. The king had attended as many as he could, slipping into churches where prayers were spoken to the Saints, helping to move families out of areas of the city that had become unsafe. Zoya had seen little of him since she'd returned to the capital, and she was glad of that. Facing him would mean facing her failure. Instead she'd tried to help make sense of the chaos that had followed the bombings, setting up new protocols for blackouts across Ravka, lodging formal diplomatic protests with Fjerda, joining the Grisha in the lower town to help with cleanup and rescue efforts, grateful to be busy.

She hadn't been ready for the terrible quiet of the funeral, or this moment that required an accounting of what they'd suffered. No one wanted to add it up.

"Where else was hit?" asked Tolya. Better to speak of war than of love lost.

"Poliznaya took the brunt of it," said Nikolai. "We lost over half our flyers, most of our airships. Our stores of titanium are gone."

He delivered the news with little emotion, a man reporting on the weather. But Zoya knew him too well. The look in his eyes was as unmistakable as it was unfamiliar: He looked defeated.

"All of it?" asked Nadia. "We haven't begun construction on the missile shells."

"We'll have to use another metal."

But even Zoya knew what that meant. The missiles would be too heavy to attack from a safe range, and far harder for Squallers to aim at a distance.

"Os Kervo will be Fjerda's next target," Zoya said, because someone had to.

"We've issued blackout warnings throughout the city," said Nikolai, his gaze skating past her. He'd barely looked at her since she'd returned. "But I think Fjerda may hold back. They attacked us in the hope of intimidating the west and getting them to declare for Vadik Demidov. It's a strategy the Darkling used in the civil war."

"He got the best of me again." She sounded resigned, maybe angry. But there was no hint of the misery inside her, the prickling thing that kept her awake, that ate at her night and day. Rage was easy. Even sorrow. But shame? *I let him get away.* Anything the Darkling did now, anyone he harmed—the blame would lie with her.

"I agreed to let him be removed from the palace," said Nikolai. "This isn't the first time the Darkling has taken us by surprise, but let's remember his schemes never quite stick."

Not yet. This time he might win and keep winning. Maybe they should have found a way to forge an alliance with him, to truly bring him to their side. Maybe the Fjerdans wouldn't have dared attack if they'd known the Darkling had returned. But was Genya expected to work side by side with the man who had sacrificed her to a rapist? Was Zoya meant to share the war room with the man who had murdered her aunt?

"What will he do?" asked Leoni. She was seated beside Adrik. They'd been together at the funeral too. It was common for Grisha who worked undercover to fall in love during a mission, but the romances rarely lasted once the thrill had passed and the agents were back on their home soil. Adrik and Leoni seemed to be an exception, though how either of them put up with the other was beyond her. Maybe relentless gloom and persistent sunshine were the right combination.

Nikolai leaned back in his chair. "The Darkling has a gift for spectacle rivaled only by my own. He'll want to stage a very public return."

"My sister has spies and informants stationed in nearly every major town in Ravka," said Tolya. "We'll ask about newcomers and strangers."

"At least Tamar is well," said Nikolai.

Nadia looked pale beneath her freckles, but all she said was, "Thank the Saints."

Tamar's messages had confirmed that with Ehri's support for the treaty, the Shu queen's council had agreed to ratify and back their newly forged alliance. Now it was a question of maintaining their leverage and of trying to dismantle the secret *khergud* program.

"Let's make sure our soldiers on the northern border keep an eye out for signs of the Starless," said Nikolai. "I don't want them crossing into Fjerda."

"Would the Darkling join up with the Fjerdans?" asked Nadia.

"He might," said Tolya. "It's another move he's made before."

Nadia's laugh was rueful. "I don't know who to root for."

Zoya wasn't sure either. More Fjerdans worshipping Ravkan Saints meant more sympathy for Ravka and potentially less support for the war. But that faith might make it far easier for the Darkling to gain a foothold there.

Tolya crossed his huge arms. "The Apparat actively campaigned against granting the Darkling Sainthood. The Fjerdans will have to break with the priest if they want the Darkling on their side."

"Will they?" said Nikolai. "The Apparat survives. That's what he does. If he senses the Darkling can become a valued asset, we can be sure he'll have a sudden epiphany. And coming back from the dead makes for a very grand entrance. Fjerda may not have to choose between the priest and a newly risen Saint at all."

"I don't think the Darkling will join the Apparat," Genya said.

It was the first time she'd spoken. The room felt suddenly still, as if encased in glass.

Nikolai turned to her. "You knew him better than any of us, longer than any of us. Why?"

She set down her teacup. "Pride. The Darkling doesn't forgive. He punishes. He punished you for betraying him as Sturmhond. He punished me for choosing Alina. When the Darkling staged his coup, he trusted the Apparat with the capital. The priest was meant to lend his authority to the Darkling's cause. Instead he marshaled the people's faith for Alina Starkov."

"Because he believed she could be more easily controlled," said Nikolai.

"More fool him. But that's something the Darkling and the Apparat had in common," she said, her voice hardening. "They underestimated her. They underestimated every one of us. All the Darkling ever wanted was to be loved by this country, adored. He won't side with the Apparat because the priest did the unforgivable: He turned the people against him."

"Then what will he do?"

Genya's fists crushed the material of her *kefta*. "The question is, what will we do?"

"Is there anything we *can* do?" asked Adrik, and for once his miserable tone was completely appropriate. "Even with support from the Shu and the Zemeni, do we have enough flyers or missiles to face Fjerda in the field?"

Nadia and Leoni exchanged a glance, and Leoni bit her lip. "If we had a new source of titanium, we're ready to move into production immediately."

Tolya took a deep breath. "I know we're all angry and grieving. What the Fjerdans did is unforgivable, but—"

"But?" said Zoya.

He held her gaze. "What we do next will determine not only what kind of war this is, but what every war will look like after. Launching a rocket without ever needing to put a soldier or a pilot in harm's way? War is meant to have costs. At what point are we as bad as the Fjerdans?"

"Maybe that's what we need to be," said Zoya. "This is a world where villains thrive." Where men like David died buried beneath a heap of stone in their wedding clothes while the Darkling and the Apparat somehow still drew breath.

"Does that mean we become villains too?" Tolya asked, and Zoya could hear the pleading in his voice.

"You've never been the weakest person in the room, Tolya. Mercy means nothing if we can't protect our own."

"But where does it end?"

Zoya didn't have an answer to that. Nikolai had said it enough times: Once the river was loosed, it could not be called back.

Genya touched her hand gently to Tolya's arm. "David hated making war. He was an inventor, a creator. He dreamed of a time when he could build wonders instead of weapons." She reached out to Zoya, and reluctantly Zoya took her hand, feeling an unwelcome ache in her throat. "But he also knew that we couldn't forge peace alone. The Fjerdans have shown us who they are. It's up to us to decide who we want to become."

"And who is that?" Zoya asked, because she truly didn't know. All she'd ever had was anger.

"We build the rockets," said Genya. "We make them understand what we can do. We give them a choice."

Zoya wondered who would get to make that choice. Parents who didn't wish to send their children off to die? Jarl Brum and his hateful *drüskelle*? Royals eager to keep their position at any cost?

"This has always been about stopping a war," said Nikolai. "If the Fjerdans don't think we can hold back the tide, they'll roll right over us."

Nadia shifted in her chair. "But without titanium—"

"We'll have the titanium," said Nikolai.

Zoya couldn't hide her surprise. "The Zemeni have agreed to provide it?"

"No," he said. "They don't have it to sell, not processed. But the Kerch do."

Adrik snorted. "There's no way they'll sell it to us, not at any kind of price we can afford."

"That's why I don't intend to ask. I happen to know someone who can help with this particular kind of negotiation."

Tolya frowned. "Negotiation?"

"He means we're going to steal it," said Zoya.

Genya's cup clattered in her saucer. "If the Kerch find out we're involved in something like this, it will be a diplomatic disaster."

Nikolai gave Genya's shoulder a brief squeeze and stood. He looked less a king with a country to rule than a privateer about to unleash his cannons on an enemy ship.

"Maybe so," he said. "But Ketterdam is the right place to gamble."

21
THE
MONK

HE DIDN'T KNOW WHERE TO GO. He hadn't thought past the need to become whole again and finally return to himself. He hadn't even been entirely certain his plan would work. But he had clung to that piece of the thorn wood, and the orphans had offered him the perfect chance to try.

Alina.

She's alive. Yuri's voice an echo in his head, a gnat he couldn't quite seem to swat. *Sankta Alina, Daughter of Dva Stolba, Alina of the Fold. She lives.*

Yes, Alina Starkov was well and happy and living with her tracker. If you could call that living. Yuri's babbling awe droned on and on.

Her questions had troubled him, but Alina always had a talent for getting under his skin. *Why do* you *have to be the savior?* The answer to her question was as obvious as it had always been: Who else could protect the Grisha and Ravka? A reckless boy who liked to play pirate? A vengeful girl too afraid of her own heart to master the tremendous power she'd been granted? They were dangerous. Dangerous to him, to his country, even to themselves. *Children.*

His shadow soldiers carried him through forest and glade as his mind wandered too, until at last he arrived in a town by a river. This place was familiar, but most places were. He knew every pebble and branch of Ravka. But the guns and tanks and flying machines that had overwhelmed this world were new to him and unwelcome. Had his plan succeeded, had he managed to weaponize the Fold with Alina by his side, Ravka never would have been vulnerable to this march of brutality.

She is alive. Sankta Alina who gave her life for Ravka.

"*I* gave my life for Ravka," he snarled at no one but the trees, and Yuri, finally chastened, went silent.

He had the *nichevo'ya* deposit him by a high bridge over the river gorge and walked the rest of the way into the village, unsure of where he was headed. His feet were bare and he still wore Yuri's ragged black robes and trousers, the fabric bloodied where a bullet had grazed him. He longed for a bath and clean clothes. Human things.

Shopkeepers stared worriedly at him from their doorways, but they had nothing to fear from him. At least not yet. It wasn't much of a town, but he noted icons in nearly every window. Most of these backwaters were religious and had grown more so during the civil war. Alina was certainly popular, always shown with her white hair and lit as if she'd swallowed the sun. Very dramatic. He saw Juris too—a wartime Saint if there ever was one—and Sankta Marya, patron saint of those far from home. No signs of the Starless One.

All in due time, he told himself, and Yuri joined in. They could be of one mind about that.

Names crowded into his thoughts. Staski. Kiril. Kirigan. Anton. Eryk. An avalanche of memories. He'd been all of them, but who should he become now? He'd had plenty of time to consider such things in the isolation of his glass cell, but now that he was free, truly free to choose, he found that only one name suited. The oldest of them: Aleksander. He had no reason to hide his strangeness anymore. Saints were meant to live forever.

He passed into a muddy town square and saw a small church capped by a single whitewashed dome. Through the open door, he glimpsed the priest, tending to something by the altar, as a woman lit candles for the dead. It would do for sanctuary. They couldn't very well turn a barefoot beggar away.

It wasn't until Aleksander was inside, the cool shadows of the church thick and comforting around him, that he realized where he was. Above the altar hung a painting of a man with iron fetters at his wrists and a collar at his neck, his eyes looking up at nothing. Sankt Ilya in Chains.

He really did know this place. He had come back to the beginning: This church had been raised over the ruins of the home of Ilya Morozova, Aleksander's grandfather, a man thrown to his death from the very bridge Aleksander had crossed on his way into town. He had been known as the Bonesmith, the greatest Fabrikator to ever live. And yet he had been much more than that.

"Hello?" the priest said, turning toward the doorway.

But Aleksander had already sunk into the shadows, gathering them like a shroud around his body in the darkness of the side aisle.

He moved quietly to the door that he knew would lead him down into the basement, down the rickety stairs to where old pews and rotted wall hangings had been stacked. His memories were as dark and dusty as this place, but the plan of the church and what had come before it was buried in his mind, and he knew there was yet another room beneath this one. He located a lantern and went looking for the hatch.

It didn't take long. When he pulled on the metal ring, the hinge let loose a shriek. Maybe the priest would hear and try to pray away the ghosts.

Yuri rattled around in his skull at that little bit of sacrilege, but Aleksander ignored him.

I will show you wonders, he promised.

This is a holy place, Yuri protested.

Aleksander nearly laughed. What made a church holy? The gilded halos of the Saints? The words of its priest?

The prayers said beneath its roof.

He scowled in the darkness. The boy's piousness was exhausting.

Aleksander lowered himself into the room beneath the basement. Here, the floor was dirt and the lantern showed nothing but earthen walls, roots trying to push their way through.

But he knew what this room had once been—the workshop at the back of Morozova's home, the place where his grandfather had tampered with the boundaries between life and death, had resurrected creatures with the hope of building power into their bones. He'd tried to make his own amplifiers and he'd succeeded.

Aleksander had attempted to follow in Morozova's footsteps. He'd cajoled his mother into bringing him to this town, to the home she'd occupied as a child. When she'd seen the church built in the place where her father's workshop had been, she'd laughed for the better part of an hour.

"They killed him, you know," Baghra had said, tears of mirth leaking from her eyes. "The ancestors of the very men and women walking this town and praying in this church threw him into the river. Real power frightens them." She'd waved at the painted altarpiece. "They want the illusion of it. An image on a wall, silent and safe."

But power was exactly what Aleksander had found, tucked away in this basement—his grandfather's journals, the records of his experiments. They had become his obsession. He'd been sure that he could do what Ilya Morozova had done, and so he'd tried. The result was the Fold.

A gift, whispered Yuri's voice, and Aleksander was suddenly standing in Novokribirsk, watching the tide of the Fold rush toward him, hearing the screams around him. *You saved me that day.*

Aleksander peered into the darkness of the basement room. He certainly hadn't meant to save Yuri. But he was glad someone remembered the good he'd done for this country.

He felt along the wall, the soil cold and moist beneath his palm, to the niche where he'd found the journals, bound up in oilcloth. Empty now. No, not entirely. His fingers fastened around something—a piece of wood. Part of a child's toy. The curving neck of a swan fashioned with exquisite care, broken at the base. Useless.

Why did you go to Alina? Yuri buzzed away. *Why seek her out?* To reclaim his power, of course. The universe wanted to humble him, to force him to appeal to a pair of pathetic orphans like a beggar on his knees.

Why did you go to her?

Because with her he was human again. She had once been naive, lonely, desperate for approval, all the things that had made it so easy for him to manipulate his soldiers in the past. So how had she bested him? Sheer stubbornness. That pragmatic impulse that had allowed her to survive the orphanage, to endure so many years without using her power. Something more. He'd known the name for it once, a hundred lifetimes ago. *It's not too late for you.* Alina might be right, but he hadn't fought his way back from death for the sake of being saved.

There was no penance for him to make. Everything he'd done was for the Grisha, for Ravka.

And the blight? Could he add that to the list of his supposed crimes? He had to admit that it was partially his fault. Though if the boy king had been good enough to lie down and die as he was meant to, the *obisbaya* would have been completed and the Fold never would have ruptured. But how terrible could it be? Ravka had been through worse and so had he.

Aleksander looked down at the broken toy in his hands. He shouldn't have come here. He smelled the turned earth, the incense from the church above. This place was nothing but another grave.

He wanted to be out of the darkness, back beneath the watery winter sun. He closed the trapdoor behind him and swept up the stairs from the basement, but he paused at the door to the church. He could hear the priest speaking, the shuffle and murmur of a crowd. They must have entered while he'd been sunk in his thoughts.

What day was it? Had they all assembled for morning services?

The priest was telling the tale of Sankt Nikolai—the little boy nearly eaten by cannibal sailors, who had gone on to minister to the poor and hungry. It was as bloody and odd as all the Saints' lives.

Perhaps it was time for a new story, a single Saint, greater than all those who had come before him, who didn't dole out his power like some kind of banker keeping a ledger of prayers and good deeds. Perhaps it was time for a new kind of miracle.

From his hiding place behind the door, he raised his hands and focused on the painted icon behind the priest. Slowly, shadows curled from Sankt Ilya's open hands; they began to bleed from his mouth.

A gasp went up from the congregation. The priest turned and fell to his knees. Aleksander drank their fear and wonder. Heady as that cheap cherry wine he'd had in . . . he could not quite recall.

You see, Yuri. Your age of miracles has begun.

He gusted through the church, disguising himself in a whirling cloud of shadow, and the congregants screamed.

Aleksander couldn't simply appear again, resurrected. There were too many old grudges and there would be too many questions. No, there was a better story here. He would become Yuri, let the boy do the talking for him, and when the time came, the monk would be his chosen one—a boy who came from nothing, endowed with great power. They'd loved Alina's little fairy tale. They'd love this one too.

He would go to the Fold. He would find those who followed the Starless Saint.

He would teach the world awe.

22
NINA

NINA DIDN'T WANT TO MOVE from her bed. Hanne had told her parents that she was ill, that the oysters at the previous day's breakfast hadn't agreed with her.

"I forget she's not used to the luxuries of the Ice Court," Brum had said, his voice carrying through the gap in the door. "But she must join us to celebrate."

That should make me angry.

The thought came and went. She felt like she was drowning, but she didn't want to fight to surface. She wanted to lie here, in this bed, the covers heavy like the weight of water. She didn't want to think and she couldn't pretend she was all right.

She felt as if someone had cracked open her chest and carved the heart right out of her. The Fjerdans had bombed Os Alta. They'd bombed houses where children slept in their beds, markets where innocent people did their business. They'd bombed Nina's home, the place she'd found joy and acceptance as a little girl. How many of her friends had died? How many had been injured? She had been in Brum's office, she had seen the map of Ravka's capital, but she hadn't understood. If she had . . . Nina sank deeper, down, down.

The news had come during a party, just days after the royal hunt. She'd been with the Brums in the ballroom, the same room where the prince had collapsed. She was holding a plate of smoked fish and roe, idly contemplating that no spy had ever been so well fed. Word had spread that Prince Rasmus had not been permitted to join the royal hunt, but the damage to his reputation was somewhat tempered by reports of how handsome he'd looked in his riding clothes and how much stronger he seemed every day.

"We'll see," Brum muttered. "Padding the shoulders on his jacket won't make him any more a king."

The grizzled Redvin had merely let out a snort. "Let's get him up on a horse and see what happens."

"That's cruel," Hanne had said quietly. "You mock him for his weakness and then punish him when he dares to change."

Redvin had laughed. "Your girl has a fondness for that whey-faced whelp."

But Brum's face had been cold. "There is no punishment for a prince, Hanne. And you would do well to remember it. Rasmus may favor you now, but if his opinion turns sour, I will be unable to protect you."

Those words had sent a shiver through Nina, remembering Rasmus with the crop in his hand, the blood on Joran's cheek.

But Hanne had refused to drop her chin, returning her father's stare with hard determination. Nina knew she should give her a nudge, a gentle touch of the hand, a reminder that they were meant to show vulnerability and softness here so no one would guess at their strength, but she couldn't. This was the true Hanne, a girl with the heart of a wolf. Healing the prince hadn't just made Rasmus stronger; it had reminded Hanne of who she could be, who she might become if Fjerda weren't in the grip of men like her father.

Their standoff had been broken by some kind of clamor in the throne room, a buzz that had risen to a roar, then cheers, applause.

"What's happening?" Ylva had asked.

Nina would never forget the smile that split Brum's face in that moment, a look of pure pleasure.

"The Ravkan capital burns!" someone shouted.

"We bombed Os Alta!"

"We have them on the run now!"

Nina couldn't quite tell where the voices were coming from. People were shaking Brum's hand, clapping him on the back. She felt like she was standing on the shore of a wild sea, the waves striking her again and again, as she tried to find her balance.

Hanne took hold of her hand.

"What is this?" Nina whispered. She heard her own voice as if from a great distance.

"It sounds like there was a raid," Hanne replied. "Fjerdan bombers struck Os Alta."

"But that's . . . It's impossible. The city is too far away." The floor was tilting beneath her feet.

"Are you all right, Mila?" Ylva asked.

"You must rally," Hanne whispered in Nina's ear. "My father will see."

Nina summoned every bit of her strength and forced an expression of wide-eyed surprise onto her face. "Then is Nikolai Lantsov dead?" The words tasted foul in her mouth. She could feel cold sweat on the back of her neck.

"No," Brum said bitterly. "The little bastard wormed free this time."

This time. What about Adrik and Leoni? Zoya? All of the others?

"One of the pilots came back with a bizarre report of monsters in the skies above the city," Brum continued. "I think he's shell-shocked."

"Help me," Nina begged Hanne. "Get me out of here."

And Hanne had, letting the flood of well-wishers envelop her father and mother, herding Nina out of the room.

Nina hadn't known what was happening to her. She had faced battle. She had held her beloved as he died, and yet now her whole world felt like it was crumpling around her, as if it were made of paper. Her heart was racing. Her gown felt too tight. How many had died while she was playing at spy? She'd seen the targets; she just hadn't understood. She wanted to scream, to weep. But Mila Jandersdat could not do anything like that.

By the time they reached the Brums' chambers, her clothes were soaked through with sweat. Trembling, Nina seized hold of the washbasin and vomited into it, then slid down to the floor. Her legs wouldn't hold her any longer.

Bless Hanne's strength, because she must have dragged Nina to her bed and gotten her into a nightgown. Nina knew she was going to pass out. She had seized Hanne's hand.

"Make him sick," she demanded.

"What?"

"Hanne, go back to the party and act as if nothing is wrong. I need you to weaken the prince."

"But Rasmus—"

"Please, Hanne," Nina begged, clutching her fingers. "Do this for me."

Hanne brushed the hair back from Nina's sweat-slicked face. "All right," she said. "All right. Just promise me you'll rest."

Only then had Nina let herself sink beneath the waves. And that was where she had remained, buried beneath the covers, all through the night and the following day. Hanne came and went. She tried to get Nina to eat. But it was as if Nina heard her from far away. She was floating somewhere quiet and she wanted to stay there, wrapped in silence. There was too much pain waiting on land.

Until she'd heard Brum's voice outside her room.

"I don't care if she's ill. I don't care if she's on her deathbed. If the queen wishes to see her, then that fishmonger's wife will drag herself out here."

Queen Agathe. Dimly, Nina remembered what she'd said to Hanne. Her instincts had taken over and she'd had the sense to set this new deception working. But she had to pull herself together to capitalize on it.

"Surely if it's something she ate, she's feeling better?" said Ylva. "She must see the queen."

"I don't have time for this. I have to be outside the ringwall in a half hour for *Drokestering*. I won't keep my men waiting for the sake of a simpleton with a weak constitution."

Drokestering. Nina tried to remember the word. It was old Fjerdan, a *drüskelle* celebration of victory in war. It was held in the woods, usually for an entire night.

"I'll get her," said Hanne. "Just . . . just give me a moment to make her ready."

Nina pushed herself to a sitting position. Her skin had the sour smell of sweat and fear on it. Her hair was tangled, and she was dizzy from lack of food and water.

"You're up!" Hanne said, rushing to Nina's bedside. "Djel's grace, I thought you might slip away from me forever."

"I'm up," Nina croaked.

Hanne poured her some water. "Nina, the queen's servants are here. They've brought a litter. She says she heard you were taken ill and wishes for you to see her personal doctor."

Nina highly doubted that was what the queen wanted.

"Do you have anything to eat?" she asked.

"I can get you some broth or some dry toast. Did you hear me? The queen—"

"I heard you. A cup of broth, please."

"You should wash too."

"Rude."

"Honest."

Nina didn't have time for a bath, so she rinsed as best she could with cold water from the basin and dabbed her body with perfume. She didn't mind the chill. She needed anything that would wake her.

She ran a brush through her hair, but there was nothing she could do about the sallow color of her skin or the circles beneath her eyes.

"Hanne, can you help me?" Nina asked when she returned with the broth. "I need you to tailor me. Can you make me look . . ."

"Less like a corpse?"

"Better. Saintly."

Hanne moved her over to the window for better light. Her hands traced Nina's face in soft strokes.

"You don't have to hold your breath," Hanne said.

Nina bit her lip.

"Stop that!" said Hanne, grabbing her chin. "You'll ruin my work."

"Sorry."

Hanne's cheeks flushed and she released Nina's chin. She focused on her hair instead.

"Has your father said anything about the missing letters?" Nina asked.

"I haven't heard him mention them to anyone, and they haven't instituted new security protocols as far as I know."

Then Brum couldn't have realized they were missing yet, but he would as soon as that safe was opened.

"There!" Hanne said a moment later. "Done."

"So fast?"

Hanne handed her a mirror. "See for yourself."

Nina looked into the glass. Her skin shone like polished marble, a faint rose-petal flush on her cheeks. Her hair gleamed silvery blond. She looked like she'd been dipped in moonlight. "You really have been practicing."

Hanne looked almost guilty. "Quite a bit. On myself. Why does the queen want to see you?"

"Her son's health is failing."

"Because of me."

"Because I begged you to help me, to help both of our countries."

"How is the prince's suffering supposed to help Ravka or Fjerda?"

"I need you to trust me," said Nina. "And Rasmus could use a little suffering after what he did to Joran in the hunters' tent."

"He doesn't like to feel weak," said Hanne.

"No one does. But he can't just be kind when he's feeling strong."

A knock came at the door.

"Hanne." Ylva's voice was quiet but urgent. "Mila must come. *Now.*"

They draped Nina in Hanne's dressing gown and placed a shawl around her face and hair so Ylva and Brum wouldn't see the effects of Hanne's tailoring.

Leaning heavily on Hanne, Nina let herself be steered down the hall and onto the litter the queen's servants carried.

"She's heavy," complained one of the guards.

"She's more trouble than she's worth," Brum grumbled.

"Papa!" cried Hanne.

"Jarl, that's enough," said Ylva. "She's clearly unwell."

Nina lay back and stared at the ceiling as she was carried down the hallways of the White Island. She shut her eyes and reached out to the spirits in the graveyard, to Linor Rundholm, the queen's former lady-in-waiting. *Tell me what I need to know. Tell me what you want.*

The answer was clear and harsh: *An end to the Grimjer line.*

Nina couldn't promise that. Given the choice between Jarl Brum's brutality and Prince Rasmus' petty violence, she would have to choose the prince. Fjerda and fate had conspired to offer her truly rotten options.

All I can promise is revenge. Now speak to me.

The litter was brought to the same throne room where the queen had received Nina before.

"Do you need to see my doctor?" demanded the queen from her alabaster throne.

Nina sat up straight, her shawl slipping back, letting light from the windows fall on her freshly tailored face. "I need no doctor. And what good has he ever done your son?"

The queen drew in a sharp breath. "Put her down," she commanded. "Leave us."

A moment later, the servants had departed and they were alone, the queen on her throne and Nina standing before her.

"You were not ill?" asked the queen.

"I fell into a trance," Nina lied smoothly. "Where is your son, Queen Agathe?"

"He cannot rise from his bed. He . . . he has been coughing blood for days. What is happening to him? I have prayed every day, twice a day, I—"

"Your warmongering has angered Djel."

306

Queen Agathe's brow pinched. "The attack on Os Alta?"

"It was a Grisha who saved your son and brought him Djel's blessing."

"The bombing was a great military victory for Fjerda!"

Of course it was. Nina could still see Brum's triumphant face in the ballroom, hear the cheering of the crowd. But she couldn't just tell the queen what she needed her to do. Agathe had to find her way there herself.

Nina lifted her head, knowing the light was gilding the contours of her face. "Do you know what stands between the Grand Palace and the Little Palace in Ravka's capital?"

Agathe tugged at the buttons of her silver gown, as if the bodice was too tight. "The royal chapel."

"The site of the First Altar. Where the first prayers to the first Saints were said."

"A false religion." But the reply was slow, tentative.

"This was where Fjerda rained fire."

"That was Jarl Brum's directive, not my son's."

"Do you not rule this country? Was it not done in the Grimjer name?"

Agathe licked her lips. "In . . . in Djerholm, they whisper that Grisha are the children of Djel."

Finally. She'd made the leap. "Djel is a good father. He protects his children. Just as any loving parent would."

The queen clutched the sides of her head, as if the very thought of Grisha carrying divine blessing might split her skull. "This is *heresy.*"

Nina spread her hands wide, helpless. "I cannot explain these things."

"You are a liar and a heretic. You are unnatural with your trances and your predictions. You—"

Nina threw back her head, letting her eyes roll white in their sockets. "You bled and bled. You knew you were going to lose this child like all the others. You sent sweet Linor to the dungeons and had a Grisha Healer brought to you. Her name was Pavlina. You promised her freedom. But you never intended to set her free. She sat with you for hours, long into the night. She stayed with you, day after day, healing you, healing your princeling, even in the womb. She told you stories when you were restless. And when you wept, she sang you a lullaby."

"No." The word emerged as a moan.

Nina had a terrible singing voice, but she did her best to follow the melody of the dead woman crooning to her. "*Dye ena kelinki, dya derushka, shtoya refkayena lazla zeya.*" It was an old Ravkan folk song. *Up in the mountains, high in the trees, the firebird sleeps on a golden bough.*

"You . . . you know Ravkan?"

"I have never spoken a word before now. I know only what Djel shows me. Pavlina told you she had a daughter, a little girl you promised she would see again."

The queen released a sob. "I needed her help!"

"Djel forgives you all of it." *I don't*, thought Nina. *Your tree god is far more magnanimous.* "But he will not forgive the murder of more Grisha. Not when your son owes his life to one."

"I . . . how am I to stop it? Our people want war."

"Is that what you've been told or what you know? Your generals want war. The people want their sons and daughters to live. They want to sleep in their beds and tend the crops in their fields. Will you listen to your generals or to Djel? The choice is yours." Nina remembered a line from one of the Saints' stories she'd read in an old children's book: *You can choose faith or you can choose fear. But only one will bring you what you long for.*

"I don't know what to do."

"You do. Listen closely. The water hears and understands." She bowed and made to leave.

"You dare turn your back on me?"

A bold move, but Nina needed to show Agathe she wore the armor of faith. She couldn't afford to show fear.

"It is Djel you should be worried about, my queen," she said. "Take care lest *he* turn his back on you."

She slipped out of the throne room and hurried down the hall. Had she gone too far or just far enough? Would the seeds she'd planted yield a move toward peace? Or had she only endangered herself and maybe Hanne too?

She couldn't contemplate that now. She'd made her choices and there was more work to be done tonight. Earlier, she'd been too bleary to make sense of what she'd heard Brum say outside her room, but now the word rang through her head—*Drokestering*. The *drüskelle* would be in the woods tonight, far from the Ice Court, celebrating the sneak attack on Ravka.

This was her chance to break Magnus Opjer out of the *drüskelle* sector. Ravka was bleeding, and she was powerless to undo the damage their enemies had wrought. *But Nikolai Lantsov still lives.* That meant there was still hope. She could deal Fjerda a blow and maybe give her king a small advantage in this fight.

It was time to make some trouble.

23

NIKOLAI

NIKOLAI HAD MEANT TO SLEEP, and when he had tossed and turned sufficiently to determine that he could not, he rose from his unfamiliar bed in the Iris Suite with every intention of working. But he had no success with that either. He had penned a message to Ketterdam and there was nothing to do but wait for a reply. Though he tried to focus on the rocket schematics he'd had brought to him from Lazlayon, it was impossible to look at the plans David had drawn, the notations in his cramped handwriting filling the margins, and not lose his thoughts to sadness, to the endless what-ifs that might have saved his friend's life. He couldn't stop seeing David's broken body being pulled from the rubble, the blood and dust on his crushed chest.

Nikolai walked to the window. The palace grounds were covered in snow. From this vantage point, none of the damage from the bombing was visible. The world seemed quiet, ordinary, and at peace. He had sent word to Tamar to see if she could find out if the Shu queen had known about the bombing, if the Shu and the Fjerdans had come together to forge an alliance against Ravka—the bone they'd been fighting over for centuries. But he didn't think that was the case. Makhi had her own agenda. She'd seen Ravka as weak and she'd moved to claim it through subterfuge before Fjerda could claim it by force. If not for Isaak's courage and fate's love of a good plot twist, the Shu queen might have done just that. But while Makhi had failed with a scalpel, Fjerda might well succeed with a hammer. They would celebrate the buildings they'd crushed, the ships and fly-ers they'd destroyed, never knowing the true death blow they'd dealt Ravka: David Kostyk was gone.

Nikolai's friendship with David hadn't been a loud one. There had been few shared confidences, no raucous nights spent singing dirty drinking songs. Most of their time together had been spent in silence, grappling with difficult engineering problems, reviewing each oth-er's work, pushing each other forward. With David, Nikolai's power and charm had been meaningless. He'd only cared about the science.

He should have been safe here, tucked away in his workshop, far from enemy lines. But there was no safety anymore. Somewhere to the north, the Fjerdans were toasting their surprise attack and wait-ing to see how Ravka would respond. When Ravka couldn't answer, they would wait no longer. They would invade. But where? When?

Movement in the gardens below caught his eye. He glimpsed dark hair, a cloak of blue wool. Zoya. She passed beyond the hedges and fountains to the shadow of the woods.

He hadn't had a chance to speak to her since she'd returned. He couldn't blame her for avoiding him. He'd sent her into the field with-out proper backup. He'd let enemies violate their home. But where was she going now? Nikolai hadn't let himself think too much on

Zoya's late-night excursions across the grounds. He hadn't wanted to. If she had a lover, it was none of his business. And yet his mind spun possibilities, each somehow worse than the last. A member of the royal guard? A handsome Inferni? She was friendly with General Pensky, and that was Nikolai's own fault. He'd forced them to work closely together. Of course, the general was twenty years her senior and had what could only be described as an *effusive* mustache, but who was Nikolai to question her taste?

He yanked trousers over his nightshirt, lunged for his coat and boots, and was out the door and down the hallway in seconds, ignoring concerned glances from the palace guards.

"Everything's fine! As you were," he called. They were all on edge after the Fjerdan attack, and there was no reason to panic anyone as he raced off to act like an infatuated schoolboy.

What exactly was he going to say to her? *I see you're headed to an assignation, stop in the name of the king?*

Her boots had left tracks in the snow, and he followed her into the woods. But it was dark beneath the trees, hard to find the trail. *This is a mistake.* She had a right to her privacy. And he damned well didn't want to find her in the embrace of another man.

He caught a flash of movement between the branches. Zoya stood facing the thicket that bordered the western side of the gardens, her breath pluming in the night air, her face framed by the silver fox fur of her hood. Where the hell could she be going out here?

She was following a wall on the far side of the water gardens, where he'd played as a child and where the secret tunnel to Lazlayon was located. He opened his mouth to call out to her—then stopped as Zoya pushed aside a heavy mass of vines to reveal a door in the wall.

He couldn't help but take offense. That Zoya had kept secrets from him was no surprise, but that the palace should?

"I thought we were past that," he muttered.

Zoya slipped a key from her pocket and opened the door, vanishing inside. He hesitated. She hadn't closed it behind her. *Turn back*, he told himself. *No good can come of this.*

There were two stars carved into the wood—just like the stars in the mural in her rooms, two small sparks painted onto the flag of a storm-tossed boat. He'd never asked what they meant.

He needed to know what was on the other side of that door. Really, it could be a matter of national security.

Nikolai passed through the tangle of vines and into what he realized was the old vegetable garden. He'd thought it had been left to rot, abandoned to the woods after the raised beds were moved closer to the kitchens. It didn't exist on any of the new palace plans.

Whatever this place had been, it was something very different now. There were no tidy rows of cabbages, no orderly patterns of hedges favored by the palace gardeners. Willows bordered the paths, like women bent in mourning, their branches shod in ice and brushing the soft white ground like strands of hair. Flowers and shrubs of every variety overflowed their beds, all of them white with frost, a world made of snow and glass, a garden of ghosts. Zoya had lit lanterns along the old stone walls and now she stood, her back to him, her figure still as an ornamental statue, as if she'd been part of this garden all along, a stone maiden waiting to be discovered at the center of a maze.

"I'm running out of room," she said without turning to face him.

She'd known he was there all along. Had she wanted him to follow her?

"You tend this place?" He tried to imagine Zoya sweating in the sun, dirt beneath her nails.

"When my aunt was killed and I came back to the Little Palace to fight the Darkling . . . I needed someplace to be alone. I used to walk in the woods for hours. No one bothered me there. I don't remember when I found the door, but I felt as if my aunt had left it here for me to discover, a puzzle for me to solve."

She stood with her perfect profile turned to the glittering night sky, her hood sliding back. Snow was beginning to fall, and it caught in the dark waves of her hair. "I plant something new for every Grisha lost. Heartleaf for Marie. Yew for Sergei. Red Sentinel for Fedyor. Even Ivan has a place." She touched her fingers to a frozen stalk. "This will blossom bright orange in the summer. I planted it for Harshaw. These dahlias were for Nina when I thought she'd been captured and killed by Fjerdans. They bloom with the most ridiculous red flowers in the summer. They're the size of dinner plates." Now she turned and he could see tears on her cheeks. She lifted her hands, the gesture half-pleading, half-lost. "I'm running out of room."

This was where Zoya had been seen sneaking off to all those nights—not to a lover, but to this monument to grief. This was where she had shed her tears, away from curious eyes, where no one could see her armor fall. And here, the Grisha might live forever, every friend lost, every soldier gone.

"I know what I did is unforgivable," she said.

Nikolai blinked, confused. "No doubt you deserve to be punished for your crimes . . . but for what precisely?"

She cast him a baleful look. "I lost our most valuable prisoner. I've allowed our most deadly enemy to regain his powers and . . . run amok."

"'Amok' seems an overstatement. Wild, perhaps."

"Don't pretend to shrug this off. You've barely looked at me since I returned."

Because I am greedy for the sight of you. Because the prospect of facing this war, this loss, without you fills me with fear. Because I find I don't want to fight for a future if I can't find a way to make a future with you.

But he was a king and she was his general and he could say none of those things.

"I'm looking at you now, Zoya." Her eyes met his in the stillness of the garden, vibrant blue, deep as a well. "You need never ask forgiveness of me." He hesitated. He didn't want to tie himself more closely to the man she hated, but he also didn't want there to be secrets between them. If they survived this war, if they somehow found a way to keep the Fjerdans from invading Ravka, he would need to forge a real marriage, a real alliance, with someone else. He would have to secure his peace with Fjerda by marrying from their nation, or soothe Kerch's ruffled pride by binding himself forever to Hiram Schenck's daughter. But that was a future that might never come. "I sensed it when the Darkling broke free. The demon . . . the demon knew somehow. And for a moment I was there in the room with you."

He'd thought she might be repelled, even fearful, but Zoya just said, "I wish you'd been there."

"You do?"

Now she looked nothing but annoyed. "Of course I do. Who else would I rather have my back in a fight?"

Nikolai struggled not to break out in song. "That may be the greatest compliment I've ever been paid. And I was once told I waltz like an angel by the lead dancer of the royal ballet."

"Maybe if you'd been there . . ." Her voice trailed off. But they both knew Nikolai wouldn't have made a difference in that particular fight. If Zoya and the Sun Soldiers couldn't stop the Darkling, it was possible he couldn't be stopped. *One more enemy we don't know how to fight.*

She bobbed her chin toward the walls. "Do you see what grows around this place?"

Nikolai peered at the twisting gray branches that ran along the perimeter of the garden. "A thorn wood." An ordinary one, he assumed, not the ancient trees they needed for the *obisbaya*.

"I took the cuttings from the tunnel that leads to the Little Palace. It's all prickles and spines and anger, covered in pretty, useless blossoms and fruit too bitter to eat. There is nothing in it worth loving."

"How wrong you are."

Zoya's gaze snapped to his, her eyes flashing silver—dragon's eyes. "Am I?"

"Look at the way it grows, protecting everything within these walls, stronger than anything else in the garden, weathering every season. No matter the winter it endures, it blooms again and again."

"What if the winter is just too long and hard? What if it can't bloom again?"

He was afraid to reach for her, but he did it anyway. He took her gloved hand in his. She didn't pull away but folded into him like a flower closing its petals at nightfall. He wrapped his arm around her. Zoya seemed to hesitate, and then with a soft breath, she let herself lean against him. Zoya the deadly. Zoya the ferocious. The weight of her against him felt like a benediction. He had been strong for his country, his soldiers, his friends. It meant something different to be strong for her.

"Then you'll be branches without blossoms," he whispered against her hair. "And you let the rest of us be strong until the summer comes."

"It wasn't a metaphor."

"Of course it wasn't."

He wished they could stand there forever in the silence of the snow, that the peace of this place could protect them.

She wiped her eyes and he realized she was crying.

"If you had told me three years ago that I would shed tears over David Kostyk, I would have laughed at you."

Nikolai smiled. "You would have hit me with your shoe."

"He and I . . . we had nothing in common. Our decision to side with Alina was what bound us—the choice to fight beside her when we knew the odds were in the Darkling's favor. He had the more experienced fighters, years of understanding and planning."

"But we won."

"We did," she said. "For a while."

"So how did you do it? How did we do it?"

"Honestly? I don't know. Maybe it was a miracle. Maybe Alina really is a Saint."

"Grief has made you delirious. But if we got lucky with one miracle, maybe we'll get lucky again."

They left the garden and walked back through the woods. On the path, they parted as they always did—she to the Grisha, and he to the Grand Palace. He wanted to call her back. He wanted to follow her through the snow. But his country didn't need a heartsick boy chasing after a lonely girl. It needed a king.

"And a king they will have," he said to no one at all, and strode back to the dark rooms of the palace.

24

MAYU

AFTER QUEEN MAKHI HAD CLAIMED she
would think on revealing the laboratories—the laboratories she still
wouldn't admit existed—Tamar and Mayu had escorted Ehri to her
chambers in the wing of the palace known as the Nest. They were
the rooms that Ehri had grown up in, where all Taban children
were raised. The boys were educated and trained alongside the
girls before they were old enough to choose a professional path—
medicine, religion, the military. The girls were all considered possible
heirs, though the eldest daughters were often favored.

Tamar and Mayu alternated shifts watching over Ehri. They
didn't think Makhi would act against the princess, not with so much
suspicion hanging over her, but they weren't taking any chances.
Tamar had warned Ministers Nagh and Zihun to strengthen their
household security as well.

Three days after they arrived, two of Ehri's sisters came to visit in a cloud of silk and perfume. Kheru with her coffee-colored eyes, always with a piece of needlework in her hands, and Yenye with the white streak in her hair and her sharp gaze. Jhem was missing, in mourning for her daughter Akeni, lost to the blight. Tamar had slipped into the neighboring room to eavesdrop but remained at the ready in case of trouble.

Mayu didn't know the princesses well. She'd been assigned to Ehri's household, and the sisters had their own Tavgharad to guard them. They were bright and loud, each striking in her own way. They looked like jewels in their dark winter silks—emerald, amethyst, sapphire. Ehri looked like a flower from a different garden, short and pale-petaled in a mint gown and a necklace of green agate, silver combs tucked into her hair.

The sisters asked Ehri for stories of Ravka, brought gifts of flowers and fruit to welcome her home, talked of their own marriage prospects and Makhi's consorts. Both Kheru and Yenye were soon to marry, and once they did, they would no longer be possible heirs for the Taban throne.

"Kheru has delayed her wedding date," said Yenye, working her needle through a pattern of violets.

"Only because I'm trying to find the right peach silk for my gown."

Yenye lifted a brow and ran her hand through the white streak in her hair. "It's because Makhi's presumed heir died in that horrible blight."

Princess Ehri gasped. "She was only eight years old."

Yenye touched her hand to her hair again. "I . . . I didn't mean to be callous. I only meant . . ."

Kheru swallowed a bite of plum. "You meant that I would take a child's death as an opportunity for Makhi to name me her heir."

319

"Don't tell me it didn't cross your mind," said Yenye.

"It did," Kheru admitted. "But Makhi won't name any of us."

"There are rumors, though," Yenye said slyly. "About you, sweet Ehri."

Ehri kept her eyes on her unfinished plums. "Oh?"

"Rumors that you've returned without a Ravkan husband because you wish to challenge Makhi."

"What foolishness," said Ehri. "You all know I've never wanted to rule. I would happily sit on a hilltop on the coast and watch the waves roll in and tend to my garden like Grandmother."

"Then why try to marry the Ravkan king in the first place?"

"Because Makhi is the queen and she commanded me to." She met their gazes, one then the other. "And we must all do as the queen commands."

There were murmurs of agreement, and in time, the sisters finished their tea and went on their way, no doubt to dissect every word that had been exchanged.

When the door closed behind them, Ehri leaned against it with a sigh. "I can tell you don't approve, Mayu."

Mayu had no reason to deny it. "This was your chance to court them, to win them to your side and tell them what the queen attempted."

"Mayu, my sisters have even less influence than I." Ehri contemplated the vase full of orange roses that she had placed at the center of the tea table before her sisters arrived. "They would either take Makhi's side or they would use the conflict between us to make their own bid for the throne, and that would leave Shu Han vulnerable."

"Are they so ambitious?"

Ehri considered. She plucked a petal that had begun to lose its freshness and crumpled it in her palm. "No. None are born schemers.

None were groomed for the throne. But power is compelling, and we're better off keeping our secrets."

Mayu watched the princess. "Are you close to your sisters?"

"The way that *kebben* are? No. I love them, but we've never fought."

"Never?"

"Not really. Oh, we squabbled. I think all sisters do. But we've never had a proper fight. Because we never trusted the love we had to carry us through. We have always been very polite with one another. What are you smiling at?"

"I'm thinking of Reyem. The way we used to *scream* at each other. He bit me once. Hard enough to draw blood."

"*Bit* you?"

"I did deserve it. I shaved one of his eyebrows off in his sleep."

Ehri laughed. "What a monster you must have been."

"I really was." But thinking of Reyem was too painful. "He was never mean to me, and he had every chance to be spiteful. My parents favored him, but he always shared—his books, his sweets. He wanted to see me happy."

"That's *kebben*," Tamar said, entering the room and helping herself to a slice of plum. "One of us cannot be happy if the other is suffering."

"Then . . . you understand what I had to do? Why I took Makhi's mission?"

Tamar popped another slice of plum in her mouth, chewing slowly. "You murdered an innocent man. Isaak was unarmed."

"He was a liar," said Ehri, leaping to Mayu's defense. "A pretender."

"He was serving his king," said Tamar.

"Just as I was serving my queen," Mayu retorted, though the words tasted of ash.

"And yet, only one of you is dead."

She was right. Isaak had deserved better.

"But you'll help me find my brother," said Mayu. She did not phrase it as a question. She couldn't let her grief and shame overcome her, not until Reyem was free.

"I will. But not for you or your twin. The only way to stop the torture and persecution of Grisha is by locating those *khergud* laboratories."

Ehri plucked a string on the *khatuur* that rested on the tea table. "We have a long road ahead of us, and none of us can make the trip alone. Let's not waste the journey arguing. We have all suffered losses."

Mayu rested her hand on the pommel of her talon sword. "What have you lost, Ehri?"

Ehri's eyes were sad. "Don't you know, Mayu? My sister."

At that moment, fireworks burst over the city skyline in two bright showers of blue and gold. Ravka's colors.

"That's the signal," said Tamar. "Queen Makhi's messenger is on the move."

It was said that no one knew all the secrets of the palace at Ahmrat Jen, but the Tavgharad knew more than most. There were hidden entrances for the use of both guards and members of the royal family, secret chambers where royalty could be watched over without being disturbed, and of course, secret exits in case of emergency or uprising.

Mayu led Tamar and Ehri down a hidden staircase to a tunnel that ran beneath the gardens, then emerged beyond the palace walls—or what had been the palace walls. The blight had struck here. This part of the garden and the orchards looked like the remnants of a blast site, but it felt like an old mine that had been worked until it had been stripped down to nothing, a place bled dry of any sort of life.

"What is this?" asked Ehri. "What's causing it?"

"An enemy for another day," said Tamar. "Keep moving."

They followed her down a low slope into the plum orchards, where a coach was waiting, and climbed inside. Tamar spoke to two men on horseback. They were dressed as peasants but carried revolvers.

"To the queen," Tamar said. But before Mayu could get a better look at the riders, they were off at a gallop, tearing across the fields.

Though the roads near the royal palace were all well maintained, to avoid attention the coach traveled on back-country cart tracks, jouncing with every rut and bump. Mayu and Tamar were both used to hard travel, but even in the shadows of the coach, Mayu could see the princess was miserable.

In her head, Mayu counted the miles of road, seeking landmarks in the dark. If the map in her head was right, they were headed toward the valley of Khem Aba. It was mostly known for farming and ranching, but there might be crags and canyons where someone could hide a government laboratory.

The coach slowed and Tamar opened the door, perching on the step to speak to another man on horseback before he rode on.

"The facility is a mile ahead," she said as they rolled to a stop. "We should go on foot. We don't know what might be waiting."

"The airship?" asked Ehri.

"On its way."

Ehri worried her lower lip with her teeth. "What if we're wrong? What if there's nothing there? If my grandmother—"

"The time for doubt has passed," said Mayu. "We move forward."

The night was cold and dark and quiet, the only sounds the singing of frogs and the rustle of the wind in the reeds. Mayu was glad to be out of the coach. She felt safer on her feet, ready to react.

A few minutes later, she saw a large structure with a peaked roof.

"What is that smell?" asked Ehri.

"Manure," Tamar replied.

A low moo sounded from somewhere ahead.

"It's a dairy," Mayu exclaimed.

Tamar signaled them onward. "It *was* a dairy."

Queen Makhi had hidden this secret facility in plain sight. And her messenger had led them right to the door.

She'd taken the bait. Ehri had made sure to tell Makhi that she'd left Grisha guards to protect their grandmother at the Palace of the Thousand Stars. They knew that threat wouldn't stop Makhi, and they also knew that she couldn't use her Tavgharad against Leyti Kir-Taban. They would never raise a hand against a Taban queen, even if that queen no longer sat the throne. So who could Makhi use against a fighting force of Grisha? Soldiers who supposedly didn't exist: the *khergud*. To deploy them, she had to get a message to one of her secret laboratories, and Tamar's scouts had followed.

Mayu could only hope Reyem was behind these walls. There were no obvious guard posts around the dairy, just what looked like a night watchman.

"Are we sure this is the place?" she asked.

Tamar nodded. "That watchman is carrying a repeating rifle. Unless the cows are planning a breakout, that kind of firepower is excessive." She gestured to the right side of the yard, past the fence. "There's a lookout posted in those trees."

Mayu and Ehri peered into the shadows.

"How can you tell?" Mayu asked.

"I can feel his heartbeat," said Tamar.

Heartrender. Mayu sometimes forgot. Tamar was deadly enough without her axes or a gun in her hands.

"Stay here," she said.

"I've never done anything like this," Ehri murmured as they waited in the dark. "Have you?"

"Only in training exercises," Mayu admitted. She was Tavgharad. She shouldn't fear death. She shouldn't fear at all. But she'd never seen real combat, never been in a proper fight. Isaak had been the first person she'd killed.

What was waiting behind those doors? And if they were caught, what would she do? The answer came easier than she'd expected. She would fight to the death if she had to—for herself, for her brother, for Isaak who had died for nothing. She tried to summon the focus and quiet her instructors had attempted to drill into her.

Maybe she'd been in the city too long. She was unused to the deep black of the night, the spread of stars above them, the sounds of all this empty space—frogs, crickets, something chittering in the trees. She blew out an exasperated breath. "The country is much noisier than I anticipated."

Ehri closed her eyes and breathed deeply. "This is what I long for."

"A dairy?"

"Peace. I always dreamed I'd get to build my own home in the mountains, a canyon where I could place a little amphitheater, maybe teach music. You would have come with me, I suppose. You and my other Tavgharad."

A silence fell between them, the memory of the women they'd both known.

"They didn't scream," Ehri said, a tremble in her voice. "I was the only one who cried out as they burned." When she opened her eyes they were wet with tears, silver in the moonlight. "Would you have done it? If you hadn't been in the infirmary and my sister had given the order?"

Yes. If not for Reyem. If not for the debt she owed him. Even now, she knew she was betraying the oath she had taken and that she had lived by—to protect the Taban queen over all others. She was in Ehri's service, had lived in her household, but ultimately, Queen Makhi was the woman she was meant to serve. Mayu had loved that simplicity, that certainty. She would never have it again.

"I would have died with my sisters," she admitted.

"And would you have sentenced me to death as well?"

"I don't know." Mayu thought of the confusion in Isaak's eyes when he'd realized what she'd done. He'd tried to tell her he wasn't the king. But it was too late by then. "I thought I understood death. I'm not so sure anymore."

They heard a soft thump and a moment later, Tamar jogged back to them.

"Did you kill him?" asked Ehri.

"I just dropped his heart rate. He'll stay unconscious and wake up with a headache."

Mayu saw what Tamar was wearing and gasped. "Where did you get that? You have no right to wear—"

"I can't enter this place as a Ravkan soldier. And I have every right. I am Grisha. My people are being tortured behind those walls."

Mayu tried to push aside her outrage. Tamar had dressed in the black uniform of the Tavgharad, her short hair hidden by the tilted black cap, the carnelian falcon at her shoulder. Mayu knew these things, these symbols of honor and tradition, shouldn't matter to her anymore. But they did.

She tried to peer past Tamar in the dark. "Are they in there?"

"Queen Makhi's messenger arrived about fifteen minutes ahead of us. He's already gone. The lights are on, but there are no windows on the ground floor. They may be mobilizing the *khergud* for action or they may wait until morning. I don't know what we'll be walking into. Ehri, we may be headed into a combat situation—"

"I was trained to fight."

"I know," said Tamar. "I sparred with you myself, and I know you can hold your own. But the *khergud* are a different kind of soldier, and if something happens to you, all of our plans will come to nothing. We'll have no leverage against Makhi. So stick to the plan and if something goes wrong, get out. Get away and get back to Nagh and Zihun."

Ehri nodded. "All right."

Tamar gestured to Mayu. "Let's go."

Flanking Princess Ehri, they strode right up to the front doors.

"You there!" called the night watchman, holding his lantern high. "Identify—oh!" He bowed deeply. "Princess Ehri, we heard you had returned to us, but . . . we . . . forgive me, Your Highness, but we were not told to expect you. Or at such an hour."

"You received my sister's messenger?"

"Only moments ago."

"There is a change to the queen's orders, and I must deliver it." She held up a scroll marked with a blot of green wax.

"May I see that?"

"I beg your pardon?" Ehri seemed to grow six inches. Her brow arched. Her voice was cold. Despite her pointed chin and diminutive stature, she was the very picture of Queen Makhi. And it was a good thing too, because that green wax seal bore no royal stamp.

The night watchman looked like he wanted to find a deep pit to jump into.

"Forgive me, Your Highness." He fumbled for his keys.

The door slid open on a shadowy entry. Two men were seated at a table. One wore military dress and the other the blue robes of a doctor. They looked a bit bleary, as if they'd been woken from their rest. They had a stack of papers before them—and a vial of some rusty orange liquid.

"Princess Ehri Kir-Taban brings word from her most exalted sister," said the watchman breathlessly.

The soldier and the doctor rose and bowed, but their expressions were confused.

"My sister has had second thoughts about deploying the *khergud* for this particular mission," said Ehri.

The doctor raised the vial of liquid. "We haven't woken them yet. Should we scrap the whole thing?"

Ehri clasped her fingers together and Mayu knew it was to stop herself from fidgeting. "Yes. Yes, scrap the whole thing. But, while we're here, we'd like to have a look around."

The men exchanged an uncertain glance.

"My sister said I would be most impressed by the work you've accomplished here."

"The queen spoke of me to you?" the doctor said in surprise. "I'm honored."

Ehri smiled her warmest smile. "Then will you show my guards and me your remarkable project?"

The soldier eyed Tamar and Mayu in their black uniforms. "It might be best if they remained here. This is a top secret facility."

The princess gave an amused laugh. "You think my sister doesn't know that? She would never send me here without my guards." She narrowed her eyes. "Why would you ask me to make myself defenseless?"

"I . . . I would never—"

"I have enemies in the government. All of the Taban do. Perhaps you see this as an opportunity to strike at my family?"

"We should take him in for questioning," said Tamar.

"No!" The soldier held up his hands. "I have only loyalty for the Taban. Your guards are most welcome."

Now Ehri smiled again. "Very good." She gave a wave of her hand and the doctor scurried to a big metal door that had no business in a barn.

Mayu felt a chill move through her as the door creaked open. The room beyond was large and dimly lit.

"What is that smell?" Tamar asked. It was sweet, cloying.

"The sedative we use. It's necessary to control the volunteers once they're under the influence of *parem*. But they cannot do the work of creating *khergud* without it."

The volunteers. He meant Grisha.

"We also use it on our *khergud*. They tend to get restless at night, since they have no real need for sleep anymore."

What did he mean? Why would Reyem have no need for sleep?

The former dairy had been divided into three large areas. On the left was a kind of dormitory, a row of bunk beds and washbasins. Most of the occupants rested atop their blankets, their wasted chests rising and falling in rapid pants, their bodies little more than bones and waxen skin.

"How long—" Tamar swallowed. "How long can the volunteers be kept alive like this?"

"It varies," said the doctor. "The older subjects have a harder time of it, but sometimes it just seems to be a question of will."

A young man on a lower bunk lifted his head and looked at them with hollow eyes. He had flaxen hair, ruddy pink skin. He didn't look Shu at all. Mayu nudged Ehri.

"Where do they come from?" Ehri asked.

"Oh, that's Bergin. He's from Fjerda."

"And he came here willingly?" Tamar asked.

The doctor had the grace to look sheepish. "Well. Willingly enough after his first taste of *parem*." He gestured to Bergin and the Grisha rose. He wore a kind of uniform—loose gray trousers and a tunic of the same fabric. Mayu saw desperation in his face, the same helplessness the other prisoners shared. But there was something else there too: rage. He was still angry. He was still fighting. "Bergin was a translator working for a shipping concern in Fjerda, but when his powers were discovered, he tried to flee the country. Our troops intercepted him and offered sanctuary."

Fury flared in Bergin's blue eyes. Mayu doubted the doctor's story bore much resemblance to the truth. Bergin had probably been dosed by Shu troops and taken captive to serve as a "volunteer."

"We've had him working on Locust."

"Locust?" asked Tamar.

"The conversion from ordinary soldier to *khergud* is incredibly complicated, so we pair each volunteer with a soldier candidate for the duration. Of course, sometimes the volunteer dies before the work is complete, but we're getting better at managing doses to prolong their lives."

"Remarkable," Tamar said, her voice sharp as a blade begging to draw blood. The doctor didn't seem to notice, but Bergin did, his blue eyes suddenly more alert. He was leaning on one of the huge, slablike tables that took up the center of the room.

"This is where the great work is done," said the doctor.

Mayu saw drills, bone saws, long pieces of brass and steel, a contraption that looked like it had been welded into the shape of a wing. The floor was made of some kind of metal and punctuated by large drains. To make it easy to wash away the blood. *This isn't an old dairy*, she realized. *It's a slaughterhouse. This is the killing floor.*

On the far right was a different kind of dormitory. The beds here were more like coffins, sealed brass sarcophagi.

"And these are our ironhearted children, the *khergud*."

Here was the proof of Makhi's program, of the torture of Grisha, of the abominations they'd created. But was her brother among them?

Tamar laid a hand on Mayu's shoulder, and Mayu realized she was shaking.

"What are their names?" asked Ehri.

"Locust, Harbinger, Scarab, Nightmoth—"

"No," said Mayu, unable to tamp down her anger. "Their real names."

The doctor shrugged. "I don't actually know."

Mayu gripped the pommel of her talon sword, trying to control her frustration. She looked at the princess, willing Ehri to understand her need. Yes, they had their proof, but where was her brother?

"I'm curious," said Ehri. "Is it safe to open the . . . containers?"

"Oh, entirely," said the doctor, already flipping a switch on one of the sarcophagi. The lid released with an unexpected pop. "We wake them using a stimulant made from ordinary *jurda*. But they're safe in any state. The *khergud* are perfect soldiers."

Is that what I am? Mayu wondered. *A soldier who would take an innocent man's life, murder a princess, watch her sisters burn at the whim of a queen?*

The doctor lifted the lid. A woman lay inside, her breathing shallow, her brow furrowed in sleep. "They don't dream well," murmured the doctor. The sleeping soldier seemed to scent something; her nostrils flared. Tamar moved away from the container. The *khergud* were rumored to be able to smell the presence of Grisha. Perfect soldiers. Perfect hunters.

"Another, please," said Ehri.

The doctor flipped a switch, pushed open another lid. "We

331

made the sleeping chambers wide to allow for those with winged enhancements."

Mayu looked down at the man who lay in the container, his brass wings folded behind him. Metal horns curved from his forehead. Not Reyem. Was he even here? If he wasn't, how would they find the facility he was being kept at?

The doctor released the lid on a third container. He smiled. "Now, this will interest you, Princess. Something new we've been working on. This is Locust. We gave him metal pincers, fused at his spine. He's taken to the treatment well."

Mayu knew it would be her brother before she even looked.

Reyem lay sleeping inside the chamber. He had the same troubled expression as the others, as if in his dreams he was not the hunter but the prey. She hadn't seen him in almost a year, but he was the same Reyem, tall and lean, his long hair pulled back from his face in a high knot, the way he'd always worn it. He had a tiny, half-moon scar on his cheek from when he'd been hit by a rock—a rock Mayu had thrown in anger, never really meaning to hurt him. He'd cried, but he'd told their parents that he'd just taken a fall.

Wings had been attached to his back, and bent at his hips were metal pincers, jointed like insect legs. Mayu felt her stomach turn.

The doctor had moved on to the next sleeping chamber.

Bergin was staring at her from his perch by the table, but Mayu didn't care. She reached down and took Reyem's hand in hers.

"Brother," she whispered. Reyem's brow smoothed. In his sleep, he clasped her hand. Mayu felt tears sting the back of her throat. "I'm here, Reyem. It's going to be okay."

"*Kebben*," Tamar murmured. Her expression had softened. Maybe more than anyone, she understood what it was to be separated from your twin.

"We have to get him out of here."

Tamar nodded. "I've already sent our scouts back to wake the ministers. I don't want Makhi to have a chance to empty this place out before they see it."

"But we intercepted your scouts," said a high, clear voice from the doorway.

Queen Makhi stood by the metal door, bracketed by Tavgharad guards.

"Your Majesty!" exclaimed the doctor, bowing to his toes.

Tamar moved to block Princess Ehri.

"How interesting to see you in that uniform, Tamar Kir-Bataar," said Makhi, sweeping into the room.

The doctor squinted as if trying to remember where he'd heard the name.

"Sweet Ehri," Makhi said. "Did you really think I was that easily outwitted? You are so new to this game, and I have been playing since we were children."

"Reyem," Mayu whispered urgently. She squeezed his hand. "Reyem, please wake up." They needed to get free of this place right now.

"Allow me," said the queen, pressing a series of buttons on the wall. A loud hiss sounded and a faint orange mist shot from spigots at the head of the container.

"No!" Bergin cried.

Her brother's eyes snapped open as he inhaled the stimulant.

"Reyem?"

He looked at Mayu, his expression blank.

"This sentimental bond of *kebben* has never made sense to me," said Makhi. "I was supposed to be born a twin. But I murdered him in the womb. Or so my nursemaid told me. She said it was why I was

333

born with only half a soul. I'm going to enjoy watching your brother kill you all."

"Reyem, it's me. It's Mayu." He gripped her hand harder. "Yes, it's me. You know me. Reyem, you have to come with us."

"Go on," the queen said. "Do what you were made to do."

Reyem's fist clenched. Mayu screamed and collapsed to her knees as her brother broke every bone in her hand.

25

NINA

A WANING MOON HUNG OVER the Ice Court, its edges blurred by the cloudy promise of snow. Nina could hear sounds of celebration from the royal palace, noblemen drinking and dancing to rejoice in the bombing of Os Alta. Somewhere, out in the wild forests, Brum and the *drüskelle* were giving thanks to Djel and preparing for the war to come.

But Nina had been at war a very long time. And tonight, she intended to do some damage. She had destroyed Queen Tatiana's letters. Now Nina was going to take away the one man who could verify that they'd ever existed.

The plan was simple but tremendously risky. First Nina needed a way into the *drüskelle* sector. She couldn't simply waltz out of the Ice Court and back in again, so she would have to approach the sector via the secret path across the ice moat. It was not an appealing option. She'd spent the last few months doing little more than sitting and scheming. She was excellent at both, but tonight she would need the strength and agility of the soldier she'd been, not the wiles of the spy she'd become. And she'd need Hanne. Nina didn't like putting her at risk, but she could admit that they'd seem less suspicious if they were caught sneaking around together than if Nina, an outsider at the Ice Court, was caught alone.

They dressed in riding clothes—two girls out for one of Hanne's larks. Nina was just grateful to be free of her heavy skirts. They would cross the ice moat together, dressed in white, hair covered to better camouflage themselves. Assuming they weren't immediately spotted and dragged back to their chambers to await punishment, Hanne would get them up the wall.

"There's no door at the bottom?" Nina had asked. She should have been doing push-ups every morning.

"Only *drüskelle* know where it is. It won't be a problem. We just need an open window."

"And a way up to an open window."

Hanne was unfazed. "I can get climbing gear from the shed at the base of the Elderclock. They use it when they clean the spire."

"Sweet Djel, you've done this before."

"Maybe once. Or twice."

"Hanne!"

Hanne shrugged. "The first time I went over the wall, I just wanted to see if I could get to the roof of the embassy sector."

"And the second time?"

Hanne winced guiltily. "I may have wanted to go see the market-place by myself. And the third time—"

"You said twice!"

"There were whales in the bay. Was I supposed to not go see them?"

Nina laughed, though imagining Hanne making madcap escapes from the Ice Court left her feeling uneasy. If Hanne accepted a proposal at the end of Heartwood, she might be trapped here forever. But for now, Nina had to focus on Magnus Opjer.

The trek across the ice moat was harrowing, and despite her heavy boots, Nina's feet were frozen by the time they arrived on the thin rind of shore at the *drüskelle* sector. It took a few tries to get the grappling hook in place, but bare moments later, Hanne was shinnying up the rope like she was part squirrel.

"Really," Nina grumbled beneath her breath. "She could at least try to make it look hard for my sake."

Once Hanne was on the roof, she braced the rope as Nina climbed, arm over arm, grateful for the knots and loops they'd tied into the rope. From there, they had to span the gap that led to the actual building that housed the dining hall and Brum's office. Nina tried not to think about how far she was off the ground and went over the plan in her head. On her back, she carried clothing they'd pilfered from Brum's own closet. It wasn't ideal, but the man spent most of his time in uniform, and they needed something to replace Opjer's rags. Once she freed Opjer, she would take him back across the ice moat and into the gardens. Then she'd send him over the bridge with the rest of the departing partygoers and deliver him into the waiting arms of the Hringsa. Before he left, Hanne would tailor Opjer's face. His resemblance to Nikolai was too damning, and Nina didn't want a weapon like that to fall into the wrong person's hands.

At last, Nina reached the other side of the gap and flopped onto the roof of the *drüskelle* sector. Hanne made sure the rope was secured around one of the chimneys, then looped it around Nina's waist.

"Ready?" she asked.

Nina clutched the rope. "To be lowered like a sack of flour into the heart of witchhunter power?"

"This was your idea. We can still turn around."

"Do not second-guess the sack of flour. The sack of flour is wise beyond her years."

Hanne rolled her eyes and braced her feet against the edge of the roof, and Nina stepped out into nothing. Hanne released a grunt, but the rope stayed steady. Slowly, she lowered Nina down.

The first two windows she tried were locked tight, but the third gave way and she wiggled inside, landing on the carpeted floor with a thud. She was in a stairway. For a moment, she couldn't orient herself, but she descended another story, and soon she was at the door to Brum's office. This time, she didn't have a key. It had been too risky to steal it again, so she would have to pick the lock. It took an embarrassingly long time. She could almost hear Kaz laughing at her. *Shut up, Brekker. Talk to me when you've done something about that terrible haircut.* Maybe he had by now. She hoped so for Inej's sake.

Nina wasn't sure if all the *drüskelle* had gone to the woods or if some had been left behind, and she didn't intend to find out. She went directly to the door leading to Opjer's cell, already placing a finger to her lips to make sure he stayed silent.

The cell was empty. And spotlessly clean. For a moment, Nina had the eerie fear that she'd made it all up, that Opjer had never been here at all.

I know what I saw. So where was he? Had he been moved after the disappearance of the letters? No, if Brum had known about the missing letters, he would have put more security in place. And there was no way he would kill Opjer; the Fjerdans wouldn't squander an advantage that way.

She needed to find out where they'd taken him. And she didn't have much time.

Nina thumbed through the documents on Brum's desk, trying to make sure to keep everything in its place. There had to be some kind of transfer order, some discussion of where they would place such a valuable prisoner. She saw the usual plans and maps, and what looked like a sketch of intersecting parabolas beside a long series of equations. A weapon? A note above it read: *Hajefetla*. Songbird. There were designs for some kind of helmet, what might be modifications to a repeating rifle, a sea transport.

Nina hesitated. The maps, the plans—more tragedies in the making? If she'd only been able to understand the targets she'd seen on Brum's desk before, she might have warned Zoya and King Nikolai of the bombing to come. She might have saved hundreds of lives. But if she stole these plans, Brum would know someone had been in his office. There was a good chance she and the Hringsa agents at the Ice Court would be compromised before they ever got the plans where they needed to go, and Hanne could be put in jeopardy too. Nina would communicate all she could remember to the Hringsa, but she had to stay focused. She didn't have much time, and she'd come here to find Magnus Opjer.

Then she spotted a strange word: *Rëvfeder*. Foxfather.

Nina's eyes scanned the page, but she wasn't reading a transfer order. It was the report of an escape. Magnus Opjer had somehow gotten out of his cell, out of the *drüskelle* sector, and out of the Ice Court—and taken Queen Tatiana's letters with him. *Well, thank you for bearing the blame for that, Magnus.* The next line on the report made Nina's stomach lurch: A piece of what looked like sharpened bone had been found in the lock of Magnus Opjer's cell door.

Nina remembered Opjer's hands gripping her sleeves as he'd begged her to free him. She'd thought it was desperation, but maybe it had just been a performance. Could Magnus Opjer, the most valued and recognizable prisoner in Fjerda, really have escaped the Ice Court?

Wily old bastard. Foxfather indeed. He'd pilfered one of her bone darts and used it to pick the lock of his cage. If she'd needed any further proof that Opjer was King Nikolai's father, this was it.

So where was he now? Nina didn't know, and she had no way of finding out. She would call on her contacts in the Hringsa, relay the information to Ravka. For now, she was stuck. There was speculation in the report that he might head back to his home north of Djerholm to reunite with his daughter or even to Elling, where some of his shipping vessels were docked. *He is a man without means*, said the report. *He cannot book passage on a ship. He cannot hope to cross the border into Ravka. It is only a matter of time before the target is reacquired.*

Nina wondered. Magnus Opjer wasn't a noble. He was a self-made man, a shipping magnate with a lifetime's worth of connections and an established network of sailing craft. And he was Nikolai Lantsov's father. He might be lacking cash, but if he'd managed to get clear of the Ice Court, he definitely wasn't short on ingenuity.

A sound from the courtyard below drew Nina from her thoughts. The gate was opening. Could the *drüskelle* have returned so soon?

She slipped the escape report back among the papers on the desk and hurried out of the office, making sure the lock slid into place. Brum would find his office just as he'd left it.

Nina started down the stairs but heard the sound of voices below. *Damn it.*

She raced back the way she'd come, dodging down the hall on silent feet, gently trying each door, praying one would be unlocked.

At last a handle turned. She slid inside and shut the door behind her with a click that seemed to echo in her ears.

"What are you doing here?"

She whirled. Joran stood before her in his black uniform, his face furious, his eyes slitted in suspicion. Someone else must be guarding the prince tonight.

Nina's thoughts skittered wildly through her head, a panicked rush, birds startled from the quiet.

Are you really doing this? She had time to wonder before her mouth blurted, "Commander Brum told me to meet him here."

She was Mila now, lip trembling, hands wringing.

Joran's fingers hovered over his whip. "The commander would never violate these rooms with the presence of a woman."

Nina grasped the bone darts in her sleeve. She didn't want to kill Joran, but she would if she had to. The trick would be making it look like an accident. His body was healthy, untouched by any death or decay for her power to exploit.

"I'm not proud," she said, letting tears fill her eyes. "I know what I have agreed to."

Joran scowled. He never showed emotion around Prince Rasmus, and the anger transformed his face, making him look like the brutal witchhunter he was.

"He said he would be back early," she continued. "But the others came instead."

"I don't know what game you're playing at, but the commander will hear of it."

"He showed me the secret path across the ice moat," Nina said, feeling the darts slide between her fingers.

Joran stopped short at that. No one knew the secrets of the ice moat except the *drüskelle*. "That cannot be."

She would have to be precise. Two darts through the inner corners of his eyes, driven directly into the brain. She could extract them before she left and hopefully keep any blood or mess to a minimum. It would look like he'd been taken by some kind of fit.

Nina stepped to the left, maneuvering so that the light shone directly on Joran's face to aid her aim—then paused.

"Those are relics." Bones spread out on an altar cloth, laid atop a trunk for clothes. A woodblock carved with the rough shape of a sun propped against the wall.

Joran tried to move his body to block her view, but it was too late.

"That's an altar," Nina said. "To the Saints. That's why you're not with the prince tonight. You came here to pray."

Joran didn't deny it. He stood as if rooted to the spot, motionless in the way of an animal sensing danger. He didn't know the half of it. She could kill him now. Quickly. Easily.

"Whose bones are those?" She kept her voice gentle, easy, as if she were asking about what he'd had for dinner last night and not heresy committed within the walls of the Ice Court.

Joran opened his mouth. She saw his throat bob, the words seeming to fight their way out. "Alina's," he rasped. "I . . . I bought them down in Djerholm. I know they're probably fake, but—"

"But they brought you comfort." People all over Ravka, and maybe now Fjerda too kept relics that had supposedly belonged to the Saints. Finger bones, a fragment of spine, scraps of an ancient garment. Nina's power told her that the bones Joran had purchased weren't even human.

"She was a soldier," he said, almost pleading. "She saved people. Fjerdans and Ravkans alike."

"Is that what you want?" Nina drew a little closer. She could hear voices in the hall. She needed to get out of here, get back out the window and down to the ice moat with Hanne. But she also needed Joran to trust her. If he mentioned her presence here to Brum, she was done for.

"I want to be . . . good." He shook his head, fighting his own logic. "Soldiers aren't good. They're loyal. They're brave."

He had never seemed so young. She forgot sometimes that he was only a boy really, not even seventeen.

"They can be good too."

"Not us." He looked at her then, his blue eyes haunted. "Not me."

"Alina Starkov wasn't just a soldier," she said very quietly. "She was Grisha."

He squeezed his eyes shut, head bowed as if ready to take the beating he knew he deserved. "I know." His voice was harsh. "I know it is sacrilege."

"Not necessarily."

Joran's eyes snapped open.

"Maybe Grisha power isn't quite what we've been led to believe," she said. They were Matthias' words from so long ago. They'd been a balm to her, a gift that had helped her heal and accept who she was. "Maybe their power is a gift from Djel, one more way he shows his strength in this world."

"No . . . no, that's blasphemy, that's—"

"Who are we to say we know the mind of god?"

Joran peered at her as if he could find the truth somewhere in her features. "Does the commander . . . does he know you think this way?"

"No," Nina said. "It is not seemly. But I cannot help the pattern of my thoughts."

Joran placed his hands to his head. "I know."

"Are there others among you who feel this way?"

"Yes," said Joran. His jaw jutted forward. "But I will not give you their names."

"I didn't ask for them. I never would." She wasn't going to inform on Joran—why would she? But after failing so thoroughly tonight, knowing that the religion of the Saints had spread to the ranks of men trained to hate Grisha was a tiny thread of hope to hang on to with both hands.

"Can you help me get back to the White Island?" she asked.

"Why do you not wait for Brum if he is your . . . if you are his . . ."

A dark bubble of mirth rose in Nina. How easily these men played with bloodshed and suffering, but at the mere thought of pleasure, their minds went slack.

Nina grasped Joran's arm. "I will tell him I was never here tonight, that I could not raise the courage to come. If he knows that I wandered away from his rooms, that I dared to speak to you, I would . . . I would have to tell him what I found."

Joran stiffened. "I would be put to death."

"I am a woman alone in a powerful man's house. I have no true allies. I will do what I must to survive."

Joran looked almost startled. "You did not want to be his whore?"

The word made Nina bristle. "Is that so hard to believe?"

"Commander Brum . . . he would never. He would not force—"

"He has no need to resort to force. He prefers a different kind of submission." At that, Joran's expression changed. *He knows it's true. He's seen Brum's love of power.* "A woman in my position has no language for refusal. Without Commander Brum's generosity, I would be lost. And if a man like Jarl Brum chose to impugn my reputation . . ."

Joran's eyes darted left and right. She could see a sheen of sweat on his forehead. He was at the crossroads. He didn't know what was true or right anymore; the altar behind him made that perfectly clear. He nodded once as if in debate with himself, then again.

"Yes," he said. "I'll help you."

Nina felt an ache in her throat. There was honor in Joran, the honor she'd hoped to see in Prince Rasmus. He didn't want to be a killer. He didn't want to be cruel. Brum's hatred hadn't twisted him completely yet. *Save some mercy for my people.* For this boy, still striving for some kind of goodness, she could.

"We have to go now," said Joran. He hesitated, noticing her attire for the first time. "Why are you wearing riding clothes?"

"He told me to. He wished to chastise me."

Joran's face went crimson at the possibilities. Nina almost blushed at that one herself. She could hear Hanne whisper in her ear, *Shameless.*

"Where did you enter the sector?" he asked.

"The secret door," she lied.

Joran shook his head, disgusted that Brum would give up the mysteries of the *drüskelle* for a tawdry affair. "I can get you back there."

He tidied up his altar, locking everything away inside the trunk, and disappeared into the hallway. A moment later, she heard voices, Joran saying something to whoever was there. For a moment Nina was certain he would sound the alarm and give her up to his brothers, that his sympathy had all been a ruse. Then he pushed the door open and waved her along.

At the end of the hall, he lifted a tapestry of a white wolf with an eagle in its bloody jaws and pressed one of the stones. The wall slid back, revealing a narrow, winding staircase carved into the rock. Nina hid her surprise. She was supposed to have come this way.

At the base of the dark stairs, she heard scraping sounds. The door opened, bringing with it a gust of cold air. From here, it looked as if the ice moat was nothing but a sheer skin of frost and freezing water lurking below it. But Nina knew there was a transparent glass bridge beneath it. She glanced up in time to see Hanne's startled face disappear high above, and the rope rapidly vanishing up onto the roof.

"I will go on my own from here," Nina said.

"You'll be all right?"

"I would not ask you to risk capture for my sake."

Joran's face was pained. "He'll punish you for not waiting. For not doing as he bid."

"I know," she said, lowering her eyes.

"You must find a way out of his household."

She would. When her work was done and not before. "I will, but I cannot leave Hanne." As she said the words, she knew they were true.

Joran hesitated. "It would be better if you kept her away from the prince. He's not . . . he's weak."

"He grows stronger every day."

Joran gave a sharp shake of his head. "I've known plenty of wounded men, people who have lost limbs, who live with pain or sickness. They bear their suffering without ever playing the games that Rasmus does. The flaw is not in his body. It's in his soul."

"He's been nothing but good to Hanne." Flimsy words after what she'd seen Rasmus do to Joran. "At the hunt, he was humiliated—"

"That wasn't the first time he lashed out. I saw him knock a boy from his horse and claim it was a joke. The child split his skull on the cobblestones, but no one said a word, because Rasmus is a prince."

Could it have been an accident? A bit of fun gone wrong? Nina couldn't quite make herself believe it.

"He's changing," she said with more hope than she felt. "The stronger he feels, the less he'll need to prove his strength."

"He was *testing* his new strength," said Joran, "waiting to see who will stop him. And you know no one will."

Nina set her foot on the invisible path, feeling the cold of the water through her boots. She made herself go slowly, carefully, when all she wanted was to run from the *drüskelle* sector and the truth in Joran's words.

She clutched her coat tight against the chill in the air. There was nothing else to do but keep moving forward. You chose your path. You walked it. You hoped to find a way home again.

26
THE
MONK

ALEKSANDER STOLE CLOTHES and shoes from the back of a wagon on his way into Polvost. Finding the Starless had been more difficult than he'd anticipated, and he was growing weary of the march. He bent beside a stream to drink, but he didn't need to waste time hunting. He wasn't hungry. He remembered how Elizaveta had craved sensation—the taste of wine, the touch of skin, the feel of soft earth beneath her feet. Aleksander cared for none of this. He only wished that it wasn't winter. He wanted to turn his face to the sun and feel it warm him. The cold frightened him now. It felt like death, like the long silence of not being, without sense of time or place, only the understanding that he must hold on, that someday, there would be an end to the terrible stillness. He'd been a long time in the dark.

But eventually he realized that he was growing weak. Yuri's body needed sustenance, and so he made his way to a beer hall in Shura. Aleksander had no money, but he offered to chop wood and fix the roof in exchange for a meal. The young men of the town were already gone, back in uniform, readying to face the Fjerdans.

"And what do you think of the king's war?" he asked a group of old men gathered on the porch.

The gray grandfather who answered was so wizened he looked more walnut than man. "Our Nikolai didn't ask for a war, but if it's what them cold northern bastards want, he'll give it to them."

His wrinkled companion spat onto the wooden slats. "You'll be kissing the icy asses of those northern bastards when they march through. We don't have the tanks and guns the Fjerdans have, and sending our children to die won't change that."

"You saying we should just let them drop bombs on our cities?"

On and on it went, the same old story. But they did love their king.

"You'll see, he'll find a way out of this trap, same as the last. The too-clever fox always does."

Aleksander wondered if they'd actually read that particular story. He seemed to recall it had a very bloody end. The fox had lost his hide to the hunter's knife. Or maybe he'd been rescued? Aleksander couldn't recall.

He sat at the end of a table in the beer hall, ate tough rye bread and strips of lamb stewed so long they tasted like they'd already been chewed. *This* was what it meant to be alive. Elizaveta should count herself lucky. To think Zoya had been the one to kill her. He supposed it saved him the trouble of doing it himself. And if Zoya ever learned to harness the power she'd been given? She was still vulnerable, still malleable. Her anger made her easy to control. When this war was done and the casualties counted, she might once more be in need of a shepherd. She had been one of his best students and soldiers, her envy and her rage driving her to train and fight harder than any of her peers. And then she'd turned on him. Like Genya. Like Alina. Like his own mother. Like all of Ravka.

She will return to you.

He didn't want Yuri's sympathy. He drank sour beer and listened to the customers gossip. All the talk was of the war, the bombing of Os Alta, and of course, the blight that had vexed the king and his general so.

"Pilgrims camped in Gayena. They tried to set up their blasted black tents here, but we drove them out. We'll have none of that unholy talk."

"They say the blight's a punishment for not making the Darkling a Saint."

"Well, I say make him a Saint if it will bring that pasture back to life. Where am I supposed to graze my cattle?"

"If he can get my lazy husband out of bed, I'll make a pilgrimage to the Fold myself."

Gayena. At last he had word of the Starless. He finished his awful meal and ducked out of the beer hall, but not before he'd used his shadows to help him snatch a pair of spectacles from one of the tables. As he walked, he let Yuri's features return to the fore, the long face, the weak chin. No beard, of course. He was no Tailor. And the weak body would remain in exile too. Aleksander would need every bit of his strength. He placed the spectacles on his nose. He would have to look over the lenses. Yuri's faulty eyesight from all those years bent over books was another thing he didn't care to restore.

He could feel the boy's elation at the prospect of rejoining the faithful. *This is my purpose. This is the reason for all of it.*

Yuri wasn't wrong. Everyone had a part to play.

Aleksander found the Starless camped under a bridge like a gathering of trolls, their black banners raised over their tents. He took quick stock of their defenses and assets. It was a surprisingly young group, and almost all men, all of them dressed in black, many in tunics clumsily embroidered with his symbol—the sun in eclipse. He spotted a mule, a few scrawny horses, a box covered with a tarp In a wagon—a weapons cache, he assumed. *This* was what he had to work with? He wasn't sure what he'd expected. If not an army, then the makings of one, but not this pathetic gathering.

I shouldn't have left them. Yuri again. His presence was more insistent now, as if allowing the little monk's features to emerge had made Yuri's voice stronger—less a single gnat than a swarm of them.

"Yuri?" A barrel-chested man with a salt-and-pepper beard approached.

Aleksander searched for his name and Yuri's memories provided it. "Chernov!"

He was swept up in a musty, muscular embrace that nearly lifted him off his toes. It was like being hugged by a bearskin rug badly in need of cleaning.

"We feared you were dead!" Chernov cried. "We'd heard you were traveling with the apostate king and then, not a word from you."

"I have returned."

Chernov frowned. "You sound different. You *look* different."

Aleksander knew better than to try to make excuses. Instead he grabbed Chernov's arm and met his gaze. "I *am* different, Chernov. How many are gathered here?"

"At last count, we had thirty-two of the faithful. But we're feeding a few travelers who have not yet found the Starless path."

"We are?" Valuable resources squandered.

"We are," said Chernov. "Just as you preached. All are equal in the dark."

He had to stop himself from laughing. Instead he nodded and repeated the words with fervor. "All are equal in the dark."

Chernov led him through camp, and Aleksander greeted those who seemed to recognize him as an old friend. If they only knew. As they walked, he inquired casually about the other places the Cult of the Starless Saint had taken hold. By Chernov's count, the cult's following had swelled to nearly one thousand pilgrims. A meager number, but it was a start.

"We've decided to head south to warmer climes, get away from the northern border. We don't want to get caught in the crossfire when the fighting breaks out."

"And then?"

Chernov smiled. "And then we continue the good work of spreading the Darkling's name and championing his Sainthood. Once King Nikolai is deposed, Vadik Demidov will be crowned and we will petition—"

"Demidov will be a Fjerdan puppet."

"What do we care for politics of that kind?"

"You'll care when they stack Grisha on the pyre."

"Grisha?"

Aleksander had to work to hide his anger. "Was not the Darkling a Grisha?"

"He was a Saint. There is a difference. What has come over you, Yuri?"

Aleksander smiled, regrouping. "Forgive me. I only meant that we may still find new followers among the Grisha."

Chernov clapped him on the back. "A worthy goal once the war is over."

He contemplated tearing Chernov's arm from its socket. Instead he shifted his approach. "But what of the Apparat? The priest will return to Ravka with Demidov, will he not? He's fought the Darkling's Sainthood at every turn."

"We believe we can win him to our cause in time."

This is all wrong. On that, Yuri and Aleksander could agree. Yuri had been a member of the Apparat's Priestguard for a time. He'd watched the Apparat side first with the Sun Saint and then with no one at all, waiting for Alina and the Darkling to wage their battles as he and his followers stayed safely underground. The Starless shouldn't be content to plead for scraps from the priest's hand, no matter what sway he held with Ravka's people.

"The sun will be setting soon," Chernov said as the Starless gathered, facing to the west. "You're just in time for services. Brother Azarov will be speaking."

"No," said Aleksander. "I will speak."

Chernov blinked. "I . . . well . . . Perhaps it would be best to take some time to settle in, to reacquaint yourself with——"

Aleksander didn't wait to hear the rest. He strode to the front of the congregation and heard a few murmurs of "Yuri!" and "Brother Vedenen!" from those who had not yet seen him in the camp. Others were strangers, people who had joined the Starless after Yuri had left their ranks.

"Brother Azarov," Aleksander said, approaching the young man with yellow hair who was preparing to speak. He had the pallor and charisma of a glass of milk.

"Brother Vedenen! I'm so pleased to see you again. Your preaching was sorely missed, but I've been trying my hand at it."

"Chernov has an urgent matter he wants you to attend to."

"He does?"

"Indeed. Extremely urgent. Go on now." He strode past Brother Azarov and took his place where he belonged, in front of the crowd.

Aleksander looked out over their faces, confused but eager, waiting for someone to give them something to believe in, a spark of the divine. *I will give you a conflagration. I will give you a new name for fire.*

Yuri's joy coursed through him. The boy had been a preacher himself. He understood this exultation.

"Some of you know me," he said, his voice carrying over the crowd as the light from the setting sun turned golden and washed over their faces. He heard them react to his unfamiliar voice with whispers and gasps. "I am not the man I was. I traveled to the Fold, and there I was visited by the Starless One himself."

"A vision?" asked Chernov, amid the startled exclamations of the crowd. "What did you see?"

"I saw the future. I saw how we are best meant to serve the cause of the Starless One. And it is not to live as cowards." Troubled murmurs rose from the pilgrims. "We will not march south. We will not hide from this war."

Chernov took a step forward. "Yuri, you cannot mean that. We have never troubled ourselves with politicians and their games."

"This is no game. The Apparat betrayed the Darkling. He fought against naming him a Saint. He allies himself with Ravka's enemies. But you would go to ground, trembling like animals without teeth or claws."

"So that we may survive!"

"So that we can run back to a corrupt priest when he joins Demidov's court? So that we can return to begging for his notice by chanting outside the city gates? We were meant for more." He met the eyes of those watching him, exchanging angry whispers. "No doubt some of you joined this group for the very purpose of avoiding battle. You didn't want to pick up a gun, so you put on a robe and carried the Starless banner. I will tell you right now, we do not want you here."

"Yuri!" cried Chernov. "This is not our way."

Aleksander wanted to cut him down where he stood, but it was not yet time to show his true power. He'd endured lifetimes of hiding just how strong he was. He could wait a little longer.

He spread his hands wide. "You are afraid. I understand that. You are not soldiers. Neither am I. And yet the Darkling spoke to me. He promised that he would return. But only if we make a stand in his name."

"What are you suggesting?" Brother Azarov asked, his face fearful.

"We march north. Toward the border."

"Toward the war?" he sputtered.

Aleksander nodded. He didn't intend to waste his time traveling from village to village, winning over tiny congregations with parlor tricks. No, he required a moment of spectacle, something grand with plenty of witnesses. He would stage his return on the field of battle with thousands of Ravkan and Fjerdan soldiers as his audience. There, Yuri's transformation from humble monk to chosen savior would be completed. There, Aleksander would teach them awe.

The Fjerdans were better armed and better provisioned, and when young King Nikolai faltered, as he inevitably would, then and only then would the Darkling return, and show Ravka what strength really looked like. He would save them. He would offer them a miracle. And he would become Saint, father, protector, king.

"Yuri," said Chernov. "You ask too much."

"I ask nothing," said Aleksander, spreading his arms wider. "It is the Starless One who gives this command." Shadows began to bleed from his palms. The crowd cried out. "You must decide how you will answer."

He threw his head back, letting the shadows billow out over the crowd. They went to their knees. He heard sobbing. He was fairly sure Brother Azarov had fainted.

355

"Will you run to the south or will you carry our Saint's banners north?" he demanded of the crowd. "How will you answer the Starless One?"

"North!" they cried. "North!"

They clung to one another, weeping, as the shadows blocked out the setting sun.

"I'm sorry I doubted you," Chernov said, approaching with tears in his eyes.

Aleksander smiled, letting the shadows recede. He placed a hand on Chernov's shoulder. "Don't apologize, brother. You and I are going to change the world."

27

NIKOLAI

THEY JOURNEYED TO KETTERDAM aboard the *Cormorant*, a large airship that would allow them to transport the titanium back to Ravka—assuming they were able to acquire it. But they couldn't approach the city in a Ravkan vessel, so they moored the giant craft at a smuggler's island off the Kerch coast. Adrik and his Squallers would keep it wreathed in mist while Zoya and Nikolai met up with the *Volkvolny*, the privateer Sturmhond's most famous ship.

Numerous people had stepped into the role of Sturmhond since Nikolai had created the identity for himself. It had made it easy to keep the privateer's legend and influence alive while he sat the throne. And, of course, there were things a privateer with no known allegiance might accomplish that a king bound by the rules of diplomacy could not. Sturmhond's gift for making and breaking blockades and acquiring stolen property had served Ravka's interests more than once. It felt good to slip into the familiar teal coat and strap Sturmhond's pistols to his hips.

Zoya was waiting on the deck of the *Volkvolny*. She had dressed as a common sailor in trousers and a roughspun shirt, and braided her hair, but she looked completely ill at ease out of her *kefta*. Nikolai had seen the way Nina disappeared into a role, changed the way she walked, the way she spoke, seemingly without effort. Zoya did not have this gift. Her posture remained razor sharp, her chin lifted slightly, less like a rough-and-tumble sailor than a beautiful aristocrat who had taken it into her head to spend the day among commoners.

Her eyes scanned him from the crown of his head to the toes of his boots. "You look absurd in that outfit."

"Absurdly dashing? I agree."

She rolled her eyes as the ship surged forward to find its berth in the Ketterdam harbor. "You like playing the pirate too much."

"Privateer. And yes, I do. There's freedom in it. When I wear this coat, my responsibility is the people on this ship. Not an entire nation."

"It's a game of pretend," she said.

"A welcome illusion. One might be anything or anyone aboard a ship."

They leaned on the rail, watching as the sprawl of the city and its busy port came into view.

"You miss it, don't you?" she asked.

"I do. Maybe if this all goes to hell and Vadik Demidov takes my crown, I'll simply return to being Sturmhond. I can serve my country without wearing a crown."

He was unnerved by how much the idea appealed to him. It wasn't the work of being a king he minded. Problems were meant to be solved. Obstacles defeated. Allies won through charm or the occasional bribe. He was happy to pick up a sword or a pen on Ravka's behalf, to go without sleep or comfort in order to see a mission through. But kings didn't take action—not the way that a privateer or even a general could. Being a king meant second-guessing every move, considering countless variables before making a decision, knowing that each choice might have consequences that others would pay for. *We need a king, not an adventurer.* Zoya was right, but that didn't mean he had to be happy about it.

She cast him a curious glance. "Could you do it? Give up the throne?"

"I don't know. When you've wanted something so long, it's hard to imagine a life without it." He supposed he wasn't just talking about Ravka.

Zoya stood a little straighter, all propriety. "Growing up means learning to go without."

"What a depressing thought."

"It's not so bad. Starve long enough, you forget your hunger."

He leaned closer. "If it's so easy to lose your appetite, maybe you were never truly hungry at all." She looked away, but not before he saw the faintest blush tinge her cheeks. "You could come with me, you know," he said idly. "A Squaller is always welcome on a ship's crew."

Zoya wrinkled her nose. "Live on salt cod and pray to the Saint of Oranges that I don't get scurvy? I think not."

"No small part of you wishes for this kind of freedom?" Because, all Saints, he did.

She laughed, tilting her face to the salt breeze. "I long for boredom. I would gladly sit in a drawing room at the Little Palace and sip my tea and maybe fall asleep in the middle of a tedious meeting. I'd like to linger over a meal without thinking of all the work yet to be done. I'd like to get through one night without . . ."

She trailed off, but Nikolai understood too well how to finish her thought. "Without a nightmare. Without waking in a cold sweat. I know."

Zoya rested her chin in her hands and looked out at the water. "We've been promised a future for so long. A day when the Grisha would be safe, when Ravka would be at peace. Every time we try to grab for it, it slips through our fingers."

Nikolai had sometimes wondered if it was in his nature to be restless, in Zoya's nature to be ruthless, and in Ravka's nature to be forever at war beneath the Lantsov banner. Was that part of what drew him to this life as king? He longed for peace for his country, but did some part of him fear it as well? Who was he without someone to oppose him? Without a problem to solve?

"I promised you that future." He wished he'd been able to make that dream come true for both of them. "I didn't deliver."

"Don't be ridiculous," she clipped out, haughty and imperious as a queen. But she didn't look at him when she said, "You gave Ravka a chance. You gave me a country I could fight for. I'll always be grateful for that."

Gratitude. Was that what he wanted from her? Nevertheless, Nikolai found he was pleased. He cleared his throat. "I believe we've arrived."

The crew lowered the gangway, and Nikolai and Zoya strode up the Fifth Harbor dock.

Zoya planted her hands on her hips, surveying the tangle of people and cargo around them. "Of course Brekker couldn't be bothered to meet us."

"Best not to announce our association on the Ketterdam docks." It would have been safer and simpler to send a delegation on the crown's behalf, but Brekker had ignored every message until Nikolai had penned the letter himself. He and Zoya had worked with the young thief before. They weren't friends or even trusted associates, but they had a better shot of winning Kaz Brekker's help than strangers.

"You are a king."

"Not while I wear this coat."

"Even with a pelican on your head, you'd still be the king of Ravka, and it wouldn't kill that Barrel rat to show a bit of respect." They plunged into the crowds of tourists and sailors on the quay. "I loathe this city."

"It's lively," he said, switching to Kerch.

"If by lively you mean a rat-infested, coal-dust-covered lump of human misery," she replied in kind, her accent heavy. "And I don't like their language either."

"I like the bustle. You can feel the prosperity of this place; I want Ravka to have a piece of this—trade, industry. Our country shouldn't always have to be the beggar at the door."

Zoya's face was thoughtful as they turned onto East Stave, both sides of the canal lined with gambling dens, some grand and some squalid. Each facade was more garish than the last, meant to entice tourists looking for fun. Barkers shouted from every doorway, promising the biggest pots and the liveliest play.

"You don't agree," he said with some surprise.

Zoya eyed an imposing building that Nikolai could have sworn had been called the Emerald . . . Empire? Palace? It had once been done up in Kaelish green and gold. Now it was outfitted in heaps of fake jewels, and a sign over the door read THE SILVER SIX.

A barker shouted at an old panhandler, chasing him from his roost beside the door. "Go on with you! Don't make me call the *stadwatch*." The man hobbled a few steps off, nearly toppling over his walking stick, his old body twisted by time and trouble.

"Spare a coin for an old fool what's lost his luck?"

"I said go! You're scaring off the pigeons."

"Easy now," said Nikolai. "We're all someone's uncle."

"I don't have no brothers or sisters," said the barker.

Nikolai tossed a folded *kruge* into the old man's cap. "Then let's all give thanks your parents didn't make more of you."

"Hey!" snarled the barker, but they were already moving on.

"That's what I mean," said Zoya as they crossed another bridge. "This city is all about the next bit of coin."

"And they're richer for it."

The energy of the Barrel felt contagious—the street vendors hawking paper cones full of sizzling meat and syrupy stacks of waffles, two-bit magicians daring passersby to try their luck, drunken tourists outfitted as the Gray Imp or the Lost Bride, and smooth-limbed creatures of impossible beauty, bodies clad in bare scraps of silk, cheekbones dusted with glitter, luring the lonely or curious across one of the many bridges to the pleasure houses of West Stave. The sheer amount of money passing through this place, the endless tide of people—there was nothing like it in Ravka.

She shook her head. "You see this city from the position of a king. A prince who came here as a student, a privateer who rules the seas. From where I stand, the view is not the same."

"Because you're Grisha?"

"Because I know what it is to be sold." She gestured to the busy street and the canal teeming with *gondels* and market boats. "I know we need this. Jobs for our people, money in our coffers. But Ketterdam was built on the backs of the vulnerable. Grisha indentures. Suli and Zemeni and Kaelish who came here for something better but weren't permitted to own land or hold positions on the Merchant Council."

"Then we take what we like from the Kerch and leave the rest. We build something better, something for everyone."

"If fate gives us half a chance."

"And if fate doesn't give us the chance, we steal it."

"Ketterdam is rubbing off on you." A small smile curled her lips. "But I think I believe you. Maybe it's the coat."

Nikolai winked at her. "It's not the coat."

"Come closer so I can push you into the canal."

"I think not."

"I do want prosperity for Ravka," said Zoya. "But for all of Ravka. Not just the nobles in their palaces or the merchants with their fleets of ships."

"Then we build that future together."

"Together," Zoya repeated. Her expression was troubled.

"What doomsaying is happening behind that gorgeous face, Nazyalensky?"

"If we survive the war . . . Once peace is struck, you should station me elsewhere."

"I see," he said, unwilling to show how much those words bothered him. "Did you have someplace in mind?"

"Os Kervo. We'll need a strong presence there."

"You've thought it all out, then."

She nodded, two quick bobs of her chin. "I have."

All for the best. Peace would mean seeking a new alliance, a bride who could help keep Ravka independent. A memory came to him, the fleeting image of Zoya at his bedside. She'd pressed a kiss to his forehead. Her touch had been cool as a breeze off the sea. But that had never happened and never would. He must have dreamed it.

"Very well. You may have any command you wish. Assuming we survive."

"We had better," she said, tugging at her roughspun sleeves. "It's going to take me two days to wash off the stench of cheap perfume and bilgewater. How can we be sure Brekker will help us at all?"

"He's a man who believes everything has a price, so I think he will."

"But *can* he help us?"

"That I can't be sure of. But we don't have time to gather the intelligence we'd need to steal the titanium on our own. He knows this city and its dealings better than anyone."

"Saints," Zoya gasped as the Crow Club came into view. It looked like a great black bird of prey among a sea of gaudy peacocks. It was three times the size of any other establishment on the block.

"It seems Mister Brekker has expanded."

"Why would anyone enter that place?" Zoya asked, even as two giggling Zemeni girls in country frocks stepped inside. "It looks like a demon dance hall."

"Because they love a good thrill," said a voice behind them—the old beggar had followed them down the Stave. But now he stood, unfolding from his bent posture, and cast off his foul-smelling cloak along with the gray wisps of what must have been a wig. The walking stick in his hand was topped by a crow's head.

Kaz Brekker wiped the putty from his face and ran a gloved hand through his dark hair. "Didn't you know, General Nazyalensky? Thrills are what all these pigeons come to the Barrel for."

Zoya looked like she wanted to send the thief to a soggy death in one of the canals, but Nikolai had to laugh. "Mister Brekker. I should have known."

"Yes," Kaz said. "You should have. But I can see you have plenty to distract you these days."

He could have meant the war. He could have meant any number of things, but the slight quirk of Kaz's brow made Nikolai feel as if he was standing naked on the Stave with his heart's desires tattooed in capital letters on his chest. He was grateful when Brekker turned his attention back to Zoya.

"For the record, General Nazyalensky, Kerch is a country without mercy or law, but it is at least a place where a man might make something of himself without noble blood or magic in his veins."

"The Grisha do not practice 'magic,'" Zoya said with disdain. "It is the Small Science. And it's rude to eavesdrop."

"Better to get fat on information than starve on good manners. Shall we?"

The doormen came to attention as Kaz led Zoya and Nikolai beneath the widespread wings of the crow and into the club. He directed them to a discreet door set off to the side of the gambling floor, guarded by two heavyset men.

"Why the charade?" asked Zoya. "Or do you just like the opportunity to dress up?"

"I like to know what I'm dealing with, and I like to know just how desperate the situation is. I could sit across a table from you and hear the polished pitch you no doubt practiced on your journey, or I could get the straight facts right from your lips."

They passed through a card room. Kaz unlocked another door, and they entered a tunnel barely high enough to stand in, dimly lit by the green tinge of phosphorescent bonelight. A few minutes later, the floor began to slope downward slightly and the air turned cool and damp.

"We're passing beneath the canals, aren't we?" asked Nikolai, unable to keep the excitement from his voice. "When did you build this tunnel?"

"When I needed to. You want to go after the titanium the Kerch army has stockpiled at Rentveer."

How did Brekker get his information? They'd shared no details of the proposed mission, only requested an opportunity to meet and negotiate. "We do."

"That's a fortified military base on one of the roughest sections of the Kerch coastline. It's unreachable by sea without divine intervention and impossible to approach by air without being shot down. There's only one road in or out, and it's heavily guarded. All that adds up to an almost guaranteed chance of capture. I have a long list of enemies who would like nothing better than to catch me at something illegal and throw me in Hellgate."

"So you've left off criminal enterprise?" Zoya asked skeptically.

"I know which chances to take. Why should I take this one?"

"Because you like a challenge?" suggested Nikolai.

"You have confused me with some other thief."

"I don't think so," said Nikolai. "I have something you want. Safety for the Wraith."

He didn't miss the slight bobble in Brekker's step.

"Speak," said Kaz.

"It is my understanding that a certain ship, captained by a young Suli woman and flying under no country's banner, has thrown the human trade in and out of Ketterdam into upheaval. I particularly liked the tale of the two slavers she left slathered in tar and crow feathers at the entrance to the Stadhall. I do admire her theatrics, though the Merchant Council was less impressed, perhaps due to the note pinned to the captain's chest that read, 'Gert Van Verent's new mansion was paid for in bodies.' It made for quite the story in the papers, and Mister Verent—a former member of the Council in good standing—is now under investigation."

"He isn't."

"No?"

"He was found guilty and sentenced to two years in Hellgate. His political rivals have already carved up his fortune."

"How swift is Kerch justice when there's money to be made," Nikolai marveled. "The captain and her ship are known only as the

Wraith, but I have it on good authority that this mysterious Suli woman is Inej Ghafa."

"Never heard of her."

"No?" Nikolai feigned shock. "That surprises me, given her association with the Dregs and her considerable talent for puncturing people with all the zeal of a nearsighted auntie trying to embroider a quilt. But it may be for the best that you have no personal connection."

"Is that so?"

They had stopped at a huge iron door with an elaborate locking mechanism.

"Have you heard of the *izmars'ya*?" Nikolai asked.

"My Ravkan is rusty."

Even if that were true, Nikolai had no doubt Brekker knew exactly what the *izmars'ya* could do. But if he wanted to play, they would play.

"They're submersible warships that travel beneath the sea. They can attack any vessel unseen, and are almost impossible to evade. Some very powerful people in Kerch possess this technology. If the Wraith's enemies convince the Kerch government to use these weapons against her, the Wraith and her crew could be blown from the water at any time."

"A dire situation for her, no doubt." Kaz's voice was even, but Nikolai saw the way his gloved hand gripped the silver crow's head of his cane. "And perhaps for the person who invented such a menace."

The threat was obvious.

"No doubt. But it so happens that when this technology was granted to the Kerch, the very wise king of Ravka—have you met him? Unusual for someone to be so smart and so good-looking—had the hulls of the *izmars'ya* imbued with bits of rhodium, so that with the help of a Fabrikator and a certain device in his keeping, a ship could receive early warning of any submersible within a three-mile radius and take evasive maneuvers. If said ship was so inclined."

"An early warning system."

"Precisely."

Brekker reached for the handle of the door. "And you have this clever invention in your possession?"

"Not on my person," said Nikolai. "I know better than to fill my pockets with valuable merchandise around a thief known as Dirtyhands. But the device is well within reach."

Brekker gave the handle on the iron door a spin. "Come with me, *Sturmhond*. If we're going to pull this off, we'll need some very particular help."

28

ZOYA

THEY EMERGED FROM THE TUNNEL in an unfa-miliar part of the city, and Zoya wondered if Brekker was deliber-ately trying to disorient them.

"We're in the Geldin District," Nikolai murmured. "The favored neighborhood of wealthy merchants."

Leave it to Nikolai to have an accurate map in his head. It was as if they'd traveled to a different country, not a different part of town. The streets were tidy and lovely, all neat cobblestones and clean brick facades. Zoya noted the curtains in the windows, a woman walking home with her groceries, a housekeeper sweeping a stoop. Ordinary people, living ordinary lives. They did their shopping, ate their meals, lay down at night thinking of the health of their children or the work waiting to be done in the morning. Could they find a way to give this peace, this ease, to Ravka? Would there ever be a time when Grisha were free to choose their paths instead of living as soldiers? It was something worth fighting for.

They arrived at an elegant mansion with red tulips painted over the entry. Brekker rapped twice on the front door with the head of his cane.

Zoya recognized the young man who popped his head out— Jesper Fahey. They'd met him when they'd last been forced to work with Brekker's crew. He was brown-skinned and gray-eyed and wore his hair shaved close to the scalp. If memory served, he was some kind of expert sharpshooter.

"I'm not supposed to let you in," Jesper said.

Brekker seemed unperturbed. "Why not?"

"Because every time I do, you ask me to break the law."

A voice from behind Jesper said, "The problem isn't that he asks, it's that you always say yes."

"But look who he brought," Jesper said, gazing at Nikolai with delight. "The man with the flying ships. Come in! Come in!"

Jesper threw open the door, revealing a grand entryway and his shockingly bright combination of turquoise waistcoat and houndstooth trousers. The ensemble shouldn't have worked, but Zoya was forced to admit it did. He could give Count Kirigin some lessons.

"I've been keeping up on your exploits, Captain Sturmhond," Jesper whispered conspiratorially.

Kaz Brekker had sussed out Nikolai's real identity at their first meeting long ago, but Zoya didn't think he'd shared it with his crew. They all still believed they were dealing with the legendary Sturmhond, rather than Ravka's king.

"You should join up with us sometime," Nikolai said smoothly. "We can always use a sharpshooter aboard."

"Really?"

"Are you forgetting how much you hate the open sea?" asked a slender boy with ruddy gold curls and luminous blue eyes. Wylan . . . something. She couldn't remember his last name, only that Genya had helped to tailor him as part of their plan to secure Kuwei Yul-Bo and his knowledge of *jurda parem*.

"I can change," said Jesper. "I'm extremely adaptable."

They followed Wylan and Jesper across a cluttered parlor strewn with musical instruments in various states of repair and a desktop littered with what looked like tiny piles of gunpowder. Through the tall windows, Zoya glimpsed a garden and a woman painting at an easel, and beyond her the slow-moving gray waters of the Geldcanal.

The house had the starchy lines and precision of any rich merchant household in Ketterdam, but it felt as if it had been taken over by a combination of circus performers, street hooligans, and mad scientists. The dining room table was laden with paints and newly strung canvases as well as what seemed to be the bits and pieces of some kind of chemistry experiment.

Zoya picked up a swatch of fabric that looked like the color had been bled from it. "Is there a Fabrikator living here?"

"A friend of ours," said Jesper, throwing his lanky frame down in a chair. "An indenture who likes to pop by for meals. Quite the sponger."

"Has he never been trained? The work seems rudimentary."

Jesper sniffed. "I thought it had a certain rustic elegance."

"No," said Wylan. "He hasn't been trained. He's stubborn that way."

"Independent," corrected Jesper.

"Pigheaded."

"But stylish."

Kaz rapped his cane on the floor. "And now you know why I don't visit more often."

Jesper folded his arms. "No one asked you to visit more often. And I don't remember issuing an invitation for lunch."

"I have a job that requires both of your skill sets."

"Kaz," Wylan said, carefully collecting some of the half-full glasses around the room. "We'd prefer not to do anything illegal."

"That's not strictly true," said Jesper. "Wylan would prefer it, and I want to keep Wylan happy." He paused, unable to hide his interest. "*Is* it illegal?"

"Highly," said Kaz.

"But the pay is excellent," offered Nikolai.

"We don't need money," said Wylan.

"Isn't it glorious?" Jesper sighed happily.

Kaz smoothed a gloved hand over his lapel, looking at no one. "It's for Inej."

Wylan set down the dirty glasses. "Why didn't you say so? What do you need?"

"To break into the base at Rentveer and misappropriate a very large supply of titanium."

"That shouldn't be a problem," said Jesper, clearing a space on the table, as Wylan rolled out a long sheet of paper beside a map of the Kerch coastline. "Their security is terrible."

Nikolai raised a brow. "Mister Brekker led us to believe the job was nearly impossible."

Zoya scowled. "He wanted to drive up his rate."

"Thank you, Jesper," said Kaz sourly.

Jesper shrugged. "What can I say? I have a naturally honest disposition."

"And I have a golden top hat," grumbled Kaz.

"If you did, I would borrow it," said Jesper. "Now, the first question is how we move that many pounds of metal."

Nikolai nodded. "We have an airship docked on Vellgeluck."

"Of course you do."

"It's equipped with cables and winches and can manage a big cargo load."

Kaz pointed to the map. "The base is located on a scrawny spit of land that juts out into the sea. The weather there is perpetually bad. High winds, rain."

"I can manage that," said Zoya. She could silence a storm as easily as she could summon one.

"The problem is getting any boots on the ground inside the base. There's an armed checkpoint blocking the road in, and we don't have time to gin up fake credentials."

"Not to mention, we're all extremely recognizable," Wylan said.

Kaz lifted a shoulder. "One of the unfortunate side effects of success."

"Is there any chance we can approach by sea?" asked Nikolai.

"There's no safe place to land even if you're flying Kerch flags. Our only way in is to create a distraction for the guards and disable the spotlights in the towers. Then we just cut through the fence."

"Sounds like an opportunity to be noisy," said Jesper, fingers tapping the table in an eager rhythm.

"Like I said," Kaz continued, "we have need of your particular skill sets. Once we enter, we can locate the titanium and signal our people in the air. But we'll need a way to cover the sound of the airship moving into place."

"I can provide some rolling thunder," said Zoya. "How is it you know so much about how to get into this place?"

Nikolai grinned. "Because he was thinking about stealing the titanium himself."

"Truly? What possible use could you have for so much titanium?"

Kaz's gaze was cool. "If someone wants it, I can sell it. It's as simple as that."

Maybe, thought Zoya. Or maybe Kaz was like Nikolai, a boy with an unquiet mind, a man in perpetual need of challenge. He'd decided the base was a puzzle and he couldn't resist finding its solution.

"One question," said Wylan. "What are you going to use the titanium for?"

"Why does it matter?" asked Nikolai.

"Because unlike Kaz, I have a conscience."

"I have a conscience," said Kaz. "It just knows when to keep its mouth shut."

Jesper snorted. "If you have a conscience, it's gagged and tied to a chair somewhere."

"This is a lot of metal," said Wylan, unwilling to let the subject go. "You're going to use it to build a weapon, aren't you?"

Zoya waited. It was up to Nikolai to decide what to disclose to this little band of monsters.

To her surprise, he reached into his coat pocket and tossed a sheaf of papers onto the table. David's rocket schematics.

Wylan unrolled them, his eyes moving rapidly over the plans. "These are missiles. You need the titanium to improve their range."

"Yes."

"And you want to build something bigger."

Now Nikolai looked surprised. "Yes. Maybe."

"This is for Ravka. Because of the bombing at Os Alta. You blockaded Fjerda for them and now you're helping them build a weapon."

"That bombing was a test. It was meant to provoke. If Ravka doesn't respond, Fjerda will know they can't. They'll march and they'll keep marching until every Ravkan is under Fjerdan rule and every Grisha has been thrown into a cell."

"Or worse," added Zoya.

Jesper went to the sideboard and pulled a gun belt from the drawer. He slid twin pearl-handled revolvers into their holsters. "When do we leave?"

But Wylan looked less sure.

"This titanium could stop a war," Nikolai said.

Wylan ran a finger over one of the schematics. "And you can really arm and aim these things?"

"We can. Mostly. Hopefully."

"I have some ideas," said Wylan. "The problem is the nozzles, right?"

"Nozzles?" said Jesper.

"Yes," said Nikolai. "For launching and directing the rocket."

"That is a ridiculous word," said Jesper.

"It's an accurate word," objected Wylan. "And slightly ridiculous. May I?"

Nikolai nodded, and Wylan began to sketch something onto the schematic.

Zoya felt a sudden sharp sting to her heart. It was too easy to imagine David in this room, his head bent over those plans, the pleasure he would have felt encountering another person who could speak his language. She knew from the look in Nikolai's eyes that he was thinking the exact same thing. The knowledge of what they'd lost was like a tether between them, a hook in both of their hearts. Maybe she shouldn't have asked to be reassigned to Os Kervo. She wanted to work with him for the future they both dreamed of. She wanted to build a peace with him. Even when he married, she could stay at the palace, serve by his side. That was the right choice, the noble one—and the thought of it made her feel like snatching a bottle of whiskey from the sideboard and downing the whole thing. It didn't help that the idea of losing her hadn't seemed to bother

Nikolai a bit. *That's good*, she told herself. *That's the way it should be.* And what was there to lose, really? They were compatriots, friends; anything else was illusion, as cheap and false as the performances on East Stave.

"We should get started," she said briskly. "We have a lot of ground to cover."

It took another few hours to hash out what they intended, get the supplies they needed, and message the *Cormorant*. The plan seemed easy enough, and that made Zoya nervous. Wylan and Jesper would ride ahead to gather ground intelligence, then meet them at a bay only a few miles from the base. It was the easiest place for Zoya to board the *Cormorant* so that she and her Squallers could guide it into position over the base once Kaz and Nikolai were inside. Sturmhond's *Volkvolny* would remain docked at Fifth Harbor lest any accusations fly after the robbery. Though if all went according to plan, there would be no outcry, no alarm. They would be in and out of the base without anyone knowing, and the stockpile of titanium would appear as plentiful as before. Only now, most of it would be aluminum.

"I don't think it's fair that I don't get to ride in the airship," Jesper said as Kaz hustled them out of the dining room.

Nikolai winked. "The king of Ravka will be grateful for what you're doing, and he has plenty of airships. Os Alta's gates will always open to you."

"To all Grisha," Zoya murmured as she drifted past. If Jesper wanted to hide his gift, that was his business, but the dragon had smelled his power the minute they'd entered the house. Zoya couldn't blame him for wanting to keep his abilities secret, to live his life full of love and misadventure without forever looking over his shoulder. Maybe someday being Grisha wouldn't mean being a target.

Kaz, Zoya, and Nikolai traveled to the bay by oxcart. Jesper had told them there were new motorized trucks that had appeared among some of the wealthier merchant families, but they were useless in the narrow streets of the city. Besides, they wanted to be as quiet and inconspicuous as possible.

As soon as they arrived at the cliffs Kaz had proposed for their meetup with the *Cormorant*, Zoya felt something was off. In the distance, she could see the lights of the naval base twinkling through the fog. But here on the cliff tops, there was an eerie quality to the mist rolling in, and her dragon's mind stirred as if recognizing danger. She could only hope that ancient intelligence would stay quiet. She couldn't afford the emotional cost of the dragon's eye opening, not when they had a mission to complete.

Far below, the beach was little more than a sliver of sand, bright and slender as a crescent moon. Waves broke against thickets of white rocks, jagged, hulking phantoms gathered at the shore as if to stand vigil. *They're guarding this place*, Zoya thought. No boat was meant to find safe harbor here. *And we're not meant to be here either.* If the beach outside the naval base was anything like this, Zoya could see why no one attempted to approach from the water. The wind howled over the cliffs, a mournful chorus.

"Going to be tough to bring the airship over the base and have it hover," said Kaz. "There's no way we'll be able to get cargo up and down the lines."

Zoya lifted a hand, settling warmth and calm around them as the wind stilled. "That won't be a problem once I'm aboard."

"Be as subtle as you can," instructed Nikolai. "We don't want the guards realizing they're in the eye of a storm."

"Somehow I'll manage it."

Hoofbeats signaled the arrival of two riders.

"We have a problem," said Jesper, sliding from his horse with ease. Wylan dismounted slowly, clearly less accustomed to the task. "They've locked down the goods."

"How?" asked Kaz.

"There's some kind of new metal shell they've installed, protects cargo from the elements."

Zoya frowned. "Titanium doesn't rust."

"But there's other cargo in the yard on base," said Kaz. "Iron. Potentially lumber that will rot if it gets wet. They used to just secure everything with tarps, but I guess the military is getting more particular."

"This wasn't part of the intelligence you gathered?" Zoya asked, her temper rising.

"It must have been installed in the last three weeks. And when you rush a job, you don't get to complain when the job goes wrong."

"You take your time or you take your chances," said Jesper.

"And I don't take chances," added Kaz.

Zoya flicked her braid over her shoulder. "You're telling me you can't get past a metal roof?"

"Of course I can. But with a bigger crew. This isn't a bank vault, it's a military base. If Jesper and Wylan are handling the watchtowers, I'll need to get inside, locate whatever mechanism opens the shell, and get it to work without anyone in the base noticing. We don't know where the guards are posted inside or what kind of alarms are rigged up. Assuming we could even get inside, we'd need time to suss it out and at least two lookouts."

"Surely the greatest thief in Ketterdam can outthink such a problem," said Nikolai.

"I'm not susceptible to flattery, only stacks of cash. This can't be done, not if you want it quiet and bloodless. If you're willing to take out a few guards or let Wylan blow a hole in this thing—"

"No," said Nikolai firmly. "Ravka's relationship with Kerch is strained enough, I don't want to give them an excuse to ditch their neutrality and use the *izmars'ya* to help Fjerda break my blockade."

"If Inej were here—" said Jesper.

Kaz's gaze was hard as flint. "You can keep saying that, but she isn't. The best we can do is wait. I can get two more Dregs here by tomorrow. Anika. Rotty, maybe."

A high wail sounded from somewhere in the distance, a shrill cry that might be human or animal or something else entirely. Zoya felt a chill pass through her that had nothing to do with the cold. *This place isn't meant for us.* She felt it in her bones.

"Saints," said Jesper, "what was that?"

Another wail followed, long and piercing. The fog seemed to seethe around them, forming shapes that melted into nothing before Zoya could truly make them out.

Jesper set his hands on his revolvers. "These cliffs are supposed to be haunted."

"You don't actually believe that," said Wylan.

"I believe in all kinds of things. Ghosts. Gnomes. True love."

Now another sound—a low hiss—seemed to crawl up from the sea, rising and falling in undulating waves. Zoya felt it like fingers brushing up her spine, making the hair on her arms rise.

"Enough," she snapped. She'd had all she could stand of this Saintsforsaken country. She lifted her hands and the fog rolled back in a gust—revealing a circle of people around them, some of them in jackal masks, others with dark scarves pulled up to hide their faces. Moonlight glinted off the barrels of their guns.

"Suli," whispered Jesper.

"You're not welcome in this place," said a gruff voice. It was impossible to tell which side of the circle it had come from. That same low, crawling hiss followed.

"We don't mean any harm," Jesper began.

"That's why you snuck up on our camp in the dead of night?"

"We should let the sea have them," said another voice. "Send them screaming over the cliff tops."

"My apologies," Nikolai said, stepping forward. "We had no intention of—"

Click click click. Like fingers snapping. The sound of triggers being cocked.

"No," said Zoya, putting a hand out to stop him. "Don't apologize. That will only make it worse."

"I see," said Nikolai. "Then what *is* protocol for an ambush?"

Zoya turned to the circle. "Our goal is to stop a war. But this place was not ours to trespass on."

"Perhaps you came looking for death," said another voice.

Zoya reached for the words her father had taught her, that she hadn't spoken since she was a child. Even then, they had only been whispered. Her mother hadn't wanted Suli spoken in their house. *"Mati en sheva yelu."*

This action will have no echo. The phrase felt sticky and unfamiliar on her tongue. She sensed Nikolai's surprise, felt the stares of the others.

"You speak Suli like a tax collector," said a man's voice.

"Hush," said a woman in a jackal mask, stepping forward. "We see you, *zheji.*"

Zheji. Daughter. The word knocked the breath from her, an unexpected blow. The mask was the type worn all over the Barrel, but those were cheap knockoffs, souvenirs for tourists who didn't know what they meant. Among the Suli, the jackal mask was sacred and worn only by true seers. *Daughter*. It wasn't a word she'd wanted from the mother who had betrayed her, so why should it mean so much from the lips of a stranger?

"We see the walls raised round your heart," the woman continued. "That's what comes of living far from home." The jackal turned, surveying them. "Shadows all around."

"What did you say?" Nikolai asked Zoya beneath his breath. "How do you know those words?"

A hundred lies came to her lips, a hundred easy ways to walk away from this, to keep being the person she'd always been.

"Because I'm Suli." Simple words, but she'd never said them aloud. She could feel her mother's hands combing out her hair, placing a hat on her head to keep her out of the sun. *You're pale like me. You have my eyes. You can pass.* The family had kept her mother's name so that they wouldn't draw attention. Nabri, her father's name, was rubbed away like a stain.

It was as if the woman in the jackal mask had heard her thoughts. "Your father faded as we all do when we don't live among our own."

"I haven't," Zoya said. A protest? A plea? She hated the tremble in her voice. These people didn't know her. They had no right to speak about her family.

"But think how brightly you might have burned if you hadn't always walked in shadow." She waved them forward. "Come with us."

"Are they going to march us to our death now?" asked Jesper.

"No idea," said Kaz.

Jesper cursed. "I wish I'd worn a nicer suit."

"Might be worth playing the king card now," Kaz said to Nikolai. "Don't you think?"

"What king card?" asked Wylan.

The jackal's voice carried through the mist. "There are no kings we recognize here."

"I might find that humbling," said Nikolai. "If I'd any practice with humility."

They descended a long path down the cliffside as the wind shrieked up from the water. Zoya's heart thumped wildly, a small creature caught in a snare. This was panic—skittering, mindless panic. *Why?* She knew Nikolai didn't disdain the Suli. He never would. And she didn't care what these Barrel rats thought. So why did she feel as if the rock was about to crumble beneath her feet? Just because she'd told them what she was? Was that all it took? Was this the terror of being seen?

Halfway down, they passed behind a boulder, and Zoya saw the entrance to a cave, its yawning black mouth carved into the side of the cliff.

Again the jackal spoke. "If you wish to enter the base, this tunnel runs under the watchtowers and opens in a basement beneath Rentveer."

"Where did it come from?" asked Nikolai.

But Kaz didn't seem surprised. "The Kerch used Suli labor to build the base."

"We always leave a back door," said the woman in the jackal mask. "There are two guards who patrol past the entrance to the basement. The rest is up to you. Daughter, you may use the cliffs to board your ship."

"Why are you helping us?" Zoya asked.

"Can't we just say thank you and be on our way?" said Jesper.

The jackal-masked woman drew Zoya aside. "Your heart does not belong to you alone. When this is over, when it is *all* over, remember where you came from."

"The king—"

"I speak of queens, not kings, tonight. Remember, daughter." Then she vanished into the shadows.

Suddenly, they were alone at the tunnel mouth. The Suli were gone.

Zoya whirled on Kaz. "You knew, didn't you? You never planned to go through the fence at the base. You knew the Suli were camped here. You knew they had a way in."

Kaz was already limping into the tunnel. "I don't walk through a door unless I know there's a window to climb out of. Jesper, Wylan, get back to the cliffs and take out the spotlights. Nikolai and I will tackle the metal shell from inside."

"How could you be sure I spoke Suli?" she called after him.

"That was a spin of Makker's Wheel. Lucky for me, my number came up."

"One day your luck will run out, Mister Brekker."

"Then I'll just have to make some more." He paused and turned to look back over his shoulder at her. "The Suli never forget their own, General Nazyalensky. Just like crows."

29
MAYU

MAYU CRUMPLED TO THE FLOOR as Reyem rose
out of his sleeping chamber. He still had her hand crushed in his fist.
The pain was beyond anything she'd ever known, wildfire searing
her veins.

Silver flashed across her vision and she saw an axe lodge itself in
Reyem's forearm.

He released her and launched himself across the room at Tamar.

Tamar hurled another axe, mere distraction as her hands curled
into fists. Reyem clutched his chest, then seemed to shake off the
Heartrender's power and charged forward.

He slammed into Tamar and her body struck the wall with a terrible clang.

She hit the floor but was back on her feet in an instant.

"Get Ehri out!" she snarled at Mayu.

But how? She had one good hand and Makhi stood between her and the door, surrounded by her Tavgharad. Mayu drew her talon sword awkwardly with her left hand. She scanned the walls, looking for another exit,

"The floor," Bergin said, his voice hoarse, as if even the effort of speaking fatigued him. "There's a sluiceway."

Of course. The drains had to go somewhere.

"Get behind me!" she said to the princess, and brought her boot down hard on the nearest grate—once, twice. It gave way. "Go! I'll hold them off."

Mayu shoved Ehri into the drain, hoping the princess had the sense to run as far and as fast as she could.

"Stop her," Makhi commanded. "And dose the Ravkan traitor with *parem*."

Mayu planted her body, trying to block the Tavgharad, but they barreled through her and leapt into the sewer after Ehri. The doctor lunged for a control panel. He pulled one of the levers, and a cloud of orange mist gusted from the vent nearest Tamar.

Tamar shouted and tried to dodge it, but Reyem grabbed her and threw her to the ground, his pincers pinning her arms as she fought to keep from inhaling the poison.

"No!" Mayu cried. She knew Tamar had antidote in her pocket, but Tamar was trapped by Reyem. There was no way for her to reach it.

"Another volunteer for the cause," said the queen.

Mayu scrambled for Tamar.

Reyem struck her; his fists felt like rocks. They must have been buttressed with metal. He grabbed her by her collar. Mayu knew he was going to throw her. She would break her ribs, maybe her skull.

"Reyem!" she cried. "Please."

"Dje janin ess! Scön der top!"

Reyem froze.

"Scön der top!" Bergin repeated, his fragile body shaking.

Mayu had no idea what it meant. She didn't speak Fjerdan, and as far as she knew, Reyem didn't either.

"What are you waiting for?" Queen Makhi shouted. "I'll wake all my monsters if I have to. There will be no mercy. There will be no escape." She pressed a sequence of buttons and the lids of the sarcophagi opened. "Who will save you now?"

Reyem's head snapped up, as if he had at last woken from a long, terrible dream.

"I will," he growled. He dropped Mayu with a thud and retracted his pincers, freeing Tamar. She grabbed a pellet of powder from her pocket and shoved it in her mouth, her body convulsing.

Reyem leapt up and seized the doctor, slamming him against the wall, smashing the controls as if the metal were driftwood. He whirled on Makhi's two remaining Tavgharad. They strode forward to meet him, their blades flashing, but they were no match for the weapon Reyem had become.

He didn't bother deflecting the attacks. It was as if he didn't even feel the slash of their blades. He seized each guard by the throat and hurled them against the wall beside their queen. They slumped to the ground, and Mayu knew they would not rise again. Reyem grabbed the queen around the neck.

"Who will save you now?" he bit out.

"Locust!" shouted the doctor.

But he wasn't Locust anymore.

"Set her down," Tamar said, coughing, her face damp with sweat. "We can't kill her, much as I might like to in this moment."

"Reyem?" Mayu asked, not certain if he would hear or obey her.

He dropped the queen in an unceremonious heap, then smashed the controls that would have allowed her to close the other sleeping chambers.

Makhi lay on the floor, gasping for breath.

Reyem turned. "Mayu." His face was haunted. He was her brother and yet he wasn't. There was a stillness in him, a coldness that hadn't existed before. "I knew you would come."

A sob shook Mayu and she ran to him. Her broken hand throbbed as she threw her arms around her brother. His body felt strange, the hard lines of his wings folded against his back. Her mind couldn't quite make sense of it. Her twin. *Kebben.*

"Bergin," Reyem said to the Fjerdan Grisha. "Are you all right?"

"No." Bergin was shaking badly. "I need . . . please."

"He needs another dose of *parem*," said Reyem.

Tamar rose, limping slightly. "Try this instead." She handed him a pellet of antidote.

"What is it?"

"Freedom."

Bergin placed the pellet in his mouth and chewed slowly. His body started to spasm.

Reyem went to him, bracing Bergin's emaciated body against his massive frame. "What's happening to him? What did you give him?" His voice was hard as iron.

"Antidote," said Tamar. "Whatever is in the *parem* he was dosed with is strong. I felt it too, but I didn't get a full dose, and his body is weakened. He'll be okay."

Shouts sounded from below, the sound of the Tavgharad returning, no doubt with Ehri in tow.

Tamar grabbed Makhi by the front of her gown and propped her against the wall. "Call back your falcons. Tell them to bring Ehri." Despite everything it troubled Mayu to see a Taban queen treated so roughly.

"I'll tell them to choke her where she stands."

"No doubt you would have already if you thought you could get away with it. But Ehri dying would be tough to explain to your ministers, wouldn't it?"

Mayu could see the queen weighing her options, calculating her next move.

"Bring her up!" Makhi shouted at last.

The Tavgharad emerged through the grate, covered in blood and muck. They dragged Ehri up behind them, keeping her arms restrained. She couldn't have gotten far in the tunnels.

In the distance, Mayu heard the thrum of what might have been an airship engine.

Princess Ehri looked around, taking in Tamar, the queen, the unconscious doctor. "Did we . . . did we win?"

Queen Makhi began to laugh. "'Did we win?'" she singsonged. "This is the fool who seeks to decide the fate of a nation? What do you think you've accomplished here tonight? There are no ministers here to witness my supposed crimes. By the time you rally them, I'll have the *khergud* transported and this facility burned to the ground."

"We're not going to give you that chance," said Mayu.

"I am a *queen*. Is that so hard to grasp? Do you think you can just march me back to the palace with your Ravkan bodyguard? They'll hang you for a traitor. I have troops surrounding this building, and any messenger you send will be intercepted. So to answer your question, little sister: No, you haven't won."

"Look around you, Makhi," Ehri said. "Is this what you want your legacy to be? Torture?"

"What you call torture, I call science. If I were building tanks like the Fjerdans or missiles like the Ravkans, would you find that more palatable? People die. That is what war is."

Reyem slammed his fist into the wall, leaving a deep dent. "To be *khergud* is to die a thousand times."

"You had no right," said Mayu, rage coursing through her. "You are a queen, not a god."

Makhi drew in a breath, looking down her nose at all of them. There could be no doubt she had been born to rule. "It was not my right. It was my *duty*. To make my country strong."

"You need bear the burden of that duty no longer."

They all turned. Leyti Kir-Taban, Daughter of Heaven and Taban queen, entered the laboratory, dressed in a gown of green velvet embroidered with roses the color of flame. She was surrounded by her Tavgharad, some of them with hair as gray as hers, and by Grisha in their gem-colored *kefta*.

"Grandmother?" Makhi said, blinking as if she might clear the image from her eyes. "But you were at your palace."

"I am not quite the fool you think I am," Princess Ehri said gently. "I never would have left our grandmother at the Palace of the Thousand Stars. I know you too well for that. As soon as Tamar's scouts saw you had called for the *khergud*, we sent word to our grandmother's hiding place."

Mayu remembered the two riders dressed as peasants. *To the queen*, Tamar had said. Mayu had assumed she meant Makhi.

Leyti gave a nod of confirmation. "I thank you for the use of your airship, Tamar Kir-Bataar."

"It is Ravka's honor," Tamar said with a bow.

Makhi tried to straighten her gown. "There's been a misunderstanding."

"I understand quite well," said Queen Leyti. "I assert my right as Taban queen and rescind my blessing. The crown is yours no longer."

30
NINA

GELIDBEL WAS THE CROWNING EVENT of Heartwood, the last formal ball before proposals were issued.

Brum had been as good as his word and had secured new fabrics for Mila Jandersdat's gowns. Most had been modest and understated. But the ball gown Nina wore tonight was all sparkling silver; dagger-shaped beads like icicles shifted with her every move. Her figure wasn't suited to the long, high-waisted styles popular in Fjerda, but the dress was beautiful.

I'd rather be in a kefta, Nina thought as she looked in the mirror. Her country was on the brink of war and she was stuffed into a ball gown and velvet slippers.

"You look like a winter morning," said Hanne, who came to stand beside her.

"And you look like dragon's gold."

Hanne's gown bordered on the scandalous, sheer panels of amber silk alternating with tiny beads that glistened like droplets of molten gold. It was impossible to tell what was fabric and what was skin. Ylva's dressmakers had outdone themselves.

But Hanne kept her eyes on Nina, avoiding her own reflection. "I'll take your word for it." She smoothed the folds of her gown, then curled her fingertips, as if the feeling of the silk over her skin displeased her.

"Hanne, what's wrong? You look like magic."

"It isn't . . . that isn't me." Hanne closed her eyes and shook her head. "Do you know the one thing I miss about the convent?"

"The Wellmother's warm and loving disposition?"

A smile quirked Hanne's lips, and Nina felt a rush of relief. She could feel the pain radiating from her and she didn't understand why.

"No mirrors," Hanne said. "We weren't meant to be vain or care about our appearance. But this house? I feel like there's a mirror on every wall."

"Hanne—"

"Don't say I look beautiful. Please."

"Okay, but don't cry," Nina said helplessly. She brushed a tear from Hanne's cheek with her thumb. "You'll be blotchy for the party."

"Cry?" said Ylva, bustling through the doorway. "Is something wrong?"

Nina and Hanne jumped at the sound of her voice, and Nina felt a flush heat her face, as if she'd been caught at something.

Hanne mustered a smile and said, "I don't think Papa is going to approve of this gown."

"Heartwood is not about your father's approval," Ylva said, beaming. "You will be the talk of the ball, and that can only be good for securing a husband."

Saints, Nina couldn't stand those words. They'd been playing a game with Heartwood and it hadn't been without its victories, but what would the end of it mean for Hanne?

They gathered their wraps and joined Ylva to wend their way to the palace. Brum was nowhere to be seen, and Nina wondered if he was hunting Magnus Opjer or if Fjerda's royal family even knew that their most valuable prisoner was missing.

The ball was held in the same cavernous room where they'd first met the prince, but the place was nearly unrecognizable. White trumpet lilies crowded every surface, wound around columns, twined in chandeliers, their petals spread like bursts of fireworks, their sweet scent thick in the air. Nina felt like she was walking through a tide of honey. Had these flowers simply come from Fjerdan hothouses or had Grisha power made them bloom?

Musicians played, and the buzz of laughter and talk rose and fell in giddy waves. It was as if no one cared a war was looming. *No*, she realized, *it's that they're not afraid. They know they're going to win.* The king and queen sat their thrones, watching the proceedings with impassive faces. Nina saw prayer beads clutched in the queen's left hand.

At the center of the room, above the fountain consecrated to Djel, hung a huge wreath of lilies and green ash boughs. This was life in winter, the Wellspring as the father of renewal, the flowers symbolizing fertility. Nina glanced at Hanne, at the other girls who had been presented at Heartwood, all displayed in their finery, blossoms in their hair. This was the last moment of their girlhood, before they were expected to become wives and mothers.

"They're eager," she said, more than a little surprised.

Hanne's eyes roamed over the girls—some talking, others standing nervously beside their mothers or chaperones, trying to keep from mussing their hair in the heat of the ballroom. "They want to make their parents proud, stop being a burden on their families, manage households of their own."

"And you?" Nina asked.

"Honestly?"

"Of course."

Hanne cast her a single glance. "I want to throw you onto my horse and ride as fast and as far away from here as we can get. Not sidesaddle."

Before Nina could even think of a reply, Hanne was drifting toward the refreshments table.

Nina watched the long line of her back. She had that same startled feeling she'd had when Joran discovered her in the *drüskelle* sector. Did Hanne mean it? Or had she just been joking? Nina set her hands on her hips. She damned well intended to ask. Because yes, she was a soldier and a spy and her duty belonged to Ravka, but . . . but the idea of riding into a new world with Hanne Brum was not a chance you just let slip by.

No sooner was Nina at Hanne's side than Joran appeared to take them to the prince. Ylva shooed them on their way with a happy smile and a wink. She was delighted at the attention her daughter had garnered from Prince Rasmus. Hanne and Nina had visited with him every day this week, and Hanne had begun to heal the prince aggressively. There were talks of an alliance forming between Fjerda and West Ravka to unseat Nikolai, and Nina had to hope that a healthy prince might dare to face Brum and finally assert himself as a king-to-be. If she just had a little more time, she might be able to turn both Rasmus and his mother toward peace.

As for Joran, Nina knew that if he'd spoken a word to Jarl Brum, she would have long since been dragged away in chains. The prince's guard gave no indication of what he'd seen or the conversation they'd shared.

The crown prince had staked out an entire corner of the ballroom to himself beneath an arched alcove. The lilies were so heavy here it was as if they'd entered some kind of enchanted bower, and Rasmus looked every inch the fairy prince, lording over the caves of Istamere. His color was high, his shoulders straight. Quite a change from the week before, when he'd suddenly lost so much of his vigor. Nina almost felt guilty, but that feeling evaporated when she thought of the bombs that had fallen on Os Alta, when she remembered him striking Joran, that excited laugh escaping his lips. He held court amid a group of lords and ladies but had eyes only for Hanne as she approached.

"All the works of Djel," the prince exclaimed. "You look extraordinary, Hanne."

Hanne curtsied and smiled, any hint of wild rebellion, of galloping away from the Ice Court to freedom, gone. Despite her short hair and her scandalous gown, she radiated demure Fjerdan womanhood. What an actress she'd become. Nina hated it.

"Go," said Rasmus, waving his hand at the courtiers who had gathered around him. "I want no distraction from gazing at this marvelous creature."

The nobles left with a few knowing glances directed Hanne's way, but they made no objections, accustomed to obeying the prince's whims.

"You look well too, Enke Jandersdat," said Joran as Hanne and Nina settled on the low chairs before Rasmus.

"Poor Joran," said the prince. "Do you think I've been rude ignoring Mila in her cheap silver sparkles?" Joran's cheeks flamed bright red, and Rasmus' brows rose. "Has my loyal guard been struck by an infatuation? She's too old for you, Joran, and you're here to be my vicious bodyguard, not moon over a fishwife."

Nina gave a merry laugh. She didn't care what the prince thought of her, and she understood that the remark about her gown was a jab at Brum, who had paid for it.

"Now you *are* being unkind, Your Highness," she said. "But I am happy to orbit Hanne's sun. You're looking very well yourself, if I may say so."

"You may—though you will make our friend Joran jealous. Perhaps you should pay him a compliment too."

Nina smiled at Joran. *Your secret is safe with me.* "You look slightly less stern tonight, Joran."

"Does he?" Prince Rasmus mused. "Maybe a bit around the forehead."

"It's quite a crush tonight," said Hanne. "I've never seen this ballroom so full."

"They all want to gawk at me, and I'm happy to let them. And of course, everyone wants to talk about the war."

"I see Vadik Demidov here, but not the Apparat," said Nina.

"Demidov is happiest at a party, eating someone else's food and drinking someone else's wine. As for the priest, he's been most secretive lately. Your father isn't happy about it. He wants my family to banish him back to Ravka or the underside of whatever rock will have him."

A glorious idea, thought Nina. The less she saw of the priest, the better.

"And what will your family do?" Nina asked.

Rasmus grimaced. "My mother has become strangely superstitious and won't part with the priest. She's in Djel's chapel day and night."

I just bet. But Nina left it to Hanne to say, "Oh?"

Rasmus lowered his voice and leaned in. "She doesn't want to let Brum bomb any more civilian targets. She's talking like some kind of peasant who claims to see the face of Djel in a loaf of bread. Saying that the spirits of the dead spoke to her and that Djel will make me sick again—just because I backslid a bit."

Hanne's eyes dropped guiltily away and she touched her fingers to a spray of lilies in a silver vase.

"Perhaps it's superstition," said Nina. "But if it was Brum's choice to bomb the city, you could choose a new policy and show him you have other plans for Fjerda's future."

"Interesting," Rasmus said, assessing first Nina and then Hanne. "The fishwife has discovered politics. She's criticizing your father's strategies, Hanne. What do you think of that?"

Hanne cocked her head to the side, considering. "I think strong men show strength, but great men show strength tempered by compassion."

Rasmus laughed. "You have a gift for diplomacy, Hanne Brum. And I do like taking a larger role in our military decisions. Though I can tell you our generals were most surprised to see me join their meetings."

That was good. At least Nina hoped so. *Better than Brum. That's all we need.* Strength tempered by compassion. A prince who might choose peace over war if given the chance.

"I'm glad you felt well enough to attend," said Hanne.

"I admit I enjoyed it. We spent most of the time discussing plans for a fascinating addition to our armory."

"A new weapon?" Nina asked. Were those the plans labeled *Songbird* she'd seen on Brum's desk?

"Something like that. But let's not talk of war and stuffy commanders."

"It's good for them to remember who will rule our country," said Hanne.

Rasmus sat a bit straighter, looking satisfied. "Yes. They should remember, much as some would like to forget. I'll have you know I've danced three times already this night. You and I will have a dance later, Hanne. I cannot wait to shock the court with your dress."

"I'd be honored, Your Highness."

"Everyone says that. But it's not always so. The court ladies used to suffer through their dances with me. I couldn't keep up. I ended each dance wheezing. I was something to be endured, like a child's piano recital."

Hanne's expression was thoughtful. "I know that feeling well. Every time a soldier asked me to dance, I knew it was just an attempt to curry favor with my father. Each minute I spent with them, I could tell how anxious they were to be away from me."

"Because you were too tall, too strong. We are opposite sides of the mirror. Perhaps we should take to the floor now and truly make them talk."

Hanne laughed. "But they're not playing music to dance to."

"If His Royal Highness wishes to dance, then they will."

He offered her his hand and Hanne took it, smiling. Nina felt something in her heart twist. *Oh, that's small of you, Zenik. It's not as if you and Hanne could have had a future here.* Hanne could talk of riding off somewhere, but that was just nerves speaking, the prospect of facing down another party, another night of idle small talk. She wouldn't abandon Fjerda and Nina wouldn't abandon Ravka. And when Nina's mission was complete? She certainly wasn't going to remain in this simpering disguise at the Fjerdan court.

Nina watched Hanne and Prince Rasmus drift into the sea of bodies as the musicians struck up a swaying rhythm. She loved to dance and she was good at it. Or she had been. She hadn't been free to dance for a long time—or sing, or behave as she wished. *Be glad for Hanne. Be glad for both of them.* She bit her lip. She was trying, damn it. Around Hanne, Rasmus' bitterness lost its edge;

Nina could see the glimmer of the man he might become if they could drain him of Fjerda's poison, of the demands it placed on its rulers and its men. And Hanne? It was easy to see what she'd sacrificed to become a girl who might garner the interest of a prince, but what had she gained? She'd spent her whole life being excluded. She didn't look like the delicate beauties of the court. She and Rasmus stood eye to eye, evenly matched in height and stature. But Hanne didn't have to look like everyone else. Now she walked among the Fjerdans, shining, unique, triumphant, an object of envy instead of scorn. *Wolf-blooded.*

"I need to thank you," Joran said, drawing Nina from her thoughts. "You could have revealed me to Brum. I'm grateful you didn't."

Nina knew she had to tread carefully. "Your faith isn't something to be ashamed of."

"How can you say that?"

With Joran, Nina could let the Mila mask slip a bit more. He didn't require the performance of servile bumbling that Brum or Rasmus did. "There's altogether too much shame in Fjerda. I don't see why you shouldn't take comfort from your Saints."

"Commander Brum says the Saints are false gods sent to turn us from Djel."

"Surely not all the Saints," Nina said, though she knew that was exactly what Brum meant. "Not Sënj Egmond, who built the Ice Court, or Sënje Ulla of the Waves."

"Brum doesn't believe they were Saints, only men and women blessed by Djel. He says if we open our doors to heathen religion, Djel will forsake us and Fjerda will be doomed."

Nina nodded slowly, as if considering. "I have heard there are cults of false Saints, like the Starless One. I've heard stories of the blight that some say is a sign of his return. Do you think his followers could gain a foothold here?"

"It's hard to believe, but . . . Brum says people are desperate for hope and will be taken in by any cheap spectacle."

Nina certainly hoped so. "And what of the miracles here? In Ravka? The men who were saved from drowning in Hjar? The bridge of bones in Ivets?"

"Theatrical fodder for feeble minds. That's what—"

"What Brum says, I know. Do you believe everything Commander Brum says?"

"That's what I was trained to do."

"But *do* you?"

Joran looked out at the dancers whirling on the floor. "You're angry because of . . . because of his behavior toward you."

"I am," Nina said, maybe the truest words she'd ever spoken in the Ice Court. "But you've begun to wonder too. What if Brum is wrong?"

"About what?"

Nina kept her voice even, conversational. "The Grisha. Djel. The way war should be waged. All of it."

Joran's face went ashen. "Then there is no hope for me."

"Not even among the Saints?"

"No," he said, his voice flat. "The Saints don't want a soul like mine."

Nina rose and went to him. There had to be a way to reach this boy. With the right prodding, he might even give up the secrets of Fjerda's new weapon. "All soldiers kill. And no soldier can say each death is righteous."

Joran turned, and Nina drew in a breath at the bleakness in his eyes. He looked like a man who had stopped searching for answers. He was alone on the ice and his heart was howling.

"You don't understand," he said.

"You might be surprised." She had done her fair share of killing.

"I murdered an unarmed man."

And Nina had let a horde of undead women tear the Wellmother to pieces. "Maybe so, but——"

Joran seized her arm. "He was my brother. He was a traitor. I shot him and left him to die in a foreign city. I——"

My brother. A traitor.

"Be silent," she gasped. Whatever Joran was going to say, she didn't want to hear it. She didn't want to know.

But Joran wouldn't stop. "He told me . . . He said there was so much in the world that I didn't have to be afraid of, if I would only open my eyes. And I did." His voice broke. "And I am afraid of *everything*."

The *drüskelle* had been in Ketterdam for the auction. They'd put a price on Matthias' head. Nina felt like she was falling. She was kneeling on the cobblestones, watching the light fade from Matthias' beautiful eyes. She was holding him, trying to keep him with her. He was dying in her arms.

"You *should* be afraid," Nina growled, shoving Joran into the shadows of the alcove, away from the eyes of the crowd. He was too startled to fight her, and in the next breath, she had the sharpened tip of a bone dart hovering above his jugular. "You should tremble in your bed and weep like the base coward you are. You are the man who killed Matthias Helvar. Say it."

His eyes were wide, confused. "I . . . Who are you?"

"*Say it.* I want your confession before I end your worthless life."

"Mila?"

Hanne's voice. She sounded so far away.

"What is this?" asked the prince.

Joran's hand closed over Nina's, hiding the bone dart. He forced her rigid body to turn. "I presumed upon Enke Jandersdat and she rightly put me in my place."

"Is this true?" asked the prince.

Nina couldn't speak. Her jaw felt wired shut. If she tried to wrench it open to speak, she would start screaming and she wouldn't stop.

Hanne came to her and wrapped an arm around her shoulders. "I should take her home."

"Don't be silly," said Prince Rasmus. "She's fine. It's not as if he put her up against the wall and lifted her skirts."

Hanne stared at him. "That's not the point."

"She's a widow, not an untried maiden, Hanne. Don't be difficult."

"Joran said—"

"Joran gave a lonely widow a little attention. It was probably a thrill for her."

Something shifted in Hanne's face, rage overtaking her beautiful features. "Does she look thrilled?"

Nina had no idea what she looked like in this moment. A ghost. A spirit sent to seek vengeance. A woman undone.

"Oh, Hanne, don't be such a killjoy. You're worse than one of my tutors."

"And you are being thoughtless and cruel."

All of the prince's warmth vanished. "Watch your tongue, Hanne Brum. I won't be bullied by you or your father."

Joran said, "The fault was all mine, Your Majesty. I can only beg Enke Jandersdat's forgiveness."

"I tell you when to beg," said Rasmus. "You serve no master but me." Then suddenly he was smiling. "Oh, everyone stop glowering and be merry. I shall be good and kind and patient—just as Hanne is. Joran, go fetch us something stronger than punch to drink."

Joran bowed and Nina clutched at Hanne's arm, afraid that if she let go, she would chase the guard down and wrap her hands around his throat.

"Now smile for me, Hanne. Sometimes princes are cruel. It's their prerogative."

Hanne's fingers tensed on Nina's arm, but she forced herself to smile and curtsy. "Of course, Your Highness."

I taught her that, Nina thought. *I taught her to lie and feign compliance. I took a wild thing and showed her how to wear a leash.* It might be pretense now, but Nina knew—act the part long enough and the show of being tame could become reality.

Hanne's performance was enough for the prince.

He grinned, eyes twinkling. "What a pretty bride you'll make for someone. Shall we have another dance? We can take poor Mila to sit with your mother, and Joran will be left to turn in circles with his hands full of punch glasses."

"It would be my great pleasure, Your Highness," Hanne said sweetly.

"There now. I've bent a Brum to my will. That wasn't so hard."

The prince laughed, but Nina could not make herself join in.

Nina left the ball early. She didn't want to abandon Hanne, but Ylva insisted.

"I think you've taken ill again, Mila. Your hands are ice cold and I've never seen you so pale."

She returned to her room, but she didn't know how to make herself go through the motions of preparing for bed. She lay down on her covers, fully dressed in her silver finery. She couldn't stop remembering the weight of Matthias' body. She could still feel him in her arms, a burden she would carry forever. When he'd taken her hand, his fingers had been wet with his own blood.

She screamed into her pillow, needing to put this pain somewhere, anywhere. All she could hear was his voice.

I need you to save the others . . . the other drüskelle. *Swear to me you'll at least try to help them.*

Matthias had been shot in the gut. He'd been facing his killer. He'd known who it was. A *drüskelle* like him. A boy, really. And that boy hadn't been operating under orders from his commander. If Joran had been sent after Matthias, he would have been rewarded for the killing. Instead he'd been made the prince's personal guard—a reminder that he'd disobeyed his commander, that he'd killed one of their own. But not a real punishment either. Not for murder.

There has to be a Fjerda worth saving. Promise me.

She had promised, but all Saints, she hadn't known what that promise would demand.

The door opened and Hanne rushed in. "I got away as soon as I could."

Nina sat up, trying to brush the hot tears from her cheeks.

Hanne threw her arms around her and pressed her forehead against Nina's. "I'm so sorry. I'll kill him if he hurt you. I don't know why the prince—"

"No," said Nina. "Joran didn't . . . He didn't make advances."

"Then what happened?"

Nina didn't know how to say it, how to unravel all of it. "He wronged me. Badly. I . . . I wanted to kill him. I still want to kill him. I told him so."

"You threatened the prince's bodyguard?"

Nina covered her face with her hands. All her talk about maintaining her cover, about how careful they had to be. "I did. He may go directly to your father. He knows I'm not who I've claimed to be." Then a fresh bolt of fear shot through her. "Why are you back so soon? Did something happen with the prince?"

"No. The ball ended early. The *drüskelle* left. The other soldiers escorted out the prince and the rest of the royal family."

"The war," said Nina. "It's starting."

Hanne nodded. "I think so."

Nina pushed up from the bed and paced the room. She couldn't order her thoughts. She had put herself and Hanne in danger, but she also had a narrow opportunity to act. War had come, and that meant the *drüskelle* would be deployed against Ravka's Grisha forces. She might never have a chance at vengeance again.

"Hanne, I'm sorry. I have to go."

Hanne's eyes were steady. "Where?"

"I . . ." If she did what she intended, if she murdered Joran, there would be nowhere to hide. It would mean a death sentence. And if she somehow managed to escape? She would never see Hanne again.

Hanne rose slowly. "This is because of Matthias."

Nina flinched backward. Hanne had never spoken his name.

"I know you loved him," Hanne continued. "My father cursed the name of Nina Zenik, the Grisha whore who had beguiled his favorite pupil."

"You knew him?" Nina whispered.

"Only in passing. Only as one of my father's soldiers."

"He . . ." Nina's whole body shook. She felt as if the room was crowded with ghosts, the person she'd been, the boy she'd loved, the girl she loved now—brave and kind and full of strength. This girl she didn't deserve. "Joran murdered him. He said it himself. He shot an unarmed man and left him . . ." Her voice caught. She was choking on the words. "He left him to die. But Matthias found the strength to make his way to me." For one last kiss. There had been so few. Nina's hands closed into fists, that overwhelming tide rising inside her. "This may be my only chance."

"At what?"

"To settle the score," Nina bit out. "To see justice done."

"Joran is not yet seventeen," Hanne said quietly. "He would have been fifteen when Matthias died."

"Matthias didn't *die*. He didn't pass away peacefully in his bed. He didn't step in front of a horse cart. He was murdered in cold blood."

"And did he tell you who killed him?"

Nina turned away. "He refused to."

Save some mercy for my people. Matthias could have told her it had been a young *druskelle* who had murdered him; maybe he'd even known Joran's name. Instead he'd pleaded for his country and his brothers. He hadn't wanted her to seek revenge. But what about what she wanted? What about the sorrow she would never be free of?

Hanne laid a hand on Nina's shoulder, gently turning her. "Joran was a boy raised on hate. The way Matthias was. And Rasmus. And me."

"You don't understand." The same words Joran had spoken hours before. He believed he was beyond salvation. Maybe Nina believed the same thing of herself.

But Hanne only shook her head. "None of us understand until it's too late. If you do this, you'll be found out. You'll be executed."

"Maybe."

Hanne's jaw set. "Is it so easy then? To leave this place? To abandon me?"

Nina looked up into Hanne's eyes. Was that what she was doing? How could she abandon something that had never been named, never spoken, that could never be?

"Prince Rasmus wants to marry you," Nina said.

"I know."

"You do?"

"I'm not a fool. It's because of my father, not me."

"That's not true," Nina said. "I've seen the way he looks at you."

Hanne's laugh was brittle, cold and sudden, hail on a window-pane. "Oh, I know it. Like something to be conquered. A Brum to be bent to his will. I understand where his cruelty comes from. He's spent too long envying others and hating himself. I know that disease."

"But there's nothing cruel in you."

"You might be surprised. But maybe I could heal his heart too, over time."

Nina pressed her lips together. "You would be queen."

"I could help to guide him, change his thinking. We might shape Fjerda anew."

"And could you be happy with him?" She had to force the question from her mouth.

"No. Not with him. Not with any man." Hanne bowed her head. "Maybe I can't be happy at all."

"When we started Heartwood—"

"I know. I thought I could will myself to want this life, to want marriage, to be . . . like everyone else. I thought if I played the part long enough and well enough—"

"The performance would become reality."

Hanne's calm had drained away. She sat down on the bed, and when she looked up at Nina, her expression was lost, frightened. "I don't know what to do. We baited our hook and caught a prince. If he asks for my hand, I cannot deny him. But Nina . . . Nina, I can't say yes."

Nina knew she had to go to find Joran now, before the prince left Djerholm, before she lost this chance. But she couldn't leave Hanne.

"I did this," she said. "With my lies and my scheming." She sat down hard on the covers beside Hanne. Her vengeance could wait. It was one thing to sacrifice her own life, but she wouldn't leave Hanne captive to a future she'd never wanted. She wouldn't abandon her to fend for herself in this place. "The queen was right. You're good and I'm . . . I led you to this. I've never been good for you."

Hanne held her gaze. "Sweets aren't good for me. I've been told riding will make me mannish and the wind will chafe my skin and age me. I know all the things that aren't good for me. And I want them just the same."

Nina's throat was dry. "Do you?" she asked quietly. "Want them?"

Hanne's copper eyes glowed like topaz. Slowly she nodded. "Since the moment we met. Since you charged into that clearing like a girl I had dreamed into being."

It had been too much tonight—learning what Joran had done, watching Hanne with the prince, knowing she'd set them on this path. *Maybe this is my fate*, she thought, *to find love and lose it*. But Nina made herself say the words. She wouldn't rob Hanne of the chance to stay with her parents, to live among her people, not if it was what she truly wanted. "If you can love him, I'll find a way to let you go."

Hanne leaned forward and brushed a damp strand of hair from Nina's cheek. Nina felt the strong curve of Hanne's fingers against the nape of her neck, Hanne's breath on her lips.

"Never let me go," Hanne whispered.

"Never," Nina said, and closed the distance between them, feeling the soft press of Hanne's mouth, the thin silk of her dress, this moment like light on water, brief and startling, blinding in its beauty.

31
NIKOLAI

NIKOLAI WATCHED UNTIL ZOYA had clipped herself to the harness and been lifted into the *Cormorant*. He knew she would be fine. Of all of them, she was the least fragile, the least vulnerable. He wasn't being logical, but she'd seemed shaken by their encounter with the Suli and her confession that shouldn't have had to be a confession. When war came, he wouldn't be able to protect her any more than he'd protected David. So, for a brief moment, he watched over her, logic be damned.

When the mists closed around the airship, he jogged down the tunnel in the cliffside to catch up to Kaz. The damp walls gleamed shiny and black in the light from Brekker's lantern.

Their entry into the base was smooth, just a question of keeping quiet and waiting for the guards to pass through the rooms above the basement, then move on to the rest of their rounds. Nikolai and Kaz followed on silent feet, Kaz limping more heavily after their long journey down the tunnel. He wouldn't have to repeat the trip. They would leave by air along with the stolen titanium.

Two picked locks later, they were waiting in a darkened doorway, peering through a small circular window. The base was built around a central yard full of building materials, which had once been open to the air. But now, most of the cargo was protected by the metal shell connected to the base walls, its roof humped like the back of a whale. There didn't seem to be too many guards, and Nikolai was eager to move.

"The yard doesn't look well protected."

"It isn't," said Kaz. "They're relying on their external defenses. They've gotten comfortable."

Nikolai wondered if the same thing might be true at Ravka's more valuable targets. Maybe he should rethink the security at his own military bases and at the palace. Brekker would probably make an excellent security consultant—if Nikolai didn't think he would steal the golden domes right off the Little Palace roof.

"You're twitchy for a monarch," said Kaz, eyes on the yard.

"Have you met many?"

"Plenty of men who call themselves kings."

Nikolai glanced through the window again. "The fate of a nation resting on one's shoulders does make a fellow restless. Shouldn't we get going?"

"You get one chance to make a move like this. Assuming we open that shell without the guards hearing us or some alarm going off, we'll have about thirty minutes to exchange the aluminum for the titanium."

"Tight. But I think we can manage it."

"Not if our timing is off. *About* thirty minutes is meaningless. So we watch the guards do their rounds until we know what their pace really is."

Thunder rumbled over the yard. Zoya's signal. That meant the airship was in place above the steel hull protecting the cargo.

Finally Kaz said, "Stay alert."

He pushed the door open and they were creeping across the yard.

The storm was raging now, Zoya and Adrik conducting it from above like maestros. Nikolai could hear thunder, the rough patter of rain against the metal roof. They needed those sounds. Locating the operating box was easy enough, but the awful shriek that went up from the metal hull as it creaked open was far louder than Nikolai had expected.

"Kerch engineering," muttered Kaz.

But at last the shell split to reveal the roiling clouds of the night sky and the *Cormorant* hovering above. Though thunder and lightning crashed around them, thanks to the Squallers above, not a single drop of rain fell on the cargo below.

The bay doors of the airship opened and a cable was lowered.

"Go," said Kaz. "I'll keep the watch."

Nikolai ran out into the yard, suddenly grateful for Kaz's vigilance. He didn't like the feeling of being this exposed. He had to hope the guards would stick to their routine, walking the perimeter outside. He grabbed the end of the cable and hooked its anchor to a metal beam at the base of the shell. A platform followed on a separate cable, descending in the calm that the Squallers had created. It was stacked with aluminum. Carefully, Nikolai steered the platform into position and set it beside the sprawling stash of titanium.

He took the hooks attached to the platform cables and fastened them to a pallet of titanium. It would have been easier with more hands, but they needed Kaz on lookout. And at least the titanium was light enough that it was easy to manage on the ascent.

Platform, pallet, platform, pallet, Nikolai sent titanium up and directed aluminum down as the wind howled, their progress impossibly slow. His arms and back began to ache. He wasn't sure how much time had passed when he heard Kaz give a low whistle. A moment later, the thief appeared.

"Guards approaching. We need to get out now."

"It can't have been thirty minutes. We've only got half the titanium on board. Maybe less."

"You can have half or you can have a gunfight. Jesper will be very sad he missed out."

They couldn't afford a brawl. No Ravkan agent could be found on this base, let alone the king of Ravka, regardless of his disguise.

Nikolai looked up at the airship and signaled to Adrik, leaning over the bay doors. "Let's go."

Kaz hit the controls and the metal shell slowly began to close. They leapt onto what would be the final pallet of titanium and the crew of the airship drew them up.

Less than one hundred feet from the bay doors of the airship, Nikolai realized something was wrong.

He peered down at the cable still hooked to the beam below. "The anchor line isn't releasing." Nikolai gestured up at Adrik to try the release again, but the mechanism was stuck. The anchor didn't budge. "I have to go back down. I'll disengage it manually."

"There isn't time," said Kaz. "Those hull doors are going to close first. They can eject the cable when we get to the top."

"No good." If they simply released the cable, the anchor would be trapped inside the yard, evidence that someone had been where they shouldn't be. An investigation could lead back to Ravka.

Nikolai saw lights moving along the western side of the building. The guards were coming.

"How long do I have?"

"Two minutes. Maybe three. Take your medicine, Sturmhond. They won't be able to prove the cable is Ravkan. Not right away."

"I can't let that happen." Nikolai glanced up at the airship, at the faces of the soldiers and Grisha looking down. He wished he could order them to avert their eyes. There was no way to disguise what he was about to do. "Tell me, Brekker, do you believe in monsters?"

"Of all kinds."

"Prepare to meet another."

He closed his eyes and let the demon uncoil. It wasn't hard. The monster was always waiting for its chance.

Kaz raised his cane as the shadow emerged, taking shape in the air before them. "All the Saints and their ugly mothers."

The demon spread its black wings and hurtled toward the opening in the hull doors. Nikolai's hands still clung to the cable, but he couldn't do much more than that. He was seeing through the demon's eyes. He felt its arms—his arms—extend, muscles flexing, claws reaching. A moment later the monster wrenched the anchor free. The cable recoiled with sudden force and slammed against one of the carefully stacked pallets of aluminum with a reverberating clang, sending bars of metal sliding.

"So much for leaving no trace," said Kaz, though his eyes were big as moons as he watched the demon soar upward back to them.

"They might not notice," Nikolai said hopefully.

The anchor cleared the crack in the hull a bare breath before the shell clamped shut. But the demon was trapped inside.

"Now what?" said Kaz.

Nikolai could feel the demon speeding toward the shell. *No.* He tried to command it, slow its progress, force it back into shadow, but it was too wild with its own freedom. It slammed through the metal shell, leaving a gaping hole in its wake.

"Think they won't notice that?" Kaz asked.

Nikolai glanced up and saw Zoya bring her hand down in a swift arc. "Hold tight!"

A bolt of lightning sizzled through the air beside them, its heat searing the sky.

It struck the shell at the edge of the hole the demon had made, scorching the metal, making it look as if the storm had savaged the metal rooftop.

Rain spattered Nikolai and Kaz in a gust as Zoya let it pour through to the yard below. Adrik swathed the airship in clouds to hide the sight of it from any guards peering up through the damaged shell.

Moments later, they were inside the airship bay, soaked to the bone.

For a moment the demon hung on the wind, feeling the swell of the storm, fearless in the lush black night and still hungry for blood and damage. Nikolai didn't want to draw it back—and not because he dreaded its presence inside him. Some part of him hated to cage it once more.

But the demon didn't fight. Maybe the divisions between them were eroding. And maybe that was a problem. He couldn't deny the remorse he felt as he tugged the darkness back.

You'll fly again, he promised.

The airship doors banged shut. The crew stared at him. Nikolai had known what unleashing the monster's power meant, what he was revealing. But for a moment he'd lost himself in the demon's exultation. Zoya was shaking her head, though Kaz seemed only intrigued now that his initial fear had passed.

What happens now? he wondered, as these Ravkan soldiers faced him. He could see the terror in their faces, their bewilderment. Adrik stood several steps back, arm raised as if ready to summon a storm to fight with. For once he looked shocked instead of morose.

Show them weakness when they need to see it, never when you feel it. Words of advice he'd given to Alina years ago. This seemed like an excellent time to take it. For once in his life, he was going to embrace understatement.

He clapped his hands together, rubbing his palms like a lord of the manor returned from the hunt, in need of a good meal and a warm fire. "That went about as well as could be expected," he said in the most ordinary, jovial tone he could manage. "Who needs a drink?"

⌁

It didn't work. Not entirely. Some of the crew sat and drank with him, downing his brandy a little more quickly than they might have otherwise, eager to fall back into the trust he'd built with them before this dark revelation.

When one of them dared to hazard, "What was . . . what was that thing?" Nikolai simply said, "Another weapon in our arsenal."

"Looked like a gargoyle."

Nikolai refilled his glass. "Hush now. It'll hear you."

The crewman blanched. "I didn't mean nothing by it."

But Nikolai only laughed and the others followed suit, nervous but obliging. These were friends, compatriots who knew him well and who wanted to find a way to accept or at least ignore what they'd seen.

That wasn't enough for some of them. Nikolai knew exactly how many soldiers and Grisha were aboard, and he knew that more than half the crew hadn't chosen to drink with a monster. Zoya would speak to the Grisha. She would do her best to answer their questions and soothe their nerves. But there was a very good chance that they would desert. And that they would talk.

Maybe this was the end then. It had been foolhardy to believe he could keep a secret like this forever.

But I could have kept it, he realized as he filled the glasses for another round. He could have let them detach the cable and leave the anchor behind for the Kerch guards to find. Yes, they would have guessed that Ravka was involved. They might have realized the titanium was missing. They might have taken action to exact revenge. None of it good. But his secret would still have been his.

Another weapon in our arsenal. It might be truer than he'd realized. David had known that once technology existed, it was impossible to control. Tanks got bigger. Guns fired more rounds. Bombs did more damage. On the night of the sneak attack against Os Alta, the demon had become a weapon in Nikolai's hand. Maybe it was no surprise that he'd chosen to use that weapon again. But it was one thing to have sent an enemy pilot home with a tale to frighten the Fjerdans, another to try to command soldiers who'd lost trust in their king. Nikolai could only hope that the soldiers who did try to spread the story of this night wouldn't be believed and that those who stayed in his service would find a way to have faith in him again.

Jesper and Wylan were waiting for the *Cormorant* on the cliffs, looking dirty but otherwise unscathed. The Suli were nowhere to be seen, but Nikolai suspected they were nearby, watching.

When Kaz was preparing to descend to the cliffs, Nikolai and Zoya joined him at the wind-buffeted bay doors.

Nikolai handed him a metal box. "For the Wraith," he said.

Kaz took it, tucking it under one arm. "An infernal gadget to contend with your other infernal gadgets."

"I have a gift for order and a taste for chaos."

Kaz raised a brow. "The man with the monster inside."

"I see the wheels turning in your head, Mister Brekker, wondering what you might do with this information. I would ask, one liar to another, that you keep it to yourself."

"I find secrets are the most reliable stocks. The longer they're kept, the more their value rises."

"We could shove him out of the airship now," suggested Zoya.

"We could, but we're not going to."

"Why is that?"

"Because Mister Brekker has the best insurance of all. He's proven himself useful."

"Speaking of secrets," said Kaz, taking hold of the cable. "I've had word from the Kerch colonies. A certain monarch and his wife are no longer in exile."

"By whose order?" Nikolai said, tension snapping through him.

"Jarl Brum and the Fjerdan government. This is the problem with letting your enemies live."

"They're my parents."

"Your point?" Kaz settled his cane more firmly in his grip and nodded to the cable operator, ready to descend. "A word of advice, from one bastard to another: Sometimes it's best to let the demon have its day."

The cable dropped and Kaz Brekker was gone.

※

Nikolai had meant to try to rest, but instead he found himself in the darkened cargo hold. He lay down on the cold floor beside one of the stacks of stolen titanium, now secured with cables and tarps. It was quiet here, empty, the only sound the heavy thrum of the airship's engines. It was almost enough to lull him to sleep.

At some point, he heard a flyer being guided into the neighboring landing bay. He knew it was the messenger they'd been set to rendezvous with over the True Sea. He heard raised voices, running footsteps. The news couldn't be good. Another city bombed? The Fjerdans already marching?

He wanted to be back at the Kerch base, racing against discovery, listening to the crackle of the storm. Better that than grappling with the actuality of a war he'd failed to prevent. The *Cormorant* would proceed directly to Lazlayon, where hopefully, Nadia and the rest of the Fabrikators would be able to use their meager supply of stolen titanium to give Ravka an edge in the battles to come. As for the *Volkvolny*, his beautiful Wolf of the Waves would sit in the Ketterdam harbor for another two days to be inspected by any nosy members of the Merchant Council. Privyet would greet them as Sturmhond, wearing the splendid frock coat that Nikolai had already sent back to the ship. He'd been sorry to let it go. The coat was the open sea, the dream of another life he might have lived. *Could you do it?* Zoya had asked. *Give up the throne?* He'd fought so hard for so long, but some wayward voice inside him said, *Yes.* Like the demon, he hungered for freedom. And yet he knew he could never forsake Ravka the way his father had, ceding his duty to his own desires. His messy, exasperating country might demand everything, might punish those who loved it for their devotion, but he wouldn't turn his back on his people.

Nikolai heard the door open, scented wildflowers somewhere in the cargo hold.

"Are you hiding?" Zoya asked as she shut the door behind her.

"I'm skulking. It's much more purposeful." He patted the floor next to him. "Join me?"

He expected her to roll her eyes and tell him to get off his ass. Instead she lay down beside him, her shoulder almost touching his own. *All Saints*, Nikolai thought. *I'm lying next to Zoya Nazyalensky.* Somewhere Count Kirigin was crying into his soup. They stared up at the shadowy roof of the hold, at nothing at all.

"Did you sleep?" she asked.

"Of course not. Someday we'll see an end to war, and then you and I will take a nap together."

"Is that your idea of seduction?"

"These days? Yes."

"I'll be honest—it's incredibly compelling."

"I heard our messenger arrive," he said. "War?"

"War. Our scouts have reported Fjerdan troops mobilizing again."

"Do we know where they're headed?"

"We're waiting on intelligence." She inhaled deeply. "I like the way it smells down here. Sawdust. Oil."

"I never knew you had a fondness for shipyards."

"Maybe anything smells good after Ketterdam." He could see her profile in the dim light. "There isn't enough titanium, is there?"

"No," he admitted. "Maybe David could have found a way to make it work, but . . . Nadia and Leoni and the others should be able to get some use out of these materials. Wylan offered up some new sketches on the diagnostics that will help. He has a way with destruction."

"Perhaps if the Fjerdans see the smaller missiles, the threat of something larger will be enough."

"Not if Jarl Brum is left unchecked." Nikolai and his engineers had tried to piece together the details on the weapons and plans Nina had sent to them through the Hringsa, along with the intel from Tamar's spies, but he still couldn't be sure what they were up against.

"Nina thinks Prince Rasmus may be a counter to his warmongering," Zoya said. "I wanted to bring her home, but . . . maybe she's safer among the Fjerdans."

"I beg your pardon?"

"I know, I know. I can't believe I'm saying it either."

"The whim of a prince isn't much for insurance."

"You were a prince once."

"Yes, but I'm *me*. Tell me something, Nazyalensky. When Fjerda gets their puppet king, assuming the Fjerdans let either of us live, do you think you can control Vadik Demidov?"

"We do have to lose first, Nikolai."

He peered at her. "That sounds suspiciously hopeful. What have you done with my doomsaying general?"

"We're not helpless. Novels are full of ragtag bands facing impossible odds."

"Do you read novels?"

"When I have the time."

"So, no."

"I read when I can't sleep."

"So, regularly then. If the Fjerdans have testimony from my mother, that will be the end of it all."

Zoya hesitated, and he knew she was weighing her words. "Would she betray you that way?"

He didn't want to think so, but he couldn't afford to pretend. "I sent her from her country and stripped her of a crown. The argument might be made that I betrayed her first."

"I haven't spoken to my mother since I was nine."

When she'd tried to marry Zoya off to some rotten old noble with bags full of money. "Always wise to get a head start on estrangement."

"The terrible thing is . . . I didn't miss her. I still don't. Maybe I miss something I never had."

Nikolai knew that feeling, the longing for a father he could trust, an older brother who might have been his companion instead of his rival. A real family. "I wish my parents had been different people, but they owe me nothing. If my mother chooses to speak against my parentage, I can't blame her." But it would still hurt like hell.

Zoya pushed herself up on her elbows. "None of it will matter if we win, truly win. Ravka loves victory more than it loves royal blood."

And it had been a very long time since Ravka had been given much cause to celebrate.

"That's why the Darkling expanded the Fold, isn't it?" Nikolai mused. "He was looking for a weapon that would leave no one in doubt of Ravka's power. He knew if he gave the people victory, they would finally love him. What did your Grisha say about what happened at the base?"

"About your demon?" She sighed and lay back down. "They're shaken. Adrik lost his arm to one of the Darkling's *nichevo'ya*. It's hard for him to see that creature and not go back to those terrible days. I remember Tolya trying to heal him, the blood . . . He left a lake of it on the deck of the ship we escaped on."

"Will Adrik leave?"

"I don't think he'll desert. But I can't vouch for the others. Some secrets need to be kept."

"Do they?" He turned his head, trying to decipher the dark slash of her brows, the black of her hair. She looked just as she always had—beautiful, impossible Zoya. "Why didn't you tell me you were Suli?"

"I think you know, Nikolai."

"You really believe it would have changed the way I see you?"

"No. Not you. But ask yourself, would your First Army generals treat me so respectfully if they knew I was Suli?"

420

"If they didn't, they would stop being my generals."

"Do you really think it's as simple as that? That they would make it that easy?" She shook her head. "They never come at you with hatred. They come at you with pity. Did you learn to read in the Suli caravans? Was it hard growing up in such squalor? They giggle about the dark hair on your arms or say that you look Ravkan like it's some kind of compliment. They don't make it easy to fight them." Zoya closed her eyes. "I passed because it was safer to be Zoya Nazyalensky than Zoya Nabri. I guess I thought it would keep me safe. Now I'm not so sure. The woman on the cliffs called me daughter. That word . . . I didn't know I needed that word. I don't regret turning my back on my parents. But it's hard not to wonder what might have happened if my father had stood up for me. If we'd gone to live with his people. If I'd had someplace other than the Little Palace to run to, someone other than the Darkling to make me feel capable and strong."

"It isn't too late, Zoya. They chose to help *you* on the cliffs, not me, not Kaz Brekker."

Now Zoya's laugh was harsh. "But they don't really know me, do they?"

"I would choose you." The words were out before he thought better of them, and then there was no way to pull them back.

Silence stretched between them. *Perhaps the floor will open and I'll plummet to my death*, he thought hopefully.

"As your general?" Her voice careful. She was offering him a chance to right the ship, to take them back to familiar waters.

And a fine general you are.

There could be no better leader.

You may be prickly, but that's what Ravka needs.

So many easy replies.

Instead he said, "As my queen."

He couldn't read her expression. Was she pleased? Embarrassed?

Angry? Every cell in his body screamed for him to crack a joke, to free both of them from the peril of this moment. But he wouldn't. He was still a privateer, and he'd come too far.

"Because I'm a dependable soldier," she said, but she didn't sound sure. It was that same cautious, tentative voice, the voice of someone waiting for a punch line, or maybe a blow. "Because I know all your secrets."

"I do trust you more than myself sometimes—and I think very highly of myself."

Hadn't she said there was no one else she'd choose to have her back in a fight?

But that isn't the whole truth, is it, you great cowardly lump. To hell with it. They might all die soon enough. They were safe here in the dark, surrounded by the hum of the engines.

"I would make you my queen because I want you. I want you all the time."

She rolled onto her side, resting her head on her folded arm. A small movement, but he could feel her breath now. His heart was racing. "As your general, I should tell you that would be a terrible decision."

He turned onto his side. They were facing each other now. "As your king, I should tell you that no one could dissuade me. No prince and no power could make me stop wanting you."

Nikolai felt drunk. Maybe unleashing the demon had loosed something in his brain. She was going to laugh at him. She would knock him senseless and tell him he had no right. But he couldn't seem to stop.

"I would give you a crown if I could," he said. "I would show you the world from the prow of a ship. I would choose you, Zoya. As my general, as my friend, as my bride. I would give you a sapphire the size of an acorn." He reached into his pocket. "And all I would ask in return is that you wear this damnable ribbon in your hair on our wedding day."

She reached out, her fingers hovering over the coil of blue velvet ribbon resting in his palm.

Then she pulled back her hand, cradling her fingers as if they'd been singed.

"You will wed a Taban sister who craves a crown," she said. "Or a wealthy Kerch girl, or maybe a Fjerdan royal. You will have heirs and a future. I'm not the queen Ravka needs."

"And if you're the queen I want?"

She shut her eyes. "There's a story my aunt told me a very long time ago. I can't remember all of it, but I remember the way she described the hero: 'He had a golden spirit.' I loved those words. I made her read them again and again. When I was a little girl, I thought I had a golden spirit too, that it would light everything it touched, that it would make me beloved like a hero in a story." She sat up, drew her knees in, wrapped her arms around them as if she could make a shelter of her own body. He wanted to pull her back down beside him and press his mouth to hers. He wanted her to look at him again with possibility in her eyes. "But that's not who I am. Whatever is inside me is sharp and gray as the thorn wood." She rose and dusted off her *kefta*. "I wasn't born to be a bride. I was made to be a weapon."

Nikolai forced himself to smile. It wasn't as if he'd offered her a real proposal. They both knew such a thing was impossible. And yet her refusal smarted just as badly as if he'd gotten on his knee and offered her his hand like some kind of besotted fool. It stung. All Saints, it stung.

"Well," he said cheerfully, pushing up onto his elbows and

looking up at her with all the wry humor he could muster. "Weapons are good to have around too. Far more useful than brides and less likely to mope about the palace. But if you won't rule Ravka by my side, what does the future hold, General?"

Zoya opened the door to the cargo hold. Light flooded in, gilding her features when she looked back at him. "I'll fight on beside you. As your general. As your friend. Because whatever my failings, I know this: You are the king Ravka needs."

32
MAYU

THEY COULDN'T RETURN TO the palace. Not without creating upheaval that no one wanted.

Well, that almost no one wanted.

"Bring us all to Ahmrat Jen," Bergin demanded, gesturing to the other sickly Grisha prisoners. They had been treated with antidote, but they were weak and there was no telling what permanent damage had been done to their bodies.

Mayu leaned against the wall by the control panel Reyem had smashed. Her brother stood at attention, perfectly still. Too still. It was as if he were as mechanical as the wings on his back, a clockwork soldier who needed no rest. What did he need? Who was he now?

Outside, Ehri and her grandmother conversed beneath the night sky. Makhi had been taken to Leyti's coach, where she was being guarded by the Tavgharad, who no longer served her, because she was no longer queen.

Bergin took a sip of water. The tremors had left his body, and though he still looked frail, his gaze was bright with anger. "Take us to the capital and let them see what Queen Makhi calls science."

Mayu thought Tamar would speak up to agree with Bergin, but she only shook her head.

"Look around you," she said, her hands resting on the Grisha captive's bony wrist, monitoring his pulse. "This is one laboratory. Our intelligence suggests there are more. I know there's one near Kobu, but we need the other locations."

"The doctor can give them to us," said Bergin.

"That isn't the only issue."

"Then what is? I've spent nearly three months here in a state of delirium, being dosed with *parem* and forced to do the unspeakable. The only thing that kept me human was Reyem."

Their eyes met, and Mayu sensed the strength of the bond between them.

But Reyem looked down. "I don't know if I'm human anymore."

Mayu wasn't sure either. It wasn't just the wings and the monstrous pincers, but some spark in him had been extinguished. Or maybe replaced with a different kind of fire. *Who are you now, Reyem? What are you?*

"You spoke Fjerdan and he came back to himself," Mayu said to Bergin. "How did you do it?"

"I didn't know I could," he admitted. "The work of conversion is grueling. It was painful for both of us."

Reyem's big shoulders shrugged. "I hated you, just as I hated the doctors and the guards. Until I saw that you were suffering too."

Bergin rested his head against the metal frame of the bunk. "Most times, there was just the pain and the work. They made me . . ." He hung his head. "I'm sorry, Reyem."

A silence fell, weighted with the horrors Bergin and her brother had seen.

Mayu touched her good hand to her twin's, and he took it gently in his. Tamar and Bergin had done what they could for her other hand, and the pain had receded to a low throb.

Quietly, she said, "You told the queen you died a thousand times."

A muscle ticked in his jaw. "To have your heart stopped in your chest, your flesh torn from your bones, to fall into oblivion, then wake to nightmare again and again and again. All for the sake of being reborn as a weapon."

"I started teaching him Fjerdan," said Bergin. "To distract him from the pain. Swear words, mostly."

"What did you say to get him to wake up?" asked Tamar.

Bergin grinned. "You don't want to know. It was incredibly filthy."

Ehri entered the lab. Her face had been washed clean, but she was still covered in sludge. "We can't stay here any longer. It will be dawn soon. There's a small summer palace between here and the city. Queen Leyti commands that we travel there. We can eat, bathe, change our clothes, and figure out what we're going to do."

Bergin struck his fist against the bunk. "There will be no punishment for Makhi, for any of them. Just watch."

"Why not?" Mayu asked. She felt naive asking, like a child trying to keep pace with her brother once more.

"Because they're all Taban," said Reyem. "A mark against one is a mark against all of them."

"Not Ehri," said Mayu. "The people love her. And they know she would never do anything like this. There will be justice."

She looked to the princess, but all Ehri did was gesture to the door. "Come. There will be time to talk when we've eaten and rested."

It took a while to sort out the laboratory. Tamar brought the doctor back to consciousness and he, in turn, woke the other *khergud* as Queen Leyti and Ehri looked on. There were four including Reyem, but none of the others remembered their true names. They asked no questions, made no requests. They simply stood—some with wings, some with horns, some with claws—waiting for orders. Perfect soldiers. Had they been further along in their transformation than Reyem? Or had none of them had a Bergin, someone to remind them that they were more than pain and anger?

Mayu watched as they locked up the laboratory, and Bergin and Reyem took their last look at this nightmare place. It was evidence and would be left intact for now.

But I'll come back, she promised herself. She might never banish the emptiness from her brother's eyes, but she would pull this place apart piece by piece if she had to. She would watch it burn to the ground.

The journey to the summer palace didn't take long. It was located in a green dell beside its own gleaming lake, a getaway for members of the royal family or important guests of the crown in the hot months.

Mayu sat with her brother and Bergin in one of the garden rooms, the windows framing the sun slowly rising over the lake. The other Grisha and the *khergud* had been placed in separate, heavily guarded chambers, but Bergin had been allowed to remain with Reyem.

"What happens now?" he asked. "I can't return to Fjerda."

Mayu didn't know. She hadn't thought past finding Reyem and

freeing him. "We could go home," she suggested. "Mother and Fath—"

"No," Reyem said harshly. "I never want them to see me like this."

"They think you're dead."

"Good. Let them mourn me."

"Reyem," pleaded Mayu. She needed to know they could take some part of their lives back. "They love you. More than anything. More than me. More than life. They'll love you this way as they loved you before."

"But I don't know that I can love them back."

Mayu looked away. She couldn't bear to think of her sweet, laughing, generous brother, and know that he was gone.

A knock came at the door and Tamar appeared. "They want your testimony."

Mayu rose and felt a brush of fingers against her hand.

Reyem was looking at her. "Sister. *Kebben*. Let this be enough."

All she could do was nod and try to smile. He would forever be her brother, no matter what he'd been robbed of.

Queen Leyti was waiting in the temple hall, seated on a throne and bracketed by Tavgharad, Ehri to her right. Statues of the Six Soldiers glowed in sunlit niches on the walls. Makhi had been seated on a low cushion to the queen's left, a position meant to humble her. But she sat with perfect poise, her face serene, as if she were the one on the throne.

"Mayu Kir-Kaat," said Queen Leyti. "Will you tell us your story?"

Mayu couldn't hide her surprise. She'd expected she would only have to confirm what Ehri had already said, as she had with Ministers Nagh and Zihun. She looked to Tamar, then to Ehri, who gave her a gentle nod of encouragement.

"Begin with your brother," said the princess. "When did you know he had disappeared?"

Mayu took a deep breath. "They told me he was dead, but I didn't believe them. I'd heard whispers of the *khergud*, as all of us had. So I set out to find him." The words came haltingly at first. Mayu felt as if she was struggling to tug them free, but slowly the tale began to unspool, and then it was dragging her along and she could only follow. At some point, she realized she was crying. She'd never unraveled her story, Isaak's story, never told anyone, never had the chance to fit the beginning to the middle to what might be the end.

When she was done, Queen Leyti said, "You have served the crown well, Mayu Kir-Kaat. I would ask you to remain one of our falcons. Ehri will need protection from someone she can trust in the years to come."

Mayu saluted. "I will gladly serve our future queen."

"But I will not be your queen," said Ehri softly.

"Then——"

Leyti held up a hand. "I will rule until one of my great-grandchildren is old enough to serve. Ehri and Makhi will then act as her regents."

"You can't mean that!" Mayu cried. The soldier she'd been might have stayed quiet, would have known her place, but the sight of that laboratory had forever banished that girl to the past, and someone had to speak for the victims of Makhi's violence. "Makhi violated your wishes even before she was queen. She's the reason *jurda parem* exists. She's the reason my brother . . . None of those people will ever be the same. They were soldiers who served your family and this country. They deserve better."

"The laboratories will be shut down," said Queen Leyti, "and Makhi will no longer have authority over the dispersal of funds. She will not be able to start up the program again. The *khergud* will be offered sanctuary."

"Sanctuary?" Mayu said. "You mean exile, don't you?"

"They must remain a secret. For now, they will stay here at the summer palace to rest and recover while we continue on to the capital."

Mayu couldn't believe what she was hearing. "Bergin was right. He said there would be no justice. That Makhi and her lackeys wouldn't face punishment." She turned her anger on Ehri. "I told him you were better than that."

But it was Tamar who spoke. "If what Makhi has done becomes widely known, chaos will erupt. Each of the Taban sisters will become contenders for the throne."

"They're murdering Grisha!" Mayu shouted. "Your own people! Don't you—"

Tamar didn't flinch. "I am Grisha and I am also Shu. I don't want to see this country torn apart by civil war the way Ravka has been."

"You don't care about Shu Han. You just want an ally to help fend off the Fjerdans. Makhi should face trial."

"There will be no trial," said Queen Leyti. "Makhi will claim she's ill and will gratefully serve the crown alongside her sister."

Mayu threw her hands up. What had been done to her brother, to the Grisha, to her, to Isaak, did none of it mean anything? "You know she won't settle for that. Makhi can't be trusted."

"I couldn't agree more," said Queen Leyti. "That is why I have arranged for insurance." She gestured to her guards and Minister Yerwei entered, the man who had served as doctor to three Taban queens.

"Him?" Mayu said in disbelief. "Yerwei is her closest confidant."

But Makhi didn't look triumphant. For the first time her serene expression faltered and her face paled. Queen Leyti watched her granddaughter with sad eyes. "I hoped there was no truth in it," she said. "But I see now that Minister Yerwei did not lie. Ehri was meant to be your mother's heir."

"That . . . that can't be," said Ehri.

Makhi's lips pulled back in a sneer. "She said I had been born with all the Taban guile but none of the Taban heart."

"I fear she was right," said Queen Leyti. "Minister Yerwei, you have prepared a confession, have you not?"

"I have, Your Majesty. Four copies, as you commanded."

"Makhi, you will sign these confessions too. Then they will be sealed. One will remain with me, one with Ehri, one with Ministers Nagh and Zihun—who have no idea of the contents. One will go to Ravka with Tamar Kir-Bataar. You will abide by the terms I have set before you and the treaty you yourself signed, or your crimes against the crown will be revealed and you will be tried as a traitor to the Taban line."

"I will never bow to another Taban queen," Makhi spat.

"That is your choice. In which case, you may absent yourself from court and spend your days in a palace of your choosing, guarded by the Tavgharad of *my* choosing. If you're in need of a hobby, I recommend gardening."

"Your Majesty," said Tamar, stepping forward. "I would ask—"

"I know what you will ask, Tamar Kir-Bataar. I cannot send troops to aid your king."

"Queen Makhi signed a treaty. An attack against Ravka is an attack against the Shu."

"We will send the Ravkan king our most sincere apologies and a confirmation of our friendship, but we cannot send our soldiers to die in a foreign war."

"Grandmother," said Ehri, "it was Nikolai Lantsov who saved my life."

"We owe him a debt," Mayu agreed. She had no love for the Ravkan king, but she and her brother owed him their lives. He could have put her to death for the crimes she'd committed. He could have married Ehri to forge an alliance and forsaken the Grisha and the *khergud* soldiers trapped in secret laboratories. "We can't abandon his country."

Leyti held up a hand. "We fulfill this debt by honoring our treaty and agreeing to support the rights of all Grisha. We cannot do that if we are seen as Ravkan puppets."

Tamar was watching Leyti, and Makhi, and Minister Yerwei. "You've made some kind of agreement with Fjerda, haven't you? They want you to stay neutral."

"Fjerda has let us know that, should they occupy Ravka, they will honor our shared border."

Slowly, Tamar shook her head. "You had best hope they're more trustworthy than you and your granddaughter."

"We cannot send the Lantsov king aid. The ministers will balk and they're right to. It's not our war."

"It will be when there's no Ravka to stand between you and the Fjerdans."

Queen Leyti Kir-Taban, Daughter of Heaven, was not moved. "If the wolves come howling, we will face them then. For now, the fox will meet them on his own."

33

THE
MONK

ALEKSANDER SURVEYED HIS ARMY of the faith-
ful, his acolytes, the people with whom he would build a new age.
For the first time in several hundred years, he wished for whiskey.

"They are ready," said Brother Chernov, brimming with pride,
his gray-flecked beard nearly bristling with excitement.

Ready to die, I suppose, Aleksander thought, but let none of his
frustration show.

He clapped Chernov on the back. "Onward to revelation."

The big man trailed him as they walked the camp together.
Aleksander had no way of knowing where the Fjerdans would attack,
so he'd brought his followers—and they *were* his now—to the area
north of Adena to await word of battle. But they'd insisted on jour-
neying west into the Fold to spend their nights in communion with

the Starless One. *I'm right here*, he'd wanted to shout. He had no choice but to oblige them in a pilgrimage to the holy sands.

He didn't care for it. It was, in part, a question of practicality. There was no shelter on the Fold, no plants to forage, no game to hunt. All they had to eat was the hardtack and dried meat they'd brought with them, a few barrels of flat beer, and the water in their canteens. They slept on hard ground with no trees or rocks to take the brunt of the winter wind. And yet, his companions were jubilant. They held services every sundown, and during the days, they alternated praying and training. They were going into a battle, after all, and though Aleksander did not intend for them to do much fighting, they needed to look like they knew what they were doing.

"Where did you come by such military knowledge, Yuri?" Brother Azarov asked as Aleksander put the pilgrims through another round of sprints. He'd been a soldier himself before he'd deserted to join the ranks of the Starless.

"During my time with the Priestguard," he lied.

Yuri had never so much as held a gun. He'd been happiest confined to the library.

"We need more weapons," he said.

Chernov's furry brows rose. "Why? When the Starless One—"

"We don't dictate the arrival of the Starless Saint. We have to be ready to defend ourselves."

Are they all so eager to die? he wondered.

They believe, came Yuri's reply. *They believe in you.*

All for the best, but war was war.

"There's a cache of weapons at the old fort east of Ryevost," Brother Azarov said. "I was stationed there for a time."

"You think they'll still be there?" Aleksander asked.

"If the Starless One watches over us, they will be."

Aleksander had to fight not to roll his eyes. If he remembered correctly, the old fort had been all but decommissioned and used as an ammunitions stockpile.

"We'll go there tonight," he said.

"After services."

"Of course."

After nightfall, they hitched a wagon to two of their horses and traveled to the old fort. Getting past the guards was easy enough. The only challenge had been summoning shadow to cloak their movements without revealing his power to Brother Azarov.

But their luck had quickly turned.

"This is it?" Aleksander asked, looking at the crates of decrepit weapons. He picked up one of the old, single-shot rifles. "We might as well try to slap them to death."

"The Starless One will protect us."

Aleksander studied Brother Azarov in the dark room. "You're a soldier—"

"I *was* a soldier."

"Very well. You were once a soldier and you would walk onto a battlefield with nothing but your faith to protect you?"

"If that is what our Saint requires."

Aleksander should be glad of that faith, that all it had taken was a bit of shadow play to get these people to march into a war with him. So why was he left uneasy?

Will you protect them?

He could. He would if need be. His powers had returned to him. He could form *nichevo'ya* to fight on his behalf. His pilgrims could enter the field with picks and shovels and they would still emerge victorious.

And yet, his mind was troubled.

They packed up the few weapons that looked like they might be of use and rode back toward Adena in silence. Since they had the cart, they would meet with Brother Chernov and some of the others outside the village to help them transport supplies from the market.

Aleksander couldn't help but think of the first army he'd built. Yevgeni Lantsov had been king then, and he'd been at war with the Shu for the entirety of his reign. He couldn't hold the southern border and his forces were stretched to their very limit. Aleksander had gone by a different name then. Leonid. The first Darkling to offer his gifts in service to the king.

His mother had warned him not to go. They'd been living near an old tannery, the stink of the chemicals and the offal always thick in the air.

"Once you are known, you cannot be unknown," she'd warned him.

But he'd been waiting for a ruler like Yevgeni—practical, forward-thinking, and desperate. Aleksander traveled to the capital and sought an audience with the king, and there he'd let his shadows unfurl. The Grand Palace hadn't even been built then, only a ramshackle castle of rickety wood and ragged stone.

The king and his court had been frightened. Some had called him a demon, others had claimed he was a trickster and a fraud. But the king was too pragmatic to let such an opportunity pass him by.

"You will take your talents to the border," he'd told Aleksander. "Be they true sorcery or mere illusion, you will use them against our enemies. And if our army finds victory, you will be rewarded."

Aleksander had marched south with the king's soldiers, and when they'd faced the Shu in the field, he'd unleashed darkness upon their opponents, blinding them where they stood. Ravka's forces had won the day.

But when Yevgeni had offered Aleksander his reward, he had refused the king's gold. "There are others like me, Grisha, living in hiding. Give me leave to offer them sanctuary here and I will build you an army the likes of which the world has never seen."

Aleksander had traveled throughout Ravka, to places he and his mother had visited before, to distant lands where he'd gone on his own to study. He knew the secret ways and hiding places of Grisha, and wherever he went, he promised them a new life lived without fear.

"We will be respected," he'd vowed. "Honored. We will have a home at last."

They hadn't wanted to come with him to the capital at first. They'd been sure it was some kind of trick and that once they were within the city's double walls, they would be killed. But a few were willing to make the journey with him, and they had become the soldiers of the Second Army.

There had been objections from noblemen and priests, of course, accusations of dark magic, but as their military victories had continued, the arguments grew weaker.

Only King Yevgeni's Apparat continued to campaign against the Grisha. He railed that the Saints would forsake Ravka if the king continued to harbor witches beneath his roof. Each day he would stand before the throne and rant until he was short of breath and red in the face. One day, he simply keeled over. If he'd been helped to his death by a Corporalnik posted by a shaded window, no one was the wiser.

But the next Apparat was more circumspect in his objections. He preached the tale of Yaromir and Sankt Feliks at the First Altar, a story of extraordinary soldiers who had helped a king unify a country, and two years later, Aleksander began work on the Little Palace.

He had thought he'd accomplished his task, that he'd given his people a safe haven, a home where they'd never be punished for their gifts.

What had changed? The answer was everything. Kings lived and died. Their sons were honest or corrupt. Wars ended and began again—and again and again. Grisha were not accepted; they were resented in Ravka and hunted abroad. Men fought them with swords, then guns, then worse. There was no end to it, and so he had sought an end. Power that could not be questioned. Might that could not be reckoned with. The result had been the Fold.

His first soldiers were dead now. Lovers, allies, countless kings and queens. Only he continued on. Eternity took practice, and he'd had plenty of it. The world had changed. War had changed. But he had not. He'd traveled, learned, killed. He'd met his half sister, who had herself passed into legend and Sainthood. He'd searched the world for his mother's other children, hungry for kinship, for a sense of himself in others. He'd discarded his past lives like a snake shedding its skin, becoming sleeker and more dangerous with every new version of himself. But maybe he'd left some part of who he was behind in each of those lives.

Brother Azarov startled awake as Aleksander brought the cart to a stop on the sloping road that led into Adena. The monk yawned and smacked his lips. It was early morning, and Aleksander could see it was market day in the little town. Even from a distance, he could tell the mood was somber, the threat of war creeping ever closer, but the square was still full of people stocking up on provisions, children playing or working the stalls with their parents, neighbors calling their greetings.

Aleksander hopped down to stretch his legs and make sure the weapons were secure at the back of the wagon.

"Have you been to Adena before?" Brother Azarov asked.

"Yes," he replied before he thought better of it. Yuri had never been. "No . . . But I always wanted to visit."

"Oh?" Azarov peered at the town as if expecting it to suddenly unfold into a more interesting version of itself. "Why? Is there something special about it?"

"There's a very fine mural in its cathedral."

"Of Sankta Lizabeta?"

Was this her town? Yes, he remembered now. She'd performed some kind of miracle here to lure the young king to the Fold. But there was no mural in the church. "I meant the statue," he said. She'd made it bleed black tears and covered it in roses.

"Who are you?"

Aleksander looked up from the cartridges of ammunition he was sorting. "I beg your pardon?"

Brother Azarov was standing beside the cart. His yellow hair was mussed from the night's adventure and his eyes were narrowed. "Whoever you are, you're not Yuri Vedenen."

He made himself chuckle. "Then who am I?"

"I don't know." Azarov's face was grim, and Aleksander realized too late that his show of confusion over Adena had been an act. "An impostor. An agent of the Lantsov king. One of the Apparat's men. The only thing I'm sure of is that you're a charlatan and no servant of the Starless One."

Aleksander turned slowly. "A servant? No. I will serve no one again in this life or any other." He considered his options. Could Brother Azarov be made to understand what he was, *who* he was? "You must listen closely, Azarov. You are on the precipice of something great—"

"Do not come near me! You are a heathen. A heretic. You would lead us into battle and see us murdered on the field."

"The Starless One—"

"You have no right to speak of him!"

Aleksander almost laughed. "No man should be forced to grapple with irony so furiously."

"Brother Chernov!" Azarov called.

Down in the market square, Chernov looked up and waved. He and the other pilgrims carried baskets and crates full of food and supplies.

Aleksander yanked Brother Azarov behind the cart and clapped a hand over the pilgrim's mouth. "You have asked for miracles and I have brought you miracles. You don't understand the forces at work here."

Azarov thrashed in his grip. He had the strength of the soldier he'd once been. He wrenched his head free. "I know evil when I see it."

Now Aleksander had to smile. "Maybe so."

He let a *nichevo'ya* form behind Azarov, towering and bewinged. Calling on *merzost* was painful, like a breath torn from his lungs, a moment of terror as his life was ripped away to form another. Creation. Abomination. But he was used to it by now.

Azarov's eyes widened as he saw the shadow of the monster behind him. He never had a chance to turn. A whimper squeaked from his lips as the *nichevo'ya*'s clawed hand burst through his chest. He looked down at it—black talons curled around his still-beating heart. Then he crumpled.

Murderer! Yuri's distress was like an alarm ringing in his skull. *You had no right!*

Be silent. Azarov was willing to die for me and he did.

Aleksander glanced around the wagon. The pilgrims were still approaching. He had mere moments to decide what to do with the

441

body. The *nichevo'ya* could carry it away but would be seen taking flight with Azarov. He would have to bury the pilgrim beneath the weapons and hope to retrieve the body when they returned to camp.

He heard shouting from the market square. Some kind of storm was moving in, the clouds casting dark shadows over the town.

No, not a storm. It was moving too fast for that, a blot of darkness spreading over the houses. Everything it touched turned to shadow, seeming to hold its shape for the barest moment, then dissolving into smoke. *Kilyklava.* The vampire. Had he somehow drawn the blight to Adena, or was it mere coincidence?

People scattered, screaming, trying to outrun it, trying to hurl themselves from its path.

Aleksander couldn't look away. The shadow raced toward him. Brother Chernov and the others dove from the road, abandoning their bread and cabbages.

Run.

He knew he should. But it was too late. What would death feel like the second time around? The old horse had time to release a startled whinny, before it and the cart were swallowed by the darkness.

The shadow surged toward him—and parted. It coursed around him in a rush of night. It was like gazing into the black waters of a lake. Then it was gone. Aleksander turned and saw the blight pour over the road and meadow before somewhere on the distant horizon it seemed to stop.

It had come on silently, swiftly, an arrow shot from some invisible bow, and it vanished just as fast. In the town square—or what was left of it—people were weeping and crying out. Half the town was just as it had been—full of color, the market stalls packed with cured meats, heaps of turnips, bolts of wool. But the other half was simply gone, as if a careless hand had wiped it away, leaving nothing but a gray smudge, a swath of oblivion where life had been moments before.

The pilgrims were staring at him as they lurched to their feet, climbing from the ditch they'd rolled into.

Aleksander looked down at the ground. Between his boots, he saw mud, pebbles, a scraggly patch of grass. To his left, to his right, nothing but dead gray sand. The cart was gone, all the weapons. And Brother Azarov.

Brother Chernov's round face was full of wonder as he approached. "It spared you."

"I don't understand it," Aleksander said, doing his best to sound dismayed. "Brother Azarov was not so lucky."

The pilgrims didn't seem to care. They were gazing at him with awe in their eyes.

"Truly, you have the Starless One's blessing."

A scrawny young pilgrim looked back at the town. "But why would the Starless One save Brother Vedenen from the blight and not those innocent people?"

"It's not for us to question his ways," said Brother Chernov as they began their long walk back to camp. "When the Darkling returns and is made a Saint, the blight will trouble us no more."

Yet another thing Chernov was wrong about.

Aleksander glanced back at the town. He had done worse to Novokribirsk at the start of the civil war. But *he* had been in control. The vampire had no master. It could not be reasoned with or seduced. Why had it spared him? Perhaps it recognized the power that had created the Fold. Or maybe the blight was drawn to life and it had sensed something unnatural in him, something it did not thirst for.

The rest of the day was spent on the Fold, making a new plan for their travel north and where to acquire weapons and supplies. They trained, they prayed, they ate their meager supply of hardtack and salt pork, and lay down to sleep.

"Rest," he told them. "Rest and we will await the sign." When the right moment came on the battlefield, he would release his *nichevo'ya* and they would all know the Starless One had returned.

These people were outcasts, he realized, as he picked his way among the sleeping pilgrims. Just as the Grisha had once been.

It's not too late for you. So Alina had said. Or was it his mother? Or the gnat? It didn't matter. All his long life he'd been guided by clarity of purpose. It had let him kill without remorse and had given him the daring to seize power that should have been beyond his grasp. It had brought him back from the dead. That was the clarity he needed now.

Aleksander lay down in the blankets that had been set aside for him. They smelled powerfully of horse. He picked up a handful of the Fold's dead sands and let them drift through his fingers. Was this his legacy? This wound where nothing would grow? A blight that spread even as his nation marched to war?

He looked up at the stars spread like spilled treasure across the night sky. The Starless One. His followers spoke his name in tones of reverence, and in the days to come, their numbers would grow. But people didn't turn their eyes to the heavens in search of the dark. It was the light they sought.

All that will change, he vowed. *I will give them salvation until they beg me to stop.*

34
NIKOLAI

THE MOOD AT LAZLAYON was bleak. Nikolai had wanted to speak to Adrik before they landed, but he hadn't seen the Squaller. There was little room not to bump into each other on a ship like the *Cormorant*—and that meant Adrik was avoiding him.

"A word," Nikolai said as they disembarked at the misty landing strip beside the secret entrance to the labs.

Adrik looked wary but said only, "Yes, Your Majesty."

"If you don't feel you can serve any longer, you may put in your resignation. We're desperate for trained Grisha, but I can't afford a soldier whose heart isn't in this fight."

"I have no interest in resigning."

"You're sure? Think before you answer."

Adrik was younger than Nikolai, but his consistently miserable demeanor made that easy to forget. Now he looked like a boy—the boy whose body had been savaged by the Darkling's monsters and who had fought on when others had lost their will.

"Are you . . . how much of you is you and how much is that thing?"

"I don't know," Nikolai answered honestly. "But the demon isn't the Darkling's to command. It's mine."

"You're sure about that?"

Nikolai had no reason to be. And yet he was. Maybe the darkness inside him had once belonged to the Darkling, a demon born of his enemy's power. But they'd begun to make their peace when they'd faced each other in the thorn wood. It was his monster now.

"I'm sure," Nikolai said. "If I weren't, I think you know I'd never let myself lead an army."

Adrik eyed him speculatively. "I'm still on your side, Korol Rezni. For now. After the war, we'll see. Maybe I'll be killed in action and I won't have to worry about it."

"That's the Adrik I know."

Adrik shrugged, his gloom descending over him like a well-worn cloak. "This country's always been cursed," he said as he headed toward the labs. "Maybe it deserves a cursed king."

"He'll come around," said Zoya, approaching with a stack of correspondence in her hands. "Reports from our commanders. Speculation from our scouts about where and when the Fjerdans will attack."

It was hard to be grateful for a war, but he was glad that he and Zoya had plenty to talk about that *wasn't* what he'd said on the airship. Would he unsay it, if he could? He hated the skittishness he sensed in her, the way she seemed to be keeping her distance. But war was unpredictable. He might not survive the fight to come. He couldn't be sorry for speaking his heart, or at least some part of it.

"Where would you put your money?" he asked.

Zoya considered. "The permafrost. It's perfect terrain for Fjerdan tanks, and the cloud cover hurts our flyers."

"Not Arkesk?"

"It would make sense for the Fjerdans except for the little matter of Sturmhond's blockade. They won't get any support from the sea. Besides, we know they're in secret talks with West Ravka. You think they'll invade on western soil anyway?"

"Maybe," said Nikolai. If the talks were a sham, Fjerda might do just that. Arkesk was closer to the Fjerdan capital, and its rocky topography was rough but manageable. "The trees would slow them down. That could work to our advantage."

"Saints' teeth," Zoya swore.

Nikolai looked up and saw Count Kirigin bustling toward them in a remarkable orchid coat and breeches.

"So sorry to interrupt, but there's been a disturbance at the gate. There's a man asking to see the king."

Nikolai frowned. The *Cormorant* had flown directly to Lazlayon under cover of mist. There was no reason for anyone to think he was visiting Kirigin's estate.

"Who is he?" Zoya asked.

"No idea," said Kirigin. "He's a bit of a mess. You might mistake him for a pile of rags. I can have the guards send him packing."

"No," said Zoya. "I want to know why he came looking for the king here. Have him searched for weapons and brought to the house."

"He won't come in. He says he wishes to speak to the king alone."

Zoya's brows shot up. "Alone?"

"A stranger in rags who dares command a king," said Nikolai. "I'm intrigued."

"He could be an assassin," Zoya said.

"A terrible one."

"Or a very good one, since you seem willing to meet him."

"Lend me your guards, Kirigin. Let's see what this stranger has to say."

The walk to the gates was a long one, but Nikolai didn't mind it. He needed time to think. Trying to pinpoint where Fjerda would launch their attack was a deadly guessing game. Ravka couldn't afford to spread its forces too thin, but if he chose the wrong place to make a stand, Fjerda would blast through the northern border unopposed. So would the enemy choose Arkesk or the permafrost or somewhere else entirely?

Count Kirigin's description of the stranger had been apt. He was tall—and that was about all Nikolai could say regarding his appearance. He was bundled in a heavy wool coat, a hat slung low over his ears, so that little more than his bright blue eyes were visible, and he was covered in soot.

"Damn it," said Nikolai, suddenly realizing what this had to be. "He must have been in Os Alta and lost family or friends in the bombing." He'd come here looking for someone to hold accountable, and Nikolai couldn't blame him for choosing the king. Well. This wouldn't be the worst thing he'd face in the coming days.

Nikolai greeted the stranger. "I'm told I have been ordered to make an appearance."

"Not ordered. Invited." He spoke Ravkan with a faint accent.

"The hour is late. What can I do for you?"

The stranger reached into his pocket. Instantly, Zoya and Kirigin's guards lunged in front of Nikolai, hands and rifles raised.

"Best to move slowly in such situations," said Nikolai.

The stranger held up his palms, showing he had no weapon, just a small package wrapped in brown paper.

"For the king," he said, holding it out. "And only for the king."

Cautiously, Zoya reached for the package.

"Give it over," said Nikolai. "If he's going to kill me with the world's tiniest bomb, I'll at least have an interesting death."

He pulled the paper away. It was a miniature of Tatiana Lantsov, Ravka's former queen. His mother. Nikolai's gaze snapped to the stranger before him. He'd only ever seen his true father in a portrait, a miniature just like this one that had belonged to his mother. Magnus Opjer had looked the spitting image of Nikolai. Except for his bright blue eyes.

"Leave us," he said to Zoya and the guards.

"It isn't safe—" Zoya began, but she stopped when she saw the expression on his face. "All right," she said. "But we'll be just up the path. I'm not letting either of you out of my sight."

He listened to their footsteps fade but kept his eyes on the man before him.

Opjer unwound his scarf and Nikolai drew in a breath.

"Tatiana told me you took after me," Opjer said. "But I cannot quite believe the likeness."

"It's all true then."

"I'm afraid so."

Had a part of Nikolai believed it was some great joke? That his mother had been mistaken? That Fjerda's rumormongering would prove to be nothing more than gossip? But here was the proof; all the whispers were true. *He* was the pretender. He had no Lantsov blood. Not a drop of it. In fact, he was more Fjerdan than Ravkan.

Nikolai took in Opjer's ragged clothes. Why had he fled Fjerda? Why would he come all this way to see a son he'd never met before? Maybe he did have assassination in mind.

"Why come to me now, looking like a beggar, bearing a miniature of my mother? Mere sentiment?"

"I tried to get here sooner. To warn you of the bombing."

So, Nikolai was right about that much. Opjer had been in Os Alta during the attack. "You knew what they intended?"

"I overheard their plans where I was being held captive. I got here in time to sound the alarm, but it was all for nothing."

"*You* were the one who got them to ring the bells in the lower town." Nikolai had wondered how they'd somehow spotted the Fjerdan flyers before his palace lookouts.

"Yes. But still the bombs fell."

Then this man had a conscience. Or he knew how to pretend to have one.

"How did you find this place? How did you know I would be here?"

"I didn't. But I knew I had no hope of getting in to see you at the palace, and when I heard the tales of Lazlayon . . ." He lifted his shoulders. "I knew you were a frequent guest of the count's. I hoped there was more to it than it seemed."

"And did you share this knowledge with anyone?"

"No."

Nikolai didn't know what to believe. It seemed impossible that this person who had loomed in his imagination so long should be standing right before him. He had never wanted to be an ordinary man more. An ordinary man might greet this stranger properly, invite him in for a glass of whiskey or a cup of tea, take the time to understand him. But not a king.

"You haven't answered my question," said Nikolai. "Why come here tonight? Why seek me out after all these years? Is it blackmail you have in mind? Or have you come to kill Ravka's king?"

Opjer's back straightened. "Do you think so little of me?"

"I *know* so little of you. You're a stranger to me."

"I wanted to know you," Opjer said. "I kept my distance for your mother's sake. I never wanted to risk harming either of you. I came here . . . I'm here because I'm selfish, because I wanted to see my son once before I disappear."

"Disappear?"

"It is the best gift I can give you. The only gift, really. I'm going to erase myself. As long as I live, I am a threat to you."

"All Saints, you can't mean you're going to fall on your sword for the sake of my throne."

Opjer laughed, and Nikolai felt a chill race up his spine. That was *his* laugh.

"I'm not nearly so self-sacrificing. No, I will go to Novyi Zem. I have money. I have time. I'll live a new life there. Maybe I'll have myself tailored and really start fresh."

"A shame," said Nikolai. "We're extremely handsome."

Opjer grinned. "Think of all the poor souls who will never look on this face."

"That's . . . that's really all you came here for? To meet me?"

"Not all. Not entirely. You have a half sister."

"Linnea."

Opjer looked pleased. "You know of her? She's studying engineering at the University of Ketterdam. Fjerdan law prohibits passing my holdings directly to her, but I've made arrangements. I only ask . . . if the war goes your way, I would ask that you look out for her, offer her your protection as I was never able to offer you mine."

"I might like having a little sister. Though I'm not much for sharing." Even if Ravka lost the war, Nikolai would find a way to reach out to Linnea Opjer. He could do that much. Assuming he lived. "I give you my word."

"I hope you keep your crown," said Opjer. "And if you ever wish to have a longer chat, if you're ever free to travel, you can send word to me at the Golden Hour in Cofton."

"A tavern?"

"A highly disreputable one. I intend to buy it, so the staff should know where to reach me. I suppose I'll have to choose a new name too."

"I don't recommend Lantsov."

"I'll strike it from the list."

Nikolai wanted him to stay. He wanted to speak to him, to know what his mother had been like before a life of indolence and envy had hardened her heart. He wanted to talk about ships and how Opjer had built his empire and where he'd been on his travels. But every minute he spent in his father's presence put them both at risk.

"Forgive me for a certain mercenary bent, but is there anything more you can tell me of Fjerda's plans?"

Opjer smiled. He looked almost proud. "I can tell you Jarl Brum hopes to marry his daughter to Prince Rasmus."

"Our intelligence suggests Rasmus might favor diplomacy over open war."

"He might. But once he's a member of Brum's household, I would count on nothing. If Brum can't control the prince, he'll find a way to destroy him. There is a quality among Fjerdans . . . we call it *gerkenig*. The need for action. We leap in when we shouldn't because we can't help ourselves. If Brum sees an opportunity, he'll take it. I've been guilty of it many times myself."

"Recklessness."

"Not exactly. It's a need to seize the moment."

"That sounds uncomfortably familiar."

"I thought it might."

In the distance, from the direction of the laboratories beneath the Gilded Bog, they heard a series of booms.

"Fireworks," said Nikolai.

"Of course," said Opjer, and Nikolai knew he didn't believe a word of it. "I suppose this is where we say goodbye."

"I'm not sure we've even properly said hello. I am . . ." Nikolai struggled to find a word for what he felt. Sorry to see this stranger go? Longing for a father he'd never had? Grateful that Opjer was willing to give up the life he knew for the sake of preserving Nikolai's false bloodline?

The man Nikolai had believed to be his father for most of his life had been a source of embarrassment and shame. Nikolai had never understood him, never wanted to be like him. He'd read enough books and seen enough plays to understand what a father was meant to be—someone kind and steady who dispensed wisdom and taught you how to wield a sword and throw a punch. Actually, in most plays, the fathers got killed off and had to be avenged, but they certainly seemed wise and loving in the first act. Nikolai remembered what Zoya had said about her mother on the airship: *Maybe I miss something I never had.* Nikolai had never missed having a father because he'd never really had one. That was what he'd believed until this moment, standing at the gates, looking at Magnus Opjer.

"Here," said Nikolai. "Your miniature." He held out the portrait of his mother.

"Keep it. I don't want to look backward. There's too much regret there." Opjer bowed. "Good luck, Your Highness."

Nikolai watched his father go. He had to wonder at the mad ambition that had brought him here, that had driven him to pursue the crown when he might have had a hundred other lives. He might have left the future of Ravka to his brother. He might have gotten to be someone's son. He could have loved whom he wanted to, married whom he wished to—assuming the vexing creature said yes. But all those lives were gone, vanished at each crossroads, with each choice he'd made. He'd given them up for Ravka. Would it be worth it in the end?

He didn't know. But he wasn't going to stand by a gate and brood over it.

"Zoya," he called, as he jogged back to her and the guards. "Have you ever heard of something called *gerkenig*?"

"I believe it's a stew," said Count Kirigin. "Made with halibut?"

"It's not a stew," said Nikolai. "At least, not that I know of. But it's given me an idea."

Zoya tucked a strand of black hair behind her ear. "Is it a formula for quadrupling the amount of titanium we have?"

"Afraid not. This is a formula for blood."

"Our blood or the Fjerdans'?"

"Saving ours, spilling theirs."

It would mean sending Zoya away again. It would mean taking a tremendous gamble. Arkesk or the permafrost? If the Fjerdans couldn't decide where to strike, maybe he could make the decision for them.

Nikolai began the long walk back to the laboratory. Dawn was coming and he had a mission to prepare for. He would write a letter for Zoya too, ask her to take care of Linnea Opjer if he didn't survive, tell her all the things he hadn't said on that damned airship and that he wasn't fool enough to turn around and say now. He didn't pause and his steps didn't falter.

He would not look backward either.

35
NINA

YLVA FOUND THEM IN NINA'S BED, gowns half on,
a rumple of silk and mouths bruised from kissing.

She stood frozen in the doorway and then said, "Your father is
already on base and we're expected at the airfield in an hour. Pack a
small bag and wear warm clothing. And Hanne, for Djel's sake, cover
that mark on your neck."

As soon as the door shut, Nina and Hanne burst into nervous
laughter, but it didn't last.

"They're going to send me back to the convent," Hanne said.

Nina snorted. "To live in isolation with a big group of women?
That's the last place they'll send you."

Hanne groaned and began to shuck off her gown as she strode to
the dressing room and poured water into the basin. She was all lean
muscle and tawny skin, and Nina wanted to drag her back to the

warmth of their bed and stay there forever. But there was no forever. Not in Fjerda.

"You're right," Hanne said as she splashed water on her face. "They're going to marry me off."

"To a prince."

"You're so sure he'll ask?"

"Yes." And last night Hanne had been sure too. This morning they both wanted to believe there would be some kind of escape. But even if the prince didn't propose to Hanne, someone else would. She'd been the darling of Heartwood.

Nina yanked her gown over her head and exchanged it for a simpler wool dress. "Hanne . . . Let's leave."

"What?" Hanne had pulled on a skirt and blouse and was tailoring away the love bite Nina seemed to have left on her neck.

"Let's leave. Just like you said, but with less galloping. We'll go to Ravka. We'll go to Novyi Zem."

She knew what Hanne was going to say, that she couldn't disappoint her parents, that she had a duty to remain, that she could do more good for the Grisha and Fjerda as a princess and one day a queen.

Hanne pulled a knitted Fjerdan vest over her blouse. "How does that look?"

"Absolutely awful."

"I thought so." Hanne sat down on the bed to wriggle into her boots. "Do you think the Hringsa could get us out?"

Nina paused with her hands on the buttons of her dress, unsure she'd heard correctly. "I . . . Yes. I think so."

Hanne grinned at her, and it was like Nina had been punched in the chest by a ray of sunshine. She thought she might have to sit down. "Then let's leave. Not right away. If we can still help Rasmus, we have to try. But then we go."

"We go," Nina repeated, not quite believing it. They would need time to plan—and for Nina to figure out what to do about Joran.

"We'll have to be careful. My mother may try to separate us."

"I thought you were going to say no."

"Do you want to talk me out of it?"

"No! Absolutely not." Nina seized her hands and yanked her up from the bed. Saints, she was tall. "I just . . ." She didn't know what to say. That she hadn't felt real hope since she'd lost Matthias, that she'd thought she'd lost her chance at joy. Until now. Until Hanne. She stood up on her toes and planted a kiss on Hanne's lips. "Never let me go."

"Never," Hanne said. "Do you still think peace is possible?"

"Only if Ravka can push Fjerda back decisively. If this turns into an invasion, Fjerda has no reason to sue for peace. But if Ravka makes a real showing, Fjerda will have to consider its options."

"I don't think my father will retreat. Not this time. His reputation can't afford it, and peace is not the vision he has for Fjerda's future."

"Then let's hope the prince is strong enough to choose another path."

"We'll make sure he is. And then we'll get free of this place."

Free. A mad word. A magical word. Nina wasn't even sure what that might feel like anymore. But she wanted to find out.

The airship was not one of the luxury craft used by royals and nobles, but a military vessel, painted gray and blue for better camouflage against the sea and sky. They were given quarters to share with another family and traveled through the day over the True Sea. At sunset, Ylva came to collect them for the landing. She'd barely been able to look either of them in the eye.

"Where are we?" Hanne asked.

Nina peered out of the window and was baffled by what she saw below. "Is that an island?"

But as the airship descended, Nina realized that they were not landing on an island at all. It was a massive naval base. She could see huge warships docked alongside it, and flocks of heavily armed flyers parked on its runways, ready to leap into the air. Spires like giant prongs were arrayed in curving rows on either side of the base— viewing towers. They looked like teeth and gave the base the appearance of a gaping mouth. Uniformed soldiers and military personnel swarmed over the deck like insects, many of them congregating near a central structure of buildings that served as a command center. Its flat roof was painted with the Fjerdan flag—the Grimjer wolf rampant.

Dread sat heavy on Nina's shoulders, a living, muscled thing that whispered doom in her ear. She knew little about weapons of war, but she knew Ravka had nothing like this monstrosity. It was beyond imagination.

The airship set down on one of the base's landing strips, and she followed Hanne and Ylva along the gangway.

Redvin was waiting at the bottom of the ramp in his *drüskelle* uniform. He grinned, and Nina knew she would be content to live a hundred years and never see that expression of eager anticipation on his grizzled face again. "Welcome to Leviathan's Mouth."

"Where is Commander Brum?" Nina asked.

"Where he needs to be," said Redvin. "I'll show you to your quarters."

"What *is* this place?" whispered Hanne. She sounded as scared as Nina felt. All their plans and schemes seemed futile in the face of power like this.

Their quarters turned out to be a cramped box with bunk beds tucked against both walls.

"Well, thankfully we have a private washroom and we'll all be together," said Ylva. Nina suspected she meant it. Hanne's mother might never trust them on their own again.

Brum arrived in their dimly lit cabin after midnight. He looked happier than Nina had seen him in months.

"It's time," he said.

Ylva gave a tremulous smile. "You must promise me you'll be safe."

"Ask me to be brave, not safe," Brum said. "I will be with my men on the northern front. But you will be secure here with Redvin, and you'll have a bird's-eye view of the sea invasion. Our ships finally broke Sturmhond's blockade. Ravka's coast is ours for the taking."

Nina felt sick. Had the Kerch helped to smash through Sturmhond's ships? But if Fjerda intended to invade the coast . . . "You weren't really negotiating with West Ravka."

"Clever girl," said Brum. "No, we had no reason to negotiate with them in good faith. Their navy is no match for ours. With the blockade in ruins, we can invade by sea in the south and on land in the north. Our forces will crush Os Kervo like a pair of pincers."

The troops attacking from the north must already be on the move. The second front would be launched from the sea. Fjerda would use this nightmare of a base to storm the beaches south of Os Kervo. West Ravka didn't stand a chance, and once the coast belonged to Fjerda, they'd push east and take Ravka's capital.

The information was useless to her now. She had no way to reach her contacts in the Hringsa, and even if she did, the intelligence would come too late.

A bird's-eye view of the invasion. She would watch Fjerda shatter the west, and then what hope would there be? Ravka would never recover from such a blow. Peace would be impossible.

Once Brum was gone, Nina tried to rest but couldn't find sleep.

She had the sense that she was rushing toward something in the dark, with no way to stop her momentum.

Ylva roused them before dawn to lead them to one of the observation towers. "Rebraid your hair, Mila," she suggested. "And pinch your cheeks to put a little color in them. Many important men will be watching the invasion. You never know whose attention you might catch."

Nina resisted the urge to roll her eyes and obliged Ylva. If this pretense would keep her in the Brums' household a while longer, she would gladly primp and flirt as required.

When they emerged on the vast expanse of the deck, Nina could see lights glinting off the Ravkan coast. Leviathan had crept closer to land in the night.

As they were about to enter the tower, a voice called out, "Hanne Brum!"

Prince Rasmus was strolling across the deck in a military uniform, flanked by royal guards, a grim-faced Joran at his side. At the sight of the young *drüskelle*, Nina felt her rage return. She'd pushed it aside for Hanne's sake, to keep them both safe, but there would be a reckoning. Hanne might wish for Nina to look to the future, but Nina couldn't do that until she'd made peace with the ghosts of her past.

"What is the whelp doing here?" Redvin muttered. He managed a forced smile. "Your Highness, I had no idea you'd be joining us aboard Leviathan."

"Why wouldn't I?"

"It's only that it's so much safer in Djerholm with the rest of the royal family."

"Leviathan's Mouth is safe enough for Commander Brum's daughter. I think a fragile princeling like myself might dare it too. Especially when my country is at war. Besides, the Ravkans will need *someone* to surrender to. Come, Hanne, we will watch the invasion together." He held out his arm.

Redvin stepped in front of Hanne. It was the move of a soldier, not a diplomat. One did not thwart a crown prince's desires.

"What are you doing, Redvin?" whispered Ylva, panicked. "It is the prince's right. Go on, Hanne. Mila—"

"Mila can remain with you," said the prince. "I wouldn't want to leave you alone, Ylva."

At that Ylva froze, unsure of what to do. Hanne could not go with the prince unchaperoned.

Joran gave the faintest shake of his head, but Nina didn't know how to stop this. She clung to Hanne's hand.

"I'd prefer to have my friend with me," said Hanne.

"But your friend is not invited," said the prince.

"Your Highness . . ." Ylva began, taking hold of Hanne's arm. But the prince's stare brooked no opposition.

Hanne had never been alone with the prince before. It was not acceptable or appropriate. Unless he intended to offer her the promise of marriage. Was that what this was? Did the prince mean to make Hanne his bride or simply use her as a pawn in his ongoing struggle with Brum? Both could be true. If he took her to the observation tower without Mila there to act as chaperone, he would have to offer marriage or Hanne's reputation would be ruined. No one would offer for her. And if he did propose, Hanne would have to say yes. Nina wanted to scream. They should have run last night, away from the palace, away from all of it. But this was the disaster she'd built. She'd placed herself and Hanne between the prince and Brum, a bulwark against war, and now they would break like Sturmhond's blockade.

"It will be fine," Hanne said. In Nina's ear, she murmured, "We'll find a way out. There's something worth salvaging in him. I know it."

"Come along, Hanne," said the prince. He was still holding out his arm. It was not an invitation. It was a demand.

"You must let go," Hanne whispered.

Never.

Nina forced her fingers to release. Hanne smiled and drifted over to Rasmus, looping her arm into his.

"See you in victory," said the prince.

Nina met Joran's eyes and willed him to understand. *You and I have accounts to settle. Watch over her.*

"Will he . . . will he offer for her?" Ylva asked. She'd been delighted at the notice Hanne had garnered from the prince, but this was not attention any girl wanted.

"That uncooked cutlet wouldn't dare do otherwise," Redvin growled. "Commander Brum would have his head."

Redvin could bluster all he wanted. Nina and Ylva knew better. Brum didn't have the status to gainsay a prince. Though if Brum found victory today, who knew what power he might attain in the wake of it?

"She will be a princess," Ylva declared as they followed Redvin into the observation tower, as if she could cast a spell and make it so. "All will be well." Nina said nothing and Ylva took her hand, giving it a quick squeeze. "The prince must ask and she must accept. You see that, don't you? It is the only thing that can keep both of you safe." She hesitated. "You can join their household. It's not unheard of. If you're careful."

Nina made herself nod and say, "Yes. Of course. Whatever Hanne wants."

Ylva's gaze was distant. "What we want . . . what we want for ourselves and for our daughters has never been the question. Only what we can bear."

Survive this place. Survive this life. Find someone to protect you since you're not free to protect yourself. Sire children. Pray for boys. Pray the strange and willful daughter you raised will somehow find her way. Fear for her, watch over her, realize your fear and your watchfulness mean nothing when the storm comes on. Ylva couldn't see any other path for Hanne. And Nina wasn't sure she could either.

Redvin led them inside a steel elevator that carried them skyward. *Even the elevator runs better*, Nina thought miserably, recalling the clanking brass contraption she'd once ridden in at Lazlayon. Only hours ago, she'd felt sure that she and Hanne would find a way out of all this. Now her fear had swallowed that hope.

The elevator lurched to a stop at the top of the tower, and they emerged into a room lined with windows that had been fitted with different types of lenses. A large crowd of officers had gathered to watch the invasion, and the mood was tense but jubilant. In the distance, Nina could see the curve of the bay, the seagrass-covered knolls teeming with Ravkan soldiers and tanks, and churning through the water, Fjerdan ships, tank carriers, and troop carriers driving toward Ravka.

The Ravkan forces looked battered and flimsy compared to the metal beasts the Fjerdans commanded. Nina saw First Army soldiers climbing the rocks that bordered the low cliffs of the bay. Why not send Tidemakers? Had they been told to hold back? They had an antidote to *parem* now. Why wouldn't they use Grisha to raise the waves and try to sink the Fjerdan boats before they landed? Maybe the Fjerdan invasion had arrived too suddenly for them to mount a proper defense.

Nina watched the invading Fjerdan fleet draw closer, like monsters from the deep, gray-backed and hungry.

"The first strike," said Redvin. "We'll drive inland, then close on Os Kervo from the south as Brum's men close from the north. The soil will run red with Ravkan blood."

But Nina wasn't so sure. A thought had entered her head, equal parts dread and hope.

"Why do they meet no opposition?" Ylva asked.

"The Ravkans expected Sturmhond's blockade to hold. The fools concentrated their forces to the north. All that remains in the south is a skeleton crew to meet our assault."

Sturmhond's blockade. Just how had the Fjerdans broken through?

Nina bent to a long glass and trained it on the Ravkan forces. It was hard to make out much from this distance, but they seemed unnaturally still. As if they were simply waiting. She focused the lens on the figures she saw standing on the rocks—and recognized a familiar head of raven hair, lifted by the wind.

Not an ordinary soldier. Not a Tidemaker. Zoya Nazyalensky. Ravka's most powerful Squaller and Grisha general. If Ravka was making its stand on the northern front, what was Zoya doing here?

"Does it trouble you, Mila?" said Ylva. "I have long been a soldier's wife. I'm used to the realities of battle. But we don't have to watch."

"No," said Nina. "I want to see."

"At last a bit of spine!" Redvin crowed. "You'll enjoy this first taste of victory."

The Fjerdan soldiers leapt into the waves, rifles in hand, charging toward the beach, a tide of violence.

One by one the soldiers on the rocks raised their hands. An army of Squallers.

Zoya was the last. Lightning forked through the skies—not the single bolts Nina had seen Squallers summon before, but a crackling web, a thousand spears of jagged light that turned the sky a vivid violet before they struck the water.

The crowd around Nina gasped.

"Sweet Djel," shouted Redvin. "No!"

But it was too late.

The sea was suddenly alight, seething like a boiling pot, steam hissing off its surface. Nina could not hear the men in the shallows scream, but she could see their mouths open wide, their bodies shaking as current passed through them. The Fjerdan tank carriers seemed to crumple in on themselves, roofs collapsing in heaps of melted metal, treads welded together.

Sturmhond's blockade hadn't broken at all. It had deliberately given way, opening the door to the trap and letting Fjerda's navy sail through. That was what the Ravkans had been waiting for.

The lightning stopped, leaving the sky clear but for a few clouds. Zoya and her Squallers were done speaking.

The observation tower had gone silent as the officers stared at what was left of their sea invasion, the bodies of their men bobbing in the gentle waves lapping the Ravkan shore, their war machines slumped like shipwreck hulls, some slowly sinking into the sea.

Ylva had her hands clapped over her mouth. Her eyes were full of tears. Nina wondered what Hanne was feeling, watching this destruction beside the prince.

Nina couldn't celebrate the deaths of soldiers, most of whom had little choice in when they marched or what kind of war they waged. But she thought of the winter ball, of the joyful toasts, how readily Fjerda had celebrated the eve of what they believed would be another nation's destruction.

This was war. Not parades and boasts but blood and sacrifice, and Ravka would not go quietly.

"We are lost," Ylva whispered. "So many dead in an instant."

"Shut your mouth," Redvin snarled. "This is why women don't belong near the battlefield."

A woman just shoved your "taste of victory" right down your throat, Nina thought with satisfaction.

"This is nothing," Redvin continued, slicing his hand through the air, addressing the officers now. "This offensive was insurance. The Ravkans have a nightmare waiting for them on the northern front that they'll never recover from."

"More tanks?" Nina said, putting a hopeful tremor in her voice.

Redvin laughed, and the sound raised the hair on Nina's arms. "Oh no, little girl. A weapon like nothing this world has ever seen. And the royal whelp helped create it."

"Prince Rasmus?" Her surprise was real.

"Yes, he's more bloodthirsty than any of us could have hoped. Got the idea at the opera, if you please."

Hajefetla. Songbird. Was Redvin speaking of the plans she'd seen on Brum's desk, the weapon the prince had spoken of at the ball? *Rasmus* had invented this new weapon. Rasmus, who they had hoped might be steered toward peace, who Nina had encouraged King Nikolai to believe might be an ally. They had known he was cruel, but they'd hoped it was a petty cruelty, personal, childish, a habit born of frustration. They'd wanted to believe he could be purged of Fjerda's poison. But he was a warmonger, just like Brum. She remembered what Joran had said that night on the ice moat: *He was* testing *his new strength.* Rasmus didn't want to forge a new world that valued life and mercy more than strength or military might. He wanted to prove to the world he was Fjerdan to the core. She had to figure out how to warn Nikolai that the prince couldn't be counted on. But first she had to get out of this tower and find a way to Hanne.

"I cannot bear this," Nina said. "It is too terrible to see our soldiers suffer."

Ylva placed her arm around Nina's shoulder and shepherded her toward the elevator. "We'll leave the men to it." Once the doors closed, she said, "It will be all right, Mila. If Redvin says Fjerda has the advantage, we do."

That's exactly what I'm afraid of.

When they reached the deck, Nina was glad of the salt sting of the sea air. It was easy to say, "Ylva, can you go on without me? I'm not ready to be back in our cabin yet. I need to clear my head."

Ylva removed her shawl and tucked it around Nina's shoulders. "You cannot go to her, Mila. His guards will not allow it. I wish you could. I wish I'd sent you both to live with the Hedjut."

"I won't try to find her," Nina lied. "I just need some air."

"Very well. But stay out of their way, Mila. After a loss like this . . . soldiers look for someone to punish."

Nina nodded. As soon as Ylva turned her back, she started cutting a path through the flurry of soldiers and sailors on deck, trying to find her way to the base of the tower where she'd seen Prince Rasmus take Hanne. She readied her bone darts and reached out with her power, sensing the corpses in the water, some in boats retreating back to Leviathan's Mouth. She would get to Hanne. If she had to go through Joran to do it, even better. And then? She wasn't sure. She'd steal a boat, get them to safety, get them far from here.

She pulled open the door to the base of the tower and wrinkled her nose. There was a strange smell—incense and the scent of turned soil. She felt a prick against her neck and then she was falling forward, into the dark.

36

ZOYA

ZOYA DESCENDED FROM THE ROCKS on a gust of wind. She could see where her lightning had struck the beach, leaving the sheen of glass where sand had been. She didn't turn her eyes to the waters and the bodies there, but marched up the gentle hills of seagrass and joined the rest of her troops. Up close, the painted flats they'd erected above the beach looked less like tanks than what they really were—a bit of theater meant to deceive the enemy. But they'd only needed them to be believable from a distance, some sleight of hand inspired by their associates at the Crow Club. If the Fjerdans had seen the bay almost entirely unprotected, they might have sensed the trap and the storm that awaited them. Ravka's soldiers had been outfitted in rubber-soled boots instead of leather, just in case.

"So many dead," Genya murmured as Zoya approached the Triumvirate command tent and called for fresh water.

"It had to be done." She couldn't stop to grieve for soldiers she'd never known, not when her own people were mobilizing on the northern front. She had warned Nikolai that she'd been made to be a weapon. This was what she was good at, what she understood.

She strode toward the flyer they'd readied. She needed to get in the air.

"You're all right?" Genya asked, pulling on her flying goggles. She'd posed that question a lot since they'd lost David, as if the words could somehow protect them from harm.

"Just covered in salt. Word from the northern front?"

"They've engaged."

"Then let's get moving." Zoya tried to ignore the fear that seized her. They would travel low and inland to avoid being intercepted by any Fjerdans in the air. A regiment of Grisha and First Army soldiers would remain behind in case Fjerda decided to make another attempt at the beach, but Zoya thought they'd send their naval base to the northern front to bolster the invasion there.

"We do have some news," said Genya, drawing Zoya from her thoughts. "The Starless have been spotted on the field."

Zoya smacked her fist against the flyer's metal hull. "Fighting for Ravka or Fjerda?"

"Hard to tell. They've hung back from the fray." Genya paused. "He's with them."

Of course the Darkling had found his way to the field, surrounded by his followers. But what did he intend? Nikolai had said the Darkling had a gift for spectacle.

"The battle is just the backdrop for him," she realized. "He's going to stage his return with some kind of miracle." She remembered what

Alina had said to him. *Why do* you *have to be the savior?* The Darkling would wait for his moment, maybe even for Nikolai's death, and then the Saint would appear to lead them all to——what? Freedom? He'd never had to face Fjerda's new war machines. He couldn't beat them on his own, no matter what he believed. And Zoya would dose herself with *parem* before she followed him again.

"General!" A soldier was running toward her with a note in his hand. "I was asked to deliver this to you."

Genya plucked it from his fingers.

"By whom?" said Zoya.

"A man in monk's robes. He came ashore a little ways up the coast."

"Were his robes brown or black?"

"Brown and bearing the Sun Summoner's symbol."

Genya's eyes moved over the paper. "Oh, Saints."

"Give it to me."

"Zoya, you must keep your head."

"What the hell does it say?" She snatched it from Genya's hand.

The note was brief and in Ravkan: *I have Mila Jandersdat. Come to the eastern observation tower aboard Leviathan's Mouth. She will await you in the cells.*

Zoya crushed the note in her hand. The Apparat had Nina.

"This is a trap," said Genya. "Not a negotiation tactic. He wants you to do something rash. Zoya? Zoya, what are you doing?"

Zoya stalked back to the tent. "Something rash."

"We have a strategy," Genya argued, hurrying to follow. "It's working. We need to stick to it. And Nikolai needs you to help guide our rockets."

Zoya hesitated. She didn't want to leave her king without the resources he needed. And damn it, she wanted to be beside him in this fight. Every time she thought of him lying on the floor of the *Cormorant*, his arm cushioning his head as he spoke those words, those absurd, beautiful words . . . *No prince and no power could make me stop wanting you.* The memory was like drinking something sweet and poisonous. Even knowing the misery it would cause her, she couldn't stop craving the taste.

You should have said yes, she thought for the hundredth time. *You should have told him you loved him.* But what good was that word to people like her? Nikolai deserved more. Ravka required more. But for an hour, for a day, he might have been hers. And if something happened to him on that battlefield? She'd been too afraid to say yes to him, to show him the truth of her longing, to admit that from the first time she'd seen him, she'd known he was the hero of all her aunt's stories, the boy with the golden spirit full of light and hope. All Saints, Zoya wanted to be near that light, she wanted to feel the warmth of it for as long as she could.

She shook her head and plunged into the tent, stripping off the First Army uniform she'd worn to disguise her identity. "There are other Squallers," she said as she dug through her trunk for something less recognizable. "Adrik can guide the missiles. And I'll be back in plenty of time. With Nina Zenik in tow."

"She may not even be alive."

Zoya nearly tore the roughspun shirt she'd drawn from her trunk. "She is not dead. I forbid it."

Genya planted her hands on her hips. "Don't flash those dragon eyes at me, Zoya. Nina isn't a child. She's a soldier and a spy and she wouldn't want you to sacrifice yourself for her."

"She's *alive.*"

"And if she isn't?"

"I'll kill every living thing Fjerda can throw at me."

"Zoya, stop this. Please. I don't want to lose you too!"

At the break in Genya's voice, Zoya froze. The sound scraped

471

against her heart, the pain sudden and overwhelming. There were tears in Genya's single amber eye.

"Zoya," she whispered. "I can't do this alone. I . . . I can't be the last of us."

Zoya felt a tremor move through her. She could see her friend suffering, but she didn't know how to fix it, who to be in this moment. Genya was the one who offered kindness, who wiped away tears, who soothed and mended. *Give me something to fight.* Something to swing at, to destroy. That was the only gift she had.

Zoya felt like she was choking on her grief and shame, but she forced the words out. "I should have been there to protect him. Both of you."

"Protect me now. Don't go."

"I have to, Genya. The Apparat is a threat to Nikolai and always will be until he's eliminated."

Genya's laugh rang with disbelief. "You're not going to fight the Apparat. You're going to save Nina."

Zoya pressed her palms to her eyes. "It was *my* mission, Genya. When Nina was first captured on the Wandering Isle, I was her commanding officer. I pushed her harder than I should have. I let her stomp off in a huff. If it wasn't for me, Nina never would have been captured by Fjerdans. She never would have ended up in Ketterdam or fallen in love with a witchhunter. I can't lose her again." She drew in a long breath. "If the Apparat has Nina, her cover is blown. He could turn her over to Jarl Brum. I won't let her be tortured, not when I have the chance to stop it."

Genya cast her hands out. "All of the people in this camp have been put on this path because of decisions the Triumvirate made. They're choosing to stand between Ravka and destruction. That was Nina's choice too. We are all soldiers. Why were you so hard on Nina if you didn't want her to use her skills?"

"Because I wanted her to survive!"

"Zoya, do you know why the Darkling lost the civil war? How Alina stopped him?"

Zoya pinched the bridge of her nose. "No. I wish I did."

"Because he always fought alone. He let his power isolate him. Alina had us. *You* have us. You push us away, keep us at arm's distance so that you won't mourn us. But you'll mourn us anyway. That's the way love works."

Zoya turned away. "I don't know how to do this anymore. I don't know how to just go on."

"I don't know either. There are days when I don't want to. But I can't live a life without love."

Zoya slammed the trunk lid shut. "That's the difference between you and me."

"You don't know what you're walking into. You're powerful, Zoya. Not immortal."

"We'll see."

Genya blocked her path. "Zoya, the Apparat knows you're an asset who can turn the tide of this war."

Now the dragon inside her bared its teeth, and Zoya smiled. "He doesn't know anything about me. But he's going to learn."

37

NIKOLAI

A HARD WIND BLEW OFF the shore to the west, and Nikolai wondered if he'd made a terrible mistake. The terrain that stretched before him was rocky and desolate. No mud, at least. But that also meant an easier road for Fjerda's tanks. He'd hoped the forest might slow them down, but the Fjerdans simply dosed their Grisha and had the drugged Squallers level the trees, obliterating woods that had stood guard along the northern border for hundreds of years, their heavy trunks cast aside like so much driftwood. The sky was the dark slate of early morning, stars still visible above the horizon. When he peered toward the coast, he could just make out the soft gray line of the sea. Maybe some of those fallen trees would roll all the way to the cliffs and tumble into the waves. Maybe the current would carry them to a faraway shore to trouble some fisherman or maybe they would wash up on a beach and become lumber for someone's home. A family would gather beneath a new roof, never knowing they sheltered under a little piece of Ravka, a fractured part of a country that might never be made whole.

Once Nikolai's scouts and flyers had confirmed Fjerdan troop movements, Ravka's forces had set up camp on a low rise north of the tiny town of Pachesyana. The grubby little village served as their base of operations as General Pensky sent out First Army troops to dig trenches—some deep and wide enough to stop a tank, others that they would use to protect their rocket launch platforms.

Nikolai hadn't known where the Fjerdans might attack, and that had meant Ravka couldn't mount a defense. So he'd let Sturmhond's blockade give way and tempted them with the chance at a two-pronged attack—at the bay and here at the border near Arkesk. He'd given the wolf an opportunity to wrap its jaws around Os Kervo and seize West Ravka in a single tremendous bite.

A risky wager, but was it the right one? He'd know soon enough.

Nikolai didn't wait for dawn to break. In the muddy fields at Nezkii, they'd hidden until the very last moment. Not today. Today, there would be no grand subterfuge, no mines to greet the Fjerdans in the field. Instead the enemy would wake to a show of force that Nikolai hoped would make them think twice.

"Sun Soldiers!" shouted Adrik. The order moved through the ranks of gathered Grisha and First Army.

Sun Summoners, the heirs to Alina's power, stood positioned all along the front, Adrik in command, the highest-ranking Etherealnik on the field. Zoya was in the south. But there was no time to think of the dangers she faced. He could only continue to believe in her, as he always had. And if there were words he wished he'd spoken, others he wanted to take back, the time for that had come and gone. His fight was here.

Adrik raised his brass arm and gave the command. "Daybreak!"

The Sun Soldiers flooded the empty fields of Arkesk with sunlight. Nikolai squinted at the brightness, at the blighted field, at the pocked earth in the distance where a forest had once stood. He could only imagine the Fjerdans were doing the same, wondering what strange sun rose in the south. They wouldn't have long to wonder.

"Squallers prepare!" cried Nadia to her deployment of Etherealki.

"First volley!" Leoni yelled to her Fabrikators. "Deploy!"

The sound was like a crackle, followed by a low whistle as the rockets ignited, their titanium shells glinting dully in the false sunlight. They arced into the sky, silver darts shooting toward the horizon, as the Squallers held the wind from the west at bay and guided the rockets to their targets—Fjerdan tanks, Fjerdan troops.

When they struck, the sounds of impact rent the air, a staccato rhythm that shook the earth, the drumbeat relentless. Nikolai climbed a rickety staircase to the lookout tower they'd erected and peered through a double long glass. Smoke and fire rose from the Fjerdan lines. Men ran to put out the flames, to help their fallen comrades, to pull bodies from the wreckage. It was like looking out over Os Alta on the night of the bombing. From this distance, those soldiers might be Ravkans, friends, his own subjects scrambling to make sense of this sudden strike. The land was pitted by smoking black craters. How many dead in a single blow? In a matter of moments?

A game of range. The Fjerdans had thought they could ground Ravka's flyers, and they'd largely succeeded. But they hadn't counted on Ravka's titanium missiles. If they wanted to use their guns and artillery, they would have to push closer and put their troops and tanks into the line of fire. The Fjerdans had given them a very big target to aim at. Their war chests were full. Their army hadn't been battered by years of fighting on two fronts. It showed.

Nikolai had no intention of letting them recover from the first strike. He signaled his forces on the ground, and General Pensky ordered his tank battalion forward, followed by infantry and Grisha, with Adrik at the lead. This was their chance to seize the advantage and force their enemy into a hasty retreat.

"Is it too much to hope that they'll just pack up and go home?" Nadia asked as Nikolai descended to the field.

"They won't," Tolya said, slinging his rifle onto his broad back. "Not with Brum in charge."

Nikolai believed it. Brum's political future was tied to the success of this campaign—a brutal and decisive victory that would grant Fjerda most of western Ravka and put the east within their grasp. With enough titanium, Ravka could have simply stood back and fired on the Fjerdan forces until they were too weakened to advance. But they couldn't build a house from bricks they didn't have.

Nikolai was more tired and more afraid for his people than he'd ever been, but he could sense the hope in them. The night before, he had walked the camp, talking to his troops and his commanders, stopping to share a drink or play a game of cards. He had tried not to think of how many of them might not survive this battle.

"We're ready with the second volley?" he asked.

"On your order," said Nadia.

"And the Starless?"

Tolya bobbed his head toward the east. "They're encamped on the periphery of the fighting."

"No engagement?"

"None."

"Are they armed?"

"Hard to tell," said Tolya. "For better or worse, they're people of faith. They'll fight with fists and sticks if they have to."

"Maybe someone will shoot the Darkling," Nadia suggested.

"Then I'll have to send Jarl Brum a nice thank-you note." Nikolai didn't know what the Darkling intended, but the Sun Soldiers would be ready.

Leoni appeared, her purple *kefta* already thick with dust and soot. "The Fjerdan lines are forming up again."

"Second volley," said Nikolai.

She nodded, her face grim, as she and Nadia returned to their positions. Nikolai knew neither of them would forget what they'd witnessed today. They were fighters, soldiers; they'd both seen combat and worse. But this was a different kind of bloodshed, murder at a distance, final and swift. David had warned them it would change everything. Bigger rockets, with longer range, would mean they could fire on much larger targets from afar. *Where does it end?* Tolya had asked. And Nikolai didn't know. They couldn't just push the Fjerdans back today. They had to somehow beat them badly enough to make them question war with Ravka entirely.

"Tolya—"

"No word from Zoya and Genya yet."

Had they succeeded? His troops were counting on reinforcements from the Grisha and First Army in the south. And he needed to know she was all right.

Shouts rang out down the Ravkan line, and a moment later the second volley of missiles flew, lobbed even farther into the Fjerdan ranks. But this time the Fjerdans were ready. Their tanks rolled over the smoldering bodies of their own troops and their infantry surged forward.

That was it: two volleys, the last of their missiles. In the trenches, he saw Leoni's troops reloading, but he knew those shells were steel, not titanium, and empty of explosives. If any Fjerdan scouts were watching, Nikolai didn't want them to know just how vulnerable Ravka was.

Most battles were waged over weeks, long slogs through bullets and blood. But Ravka couldn't fight that kind of war. They didn't have the funds, the flyers, the bodies to sacrifice. So this would be their stand. If the Saints were watching, he hoped they were on Ravka's side. He hoped that they had protected Zoya in the south. He hoped they'd fight beside him now.

"What the hell do you think you're doing?" said Tolya. "Put down that gun."

Nikolai checked the sights on his rifle. "I can't very well plunge heroically into battle unarmed."

"We need you alive to issue commands, not blown apart by Fjerdan repeaters."

"I have officers to issue commands. This is our last chance to make a real charge. If we lose, Ravka won't need a king anyway."

Tolya sighed. "Then I suppose you won't need bodyguards. We go together."

As they drew closer to the front lines, the noise was overwhelming, the thunder of tanks and artillery like a hammer to the head. They pushed forward through the ranks, past the injured and those preparing to be called into battle.

"Korol Rezni!" soldiers shouted when they caught sight of him.

King of Scars. He didn't mind the name so much anymore.

"Who fights beside me?" he called back.

And they bellowed their names in response, falling into step behind him.

Nikolai smelled gunpowder, burning flesh, turned earth—as if the whole field had been dug as a grave. He remembered Halmhend, the bodies spread out before him, the spatter of red on Dominik's

479

lips as he died. *This country gets you in the end, brother. Don't forget it.* Nikolai had promised to do better, to build something new. But in the end, all his inventions and diplomacy had come down to this: a brawl in the dirt.

He was walking, then running, and then he was in the thick of it. Nikolai's world narrowed to smoke and blood, the sounds of gunfire, the roar of tanks. Figures emerged in flashes, and there was only the briefest moment to tell friend from foe. The Fjerdan helmets helped—a design Nikolai had never seen before but distinct from what the Ravkan soldiers wore. He shot, shot again, reloaded. Someone ran at him from his left—a gray uniform. He yanked the knife from his belt and plunged it into a soft belly. This was a feeling he had been happy to forget, the knowledge that death walked with you, breathing down your neck, guiding your hand but ready to turn the blade on you in the space of a moment.

A bullet grazed his shoulder and he flinched back, lost his footing. Tolya was there, laying down cover as Nikolai righted himself, reloaded, strode forward again. He wouldn't remember these faces, brief glimpses like ghosts, bodies underfoot, but he knew he would see them in his nightmares.

"Nikolai!" shouted Tolya.

But Nikolai had already heard the beast approaching—the gigantic transporter they'd glimpsed in their first engagement with the Fjerdans, the one that had been full of drugged Grisha. Its huge treads thundered over the earth, metal gears shrieking, the air thick with the stink of burning fuel.

Nikolai had ordered his remaining flyers to keep Fjerda's air support at bay as best they could, but to watch for the transport. Now he saw them descend, releasing clouds of the Zemeni antidote. But the Squallers who rode atop the vehicles were wearing masks this time.

They raised their hands, driving back the haze of antidote in a hard gust that sent the flyers wobbling off course.

"Those masks!" Tolya shouted over the din.

They weren't ordinary masks, like those worn on the Ravkan side. Nikolai suspected they were being used to keep Fjerda's Grisha dosed with *parem*.

The transport's huge metal mouth opened and another row of sickly Grisha emerged, masks in place. All along the Fjerdan line, soldiers were pushing strange objects into position—big metal disks somewhere between a dish and a bell shape, winter sun gleaming off their curved edges. Nina's parabolas. *Songbird.* Suddenly Nikolai understood the strange helmets the Fjerdan soldiers wore.

"Open fire!" he shouted. "Take out the drugged Grisha! Take out the bells!"

But it was too late. The Fjerdan soldiers lifted huge mallets and struck the dishes. A strange thrum filled the air. The drugged Squallers arced their arms and people began to scream.

The sound was overwhelming. Nikolai clapped his hands to his ears and all over the field he saw soldiers doing the same, dropping their weapons, collapsing to their knees. It was like nothing he'd ever heard before, rattling his mind, his bones, filling his skull. It was impossible to think.

The Fjerdan troops, protected by those strange helmets, surged forward, opening fire, picking off helpless Ravkan soldiers and Grisha. The helmets had been created to protect them from this horrifying, paralyzing sound.

Blood leaked from Tolya's ears. Nikolai felt wetness on his neck and realized the same thing must be happening to him. The vibration felt like it was pulling him apart. Ravka's missiles seemed like toys.

He'd thought he could give his country a fighting chance. He'd thought that despite their numbers and their resources, he could think his way out of this for his people. Hopeless, foolish pride. This was how it would all end. With Ravka brought to its knees.

At least he'd fought to the end as their king.

But maybe Ravka didn't need a king. Or even an adventurer.

Maybe his country needed a monster.

He had one last gambit left, a final trick for the fox to play, a bit of hope dressed in shadow—his demon. But once the troops saw what he was, once his enemies knew the truth, the crown would be forever out of his grasp. So be it.

Go, he commanded. *Stop them. Help keep my country free.*

The demon hesitated. The thing inside him *was* him, and it knew what freedom meant this time. There would be no secrets anymore.

Good. Let Vadik Demidov have the throne. Ravka would survive.

With a roar, the demon launched itself from his body.

He was soaring over the battlefield, straight toward those horrible bells. He saw soldiers look up, faces cast in horror at the sight of the demon. They pointed and screamed, eyes wide with terror.

But the sound from the bells was too much. The vibration moved through his shadow body, fracturing it, dragging it apart. He fought to pull himself back together, but the closer he got to the Fjerdans, the harder it became. His wings, his body, unspooled around him.

Another mistake. It would be his last. The demon was going to shatter and Nikolai knew he would die with it.

Ravka would fall. After thousands of years of Lantsov kings. His people, his country, the Grisha. All lost.

Pain tore through Nikolai. The demon was breaking, flying apart. On his knees in the dirt, his mortal body screamed at the sky overhead. This was all that was left. His last chance to fight for his country before he fell into darkness forever.

He gritted his teeth, felt fangs in his mouth.

We die together.

The demon shrieked its response, full of pain, and anger, and iron will. They hurtled toward the bells.

38

THE

MONK

SO THE BOY WAS GOING TO DIE. Maybe they were all going to die.

If his skull hadn't been ringing like a church bell, Aleksander might have laughed. Instead he knelt on the ground with the rest of the Starless, hands clamped to his ears, trying to find a way out of this. The spectacles he'd used as a prop had fallen from his face and lay broken in the dirt. *Wait for a sign*, he'd told them. *The Starless One will show us the way.*

He'd intended to conjure a great blot of shadow, block out the sun, fill them with awe.

There would be no sign. He hadn't anticipated a weapon like this one.

Again, he tried to summon his *nichevo'ya*, but they couldn't take shape. Fjerda's drugged Squallers were amplifying the vibrations from those bells in some way, preventing his shadows from finding their form.

He couldn't hear the screams of the Starless around him, but he could see their mouths open and wailing, their eyes wide with misery and confusion. On the Fjerdan line, he saw the emaciated Squallers forced into Fjerda's service, their bodies frail and trembling, their faces hollow and haunted. This was *parem*. He'd never seen its effects before, hadn't understood what it could do to his people. Grisha weaponized against Grisha. Fjerda had at last realized their dream of domination. And they just might realize their dream of conquest too.

He had to get out of this place and away from that sound.

Aleksander lurched to his feet, stumbling through the ranks of the Starless, all of them too lost to pain to pay him any mind.

Then he felt it, like a hook in his gut. He turned and saw the young king's demon racing through the skies, that embodiment of his own power Aleksander had last glimpsed during the *obisbaya*, when he'd sought to claim the demon for himself.

The boy had set it free. It would cost him the throne. It would cost him everything. Why? So he could die heroically for a country that would turn its back on him? Would the boy never learn?

Sacrifice. The whisper of Yuri's voice, full of reverence.

He is a fool. Your reverence belongs to me.

What good would this grand gesture do the king? Aleksander could feel the demon breaking apart just as his *nichevo'ya* had. It was stronger than they were, maybe because it had emerged whole from Nikolai instead of being pieced together from the shadows around them, maybe because it was linked to the king's consciousness. Even so, it would be no match for the bells.

But it might be. With your help.

Of course, Yuri would like nothing better than for Aleksander to sacrifice himself to this cause. *They followed you. They believed in you.*

Aleksander needed to run. He would save himself as he always had, regroup and make another plan. The Fjerdans were plowing their way through the Ravkan ranks, and once they reached the Starless, Aleksander would be as good as helpless. He had to get out of here. He had eternity to launch a new strategy, to retake Ravka from the Fjerdans, to build his following and forge a new path to victory. He'd fought too hard to return to this life to endanger it now.

Yet he couldn't deny what would happen to the Grisha if the Fjerdans won the day. And there would be no miracle, no grand resurrection for him, if there was no one there to see it.

Perhaps it wasn't too late to salvage this moment. Aleksander planted his feet and opened his hands, calling out to the shadows. This time he didn't attempt to form them into soldiers. Instead he sent them skittering over the field, fragile tendrils of darkness, blindly seeking the power they recognized. *Like calls to like.*

He released a shout as the shadows met the demon. They clung to its form.

More. Aleksander's body shook as he fought to keep his sanity, that deafening, maddening vibration traveling through his skull. His threads of shadow wrapped around the demon's body, giving strength to its limbs, banding together and binding its form.

The creature shrieked. Aleksander felt the demon's mind, Nikolai's mind.

The monster is me . . .

The ghost of a thought.

The demon's wings beat against the winter sky and it hurtled toward the bells. It slammed into one, then another, sending them crashing to the ground in a heap of metal and glass. A soldier tried to fire on the creature, but it tore the helmet from his head and slashed its claws across the soldier's face, silencing him, hot blood like a balm.

The Fjerdans scattered, terrified by the monster come to life before them. The drugged Grisha looked on without interest, their minds full of nothing except *parem*.

With a roar of triumph, the demon king smashed through the final bell. The wall of sound collapsed in blessed silence. Shouts rose from the Ravkan troops as they stumbled to their feet. They were bleeding. They were broken. But they were not done. They took up their guns, Ravka's Grisha raised their hands, and they all threw themselves into battle once more.

"What happened?" cried Brother Chernov.

Aleksander could barely hear him. His ears were still ringing with that violent sound, and helping to forge the demon had taken a toll. He watched the monster slide back to the king, a dark blot skating over the field to return to its true master. The Starless hadn't seen what he'd done or hadn't understood it. They'd been on the ground, subjugated to the bells.

"What do we do?" said Brother Chernov.

Aleksander wasn't sure. The bells were gone, but Fjerda had seized the advantage. Their troops were recovering, driving forward, and the king was surrounded.

"There are demons in the sky!"

At first he thought the monk meant Nikolai's shadow creature, but he was pointing southeast.

"Who has a long glass?" he demanded, and Brother Chernov placed one in his hands.

There was something moving toward the battlefield, though he couldn't tell what. He only knew it meant more trouble for the king. Nikolai had no allies to the south.

"Where is the sign?" pleaded Brother Chernov. "Why has the Starless One forsaken us? What do we do?"

Aleksander watched as the Fjerdans circled the king and his troops. The bells had given them the chance to cut off Nikolai's path of retreat. Aleksander supposed he could send the *nichevo'ya* to help. He could attempt to rescue Ravka's king a second time.

Or he could let him die and seize control of Ravka's forces, then lead the charge himself.

The boy had been brave; he'd smashed the bells and risked his life and his country's loyalty for it. But that did not mean he was meant to win this day.

Apologies, Nikolai. A man can hardly hope for two miracles in one morning.

"What do we do?" repeated Chernov desperately.

Aleksander turned his back on the last Lantsov king. Let him die a martyr.

"All we can do," he said, addressing his flock. "We pray."

39

ZOYA

ZOYA KNEW SHE WAS BEING IMPRUDENT, indulging in the same recklessness she'd scolded Nina for again and again, but she wasn't going to let one of her soldiers be used as a pawn. The Apparat had a game to play, and he would play it. Zoya intended to dictate the rules.

At the edge of the beach, she pulled down cloud cover slowly to avoid drawing attention, then wreathed herself in sea mist. She summoned the wind, letting it carry her low over the waves as she skated across the water. This was the power that the amplifiers at her wrists, Juris' scales, had given her. It was not quite flight and it required every bit of her focus, but the Apparat would be anticipating a disguised flyer or raft. She had a better chance of getting Nina out if she caught the priest and his men off guard.

And if Nina is dead?

Zoya had lost as many allies as she'd sent enemies to the grave. Nina wasn't even a friend. She was a subordinate, an upstart student with a gift for languages who could always be counted on to make trouble if she couldn't find some to get into. But Zoya had been her commander and her teacher, and that meant she was under Zoya's protection.

Juris' laugh rumbled through her. *Zoya of the garden, when will you cease your lies?*

As she approached the monstrous Fjerdan base, a chill swept through her. It was even bigger than it had seemed from the beach. She circled it slowly, peering through the mist she'd summoned, trying to get her bearings. The eastern tower was obvious enough, but it had to be twenty stories tall. Where was the Apparat keeping Nina? He'd said the cells and . . . there, nearly at the top of the structure, an expanse of smooth wall, its surface unbroken by windows. Those must be the holding cells.

But how was she meant to get up there? She could vault herself on the currents of the air, but not without being seen, and a sudden thunderstorm would be more than a little suspicious. She circled the base slowly and spotted a series of piers on its lower level, where small craft could dock. On one of them, two Fjerdan soldiers were repairing the battered hull of an armed boat.

Zoya stepped onto the dock and lifted her hands, clenching her fists. The soldiers gasped and clawed at their throats as the air left their lungs. She let them drop unconscious to the deck and set about stripping one of his uniform. She bound and gagged them both, then rolled them out of sight. She was grateful for the soldier's heavy coat and hat. Women didn't serve in Fjerda's military.

She crept up the dock and climbed a metal staircase onto the main deck. She kept her head down and tried to make her walk determined. Zoya was not an actress and had no gift for subterfuge, but she only needed to make it to the tower. The naval base was moving through the waves, picking up speed, heading north, she was sure, to lend support to the rest of Fjerda's forces.

Zoya reached the eastern observation tower and slipped inside. It didn't seem safe to take the elevator, but when she ducked her head inside the stairwell, she heard the clamor of footsteps coming from above. She couldn't speak Fjerdan. She didn't want to risk meeting fellow soldiers. The elevator it would have to be.

She entered and jabbed the number for the floor just below the observation deck, unsure of what she would find there. On the tenth floor, the elevator jolted to a stop. Zoya kept her eyes on the ground as a pair of shiny black boots entered. Whoever it was pushed a button and they were moving upward again. He said something in Fjerdan.

She grunted a reply, her heart racing.

Now his voice was angry. He grabbed Zoya's chin and shoved her head up.

Grizzled face. Black uniform emblazoned with the white wolf. *Drüskelle.*

He drew his sidearm, but Zoya's hands were faster. Her gust struck his chest and he slammed against the elevator wall with a clang, then fell in a lifeless heap to the floor.

All Saints. Now she had a body on her hands.

Frantically, Zoya smacked the buttons of the high floors, praying that no one would be waiting when the doors opened.

The elevator stopped at what looked like a gunnery. She could see weapons pointing down from every window. And the place seemed to be deserted—for now. She rolled the body into the corridor, then took a moment to send lightning jolting through the guns, melting their long barrels. A small thing. But as long as she was here, she might as well leave some destruction in her wake.

The elevator doors closed, and at last she arrived at what she hoped was the prison floor. If she'd gotten her count right, this place would be heavily guarded. She raised her hands.

The doors opened on silence. Zoya saw two long gray hallways curving in either direction. Both walls were lined with doors. Were there Grisha behind them?

She took the hallway to the right and dropped the pressure, dampening the sound of her steps. But she needn't have bothered. When she rounded the corner, she saw a thick-waisted woman with silky blond hair seated in a chair at the end of the hall, the Apparat behind her, bracketed by two Priestguards in their brown robes. *Nina.* Zoya hadn't seen her since she'd left the Little Palace for her mission, and she'd forgotten the extent of Genya's tailoring. It was like looking at a stranger—except for the stubborn glint in her eyes. That was pure Zenik.

The Apparat had a knife to her throat.

"Easy, General Nazyalensky. You see where you are, don't you?" He gestured to the windowless walls. "A dead end. I doubt even the inimitable Nina Zenik would survive having her jugular cut."

"Will it be so easy to explain a dead girl whom everyone knows to be a good and pious member of Jarl Brum's household?"

The Apparat smiled. His gums were black. "When I show him the bone darts we took from her clothing and expose her spies in the Hringsa, I imagine Jarl Brum will give me a medal. We've taken Nina's weapons, and her power is useless against my healthy Priestguards. Shall we see if she'd like to use her twisted gift to call some corpses to do her bidding?"

Nina said nothing, only pressed her lips together, her gaze focused on Zoya.

"I don't think she will," the Apparat continued. "She can't call the dead without destroying her cover and putting dear Hanne Brum in danger of being charged with collusion. That would spoil her betrothal to the crown prince, now wouldn't it?"

"What do you want?" Zoya said. "Take me as your prisoner and set Nina free."

"No!" Nina cried.

"You mistake me, Zoya Nazyalensky. I do not want you as my captive, but as my comrade. Though be assured," he said, "my monks stand at the ready. One step toward me and this whole room will be dosed with *parem* gas."

Zoya's eyes darted to the cells, the ceiling, the two Priestguards flanking the Apparat. There were vents in the walls, but he might be bluffing. She had antidote in her pocket. Was it worth the risk? She'd have to dose herself with antidote, then fight off the effects and the Priestguards at the same time.

Zoya shook her head. "Do you have any love for Ravka at all?"

"Ravka was meant to be ruled by holy men, and your king is not one. He is an abomination. The Saints must be freed from him."

"I think you find abomination where it's convenient. The same way you locate your Saints. What do you want? We're short on time."

"Were you seen?"

"I killed a man on the way up."

"I see," the Apparat said with some distaste. He nudged one of the monks. "Bring me the boy."

The Priestguard moved to obey, opening the nearest cell and leading out an emaciated prisoner.

"This poor soul was taken from a Fjerdan village by Jarl Brum. He's a Heartrender. Or maybe a Healer. He was never trained. But now he does whatever the drug *parem* tells him to." The Apparat removed a packet from his robes and the Heartrender lifted his head, sniffing the air, a low moan escaping his throat. "You and I are going to leave this place together, Zoya Nazyalensky. You will declare your allegiance to Vadik Demidov, the true Lantsov king. And you will become my Saint, a symbol of the new Ravka."

"And if I say no, Nina will be tortured by your monks?"

"She will be tortured by this Heartrender. One of your own. He will take the skin from her body inch by inch. And when her heart begins to fail, I'll have him heal her and start all over. Maybe I'll have Miss Zenik dosed with the drug. I understand she survived one encounter with parem. I doubt she'll be so lucky again."

For the first time, Zoya saw panic enter Nina's eyes. *I won't let it happen*, she vowed. *I will not fail you.*

"If Nina Zenik dies here today," the Apparat continued, "who will remember her name? She is no Saint, has worked no miracles."

"I'll remember," Zoya said, her fury growing. "I remember all their names."

"You and I will leave this tower. You will announce you've defected to our side and offer your service to the true Lantsov heir. You will join us and see the false king deposed."

"Where does this plan end, priest? You've told me what you intend, but what is your goal?"

"Demidov on the throne. Ravka purified and sanctified by the Saints."

"And you?"

"I will attend to the matter of Ravka's soul. And I will give you a gift that no one else can."

"Which is?"

"I know the locations of Brum's secret bases, all the hidden places where he's keeping Grisha prisoners. Men, women, children, maybe even friends you once thought dead. Not even Fjerda's king and queen know where to find them, only Jarl Brum and my spies. The witchhunter is far less stealthy than he thinks, and my followers have done their work well. I see I have your full attention."

Grisha in cells. Grisha being tortured and experimented on. Grisha she could save. "You mean to make me choose between my king and my people."

"Haven't the Grisha suffered enough? Think of all the prison doors that would fly open if you joined my cause. Imagine all the suffering your people will endure until then."

"Do you know what I think?" Zoya said, edging closer. If she could manage a lightning strike before the monks released the gas, she and Nina could make quick work of the rest of the Apparat's men. "This has never been about the Saints or restoring Ravka to the faith—only your own desire to rule. Do you resent men born of royal blood? Women with power in their veins? Or do you truly think you know what's best for Ravka?"

The priest's eyes were dark as pits. "I have been waiting for the Saints to speak to me since I was a child. Maybe you recited the same prayers, had the same hopes? Most children do. But somewhere along the way, I realized no one would answer my prayers. I would have to build my own cathedral and fill it with my own Saints." He held up the packet of *parem*. "And now they speak when I want them to. Speak, Sankta Zoya."

The Heartrender, eyes focused on the drug he so desired, twisted his fingers in the air. Nina screamed, blood leaking from her eyes, her nose.

"Stop!" shouted Zoya.

The Apparat signaled the Heartrender, who whimpered softly but went still. The priest dabbed a bit of orange powder onto the Grisha's tongue as reward.

Zoya watched the Heartrender's eyes roll back into his head, watched the blood trickle from Nina's nose.

"She's like a sister to you, no? Maybe like a daughter?" The Apparat smiled gently, serenely. "Will you be the mother she deserves? The mother they all deserve?"

Zoya remembered her own mother marching her down the aisle of the cathedral to hand her to the rich old man who would be her groom. She remembered the priest standing behind him, ready to consecrate a sham marriage for the sake of a little coin. She remembered the Suli circling her on the cliff top. *Daughter*, they'd whispered. *Daughter*.

Zoya looked at the Heartrender, looked at the cells. How many of them were full? How many cells were there in military bases and secret laboratories? Whether she chose her king or her people, she would never be able to save them all. She could hear Genya's voice, ringing in her ears: *You push us away, keep us at arm's distance so that you won't mourn us. But you'll mourn us anyway. That's the way love works.*

Understanding burned through her like fire from a dragon's mouth, leaving her weightless as ash. She would never be able to save them all. But that didn't mean she was Sabina leading her child to the slaughter.

Daughter. Why had that word frightened her so? She remembered Genya looping her arm through hers, Alina embracing her on the steps of the sanatorium. Nikolai drawing her close in the garden, the peace he'd granted her in that moment.

This is what love does. In the stories, love healed your wounds, fixed what was broken, allowed you to go on. But love wasn't a spell, some kind of benediction to be whispered, a balm or a cure-all. It was a single, fragile thread, which grew stronger through connection, through shared hardship and honored trust. Zoya's mother had been wrong. It wasn't love that had ruined her, it was the death of it. She'd believed that love would do the work of living. She'd let the thread fray and snap.

This is what love does. An old echo, but it wasn't Sabina she heard now. It was Liliyana's voice as she stood fearless in the church, as she risked everything to fight for a child who wasn't her own. *This is what love does.*

How long had Zoya feared being bound to others? How little had she trusted that thread of connection? That was why she'd shied away from the gifts the dragon offered. They demanded she open her heart to the world, and she'd turned away, afraid of what she might lose.

Daughter. We see you.

She had failed to keep David safe, but Genya hadn't turned away from her. She'd failed to keep the Darkling from returning, but Alina hadn't damned her for it. And Nikolai had offered her a kingdom, he'd offered her the love she'd been seeking the whole of her life, even if she'd been afraid to take it, even if she'd been too much of a coward to look him in the eye and admit that it wasn't Ravka's future she sought to preserve, but her own fragile, frightened heart.

Juris had known. Juris had seen it all. *Open the door.*

Love was on the other side and it was terrifying.

Open the door. The dragon had seen this very moment, this very room.

She turned her gaze on the Apparat. "How is it, through wars and kings and revolutions, you always manage to survive?"

The priest smiled. "That is a gift I can share with you. I understand men better than they understand themselves. I give the people what they need. Comfort, protection, wonder. You may live a thousand years, Zoya Nazyalensky, but my faith means I will live for eternity."

Zoya's eyes met Nina's. "Eternity may be shorter than you think."

She didn't have to lift her hands to summon the current that suddenly crackled through the air. It ignited around the Apparat's guards in sparks of blue fire. They shuddered and shook, burning from the inside, and collapsed.

"Nina!" Zoya shouted. In a flash the corpses of the guards were on their feet, commanded by Nina's power. They seized the Apparat.

I'm sorry, she said to the nameless, faceless prisoners in their cells. *I'm sorry I can't save you. But I can avenge you. I can love you and let you go.*

"Gas!" shouted the Apparat, his eyes wild.

Zoya heard the vents open, the whoosh of *parem* shooting toward them. She leapt, seizing Nina, feeling the strength of Juris and the dragon. The power of the lives they'd lived and the battles they'd fought flooded her muscles. She slammed through the wall with Nina in her arms, through stone and metal, and into the waiting sky.

Nina screamed.

You are strong enough to survive the fall.

They were plummeting toward the sea. Zoya felt Genya's arms around her, Liliyana holding her tight. She felt Nikolai's presence beside her and Juris' sword in her hands.

With a wild, gasping breath, she felt her wings unfurl.

40
MAYU

THEY WERE TOO LATE.

The battlefield was strewn with bodies and Fjerdan soldiers surrounded the king, a noose drawing ever tighter.

"Put me down!" shouted Tamar. She was carried by Harbinger, his double metal wings like those of a dragonfly.

"There are too many of them!" said Reyem. He had one arm around Bergin, the other tight around Mayu, but her heart was still pounding, certain they were about to fall.

"My wife is somewhere down there," Tamar snarled. "You put my feet on that battlefield and then you can run back south."

They dove for the ground. Mayu saw surprised faces turn toward them, Grisha raising their hands to defend themselves from the creatures of their nightmares—the *khergud*.

"Stand down!" yelled Tamar in Ravkan. "Tolya, tell them to stand down!"

The people on the ground began to shout at one another.

King Nikolai looked up at them in wonder. "Stand down!" he commanded. "They're allies." He didn't sound like he believed it. "Keep your eyes on the Fjerdans."

Some kind of shadow shape circled the Ravkan troops, trying to keep the Fjerdan soldiers at bay, making it impossible for them to aim their rifles. But they were drawing closer.

As the Fjerdans caught sight of the winged Shu, they opened fire. Reyem whirled in the air, turning his back to the gunfire, sheltering Mayu and Bergin. Bullets pelted his back and his wings, the sound like hard rain on a metal roof.

"Reyem!" she cried.

"I'm all right," he said, the calm sound of his voice so strange amid the chaos of battle.

Harbinger had his stout arms wrapped around Tamar to protect her, but Nightmoth and Scarab threw themselves at the Fjerdan soldiers, oblivious to the bullets peppering their bodies. Some Fjerdans ran screaming from the monsters descending from on high; others tried to stand their ground. But they were no match for the strength and speed of the *khergud*. They were fearless, relentless. Nightmoth lowered his head, using his horns like a battering ram. Mayu saw Scarab rip the rifle from a Fjerdan's hand, then tear the arms from his body, her metal claws flashing.

"Take us down!" Tamar demanded.

Locust and Harbinger obliged. Mayu's feet struck ground, and she went to one knee before she righted herself. Scarab and Nightmoth had pushed the Fjerdan line back, but the enemy had far greater numbers and they wouldn't stay in retreat for long.

"Dare I hope you haven't come to kill us all?" Nikolai shouted over the din of the battle.

Tamar threw an arm around her twin. "I've come to save your ass, little brother."

"Two minutes!" said Tolya. "You're *two minutes* older than me."

They drew their weapons, standing back to back. Mayu snatched a rifle from the hands of a fallen soldier.

"I thought you couldn't send reinforcements," said King Nikolai. His lip was bloodied, his uniform covered in dirt and gore. He'd been shot in the left shoulder and had a rifle in his hands.

"The queen forbade it," said Tamar.

Now Mayu met the king's eyes. "But as far as the government is concerned, the *khergud* don't exist."

"Schemes within schemes," said Nikolai. "Welcome back."

At the summer palace, Tamar and Mayu had left their audience with Queen Leyti and the princesses and found their way back to Bergin and Reyem.

"You were right," Mayu had said. "Makhi will rule side by side with Ehri as regent. No trial. No punishment. The Taban line remains unblemished."

Bergin had shrugged his gaunt shoulders. "There's a war on. They want peace and stability. Justice is a luxury people like us can't afford."

"They're going to bring the other *khergud* here," said Mayu. "To recover."

"Exile," Reyem had said. "Maybe it's for the best. We aren't fit to be around human beings."

"Don't say that," said Bergin. "We're alive. We're free."

"Are we? How long will the *khergud* be allowed to live when our very existence threatens the Taban? We're a secret they can't risk being exposed." He looked out the window, toward the shores of the lake. "And we aren't meant to live in isolation, without purpose. We were built for battle."

"Ravka won't let any harm come to you," Tamar vowed. "I won't. We have a treaty now."

"To protect the rights of Grisha," Mayu objected. "What do you care for the *khergud*?"

Tamar's golden eyes flashed. "They're victims of *parem*, just as much as the Grisha."

"It doesn't matter," Mayu said. "What good will the treaty be when Ravka falls to the Fjerdans?"

"Don't underestimate King Nikolai," Tamar replied. "He'll fight until there's no fight left in him. And so will I."

Bergin rose. "If you're going to the front, I want to go with you."

Reyem turned. "You . . . you're leaving?"

He'd said it with little emotion, but Mayu had sensed the turmoil inside him.

"Ravka may not be my homeland, but I'm Grisha. I'll fight for the king who gave me freedom."

"Then we should fight too," Mayu had said. She hadn't been sure where the words came from. But Nikolai and Tamar had brought her back to Reyem—and she knew in her bones that without Bergin there wouldn't have been a brother to come back to. Scarab, Nightmoth, Harbinger . . . they'd had friends, families, lives, and all of it had been wiped away by their rebirth as *khergud*. She had a Grisha to thank for the humanity that Reyem had retained.

"We will," Reyem said firmly. "Your cause is mine, Bergin. We'll fight for the Grisha. A *khergud* warrior is worth ten ordinary soldiers, maybe more. The others will fight too. We need a mission."

"I'm grateful," said Tamar. "Truly. But Queen Leyti—"

"Queen Leyti told us we could send no Shu troops," Princess Ehri said. She'd appeared at the doorway, her small frame seeming to hover there, a smile playing about her lips. "But she said nothing of ghosts. According to our government, my sister, and my grandmother, the *kheryud* don't exist. And phantoms may go where they please."

She'd floated away, as if she was a spirit herself, and in that moment, Mayu realized that if she survived whatever came next, she would come back to her post as Tavgharad and serve Princess Ehri gladly.

Would she ever have that chance? As she stood on the battlefield, a rifle at her shoulder, she took aim and fired, again and again, unsure of which bullets might have found purchase, terrified by the rush of blood in her ears, the jackrabbit thump of her heart. Out of the corner of her eye, she saw Scarab moving like a whirlwind through the ranks of Fjerdan troops, as Nightmoth, Harbinger, and Locust—Reyem—attacked from the air, plucking soldiers off their feet and snapping their necks with smooth efficiency.

"I'm glad they're on our side," said Tolya, wiping the sweat from his brow.

"Let's hope it stays that way," said Tamar.

Mayu heard a series of rapid explosions, and suddenly she was looking at a wall of fire crawling toward them across the Fjerdan lines. She looked up—Fjerdan flyers, dropping bomb after bomb.

She couldn't believe what she was seeing. "They're killing their own soldiers along with the Ravkans!"

"They don't care," said Tamar. "They intend to win at any cost."

Two Ravkan flyers intercepted the Fjerdans, breaking their formation, but the enemy reassembled, taking the onslaught of the Ravkan guns head-on. A Fjerdan wing caught fire, and the flyer plummeted in a spiral of flame and smoke. It crashed onto the battlefield, plowed through soldiers, struck a tank, and exploded in a yellow ball of fire. Another flyer took its place in formation. Any sacrifice for victory.

"Call for retreat!" King Nikolai shouted. "Have the Squallers and Tidemakers create some kind of cover. We need to get our people out of here."

"This is our last chance——" said Tolya.

"If they're willing to bomb their own troops, we're out of chances. They have too much firepower, and Brum doesn't care what kind of casualties he racks up as long as Fjerda wins the day. I won't line my people up for the slaughter. Retreat!"

The call went down the line as mist began to shroud the battlefield. But Mayu could see it wasn't going to matter. The Fjerdans had been given their orders, and it made no difference if they couldn't spot targets when they didn't care about taking aim. They would bomb this battlefield into oblivion.

Mayu saw Reyem speeding toward the ranks of flyers, his wings beating the air. A creature flew beside him—that shadow she'd glimpsed before, but now she saw it had the shape of a beast. They seized one of the Fjerdan flyers and yanked its wings free. Ravkan Squallers hurled the debris away from the battlefield, trying to protect the troops below.

"Come on," Reyem said as he set down beside her. He grabbed her around the waist. "I need to get you out of here."

"Go," said Tamar.

"Bergin——" Reyem attempted, but Bergin shook his head. He would not abandon this fight.

Reyem was already lifting Mayu off her feet.

"No!" shouted Mayu. "We have to get Tamar and the others out too."

"Forget it," said Tolya. "This is our fight. For every Grisha."

"For every Grisha," said Bergin.

"This is suicide," said Mayu. "There are too many of them!"

Tamar grasped the king's shoulder. "Nikolai, let the *khergud* fly you out. You can still survive this."

But the king only laughed, a laugh that was nothing like Isaak's, ferocious and maybe a little unhinged. "None of that, Tamar. If Ravka's independence dies this day, then I die with it."

Mayu heard the unmistakable buzz of the Fjerdan engines. They'd locked back into formation and were making another run over the battlefield. "They're coming back!"

The king climbed onto a tank, the shadow creature hovering above him. He turned to the *khergud*. "You have no reason to give me aid, but I ask for it anyway. The battle is lost, but if we can take out that line of bombers, we can give everyone on this field a chance to get to safety—Fjerdan and Ravkan alike."

"Nikolai," said Tolya. "Please. It's madness. If the demon dies, you do too."

The king grinned. "Manners, Tolya. If they want to send me to hell, I'm going to at least say a proper goodbye. His jacket was torn, his clothes stained with blood. He had never looked less like the boy who had courted her. He had never looked more like a king. "This is not your country. I have no right to command you, so I ask you. Fight for me. Fight for every Grisha, for every soldier, for every child who wishes to see his mother again, for every father who wishes to rest his head at night without fear of what may come tomorrow, for every artist, and carpenter, and stoneworker, and farmer who were meant to do more with their lives than carry a gun in their hands. Fight for all of us."

The soldiers who remained around the king roared their response. "For all of us!"

The shadow creature that hovered above him shrieked and leapt into the sky. *He's commanding it*, Mayu realized. It was the king's demon.

Harbinger and Nightmoth launched themselves into the air. Maybe they were still human after all, or maybe they were just hungry for a fight.

"Mayu?" said Reyem.

He would run if she told him to. They could escape this place, go back home, back to their parents. Or they could try to save these people.

This is penance, she realized. Penance for Isaak, for the innocent boy who might have loved her and who would never return.

"Take their hearts," she said to him.

"I will."

He was gone, arcing upward on hinged wings, Harbinger and Nightmoth beside him. They joined the demon in the sky, locking into formation, an arrow aimed at the Fjerdan bombers. The king's mortal body knelt on the tank, as if in prayer, all his attention focused on the attack.

"Form up!" shouted Tamar. "Protect the king."

They surrounded the tank, watching as the demon and the *khergud* sped toward impact.

"We're going to watch them die," said Tolya.

"*Everyone mourns the first blossom*," Mayu said softly. "*Who will weep for the rest that fall?*"

"*I will remain to sing for you*," Tamar continued the poem.

Tolya placed a hand to his heart. "*Long after the spring has gone.*"

Only they knew what this moment, this loss would mean.

There were tears in Tolya's eyes. "May the Saints watch over you, Nikolai," he said. "You die a king."

Mayu watched the distance to impact narrow—two hundred

yards, one hundred yards. She would not let herself look away. "Goodbye, brother," she whispered.

A roar split the air. A massive shape tore across the field, between the *khergud* and the Fjerdan bombers, sending them scattering. Silver lightning crackled through the sky.

"What the—" Tamar began. But the words died on her tongue.

They all stared at the sky and Mayu opened her mouth to scream. She was looking at a dragon.

41

NINA

"PLEASE, PLEASE, PLEASE DON'T DROP ME!"

If Zoya had the power of speech, she wasn't using it.

Because she was a dragon.

A dragon.

One minute Nina had the scent of *parem* in her nostrils, and the next she was knocked backward with Zoya's arms around her, smashing through the tower wall as if it were straw. They were falling, the air rushing past them. Nina squeezed her eyes shut, knowing her body would break when they struck the water, as surely as if they'd struck stone. And then——the fall became flight.

She'd heard a voice in her head say . . . something. *Open the door.*

Zoya's body seemed to shift around her and Nina screamed, certain that at any moment she'd be plummeting toward the sea again.

Her hands scrabbled for anything to cling to—and grabbed hold of gleaming black scales.

What had happened to the Apparat and his monks? How was she going to get back to Hanne? She couldn't hold a thought in her head for more than a moment. All logic and sense dissolved in a fizzing mix of fear and elation. She was *flying*. She was flying on a *dragon's back*.

They sped over the waves, and Nina saw the dragon's shape reflected in glimpses on the water. It was huge, its wings wide and graceful. Salt spray stung her cheeks.

"Where are you going?" Nina managed to gasp. "Where are you taking me?"

But the answer quickly became clear—inland to the front.

Nina smelled the battle before she saw it. Smoke from bombs and artillery lay over the field in a thick haze. She heard the buzz of flyers, the rumble of engines.

A squadron of what looked like Fjerdan bombers circled the field, then came together in a V formation, a sky-borne spear of gray metal and destruction. She saw something moving through the air toward the enemy craft—small, winged shapes. One of them looked different, like shredded shadow. *Khergud.* Shu soldiers engineered to hunt and capture Grisha. So why were they throwing themselves into the path of Fjerdan flyers?

And why was the dragon speeding directly toward them?

"Zoya?" she said. "Zoya, what are you—"

Nina flattened herself against Zoya's back as they hurtled into the fray. She saw the *khergud* scatter, breaking their ranks. She heard the rattle of the Fjerdan guns. A bullet skimmed her thigh and she cried out, but the gunfire seemed to have no effect on Zoya—or whatever Zoya had become.

The dragon shot skyward, whirled in the air, and dove back toward the bombers. Nina felt her stomach lurch. Zoya was going to kill her if she vomited.

The dragon opened her jaws, and it was as if the storm had been brewing in her belly. Silver lightning spewed from somewhere deep inside her. It crackled through the air, snaring the flyers in current. They burst into flame, dropping from the sky like crumpled insects. Nina smelled something sweet, almost chemical—ozone.

She clung to the dragon's back, the scales pricking her skin, the ground impossibly far below. She could see their shadow on the battlefield, soaring over the ranks of Ravkans and Fjerdans, who looked up in terror.

Nina had the sudden thought that none of this was real, that when that poor, drugged Heartrender had begun torturing her, she'd simply passed out from the pain, her mind splintering and creating this wild scenario to hide in. It seemed more plausible than that her friend and mentor had become a creature from a storybook.

The dragon laid down a trail of silver lightning, creating a wall of fire, and as they banked east, Nina understood why. She'd cut off the Fjerdan retreat. Their forces were wedged between a wall of silver flame and Ravka's soldiers.

The Fjerdan tanks turned their mighty guns on the dragon and Nina gasped as Zoya banked hard to the right, dodging their shells. Again she unleashed her lightning, the current sparking on Fjerda's war machines, melting their gun barrels and sending men diving for safety.

The dragon's vast wings beat the air. A roar thundered through her scaled body, and Nina felt it shudder through her too. She could see the corpses of fallen soldiers, Grisha with their gas masks on. She saw the Cult of the Starless Saint in their tunics emblazoned with the sun in eclipse. And there, not far from the king's forces, a line of black uniforms, a mass of *drüskelle* with their whips and guns raised, moving toward King Nikolai.

She didn't see Brum among them. Had he known Fjerda planned to bomb the battlefield with their own soldiers still in play? Maybe he'd given the order himself.

Nina kept her body pressed against Zoya's neck. She didn't know if she could be recognized from this distance, but she was taking no chances.

"Open fire!" the *drüskelle* commander shouted. But they stood dazed, petrified, heads tilted to the sky, mouths wide open.

Nina felt a rush of power. She had spent so many months frightened and unsure, wondering what would become of her country, scraping by on hope, not knowing if she and Hanne would find a way to survive. All Saints, it felt good to be the strong one, to be unafraid at last. With a mighty breath, a single exhalation of lightning, Zoya could destroy them—hundreds of Fjerdan troops and the witch-hunter monsters Brum had trained. It would be done. What soldier would dare to march against Ravka, against the Grisha, again?

Nina looked into the faces below as they craned their necks, shielded their eyes, gaping at death borne aloft on black wings. They'd always feared the Grisha, and now, in this moment, from this height, she could admit they'd had a right to that fear—Grisha were born with gifts that made them more deadly than any ordinary soldier. Fjerda had let that fear overtake them, drive them, shape their nation.

But wasn't there awe in those faces too? Awe Nina had fostered with her phony miracles, her small attempts to sway Fjerdan thought. What had that all been for if it only ended in annihilation?

Save some mercy for my people.

Damn it, Helvar.

There has to be a Fjerda worth saving. Promise me.

511

She had promised. And in the end, she could not let go of that vow. When she'd spoken those words, when she'd made that oath, she hadn't been speaking just to Matthias, but to the boy who had killed him, and to the men who cowered in the field below them now.

"Zoya!" she cried, unsure if Zoya could even hear her, if this creature *was* Zoya Nazyalensky anymore. "Zoya, please. If you destroy them, Brum's cause will never die. They will always fear us. There will never be an end to it!"

The dragon shrieked and spread its jaws wide.

"Zoya, please!"

Nina smelled ozone on the air. Heard the crackle of lightning.

She pressed her face against the dragon's scales. She didn't want to see what came next.

42

NIKOLAI

JURIS.

That was Nikolai's first thought when the dragon appeared, sunlight glinting blue off its black scales. Until lightning sparked in jagged streaks across the sky. He knew Zoya's power, recognized it instantly.

He drew the demon back to him. He had long since stopped thinking of what the soldiers around him had seen or if they would damn him for the monster he'd become. Somehow, impossibly, Ravka had seized the advantage. Zoya's lightning had ignited walls of flame, blocking retreat for the Fjerdan forces, and now she hovered above them, ready to pass judgment.

The Age of Saints. Yuri had predicted it and now, in this trembling moment, it had come. Not with Elizaveta or the Darkling, but on the wings of a dragon. Nikolai thought of all the stories, of Sankt Feliks who had become a beast to fight for the first king, of Juris who had bested the dragon only to take on its form. Zoya had become something the world hadn't seen since before legends were written.

The dragon's jaws opened and released an angry shriek. In it, Nikolai heard all of Zoya's sadness, her rage, the grief she'd endured for every soldier fallen, every friend lost, the deep loneliness of the life she'd been forced to live. The air seemed to come alive, the pressure dropping, lightning gathering.

She was going to kill them all.

Don't, Nikolai prayed. *Don't give in to this. There has to be more to life, even for soldiers like us.*

For a moment, the dragon's gaze met his and he saw her there, in that inhuman silver, those slitted pupils. He saw the girl who had rested her head against his shoulder in the garden and wept.

There has to be more.

She swiveled her scaled neck and lightning burst across the sky, crackling exclamations that scorched the air and lifted the hair on Nikolai's arms. But the Fjerdans were still standing. Zoya had spared them.

"Sankta!"

Nikolai wasn't sure where the shout came from. He turned his head and saw a figure in black, kneeling in the field.

"Sankta Zoya!" the figure shouted again.

He lifted his head, and Nikolai met the Darkling's gray gaze. The bastard winked at him.

"Sankta!" Another voice, wavering with tears.

"Sënje!" This time from the Fjerdan side.

"Sankta Zoya of the Storms!"

One of the *drüskelle* threw down his gun. "*Sënje Zoya daja Kerkenning!*" he cried, crumpling to his knees. "*Me jer jonink. Me jer jonink!*"

Saint Zoya of the Lightning. Forgive me. Forgive me.

The *drüskelle* captain strode forward, his pistol raised. Would he kill this kneeling boy? Blow his head open for daring to entertain heathen thoughts within it? If he did, what would happen?

But two Fjerdan soldiers stepped into the captain's path, seizing his arms and snatching away his pistol. The *drüskelle* captain shouted, face red, spittle flying from his mouth. *Blasphemy, heresy, treason, abomination.* All words that had been used against Grisha before. If the Fjerdans had been winning this battle, maybe those charges would have held sway. But these men didn't want to die. One by one, the *drüskelle* went to their knees. Zoya had bought their fealty with mercy.

Again, Nikolai looked to the Darkling. The Starless had surrounded him, praying. The field was full of kneeling soldiers, weeping troops, perplexed Grisha. From the north came the sound of a trumpet—the Fjerdans sounding retreat. The Darkling grinned at Nikolai as if he'd been the architect of it all.

Above them, the dragon flapped her vast wings and he saw someone on her back, though he couldn't tell who. The great beast roared and the clouds around her pulsed with light. Thunder boomed, rolling over the mountains, and lightning forked through the sky, so bright he had to avert his gaze.

When he looked back, Zoya was gone.

43

ZOYA

ZOYA COULDN'T THINK OVER the sound of Juris'
laughter in her head.

Sankta Zoya.

She was no Saint. It was podge-headed nonsense. But had she
helped buy peace for Ravka? Had she done right by leaving the Fjerdans
alive? She swooped down to the coast, searching for a place to land
that would be out of sight of prying eyes. She needed a moment in the
cool dark to pull her thoughts back together, to understand herself
again. Her mind felt different, not just her body. She couldn't grasp
the shape of who she was. It was all too much—the soldiers' panic
on the field, the Darkling's bemusement, the *drüskelle* commander's
wild rage, Nina's anguish. Nikolai. She could still feel his fear for her.
There has to be more to life, even for soldiers like us. In those brief seconds

she had believed. *We might shelter in each other.* She was tied to all of them.

Juris' knowledge echoed through her—a cave just north of Os Kervo, hewn into the cliff wall. He had flown this coastline many times before. The cave was snug, but it would do.

I should have killed the Fjerdans. I should have given them a wound from which they'd never recover. But that was an old voice, the voice of a hurt child who had no one to trust, who feared there would always be someone more powerful and more cruel than her. She would forever be a bloodthirsty, furious girl, but she might allow herself to be something else too. If she had helped to earn peace for Ravka, then maybe she could grant her own heart a bit of peace as well.

She set down with an awkward thud, nearly crashing into the cave wall before she managed to stop her speed. Utterly graceless.

"You have to take me back," Nina said.

Zoya gave a massive shrug. *Climb off or I'll throw you off.*

Nina yelped and half rolled off her, landing in a heap on the cave floor. Her clothes were soaked and her blond hair looked like someone had tried to style it with a pitchfork.

"Are you in my head?" Nina squeaked, pressing her hands to her temples. "Can you read my mind?"

Blessedly not. But she could feel. So much. It was terrifying. This was what she had always feared, this deep connection to the world. But she had opened the door. She'd burst right through it. There was no closing it now.

Nina pushed to her feet. She was staring at Zoya with huge eyes, and Zoya wondered what she saw. Her own sight was keener, her sense of smell sharper. Each breath felt strange, her belly, her lungs. What had she become?

"I . . . I still don't . . . I can't believe it's you."

Zoya couldn't quite believe it either. And yet, this was what Juris had wanted from her, it was the true gift that had come through his scales when she'd taken his life and he'd taken hers. But she didn't know how long she could keep this form. It still felt wrong to her, unstable.

She sought some kind of explanation to offer Nina. *There was a time when soldiers became beasts, and when Grisha didn't take amplifiers, they became them.*

"You didn't become a bear or a hawk, Zoya. You're a *dragon*. Can you . . . Is it permanent?"

Zoya felt a shiver pass through her, an echo of Juris' loneliness. He had been able to take human or dragon form at will. She hoped the same thing would be true for her.

I don't know.

"Zoya, you have to take me back to Leviathan's Mouth."

You will come home to Ravka.

"No, I will not. My mission isn't complete."

A deep growl rumbled through Zoya and she snapped her huge jaws at the air. *Why must you be so stubborn?*

"I could ask the same of you!" Nina said, and she had the temerity to kick Zoya's foreleg with her tiny foot.

I put my life at risk to get you back, Nina. The Apparat could still be alive. Your cover may be worthless.

"I'm going to take that chance. I have to."

Zoya huffed a breath and watched dust and pebbles billow through the cave. The cost of the dragon's form was just as high as she'd suspected it would be. She felt Nina's hurt, and it only made Zoya want to keep her closer, find a way to shield her from harm. It was unbearable.

Promise you'll come home to us.

"I can't."

Then promise you'll be careful.

"I can't do that either."

Wretched girl.

But she was going to let Nina go. Nina Zenik was a soldier. Zoya had trained her well. And she had the right to choose her own path.

Climb on and hold tight, Zoya instructed.

Nina laughed. "That I can do."

Zoya craned her neck back to look at Nina. She was beaming, her cheeks rosy. She looked nothing like the grieving girl Zoya had known. Happiness and anticipation shimmered around her as if they were her true shape, as if she wore a halo of gold.

Zoya leapt from the mouth of the cave and let Nina's joy carry her over the sea.

She shrouded them both in mist as they approached Leviathan, but absolute chaos had erupted aboard the base and there was plenty of cover. She saw rafts and boats arriving and departing in swarms as officers, soldiers, and medical personnel traveled to and from the mainland. The battle had come to a standstill for now; Zoya knew that didn't mean peace.

Saying goodbye to Nina again wasn't easy, but Zoya wasn't going to stand in the way of her decision. If she really believed she could resume her cover as Mila Jandersdat, then she could still be a valuable asset and feed vital information to Ravka. But there was more. Zoya sensed the pull of Nina's longing toward . . . someone vibrant, bright as a new sun, warm and coppery. The girl couldn't stay away from Fjerdans, it seemed. Zoya wondered if she should warn her against falling in love, against the danger it could put her in undercover. But it was foolish to think she could contain Nina Zenik's heart.

"I have to warn you," said Nina as they set down near one of the piers. "Tell the king we can't rely on Prince Rasmus. Hanne still has hope for him, but he's not who we thought he was. Not at all."

One less ally. The prince had let his country's hatred choose his road.

I'll create a distraction so you can rejoin the soldiers on base without notice.

Nina grinned. "That shouldn't be much of a challenge."

Zoya bumped Nina with her snout. It was a gesture more intimate than she ever would have been tempted to make in her human body. *Stay as safe as you can.*

Nina set a hand on Zoya's scales. She rested her cheek briefly against Zoya's head. "Thank you," she whispered, and then she was vanishing up a ramp and into the bustle of the base.

Zoya wondered if she would ever see Nina Zenik again.

She set out over the waves, then whirled back around, exploding through the mist as she arced over the naval base. She heard screams from below, felt the Fjerdans' terror like an icy wave, and reveled in it. Fear was a language universally understood. She drew in a breath and released a crackling burst of lightning, then banked to the left and headed back to the mainland, her wings spread wide, feeling the salt spray against her belly, as she coasted low over the water. She could still sense Nina's powerful heart, the steady beat of her courage.

When you are tied to all things, there is no limit to what you may know.

And apparently to what she would have to feel. All this emotion was exhausting. She was Zoya and she was the knight known as Juris and she was the dragon he had once slain.

She circled the battlefield, noted the Fjerdans in retreat. It was hard to see so many bodies on the ground, feel the grief emanating from soldiers as they tended to their wounded and mourned their dead. But she could find no sign of the Starless Saint or his followers. The Darkling had been the first to kneel, though she had no illusions that he'd suddenly come around to their side. He wasn't done, and yet she couldn't guess his intent. His presence on the battlefield had been like a gap in all that life and fear, a deep well of eternity.

Zoya turned toward the village of Pachesyana, where the Ravkan forces had set up their headquarters. The soldiers' camp came into view and then the royal command tent. She knew she needed to focus to manage a landing in this small space, but she was more tired than she'd realized. She'd done too much, too fast. She could feel her control over the dragon's shape slipping, and then she wasn't flying, she was falling.

A gust of air caught her, buffering her descent. When she struck the earth, the impact was gentle, but it still came as a surprise, knocking the breath out of her. Some part of her wanted to just give in to her fatigue and slide into unconsciousness.

She felt arms encircle her and lift her head.

"Zoya?" Nikolai's voice. The voice of a king. The voice of a brilliant, creative boy, left alone with his books and inventions, forever roaming an empty palace. His hurt and worry washed over her. "Please," he whispered. "Please."

The dragon's mind receded, leaving her mind blessedly empty of any thoughts but her own. Zoya forced herself to open her eyes. Nikolai's lip was bloodied. There was soot in his hair. But he was alive and for this brief moment, he was holding her. She wanted to curl into him and let herself cry. She wanted to lie beside him and just feel safe for an hour. She had so much to say to him and she didn't want to wait.

Zoya made herself sit up. "The Fjerdans?"

"Careful," he said, still helping to support her. "Nadia broke your fall, thank the Saints, but you hit the ground hard."

"The Fjerdans," she repeated. "They retreated?"

"We've called a truce."

Zoya saw Tolya with his big brow furrowed, Tamar biting her lip, Nadia with her goggles around her neck, Leoni holding tight to Adrik's arm, Genya with a hand pressed to her mouth. Relief flooded through her and she wanted to pull them all close. Instead she said, "We'll get no help from Fjerda's crown prince. Nina seems to have overestimated her influence."

"I wouldn't say that," Tamar mused. "An entire battlefield just declared you a Saint."

"Actually, the Darkling declared you a Saint," Nikolai corrected.

"Turning into a dragon probably helped," added Tolya.

"Did you *know* you could do this?" Genya asked. "I can't believe you didn't tell me!"

Zoya shook her head. She felt impossibly cold, as if now that the dragon's fire had banked inside her, she would never be warm until it was kindled again.

"There were *khergud* on the battlefield," she said, remembering. They'd flown beside Nikolai's demon.

"It's all right," Tolya said, squatting down. "They fought on our side. But they had to disappear for a while. They couldn't risk questions."

"They don't exist," said Tamar. "At least according to the Shu queen."

"You're back," Zoya said.

Tamar winked. "You think I'd miss a fight?" She offered Zoya her hand and helped her to her feet.

Nikolai's eyes widened. "You are wearing the most extraordinary armor."

Zoya looked down at herself. Her roughspun peasant clothes were gone. Her body was covered in a snug tunic and breeches made of metallic black scales that shimmered blue in the sun. She recognized this armor. It was what Juris had worn in human form, and it fit like a second skin. Her vanity didn't mind the effect, but she'd bloody well better be able to take it off.

Leoni cocked her head to one side. "Is it comfortable?"

"It's heavy," Zoya said, offering up her arm so the Fabrikator could feel the metal.

"It will make quite the impression in Os Kervo," said Nikolai. "Fjerda has called for talks."

"Vadik Demidov is in Os Kervo too," said Tolya. "The Fjerdans are in retreat for now, but they've switched tactics."

Tamar grunted in disgust. "They couldn't beat us on the field, so they're pushing the issue of succession. They've called for an assembly of Ravka's highest-ranking nobles."

Zoya couldn't believe what she was hearing. "*Our* nobles? They have no right to command our people."

"We can stop them," said Genya. "We'll block the assembly."

Nikolai tugged on a pair of calf-leather gloves. In the time since the battle, he'd changed into an immaculate field uniform. "On the contrary," he said. "I've ordered airships sent for them. They'll be here in a few hours."

"For Saints' sake, why?" asked Zoya. If the man could make something more difficult, he would.

"Because the longer we give them to plot and scheme, the worse it will be. Right now, West Ravka is grateful to us and angry with Fjerda for their betrayal. Genya, I'll need you to see to my cut-up lip and make me look less the rogue and more the respectable monarch. Bastard or not, if I have any hope of keeping the throne, this is it."

An uncomfortable silence followed.

Tamar broke it with a click of her tongue. "Bastardy is the least of your worries."

"They know what you are now," said Zoya. She left for a few days and everything went to hell. He'd released his monster onto the field. He'd shown all of Ravka the demon king.

"True," said Nikolai. "But they know what you are too, Sankta Zoya."

"Do not call me that."

"It has a nice ring to it," said Tamar.

"Our Lady of Dragonfire?" suggested Nadia.

"Sweet scaly vengeance?" said Genya.

Zoya turned her back on all of them and strode toward the tents. "I'm going to go live in a cave."

44
NINA

WITH EACH STEP NINA took on the naval base, she wondered if she'd hear a voice telling her to halt. She flinched at every shout, sure she was about to feel the sting of a *drüskelle* whip around her arms or that a squad of the Apparat's men would rush at her.

But the Fjerdans only had eyes for the dragon soaring above them.

"It's back!" someone shouted. "Take cover!"

Nina had to remind herself to duck down and find shelter behind a grounded flyer. "What is that thing?" she asked the pilot staring up at the sky.

"I don't know," he said, voice shaking. "I saw it before. It destroyed the eastern tower and then just flew away."

"Maybe it wasn't hungry then," Nina offered helpfully.

The pilot whimpered and curled more tightly to the side of the flyer.

She made her way back to the Brums' cabin slowly, taking in the tumult around her, and giving herself time to concoct a story. The naval base had moved north to join in supporting the battle at Arkesk. Now Fjerdan medical units were being deployed to attend to soldiers and to bring bodies back from the front. Nina could sense the change that had come over these men. They had entered one battle but had been forced to fight another. Even those who had considered the possibility of defeat hadn't thought it would come this way—courtesy of a dragon and a squadron of flying Shu warriors. No one could have imagined Fjerdan soldiers kneeling before a Grisha. If Nina's thoughts still felt like a slippery plate of dumplings, she couldn't begin to guess at what the people around her must feel.

Assuming no one had gotten a clear view of her during the battle, she only had to account for where she'd been over the last few hours. She would say that she'd needed time to recover from what she'd seen during the sea invasion, that she'd been more disturbed by it than she'd realized, and that once the base had joined the northern assault, she'd simply tried to stay out of the way.

And if the Apparat had managed to survive and attempted to expose her? She didn't know what proof the priest might have of her true identity, but she doubted it would matter. The Fjerdans would throw her in a cell and ask questions later. Nina was not going to let that happen. The Apparat's men had taken the bones from her sleeves. That might have left her vulnerable, but there was death all around, corpses on shore and on base, all of whom could become her soldiers. She just needed to find Hanne and get them both out of here.

But the Brums' quarters were empty. There was no sign of Ylva or Hanne to be found.

Nina changed out of her soaked clothes and into the rose wool dress she'd worn the previous day. She rebraided her hair and headed out onto the deck. Could Hanne still be with the prince in the western tower?

She was only a few yards from the command center when she heard a woman sobbing. It sounded like Hanne. Nina broke into a run and saw a group of soldiers gathered around someone or something. Jarl Brum stood off to the side, arguing with a group of royal guards. He had dirt on his face, the muck and blood of battle staining his uniform. She pushed through the circle of soldiers and sailors, fighting to get closer, and then stopped dead.

It wasn't Hanne crying. It was Ylva. Sobbing over her daughter's broken body.

Nina's mind tilted, unable to comprehend what she was seeing. That wasn't right. It couldn't be.

Hanne lay on her stomach in a pool of blood, her body bent at an impossible angle, her face turned to the side. Her profile looked wrong, her rosy freckles, her full lips. Nina fell to her knees, reaching for her. Hanne's blood had soaked Ylva's skirt. Her body was cold.

"The prince," Ylva cried between sobs. "The prince . . . said she fell."

Nina looked up, up to the western observation tower where Hanne had gone to watch the battle with Prince Rasmus.

Not Hanne. Not her Hanne. It was happening all over again. She was kneeling in the streets of a foreign city. She had Matthias' blood on her hands. Was this what her love did? Did it murder everything it touched? Nina wanted to scream and so she did, unable to stop the anguish that tore through her.

Hanne wouldn't jump, would she? They'd had hope for the future, hope for escape. But Nina thought of Hanne sitting on the edge of her bed, how lost she'd looked, how scared. *If he asks for my hand, I cannot deny him. But Nina . . . Nina, I can't say yes.* Two nights ago. An eternity away. A moment when Nina had still believed in possibility.

Maybe I can't be happy at all, Hanne had said.

Nina saw Joran watching, his face ashen, stricken by what looked like grief.

She lurched to her feet and seized him by the fabric of his vile *drüskelle* jacket. "What happened?" Her voice was shrill, sharp as broken glass. "What happened to her? What did you do to her?"

"I didn't see," he protested, then yanked her close, wrapping his arms around her. "You must be still. You must calm yourself." But in her ear he whispered, "I don't know what happened. There was an argument. The prince struck her, only a slap, but then he was taken with some kind of fit. Hanne told me to get help, and when I returned——"

Nina shoved away from him. She couldn't think, couldn't breathe. *Hanne. Hanne. Hanne.* Her name a blessing, an incantation, a curse. The prince had hurt her. Maybe it had just been a game to him, like the one he'd played with Joran, testing his control, a chance to see how far he could push his rivalry with Brum. *He was taken with some kind of fit.* Hanne had lashed out. She probably hadn't meant to. She'd been frightened and she'd used her power on the prince.

And then what? What had happened between them when Joran had left them alone?

"He did this!" she spat. "Prince Rasmus. Where is he? Hanne didn't just fall and there's no way she would jump. Where is he?"

Jarl Brum was suddenly beside her.

"Be silent," he growled. He clapped his big hand over her mouth. His eyes were chips of ice.

Nina thrashed in his arms, tried to bite his fingers.

Brum only squeezed tighter, startled by her strength. "You will not say such things."

Nina couldn't breathe. She looked into Brum's hateful eyes, his pupils like pinpricks, and she knew then what a coward he was. He'd lost control of his *drüskelle* on the battlefield. The invasion had collapsed. He was desperately hanging on to his position and couldn't afford any hint of treason. Even with his daughter dead at his feet.

Nina stopped moving. Slowly, cautiously, Brum released her.

"You know he did this," she said plainly. "You know what he is." And Nina had known too, but she'd let Hanne face him alone. Had Hanne admitted she was Grisha? Had she rejected his proposal? Stung his pride? Or had he simply wanted to hurt Brum and show that he was the one who truly held the power?

Ylva let loose a broken moan. "I never should have let her go with him. I never should have let her enter Heartwood."

Nina knelt and threw her arms around Hanne's mother. She could feel sobs shaking both of their bodies.

"I will kill him," Nina said. "I swear it."

"That won't bring her back."

Nina didn't care. She'd lost too much. She had spared Joran. She had begged Zoya to spare Fjerda's soldiers. Mercy, mercy, always mercy. But what good was mercy when the world took the best people from it? Matthias gone. Hanne gone.

Save some mercy for my people.

Maybe the Fjerdans deserved forgiveness, but their leaders—Brum, this monster prince—did not. She and Hanne had dared to dream of a new world, but they'd put their trust in the wrong people.

A clarion horn rang out over the deck. The prince was coming.

"Mila, you must control yourself," Ylva pleaded. "There may be an explanation."

"He killed her, Ylva. I know it and so do you."

A hand gripped the back of Nina's neck hard.

"You will be silent or I will silence you," Brum snarled.

Nina stood, breaking Brum's hold. The wild hysteria that had gripped her was gone, and only fury remained. She met his gaze and

Jarl Brum—commander of the *drüskelle*, architect of torture, Fjerda's scythe—took a step back.

She knew she was at risk of blowing her cover. She knew that Mila—sweet, meek, doting Mila—would never dare look Brum in the eye, would never show him this clean, unclouded glimpse of her rage.

"You are a coward," she said, her voice low in her throat. It was an animal growl. She spoke for Matthias, for Joran, for Hanne, for the Grisha, for everyone whose roots had been forced to drink the poison of this man's hate. "You are the lowest form of man. Without honor, without integrity. *Djel djeren je töp.*" Djel turns his back on you.

"Mila!" Ylva gasped.

Brum's lips flattened. "You are no longer welcome in our home."

Nina laughed. "I don't keep company with vermin. My place is with the wolves."

Brum could see it now, that she was not what she had pretended to be. But the other generals were approaching, the royal ministers.

"Enke Jandersdat," Joran said urgently. "Mila, you must listen. The prince has commanded that—"

But Rasmus' voice cut past the crowd. "Come, Enke Jandersdat." He stood surrounded by guards and nobles, waving her over with a lazy flick of his hand. His face was golden, glowing, warm and alive. He finally looked like a Grimjer. It was as if he'd stolen Hanne's life and swallowed it. "I must travel to Os Kervo for these peace talks, and I would have you beside me. We should be together in our grief." She heard no remorse in his words. If anything, he sounded even more vicious and amused, as if he once again held the crop in his hand. Rasmus at his worst.

Nina trembled. How would she kill him? A dart to his throat? A corpse to tear him in two? Maybe she would strangle him with her bare hands. The prince thought he was dealing with another vulnerable girl, someone kind and good. Someone gentle like Hanne.

She forced herself to curtsy. She would bear his presence, his smugness, until she could get him alone. Then Nina would end his life. She would be hung for it, she knew. Maybe burned alive on a pyre. And she didn't care. *I was a soldier before I was a spy, and I am done with lies.* She fell into step beside the crown prince of Fjerda. *I will leave this world on a hammer blow.*

45

NIKOLAI

NIKOLAI HAD BEEN INSIDE Os Kervo's city hall many times, had fought not to fall asleep beneath its stained-glass dome through countless meetings. Yet the audience chamber looked different today, the light filtering through the colored glass from above seemed brighter.

The chamber was built like an amphitheater, its terraced walls lined with long, curving benches, and Ravka's nobles had already assembled. But the Ravkan and Fjerdan delegations were conducted inside through the northern and southern doors at the same time, so that neither country was seen to take precedence.

"Something happened to Nina," Zoya whispered. "When I left her she was shining, ready to take on the world."

It took Nikolai a moment to realize whom she meant. He'd nearly forgotten Nina had been tailored. She was in the prince's retinue, which Nikolai hoped was a good sign. But that hope was dashed by her expression. Her eyes were too wide, her lips slightly parted.

Nikolai had to agree with Zoya. "She looks like she's in shock."

The prince himself was mostly what Nikolai had expected based on intelligence reports—young, of about average height for a Fjerdan. His eyes were bright and there was a nervous energy radiating from him, but that was to be expected of an inexperienced leader when the stakes were so high.

Brum looked nothing but calm, despite the defeat and near mutiny he'd suffered. This would be his attempt to resurrect his reputation and take control once more. He was flanked by *drüskelle*.

"He brought his wolf pups," Nikolai noted in some surprise.

"He wants to show he still has command," said Zoya. "He must have chosen them carefully. A calculated risk."

"He should have checked his math. They only have eyes for my general."

And who could blame them? Grisha were enlivened by their power. It fed them, extended their lives. Zoya's face was still flushed. Her hair framed her face in thick black waves, slightly damp from the sea mist. The armor she wore was less like battle gear than a clinging skin of glittering scales. She didn't look like a Grisha, or a military commander, or even quite human.

What must they make of us? he wondered as he and Zoya took their places gazing up at the seated noblemen and diplomats, surrounded on all sides. The demon and the dragon. At least Nikolai had the grace to put on proper clothes.

The people trailing Brum were like a punch to the gut. His father. His mother. And the man Nikolai instantly knew to be Vadik Demidov.

"He looks just like the old king," whispered Zoya.

"A tragedy for everyone involved," Nikolai replied. But it hurt to see Demidov flanked by his parents.

Nikolai had known it was likely the Fjerdans would involve his mother and father—or the man he'd once believed to be his father—and the Kerch had made it possible. Yet seeing them here was still hard to accept. He could feel his father's contempt from across the chamber, see it in the bitter lines of his haggard face. His mother looked frail and tired, and he wondered if she wanted to be here to speak against him or if she had been coerced. Perhaps that was wishful thinking, the hope of a wayward son who had exiled his own parents. She wouldn't meet his eyes.

Is this where all of it ends? He'd asked that question more than once over the last few days. He looked around the room at the Fjerdan delegates, the Ravkan noblemen, and the Kerch and Zemeni ambassadors stationed in Os Kervo who had joined the summit as mediators. The Apparat and his Priestguard had made their way here too, though they hadn't arrived with the Fjerdans and they stood high up in the gallery. The priest's face looked bruised.

Nikolai didn't know whom he could rely upon. He had allies among Ravka's first families, though many had opposed his reforms. Plenty of the nobles from West Ravka would have been happy to see him deposed, particularly if it meant secession for the west. But after the Fjerdan betrayal and invasion, he hoped he could count a few more friends among them. Nikolai was popular with the people, but the people weren't gathered here. They had no voice in this chamber.

Not entirely true, he considered. Dense crowds had thronged the square outside the city hall and he could hear the distant sounds of their chanting, even if it was hard to make out what they were saying through the closed shutters.

He felt curiously light. Whether or not he kept the Ravkan throne seemed almost incidental now that he might see his country and his people free. He didn't know Demidov, but he might not be the most terrible choice, especially since Zoya had the power to combat the Apparat's influence. She could remain to counsel the Little Lantsov as a voice to oppose Fjerda. And to keep the king from doing anything ridiculous. She'd essentially be occupying the same role she always had.

And Nikolai? He would be banished. There was no way that Demidov could allow him to remain as a member of the cabinet. He wouldn't be permitted to resume his experiments at Lazlayon nor take up some position in the Ravkan government. Maybe there was some freedom in that. He could return to the sea. He could become Sturmhond again and join forces with the legendary Wraith, terrify slavers, become the scourge of . . . something. It all sounded reasonable, exciting even, except when he considered leaving behind the woman beside him.

The floor of the audience chamber was set with benches like those above. But no one sat. Instead they all stood—the Zemeni, the Ravkans, the Fjerdans, the Kerch—all facing each other beneath the dome, as if about to begin a dance.

The Zemeni ambassador stepped forward. "Both nations have submitted their list of concessions for peace. His Most Royal Highness, King Nikolai Lantsov of Ravka, has the floor."

Nikolai could only handle so much pomp, so he decided to dispense with it.

"I read your list of proposed concessions, Commander Brum. They're absurd. I think intentionally so, because you don't want peace at all."

"Why would we?" Brum shot back. It seemed he was done with pomp as well.

"It wouldn't be unprecedented, given the crushing defeat you just suffered." He turned to Zoya. "This is awkward. Does he know they lost?"

Brum cut his hand through the air in dismissal. "A battle is not a war, and I do not believe Ravka has the stomach for a prolonged conflict. If you did, you would press your advantage instead of waving the flag of truce."

True, alas. "Are you so eager to see more blood spilled?"

"I am eager to see Fjerda's sovereignty protected from witches and demons and those who would see the work of Djel corrupted. We all witnessed the monster you became on the battlefield."

"I am both man and monster. Something I imagine you know quite a lot about."

"And this creature"—Brum pointed at Zoya—"the Stormwitch or whatever abomination she's become. No one should have such power."

"I'll wager the same thing was said of the first man who held a gun in his hand."

A murmur rose from the benches. To Nikolai's hopeful ears, it sounded approving. *I haven't lost them entirely.* Whatever reports of demons his countrymen had heard from the battlefield, the king who stood before them in polished boots and gilded epaulets was every inch the civilized ruler.

"You may offer all the fine talk you like," said Brum. "It won't change the size of your army or the odds that favor us."

"Forgive my indelicacy," said Hiram Schenck, the Kerch delegate, who had drunk Count Kirigin's excellent wine and denied Ravka aid. "But can you even speak for Ravka, Nikolai . . . well, whoever you are?"

A gasp went up from the crowd. This was not the polite allusion to Nikolai's parentage some had expected. It was a blatant insult—

reprisal for preserving Zemeni trade routes and handing the Kerch what amounted to worthless technology.

Nikolai only smiled. "I'm the man who still wears the double-eagle crown and the demon who just tore apart a battlefield. Let me know if you need your memory refreshed."

Brum seized his chance. "We reject this pretender, the bastard king, as the true ruler of Ravka. He cannot speak for his country when he has no right to hold the throne."

"That may well be," the Zemeni ambassador said grimly. "But who are you to speak for Fjerda? Why do we not hear from Fjerda's crown prince?"

Oh friend, thought Nikolai ruefully, *we'll find no luck in that quarter.*

There was a long pause as all eyes turned to Prince Rasmus. He had a strong, sharp jaw and unusually full lips.

The prince shrugged. "Who rules Ravka will be decided by Ravkans," he drawled. "I came here to make peace."

"What?" Nina said, stunned.

The prince gave her the faintest smile and—it was so fast Nikolai thought he might have imagined it—reached out to brush his hand against hers. Nina recoiled. She had managed the impossible: She had delivered the prince and a promise of peace. So why did she look so shocked?

Her surprise was nothing compared to the confounded fury on Brum's face.

"That is not . . . We agreed—"

"We?" the prince asked, turning hard blue eyes on him. "*We* are Fjerda. *You* are a military commander who cannot control his own men. Tell me, if we return to the battlefield, are you so sure your soldiers will take up arms against a woman they call Saint?"

Brum's nostrils flared alarmingly. "They will or I will cut their hearts from their chests."

"All on your own?" Prince Rasmus surveyed the *drüskelle*, then bobbed his chin at the bodyguard beside him. "Joran, will you take up arms against your brothers then? Will you cut out their hearts for Fjerda?"

The young *drüskelle* shook his head. "Never."

Brum stared. "You are a traitor and will die as such at the end of a rope."

Despite his height, the boy couldn't have been more than sixteen. Yet he didn't flinch.

"I deserve nothing less," said the prince's bodyguard. "I committed horrible crimes for the sake of my country, because I believed I was doing what had to be done to save Fjerda's soul. So hang me. I will die with more honor than I've lived."

Brum's face flushed dark red. "I will not cede my country's right to protect its borders and its sovereignty just because a few naive boys have had their minds tampered with by Grisha witches." He wagged a finger at Zoya. "That woman is not a Saint. She is corruption walking. And this man," he seethed, whirling on Nikolai, "is just as unnatural. Let the dowager queen give testimony. She is witness to the fact that he is not royal born."

"We will hear what she has to say," said Hiram Schenck.

"No," said Nikolai. He'd known the conversation would come to this. He'd understood that he was out of options as soon as he'd seen his parents enter the audience chamber with the "pretender." He thought of Magnus Opjer, dressed as a beggar but still standing proud, who had journeyed all the way to the capital to try to save his son and a city full of innocent people. He was an inventor, a builder. Like Nikolai.

I've never been a king, he realized. It was never the throne or a crown he had sought. All he'd wanted was to fix his country, and now, at last, he thought he knew how.

He caught his mother's faded blue eyes and smiled. "There's no reason to put Queen Tatiana through this ordeal. You will have the proof you seek in my confession. I am a bastard. I have always known it and I am not sorry. I have never wanted to be a Lantsov."

"What are you doing?" Zoya whispered furiously.

"What I must," said Nikolai.

"The Lantsovs are descended of the blood of the first kings!" seethed his father. "Of Yaromir himself!"

"Once-great men do not always remain great. It was a Lantsov king who failed to keep the Black Heretic in check and allowed him to create the Fold. It was a Lantsov king who all but abdicated rule of Ravka to the Darkling and the Apparat, and let his country and his people languish in their care. I'm sorry I cannot claim Ravka's crown, but I'm happy I cannot claim Lantsov blood."

"Nikolai—" protested Zoya.

He gestured to Vadik Demidov. "But this man has no more right to the throne than I." Nikolai cast his gaze around the chamber, gathering every bit of authority he had earned through blood and trial, on the seas as Sturmhond, on the battlefield as Nikolai Lantsov. He might have no true name, but he had victories enough. "Fjerda imposed on Ravka's noble families to come to this place. So we will do those nobles the courtesy of letting them decide who should rule this nation."

"Are you so arrogant you think they'll choose a bastard?" his father said on a cackle.

Zoya turned to him and whispered, "This is exactly what Fjerda wants. You can't let them vote and give legitimacy to such a body. You must stop."

But Nikolai didn't intend to stop. And if Zoya was angry now, he suspected he'd have to take cover momentarily.

He strode to the windows. "Yaromir, the first king, had no claim to royalty until he united Ravka's warring noblemen beneath his banner. He had the help of Sankt Feliks to do it. Only one person can unite this country and bring peace to our nations. Soldier, Summoner, and Saint."

He threw open the shutters. The winter wind blew through and on it, the sounds of the people chanting below. *Sankta Zoya. Rebe Dva Urga.* Saint Zoya. Daughter of the Wind. The only person to whom he could entrust this country he had fought and bled for, who might finally bring them an age of peace.

"I will kneel to only one ruler, and I will see only one person crowned this day. The age of the Lantsovs is over." He sank to one knee. "Let the Nazyalensky dynasty begin. All hail the Dragon Queen."

The words hung in the room like insects suspended in amber. Nikolai could hear the pounding of his heart, the chanting outside.

What happens if no one speaks? he wondered. *What if they all get up and leave? Do I just stay here?*

Then he heard a throat being cleared, and all the sweet Saints, a voice: "All hail the Dragon Queen! Moya Tsaritsa!"

Count Kirigin. The man did come through in a pinch.

Another voice shouted, "The Dragon Queen!"

Nikolai couldn't be sure who that was . . . Raevsky? Radimov? It had come from the left side of the room. And then he couldn't keep track of the voices because they crowded together, one on top of the other, as the men and women of Ravka's noble families shouted Zoya's name.

It would not be all of them, he knew that. There were voices raised in anger too, men already shuffling out the door and off to make trouble. And he knew not all of those who knelt now liked this idea, or believed in it. They would begin fomenting revolution before they ever left the building. Nikolai might have doomed both the Lantsov and the Nazyalensky dynasties in a single move. But he didn't think that was the case. The nobles of Ravka didn't want to be ruled by a Fjerdan puppet.

He glanced up and met Zoya's furious gaze.

"I am going to murder you in your sleep," she seethed.

Nikolai winked. "Go on. Say something grand."

46

ZOYA

"WHAT SAY YOU, Zoya Nazyalensky? General of the Second Army?"

The Zemeni ambassador had asked her the question, but she had no idea how to answer. She only knew that as soon as she was alone with Nikolai, she was going to throttle him. When had he decided on this ridiculous, utterly nonsensical plan?

She remembered the image Juris had thrust into her head when she'd taken his scales as amplifiers: a crown. She'd thought it was the dragon's arrogance, his wish for a Grisha queen, but now she had to wonder. Had Juris predicted this moment, just as he'd seen what would happen in the observation tower?

He'd hinted at it again and again, but she'd misunderstood at every turn. *You cannot tell me you have not contemplated what it would mean to be a queen.*

Zoya had. Of course she had. When her foolish, dreaming mind had gone wandering. But this was something different. *I can't do this.*

Can't you? She was no humble girl plucked from obscurity. She was no young princess far from home. Her life had been given in service to the Grisha, to her country, to her king. Was this any different?

Of course it was different. She wasn't thinking rationally.

We are the dragon and this is our time.

Zoya felt the eyes of everyone in the audience chamber assessing her. She could hear people chanting outside the city hall far below. All right. She was no queen and she certainly wasn't a Saint, but she was a general. She would attack this the way she would any other strategic campaign. If these were her allies, let them say so.

"I am a soldier," she said. "I've been a soldier since I was a child. Would you have a girl who has spent her life down in the trenches of battle wear a crown? Will you have a soldier queen?"

It was Pensky, general of the First Army, who stepped forward. They had been forced to work together since Nikolai had taken the throne. He'd never particularly liked Zoya, but she hoped he respected her.

He straightened his jacket, stroked his voluminous white mustache. "Better a queen who knows the cost of battle. I will have a soldier queen."

Zoya kept herself to a short, dignified nod, showing the barest fraction of the gratitude she felt. Cold sweat had coated her body, but she forced herself to continue.

"I am a Squaller, a Grisha." She cast a disdainful glance at Brum. "Some of our enemies will call me witch. And some of our own people will agree. Will you have a Grisha queen?"

"It's true," said the old duke from Grevyakin, whom she and

Nikolai had visited with months ago. She'd been miserable through the whole evening, but now she was glad she'd managed to stay awake and civil. "Some will despise you. Others will call you Saint. I want to farm my land and see my children safe. I will bow to a Grisha queen if it will bring peace."

Again she nodded, as if she had expected nothing less, as if her heart didn't feel like it was about to hummingbird straight through her chest. Zoya paused. She understood the risk she was about to take, but the crown would be nothing but an unwanted weight if she didn't. She knew the toll speculation around his birth had taken on Nikolai. She couldn't attempt to rule that way. And she didn't want to be the girl who hid any longer. *We see you, daughter.*

Zoya took a deep breath. "My father's name was Suhm Nabri, and I am his only daughter. Will you have a Suli queen?"

A murmur of consternation and confusion rose from the crowd, but Zoya didn't lower her chin. She met their gazes one by one. Some of them had probably had their servants chase Suli off their land, or maybe they'd hired them for their parties and never thought twice about them again. Others sent old clothes to Suli caravans and slept better that night, soothed by their show of generosity, while others praised the beauty of Suli women and children and patted themselves on the back for their open-mindedness. But maybe some of them knew they had Suli blood in their own families, and maybe a few would admit that the Suli had roamed this country before it had ever been called Ravka.

Count Kirigin stepped forward. He'd chosen an alarming cobalt-blue coat trimmed in scarlet ribbon today. "Are the Suli not known for their far-seeing and their resilience?" he asked the chamber.

Nikolai was going to have to give that man a medal. Or maybe Zoya would.

"That's right," said the duchess of Caryeva. "I don't care where she's from. I will bow to the only queen who can take to the skies on black wings and put terror in our enemies' hearts."

Nikolai rose. "I say yes!" he cried to the chamber, his face alight with optimism and triumph. "We will have a Suli queen, a Grisha queen, a Ravkan queen!" He had never looked more golden or more grand.

A cheer went up from the Ravkans as the Fjerdans looked on with some concern.

Maybe that could be enough. Maybe. This moment was made of glass, fragile, ready to shatter into nothing if she made the wrong move.

"If this is the wish of the Ravkan people," said Zoya slowly, "I will serve my country in whatever way I can."

"But how do we know her power is holy?" The Apparat's voice snaked through the room. Zoya had nearly forgotten about him and his Priestguard. "Are we so ready to forget the blight that has struck not only Ravka but every country represented in this room and beyond? Can it be mere coincidence that such a curse has befallen our lands when first a demon and then a dragon appear?" He spread his hands as if addressing his congregation, his questions ringing through the chamber. "How is it that Zoya Nazyalensky, an ordinary Grisha, should come to possess such abilities? She took the form of a reptile because she is one. I know this girl. I served as spiritual counselor to the king. She has a cruel, cold heart and can never be the mother Ravka needs."

Zoya could make no reply to that. She had been cruel. She had been cold. There was a hard heart of iron in her that had allowed her to survive. And how was she meant to oppose the Apparat? Nikolai hadn't thought of that, had he? The priest was believed to speak for the people, and in this chamber, his words carried as loudly as those chanting outside.

"Do you choose which Saints we're free to worship now?"

That voice. Cool as well water. The Darkling emerged from the back of the chamber. He still wore the black robes of the Starless Saint. How had he even gained access to the hall?

The Apparat scoffed. "What right do you have to be here? A nameless monk following the banner of a madman."

"Let us not concern ourselves with names," said the Darkling, stepping into the light. "I have had so many of them."

The Apparat recoiled. Most of the people in this chamber had never met the Darkling or had encountered him only briefly, and his features were still not returned to what they'd once been. But for those who knew him, who had worked with him, who had admired and feared him, there was no mistaking who he was. Genya had known it instantly. And if the sheer horror on his face was any indication, so did the Apparat.

"We have all suffered throughout these long years of war and conflict," said the Darkling smoothly. "But of the many people who might speak of kings and queens, it should not be this man. For a moment, let us put aside the fact that he has allied himself with Ravka's enemies during a time of war—"

"My only allegiance is to the Saints!"

The Darkling ignored him, seeming to drift closer to the Apparat. "This man helped the Darkling depose a Lantsov king. He was instrumental in bringing about the civil war that nearly destroyed this country, and now, he dares to challenge a woman the people worship as a living Saint?"

"Are we sure we want to let him keep talking?" Zoya murmured to Nikolai.

"Not at all."

"Everyone knows the old king was ill," the Apparat said, but his eyes were skittering about the room wildly as if searching for some means of escape. "These charges are nothing but lies."

"The king was a victim of poison, was he not?" the Darkling queried.

"He was indeed," said Nikolai.

"Poison delivered slowly over time, by someone close to him, someone who had his trust. How many people could that be? I can think of only one."

Zoya glanced at the old king. His face was red with fury, his jowls trembling like pudding that hadn't quite set. In truth, the poison had been delivered by a certain Genya Safin in just retribution. But that was hardly common knowledge. And to admit to it now, Nikolai's father would have to tell all these people just how a young girl had gained access to his body every day.

"Lies!" said the Apparat. "Lies from a heretic!"

But as he spoke, shadows began to bleed from his mouth. The people in the chamber gasped, backing away, trying to put distance between themselves and the priest.

Zoya's eyes focused on the Darkling's hands, tucked into his sleeves but moving.

"I believe this is your cue," whispered Nikolai.

One she was happy to take. Zoya slashed her arm through the air and thunder broke in an enormous *boom*.

"Enough," she said. "Seize him."

⟞❦⟝

Chaos had erupted in the chamber when the royal guards swarmed the Apparat. The Fjerdans had departed hurriedly, but not before the crown prince had agreed to prolong their truce until a proper treaty could be made.

"Can you not stay?" Zoya had said, her gaze on Nina in her guise as Mila Jandersdat. But all of Nina's attention was focused on the prince, her face a mask of confusion as she studied him with a bizarre intensity that didn't seem at all in keeping with the modest ways of Fjerdan women.

"We will return," Prince Rasmus said. "I vow it." He had a low, husky voice. "Perhaps for your coronation."

Nikolai had set guards and Sun Soldiers to pursue the Darkling, who had somehow vanished from the chamber. No matter what he'd done for them at the summit, they still had no idea of his agenda, and Zoya refused to let him hie off somewhere to scheme. Besides, if this truce held, they had to find a way to stop the spread of the blight. She didn't know if the Darkling actually possessed any knowledge of how to do that or if all his talk of the *obisbaya* had been manipulation, but she intended to find out.

Already, the nobles of Ravka were asking when she would be crowned and when she would be accepting petitions for government funds, annexations of land, the list went on. But eventually the audience chamber was cleared and only Nikolai and Zoya remained beneath the echoing dome.

With a sweep of her hand, Zoya sent a gust to slam the shutters closed, blocking out the sound of that infernal chanting.

She turned to Nikolai. "Are you quite out of your mind?"

"On occasion. I find it bracing. But I have never been more sane or sober, Zoya."

"I can't do this, Nikolai. You're the diplomat, the charmer. I'm the . . ."

"Yes?"

She threw her hands up in exasperation. "I'm the muscle."

"The crown was never meant for me. You're a military commander, you're Grisha, and thanks to Nina's work and Juris' gift, you are a living Saint."

Zoya slumped down on one of the benches. "No matter what they said in this chamber, you know they'll never accept me. All those vows and cheers will mean nothing when they don't get what they want."

Nikolai knelt before her and reached for her hand.

"Stop doing that," she snapped. "Stop kneeling." But she didn't keep him from taking her hand. His touch was comforting, familiar, something to hold on to.

"I can't. It's just what my knees do now. I noticed your tricky little turn of phrase back there. You said that you would serve Ravka, but you didn't actually say you would accept the crown."

"Because I'm hoping you'll come to your senses and see this is impossible."

Nikolai grinned. "You know how I feel about that word."

He looked positively giddy.

"How can you do it?" she asked. "How can you just give up the throne you've fought so hard for?"

"Because I was never fighting for the throne. Not really. The battle was always for this disaster of a country. The Darkling believed that he was the key to Ravka's salvation. Maybe I fell into that trap too. But it isn't too late to get this right."

She shook her head. "It can't be done."

"We'll charm them one by one if we have to, and you will lead Ravka into an age of peace."

"I'm not charming."

"But I am. I have a stockpile of wiles to deploy on Ravka's behalf."

"Dinners and parades and small talk. That sounds like hell."

"I'll rub your feet every night."

What was he offering her? He was smiling but she could sense the caution in him too, a wariness she recognized. She'd promised herself she would speak her heart when she had the chance, but now that she was here, in this quiet room, with Nikolai before her, she had never been so frightened in her life.

"There's a mural in my room," she said hesitantly, unsure of what she meant to say, afraid of the words that might come. "A stormy sea. A boat. A flag with two stars. Did you ever wonder—"

"What they mean? Only when I thought of your bedchamber. So, roughly every night."

"Can you be serious for once?"

"Once and only once."

"Those stars are me and my aunt. Liliyana. She was the bravest woman I ever knew and she . . . she fought for me, when no one else would, without any weapon. She was a woman with no status or wealth, but she risked her own life to protect me. She thought I was worth saving. She thought . . . She thought I was worth loving." When Liliyana's star was gone, Zoya had believed she would reckon with that stormy sea on her own, forever. That if she was lucky enough to be loved by one person in this life, that should be enough. Or that was what she'd told herself. "I can't do this alone, Nikolai."

"I will be by your side."

"As my adviser?"

"If that's what you wish."

She didn't want to ask. Her pride forbade it. But her damn pride had cost her enough. She looked away. "And if . . . if I wished for more?"

She felt his fingers on her chin, turning her head. There was an unwanted ache in her throat. Zoya forced herself to meet his gaze. In this light, his hazel eyes looked almost golden.

"Then I would gladly be your prince, your consort, your demon fool."

"You will grow to hate me. I'm too sharp. Too angry. Too spiteful."

"You are all of those things, but you are so much more, Zoya. Our people will come to love you not despite your ferocity, but because of it. Because you showed mercy in our darkest hour. Because we know that if danger comes again, you will never falter. Give us that chance."

Love. The word was not made for people like her. "I don't know how to believe you," she said helplessly.

"What if I say I can't bear to lose you?"

A smile tugged at her lips. "I'd say you're a liar. That claims like that belong to romantic ninnies." She raised her hand and let her fingertips trace the line of his beautiful jaw. He closed his eyes. "We would go on, you and I. If I couldn't be queen, you would find a way to win this battle and save this country. You would make a sheltering place for my people. You would march and bleed and crack terrible jokes until you had done all you said you would do. I suppose that's why I love you."

His eyes flew open and his face lit in an extraordinary grin. "All Saints, say it again."

"I will not."

"You must."

"I'm the queen. I must do nothing but please myself."

"Would it please you to kiss me?"

It would. And she did, drawing him up to her, feeling the stubble at his jaw, the soft curl of his hair behind his ear, and at last, after all these long days of wanting, his witty, brilliant, perfect mouth. Silence fell around them and Zoya's head emptied of fear and worry and anything but the warm press of his lips.

When the kiss broke, he rested his forehead against hers.

"You do realize you just referred to yourself as the queen. That means you agreed."

"I *am* going to kill you."

"So long as you kiss me again before you do."

She obliged him.

47

NINA

NINA COULDN'T THINK STRAIGHT. *Is this a game? Is he toying with me?*

She was a tangle of anger and hope and confusion. *Get your head together, Zenik,* she chastised herself. *If you ever needed to keep your wits about you, this is the time.*

Easier said than done. She was fairly sure she'd just seen Nikolai Lantsov—or maybe not Lantsov, since he'd admitted to being a bastard—give up his crown to Zoya Nazyalensky. Who was also a dragon. And possibly a Saint. And Rasmus had called for a lasting truce and a treaty with Ravka. But why? Did he truly believe in peace? Was this all some elaborate ruse, some part of his feud with Jarl Brum?

Or was something else at play here altogether? Nina had seen

Hanne's body crumpled on the ground. But what had she really seen? She remembered Hanne's hands moving swiftly over her face, drawing hair from her own head. *I've been practicing*, she'd said.

Do not hope, Nina. Do not dare to hope for this.

All was silence on the boat ride back to Leviathan's Mouth, the unease of the Fjerdan soldiers and officers palpable. She could feel Brum's anger radiating from him, the fear of the *drüskelle* who had failed him in the audience chamber.

Joran looked nearly happy, his face serene, as if he'd finally found some kind of peace for the first time. He had been the first to speak, to declare for Zoya and for an end to war. Would any of the others have dared to be first? Or only the boy full of regret, desperate to do right, to sacrifice everything as penance to the Saints? If Nina had sought her vengeance and taken Joran's life, if Hanne hadn't stopped her, what might have happened in Os Kervo?

Nina was less sure of what she sensed from Prince Rasmus. He kept glancing at her, and his expression was one she could almost believe was true concern. She couldn't stop herself from studying his profile, the color of his eyes—were the differences she thought she saw there real or imagined? She felt like she was coming undone.

They docked at one of the piers, and the prince strode toward the command center with Joran beside him. "Come along," he said to Nina.

"I would have a word, Your Highness," said Brum, his anger barely leashed.

"Then you may come along too."

The command center was much like the rest of the structures on Leviathan—all military utility, stocked with maps and equipment. Crates of gear had been stacked in neat aisles, maps and tide charts were hung on the tent's canvas siding, though the rest of the walls had been left open.

"Are you sure you wouldn't like to have a *rest*, Your Highness?" Brum asked, seeking to draw attention to the prince's frailty.

"I think not. I feel quite well."

"Of course, you were not on the field today."

"No, I wasn't I have not had my share of riding or fresh air or battle in this life. I know you think me the lesser because of it."

"I never said—"

"You've said enough. You've called me weakling and whelp."

Brum sputtered. "I never did. I—"

"Think," the prince said gently, and again Nina found herself leaning forward, wondering. His voice sounded rough, different. As if the vocal cords had been hastily altered. "Remember that the men you once called loyal no longer wish to serve you. Your friend Redvin was found dead in the ruined eastern tower. Your *drüskelle* are in shambles. Is this the time you want your honesty called into question?"

Brum did not give any ground. "I have served Fjerda with honor."

"You have served Fjerda long enough."

Brum laughed. "I see. You think the Ravkans will keep to this peace, Your Highness?"

"I do," said Prince Rasmus. "And even if I didn't, it is no longer a matter that concerns you."

"Your health—"

"My health has never been better."

Nina hesitated, then said, "All this talk of poison today."

A hush fell.

"Yes," said Rasmus slowly. "A curious thing. I've been guarded by *drüskelle* since I was a child."

Now Brum looked genuinely frightened. As far as Nina knew, he had never resorted to poison. He'd thought the prince's poor health would do the work for him. But could he prove that?

555

"If you have evidence of such rank treason," Brum said, "I demand it be presented. I will not have my honor besmirched."

"I know this has been a day of tragedy for you," the prince said. "Of terrible loss. You need a time of rest and quiet contemplation. Perhaps on Kenst Hjerte."

"That is exile," Brum said, his voice low and determined. "You cannot mean to—"

"'Cannot' is a word unfamiliar to princes."

"Your Highness," Brum tried, making his voice warm, appealing. "This is a misunderstanding and nothing more."

The prince gestured to his guards. "Take him to his cabin and keep him under guard. But be kind to him. He is . . . he is what this country made him."

Before the guards could take hold of Brum, he had a gun in his hands, pointed at the crown prince.

"No!" Nina cried.

"*Strymacht Fjerda!*" Brum shouted.

Gunshots—one, two, three, whipcrack loud.

Brum never had a chance to fire. He was on the ground, bleeding. Joran reholstered his weapon. He'd shot Brum three times—once in the leg, twice in the arm.

The prince moved forward, but Nina seized him by the elbow. "Don't. He'll be all right."

Rasmus' eyes met hers, not quite the blue they had been. "Get a medic!" he called, holding her gaze. "This poor man needs help."

Medics and soldiers rushed forward. "We should let him die," said one, spitting on the ground by Brum's body. "He tried to kill you, Your Highness."

"I have no doubt he meant to turn the gun on himself. He lost his only daughter today." Rasmus paused. "Mila, you knew her well. You were Hanne's dearest friend, were you not?"

"I loved her," said Nina, stubborn, terrible hope clawing at her heart. "I love her still."

⚜

Brum was taken to the infirmary to have his gunshot wounds treated. He would recover in time, though he would have healed faster with the help of a Grisha. Ylva insisted on remaining with him. Nina wanted to comfort her, but she scarcely knew the words to say.

They boarded the royal airship in silence. Already there was talk of Prince Rasmus meeting with his parents to discuss the treaty, of whether the peace would hold, but all Nina wanted was a chance to speak to him alone.

They entered the royal cabin, a sleek pod of golden wood and plush white silk. Through the windows, Nina could see the setting sun painting the clouds in golden light, pale rose, faint blue at the edges.

"Leave us, Joran," the prince said.

Joran paused at the door, meeting first the prince's gaze, then Nina's. "Whatever you require, Your Highness. You need only ask." He said the words as if speaking a vow. "I'll see that you're not disturbed."

He bowed and departed, closing the door behind him. There were no witnesses now, only the clouds and the sky beyond.

The honeyed light caught on the prince's features. He was watching her with an expression she'd never seen on his haughty royal face before. She saw fear there, and her own hope reflected back to her.

"Where did we meet?" she whispered.

"In a clearing by a poison stream," the crown prince replied in that soft, husky voice. "I rode a white horse, and for a moment, you believed I was a soldier."

Before Nina's mind could protest, her feet were carrying her across the room. She threw her arms around him.

557

"Never let me go," Hanne whispered against her hair, holding her tight.

"Never again." She drew back. "But . . . the prince?"

Hanne's guilty expression said all it needed to. Rasmus was dead, his head dashed by the fall. He'd died wearing Hanne's face.

"How? What happened in that tower?"

Hanne took a breath. "Prince Rasmus started drinking when Fjerda's bells were destroyed. He was all mocking words for my father and his plans. He . . . he thought it was amusing to give me a slap."

"We knew how cruel he could be. I never should have left you alone with him."

"It was a small slap."

"Hanne!"

"It *was*. It was a test. I think he wanted to see how far he could go. He told me to strike him back, just as he did with Joran. He dared me to hit him. He hit me again. He said we'd play this game whenever he pleased when we were husband and wife. Joran tried to stop him, but . . . I panicked. I didn't mean to do it."

"You used your power on him."

A tear slid down Hanne's cheek. "His heart. I think I crushed it . . . I've never hurt someone that way."

Nina cupped Hanne's face in her palms. "I know you didn't mean to. I know you never would." Hanne had always been too good and too kind for the ugliness of this world.

"I told Joran to run for help. I tried to heal the prince. But I knew he was dead."

"So you tailored him."

"Yes. And myself. As quickly as I could. But Joran . . . I think he took his time."

To help Hanne? Or because he wanted Prince Rasmus dead? *Whatever you require, Your Highness.* Could Nina call that redemption?

Did his motives matter? Joran had saved Hanne's life today. He had spoken against Brum. He'd known Nina was not Mila Jandersdat and yet he'd kept that secret to himself. Maybe it could be a beginning.

"I bound my breasts, changed our clothes, and . . . and . . . I threw his body out the window."

"All Saints."

Hanne sat down on a wide velvet bench. "What am I to tell my mother? She thinks I'm dead. You can't imagine what it was to hear her grieve, to see you on your knees weeping for me. I can't lose her, Nina."

"We'll find a way to tell her. In time. But Hanne . . . what do we do now? You'll have to face the Grimjer king and queen."

"I can tailor myself more fully before then. Though I wish I had your gift for performance."

Nina had to laugh. "You did brilliantly. I absolutely believed you were Rasmus. You're lucky I didn't murder you on the spot."

"Don't think I wasn't worried. But fooling his parents?"

Hanne had learned deception from Nina over the last months. She'd spent a good part of her life at the Ice Court learning its protocols, and she'd been so much in the prince's company that his mannerisms and ways of speech were no mystery.

"We'll practice. We have time on the journey."

Hanne didn't look convinced. "If the king and queen ask me questions about Rasmus' childhood . . . ."

"I can help with that," said Nina. After all, they had the counsel of the dead.

"Will you?" Hanne's brow creased. "Can you love a murderer?"

"I might ask the same."

Hanne hesitated. "And can you love me in this body?"

"It is your heart I love. You know that, don't you?"

Tears formed in Hanne's eyes. "I hoped."

"But where does this end? How long can you stay trapped this way?"

"I'm not trapped, Nina." Hanne blew out a breath. "What if I told you there's a rightness in this body? That ever since I understood what tailoring could do, I haven't been able to stop thinking about what might be?"

Nina remembered the guilty look on Hanne's face when she'd admitted she'd been tailoring herself in secret. She thought of the way Hanne's eyes had slid away from her own reflection. Nina hadn't understood. "You said you didn't know if you could be happy."

"I still don't. I don't know what it is to live in a body that feels like it could be mine. All I know is . . . I lost my father today, maybe my mother. But not myself. And if I have to play the role of prince for this possibility, then it's a trade I'll gladly make."

"This from the person who said she hated parties."

"It isn't the face I would have chosen. I don't want to be Rasmus."

Nina put her hands on Hanne's shoulders. "You *aren't* Rasmus. You're someone new, someone I can't wait to know."

Hanne's smile was small, a precious, fragile thing. "We wanted to change the world. Maybe this is our chance."

"The prince and the fishwife? If you live as Rasmus, you know you'll be king one day." A king who knew what it was to be a woman in Fjerda, what it was to feel alone among her people. A true warrior.

"And you will be my queen." Hanne's shy glance pierced Nina—sudden light, too bright after so much darkness. "If you'll have me."

Nina laughed. "Oh, I'll have you, Hanne Brum." Hanne's cheeks flushed. It was glorious. "Two Grisha living in secret, ruling Fjerda, guiding them toward peace with Ravka? It's too beautiful a dream. But a prince can't wed a commoner."

"Then I'll give you land and titles. If you're willing. Can you stay here with me and live this lie?"

Nina stopped Hanne with a kiss, gazing down at the person she loved, alive and happy. "It's not a lie. You are my prince and you have my heart."

"You would wear a false face forever?"

"Well, Mila may develop some new hobbies and stop wibbling and wringing her hands so much, but yes. For the dream of you, I could."

"If you want to go back to Ravka—"

"I do. And I'll miss it and make you command the chefs to cook blini and beet soup." She planted herself in Hanne's lap. "But this is where I belong."

They stayed there, curled against each other, Hanne's arms wrapped around Nina, as they watched the sky turn the deep blue of twilight. Just beneath Hanne's left ear, Nina saw two rosy freckles, missed in the panicked rush of tailoring. She did love those freckles. Maybe they could keep one of them.

What would Matthias think of all this? Nina wondered. A Grisha king. A Grisha queen. She hoped he would be glad to see her happy, that he would want her heart to heal. *Save some mercy for my people.* Sitting there, in the quiet, watching the clouds slide by, no sound to break the silence but the steady hum of the engines, Nina felt a strange sensation creep through her, an ease that she had all but forgotten. Peace.

There were battles ahead, dangers she and Hanne would have to face. What they were attempting was audacious, maybe impossible, but somehow she knew they would manage it. Nina rested her cheek against Hanne's. She'd honored Matthias, and this path, somewhere between revenge and redemption, was the right one. *My place is with the wolves.*

Nina sat up straight. "Hanne, what do I call you now? Rasmus?"

Hanne shuddered. "I can't stand that. We'll have to choose a new name. A Saint's name. To honor the prince's newfound faith in the Children of Djel."

"All Saints, you're a quick learner. That's a politician's move."

"But we have to pick a good one."

"How about Demyan? Or Ilya? He was famous. And he changed the world."

Her prince smiled. "I don't know the story."

"I'll tell it to you," Nina said. Outside, night was falling and the sky was full of stars. "I'll tell you a thousand stories, my love. We'll write the new endings, one by one."

48

NIKOLAI

THEY TRAVELED WITH SUN SOLDIERS, not only for protection, but because some of the mountain passes were still blocked by snow.

"It would have been faster by dragon," Zoya complained as they traversed yet another switchback.

"And considerably more conspicuous," Nikolai replied.

"Just keep moving," Genya said. "I don't want to spend another night in these mountains."

Nikolai glanced behind him on the trail, where Zoya was helping Genya clamber over a rock. They'd all worn the roughspun clothes of travelers—warm coats and trousers, boots lined in fur. "Is it the bobcats, the weather, or the company that displeases you?"

"I am a queen," Zoya said. "I should be borne aloft on a litter so that my delicate feet never touch the ground."

"I could ask the demon to carry you."

Zoya sniffed. "Thank you, no. The last time you let it out, it tried to bite me."

"I think it was meant affectionately."

"Are you certain?" asked Genya.

"Not entirely," he admitted.

Flyers had brought them to the plains north of Sikursk. From there, they'd been forced to continue on foot. The winds that tore through these peaks made flight too risky. Ahead of them, bracketed by Sun Soldiers, the Darkling trudged on. His hands were bound and he still wore the black robes of the Starless. It was as if he didn't feel the cold.

Nikolai wondered what might be waiting for them if they ever managed to find this monastery—assuming it even existed. He was perfectly prepared for this daft excursion to be yet another of the Darkling's deceptions, but that didn't mean he was prepared for the deception itself. Perhaps the Darkling would bring down a landslide and bury them all beneath a pile of rock or abandon them in a labyrinth of caves. The options were endless. The man had a limitless supply of unpleasant surprises.

They emerged around a bend and the valley sprawled out before them, blanketed in silver mist and ringed by the snow-capped peaks of the Sikurzoi. He could see mountain lakes gleaming like frozen coins, and far in the distance, a herd of shaggy bison moving slowly across a meadow, searching for signs of spring.

Nikolai would have preferred to wait for the thaw to make this trip, but reports of the blight had only grown more frequent, miles-wide patches of dead earth and ashen soil, men, women, and children struck down in the space of moments, scars that might never heal.

After the battle for Os Kervo, his trackers hadn't been able to locate the Darkling. The followers of the Starless One still held their services, and a few had camped outside the palace walls to petition the new queen for the Darkling's Sainthood. But the man himself had gone missing. Until one night they'd entered the war room in the Little Palace to find him slouched in his old chair, as if he'd never left.

Nikolai had reached for his guns, Tolya and Zoya had moved into combat stance. But the Darkling had merely rested his chin in his hand and said, "It seems that, once again, Ravka has a problem only I can solve."

It was fair to say that problem was of the Darkling's creation, but if he could be of assistance, Nikolai wasn't going to argue. At the very least, he'd set them on the path to the Monastery of Sankt Feliks, where he believed they would find answers. And if not? Even the Darkling, the eternal know-it-all, wasn't sure what they would do. He seemed unfazed by the prospect.

"Are you really so ready to watch the world die?" Nikolai had asked him.

He'd merely shrugged. "Imagine, if you're able, how long I've spent in this world. Do you never wonder what waits in the next?"

Nikolai supposed he had. He'd written some very bleak poetry about death and the unknown while he was at university in Ketterdam, some of it in rhymed couplets, all of it remarkably bad.

He glanced back at Zoya trudging along, her silver fur hat pulled down low over her ears, her nose red from the cold. Why think of the next world when she was in this one? Over the past weeks he'd watched her navigate meetings, diplomatic dinners, the tricky early negotiations of the Fjerdan treaty. He was there to charm and to offer guidance when she needed it, but Zoya's role as general of the Second Army had forced her to learn the ins and outs of Ravka's foreign policy and internal workings. She might never have a real passion for agricultural reform or industrial development, but her ministers would be there to help. And so would Nikolai, if she let him.

They weren't married. They weren't even engaged. He wanted to ask, but he wanted to court her first. Maybe build her something. A new invention, something lovely and useless and ill-suited to war. A music box or a mechanical fox, a folly for her garden. Part of him was certain that she would simply change her mind about him and that would be the end of it. He had wanted her for so long that it seemed impossible he should actually have her beside him every day, that he might lay down beside her every night. Not impossible, he supposed. Just improbable.

He turned, sending pebbles scattering off the mountainside.

"Kiss me, Zoya," he said.

"Why?"

"I need reassurance that you are real and that we survived."

Zoya went up on her toes and pressed her warm mouth to his. "I'm right here and I'm freezing, so move before I toss you into a gully."

He sighed happily. There she was. Bitter and bracing as strong drink. She was real, and at least for now, she was his.

⌒♦⌒

They came upon the monastery without warning. One moment they were squeezing between two sheer rock walls and the next they were staring at an elaborate stone facade of arches and columns carved into gray stone. Between them, in a series of friezes, Nikolai saw the story of the first Priestguard, the monks who had transformed into beasts to fight for the first Ravkan king but who had been unable to return to human form. Yuri had believed that Sankt Feliks had been among those monks, and that over the years, the details of his Sainthood and martyrdom had been altered by time and retelling. Feliks had endured the *obisbaya*, the Ritual of the Burning Thorn, to purge himself of a beast. And if Nikolai didn't particularly want to be freed of his monster any longer? He would still do what his country's future required. That much hadn't changed.

There was no door to knock on, only a long tunnel that led into the dark. One of the Sun Soldiers lit the way.

"The air smells sweet," Genya said, and moments later, they understood why.

They emerged into a vast, snow-dusted clearing open to the sky. The rock walls around them were pocked with arched niches like a hundred hungry mouths, and at the center of it all stood the biggest tree Nikolai had ever seen.

The diameter of its twisted trunk was nearly as wide as the lighthouse at Os Kervo. A network of thick, muscular roots radiated from its base, and high above, the canopy of its branches nearly covered the clearing, dense with red blossoms and thorns as long as a man's forearm.

The thorn wood. But its shape felt different this time.

"It looks like Djel's ash tree," said Zoya.

"All stories begin somewhere." The voice came from the shadows of one of the niches. A woman appeared, her body swathed in crimson silk, her black hair in three long braids thrown over her shoulder. She was Shu, her eyes the vibrant green of new quince, and her feet were bare despite the snow. "All gods are the same god." She turned to Zoya. "*Nae brenye kerr, eld ren.*"

Zoya bowed.

Nikolai looked from Zoya to the monk. "Beg pardon?"

"It's Kaelish," said the Darkling. "Ancient Kaelish. A language I didn't realize Zoya knew."

Zoya didn't spare him a glance. "It means 'good to see you, old friend.' Juris was here before."

"Long ago," said the monk. "He wanted to be human again and thought we could help him. Do you fear that fate?"

Zoya looked surprised. "I'm still human."

"Are you?"

Genya reached out and took Zoya's hand. "She's human enough."

But Nikolai supposed they were all in somewhat hazy territory where that was concerned.

"We know what you're here for," said the monk. "But there's no help to be found in the thorn wood."

We? Nikolai realized that figures in crimson stood beneath every arch, staring down at them. They looked to be unarmed, but they held the high ground.

"You're aware of the blight?" he asked, trying to make a count of the people in the arches. There were over fifty of them.

"It has come to our mountains once already. We're only grateful it didn't strike the thorn wood."

"As are we," said Nikolai, since the tree was their only hope. Or had been. "You're saying we can't stop the spread of the Fold?"

"Not with the *obisbaya*. The Shadow Fold is a tear in the fabric of the universe, the fabric of the first making."

"The making at the heart of the world," Zoya murmured.

"Before the making, there was nothing, and that is what seeps into our world now."

Nikolai rubbed his hands together. "So how do we fix it?" The question he would always ask. What was broken could be repaired. What was torn could be mended. "How do we close the tear?"

"You can't," said the monk. "Someone must hold it closed."

Genya frowned. "What?"

"Someone must stand at the doorway between worlds, between the void and creation."

"For how long exactly?" asked Nikolai.

"Forever."

"I see."

"What do you see?" Zoya said sharply.

"It has to be someone."

"Don't be absurd," she snapped.

The monk drew closer. He couldn't tell how old she was. "Is it the shadow inside you that makes you brave?"

"I should hope not. I was making bad decisions long before that thing showed up."

Zoya grabbed his sleeve. "Nikolai, you can't be serious. I won't let you do this."

"You haven't been crowned. I'm not sure you can forbid anything just yet."

"You told me you'd stay by my side."

There was nothing he wanted more. They'd stopped a war together, and he'd begun to believe they could build a life together, but this was something he would have to do alone. He turned to the monk. "What do I have to do?"

"Nikolai—"

"The thorn will pierce your heart, just as in the *obisbaya*, but there you will remain, in agony, courting madness. If the thorn is removed, the blight will return and the universe will crumble."

Nikolai swallowed. That sounded far less palatable than a quick and heroic death. "I understand."

"But Nikolai," Genya said. "What happens when . . . well, when you die?"

"The blight will return," said the monk.

"Just as I thought." The Darkling leaned against one of the tree's gargantuan roots. He looked bored, as if he encountered an ancient order of monks every other day. "Your grand gesture has been noted, boy king—"

"Not a king," corrected Nikolai.

"Consort or king, you're not up to the task."

Zoya looked at the thorn wood. "Is this my martyrdom then?"

"Absolutely not," said Genya.

The Darkling just laughed. "Look at the way you march to the gallows. One with heroic zeal, one with grim determination. No, Sankta Zoya, you're not powerful enough to play martyr either. It has to be me, of course."

Zoya's eyes narrowed. "Of course. A man known for selfless acts. You do nothing without first calculating your own gain. Why would you start now?"

"Because I'm the only one who can."

"Is it my imagination," asked Nikolai, "or do you sound *smug* about that?"

"I am immortal," said the Darkling with a shrug. "You possess a bare scrap of my power. Zoya is only just learning how to master hers. I am the linchpin. I am the lodestone. I move the tide."

"You did cause all of this," Nikolai said. "Remember?"

"Is this meant to be your redemption then?" Genya asked. "Your great sacrifice?"

Nikolai had been surprised that she wanted to accompany them, but she'd held firm. *I'm not letting him out of my sight again*, she'd said. *No more escapes.* She and the Darkling hadn't exchanged a single word or glance until now.

"No forgiveness for me, little Genya?"

Zoya whirled on him. "Show her respect or I will gut you where you stand."

"No, Zoya," Genya said. "He and I are due for a chat. I forgive you for these scars." He couldn't hide his surprise, and she laughed. "You didn't expect that, did you? I don't regret them. I found my way to who I was meant to be through the pain I endured. I'm stronger for it."

"Consider it my gift to you."

Nikolai saw Zoya's fists clench. It was taking everything in her not to skewer the Darkling on a bolt of lightning.

"But the rest I can't forgive," Genya said. "You gave me to the queen's household because you needed a spy. You knew the old king's gaze would turn to me. You knew what I would endure." She shut her eye, remembering. "You told me I was your soldier, that all of my suffering would be worth some future glory. It wasn't."

"The cost—"

"Do not speak of costs." Her voice rang through the clearing, her red hair burning like autumn fire. The patch she wore was emblazoned with Alina's symbol. It shone like a star. "If the *cost* was so necessary, then you should have been the one to pay it. I was a child and you offered me up as a sacrifice for your centuries-old war." She laughed, a sad, small sound. "And the worst part is that no one remembers. When people speak of your crimes, they talk of the slaughter of Novokribirsk, your murder of the Grisha who were once under your care. What I lived through stayed hidden. I thought it was my shame to bear. Now I know it's yours. You were father and friend and mentor. You were supposed to protect me."

"I had a nation to protect, Genya."

"A nation is its people," Zoya said. "Genya, me, my aunt."

The Darkling raised a brow. "When you are queen, you may find such calculations more difficult to make."

"There will be no redemption for you," Genya said. "The woman I am can forgive you for the punishment you dealt me. But for the

571

sake of the child I was, there is no penance you can perform, no apology you can speak that will make me open my heart to you."

"I don't remember asking you to."

Zoya's eyes had gone silver, the pupils slitted. "Can I kill him before we shove him in the tree?"

Nikolai didn't doubt that the Darkling deserved that and much worse, but he hesitated. "Something's off here. What's the catch?"

The Darkling lifted one shoulder. "An eternity of suffering as penance for my crimes. I ask but one thing."

"Here it comes."

"Build me an altar, so that I may be remembered."

Zoya scowled. "As a tyrant? A killer?"

"As the Starless One. Give me a place in your books. When night comes, let there be one more candle lit for one more Saint. Can you agree to that, merciful queen?" he drawled.

The Darkling seemed almost disinterested, but the demon in Nikolai sensed it was a pose.

"He means it," Nikolai said in disbelief. "He's willing to die."

"It is not death," said the monk. "Death would be a kindness."

Genya tilted her head to the side. She was watching the Darkling closely. "But it's not death you fear, is it? He's afraid he'll disappear."

Nikolai remembered what Genya had said. *All the Darkling ever wanted was to be loved by this country.* He knew that feeling well. He'd had to face it when he'd stared down his demon. There were few men Ravka loved. Saints were another matter.

"Zoya?" Nikolai asked. The Darkling wanted them to raise an altar in his name, to write his story and his legacy anew, but it was not Nikolai's choice to make. "Genya?"

Zoya and Genya stood hand in hand, and as they looked at each other, he knew they were remembering every loss they'd endured at this man's whims. He had seen Zoya's torment when she'd witnessed the Starless at their worship, when they'd stood on the Fold that had devoured her aunt and cost countless others their lives, praising his name. The woman she'd been in that moment could not have bent to this request.

"Do we let him play the hero?" Zoya asked.

Genya nodded once. "Let him do it. Let our suffering have meant something."

Zoya stood framed by red blossoms and thorns, a queen who needed no crown. "It will be done."

The Darkling turned to the monk. "Where do we begin?"

The monk studied them for a while. Then she gestured to the thorn wood, as the monks descended the walls, surrounding the trunk in a sea of red silk, men and women, old and young, Ravkan, Zemeni, Suli, Shu. Even a few flaxen Fjerdan heads.

The Darkling held up his hands. "Unbind me."

Nikolai and Zoya exchanged a glance. If this was all a ploy, he would make his move now.

"Fan out," Nikolai said to the Sun Soldiers. "Be ready."

"As long as I live, the demon will remain inside you," said the Darkling as Nikolai used a knife to saw through the ropes at his wrists.

"We've made our peace."

"Some treaties do not last."

"You do love a dire prophecy, don't you?"

"Zoya will live a very long life," the Darkling said. "Despite the demon, you may not do the same."

"Then I will love her from my grave."

A smile touched the Darkling's lips. "Brave words. Time may tell a different tale."

Nikolai almost laughed. "I'm really not going to miss you."

He sheathed his knife and stepped away.

The Darkling rubbed at his wrists, taking his time, as if enjoying the fear of those forced to watch and wait to see what he would do.

He shucked off his robe, letting it drop to the snowy ground, then stripped off his shirt and strode to the base of the tree. He stood in trousers and boots, his skin white as driftwood, his long hair black as the feathers of a crow.

"Go on," said the monk with the three braids. "If this is your wish. If you dare it."

The Darkling took a deep breath.

"My name is Aleksander Morozova," he said, his voice echoing through the clearing. "But I have had a hundred names and I have committed a thousand crimes."

The monks placed their hands upon the roots of the tree, the trunk, the hanging boughs.

The Darkling spread his arms wide, his lean body pale in the winter light. "I am not sorry."

The great tree's bark began to move and shift. *They're Fabrikators*, Nikolai realized, watching the monks concentrate. *All of them.*

"I do not repent!" said the Darkling.

One of the branches of the thorn wood began to twist, writhing like a snake, a single spike protruding from its tip. Zoya took Nikolai's hand. Now they were all joined together: Nikolai, Zoya, and Genya.

The thorn-wood bough moved back and forth, back and forth, a serpent staring down its prey.

"All I did, I did for Ravka," shouted the Darkling. "And now, I do this too. For Ravka!"

The bough struck in a sudden, sinuous lunge.

The thorn pierced the Darkling's chest and he screamed, his head thrown back, the sound pure, human, and terrible. Nikolai gripped

Zoya's hand as the demon inside him screamed too, the pain like a brand, a fire in his heart.

The thorn-wood tree drew the Darkling closer, its branches wrapping around him, lifting his helpless body, a mother cradling her son, calling him home. The massive trunk parted, and the thorn wood pulled him into the dark.

The tree closed around him, silencing his scream. Its branches stilled. The monks stood silent. Nikolai pressed his hand to his heart. The pain was gone; the demon lay quiet.

Faintly, in the pattern of the bark, Nikolai could see the shape of a hand—the Darkling's hand, pressing at the bars of his prison for eternity.

One by one the Sun Soldiers knelt.

Zoya walked slowly to the tree, her footsteps quiet in the snow. She rested her hand against the mark the Darkling had made and bowed her head.

"I didn't really think he'd do it."

"He stands at the doorway between worlds," said the monk. "Look with your dragon's eye. What do you see?"

Zoya shut her eyes, lifted her face to the sky. "The Fold . . . the Fold is blooming."

"Tell us," said Genya.

"Green grasses. An orchard in blossom. Quince trees. Their boughs are full of white flowers. They look like sea-foam."

"The blight is over," said the monk. "Do you see him too?"

Zoya hissed in a breath. "His pain . . ." She shuddered and withdrew her hand, touching it to her chest as if she felt the thorn in her own heart.

The monk nodded slowly. "You will have to decide what you can and can't forgive, *eld ren*."

Zoya looked at her. "And if I could?"

"Some hearts beat stronger than others," said the monk, and Zoya seemed to startle at the words. "Only a heart as strong as his could free him from his suffering and give him the release of death."

⚬

They thanked the monks, but there was no offer of hospitality, and Nikolai had no desire to stay in this place any longer. Whatever the Darkling had been, this clearing had become a place of mourning.

Without a word, they made their way beneath the arched entry and through the crack in the rock. Spring would come soon. The world would be made green and new. But for now, all was ice and wind and gray stone, as if the land wore a veil and spoke only words of loss. Nikolai couldn't feel sorrow for the man the Darkling had become, but he could regret the loss of someone who had begun with so much promise, so much belief in what might be accomplished if only he was clever enough, strong enough, brave enough to risk it all. Who might he have been if the world had been kinder? If Ravka had been better to its people all along?

The past lay shattered and bleak, torn by trenches, thick with mines. But the future was rolling hills and untouched forest, an open sea, a fair-weather sky.

Nikolai followed his queen through the mountains and knew hope would lead them home.

49

ZOYA

THE MORNING OF ZOYA'S CORONATION,
Genya sent the servants away and insisted on doing Zoya's hair herself. Zoya felt strange letting her friend wait on her, but she was
grateful for her presence and for her skills.

"You haven't been sleeping," Genya said, tailoring away the dark
circles beneath Zoya's eyes.

"Nothing new."

But that wasn't entirely true. Her responsibilities weighed heavy
on her, but in the weeks since their journey to the mountains, she'd
been troubled by new nightmares.

She and Genya took their time over breakfast, looking out at the
palace gardens, watching the mist burn away in the morning sun.
They'd propped their feet on the windowsill, their plates in their laps.

"I don't mind the view," Zoya said, reaching for another blini.

Genya wriggled her toes. "The Little Palace *is* short on windows. Secrecy over scenery."

Nikolai had insisted that Zoya take his chambers.

"They belong to Ravka's ruler," he'd told her. "Go on, it's an opportunity to complain about my horrible taste."

Zoya did hate the rooms, but not because of the way they were decorated. She simply missed her chambers in the Little Palace. Everything was so new, she couldn't help but long for the familiar. But on the day she'd moved in, she'd found a little wire ship on her desk, small enough to fit in the palm of her hand. From its mast flew a tiny flag emblazoned with two stars. She was glad to have a reminder of Nikolai and of Liliyana with her always.

Genya helped her dress in a gown of darkest blue velvet, the skirt and bodice embroidered with silver thread in a pattern of dragon scales. It was reminiscent of a *kefta*, but no *kefta* like this had ever been seen.

"It's perfection," Zoya said. She'd entrusted Genya with its design. "Thank you."

"Oh, we're not done yet."

Genya vanished into the dressing room and emerged with what looked like a mile of spangled silver lace.

Zoya lifted it in her hands. It was nearly weightless and glinted like captured lightning. "Did you actually skin a dragon?"

"Didn't have to," said Genya, attaching the cape to the shoulders of Zoya's gown. "I told him it was for the queen of Ravka and he shrugged right out of it."

"You're absurd."

"I'm delightful."

"The train is too long."

"Someone once told me the chapel demands spectacle." Her tone was all mirth, but Zoya could see Genya's sad smile in the mirror.

She snagged her friend's hand. "I wish he could be here with us."

Genya brushed a tear from her cheek and they stood together, as they had in the mountains. "David would have hated every minute of this. But I wish it too."

⌒◆⌒

The chapel would never be a place of celebration for Zoya. She had seen Nikolai crowned in this room, but she had also stood beside Alina here, behind this very altar on the night the Darkling had laid waste to the Little Palace and murdered half the people Zoya had ever known. They had gone underground that night, but it had been years before Zoya had really let herself emerge into the light. The wounds had been too deep, the fear too profound. She hadn't believed she could ever feel safe again.

And now? She let Vadik Demidov, the last of the Lantsovs, who had been granted a glorious estate and a considerable amount of treasure—most of it courtesy of Count Kirigin—settle Sankt Grigori's bear skin around her shoulders. She listened to Vladim Ozwal, the priest who would serve as her Apparat, preach the words of the old Saints and the new. Work had begun on a small chapel in the lush quince grove that had once been the Fold, and it was said that little altars to the Starless One had already begun to spring up in the places where the blight had struck, but that were now blooming. Zoya wasn't sure that she could make peace with the Darkling as a Saint, but she had tried to fulfill her vow.

When the time was right, she let Vladim place a crown upon her head. It was a crown born of battle—forged from their remaining scraps of titanium, set with sapphires, and formed into the shape of curving dragon's wings.

She looked out at this crowd of strangers and friends, at Genya with her single amber eye, her red *kefta* now emblazoned with a golden dragon; at Leoni, the Fabrikator David had so admired—now one of the Grisha Triumvirate—holding hands with Adrik, who had not abandoned their demon king after all, and who would take Zoya's place to represent the Etherealki.

Dignitaries had come from all over the world: delegates from the Kerch Merchant Council, including that oaf Hiram Schenck, who had done all he could to give Ravka's throne to Fjerda; the marshal from the Wandering Isle; Zemeni's ministers, without whom Ravka would not have survived the war; and even the Shu princesses and their guards—Ehri and Mayu, who had embraced Nikolai as an old friend, and Makhi, who had taken one look at the white flowers festooning the palace balustrades, the glittering courtiers at every doorway, the banners snapping in the winter wind, and said, "All the Heavens, do none of you understand ceremony?"

They had made sure Tamar and the *khergud* were long gone before the Shu delegation arrived. Zoya would never feel easy in their presence, but she was grateful to them nonetheless. They had been engineered to hunt and capture Grisha, but that meant they were perfectly suited to saving Grisha as well. Locust, Harbinger, Scarab, and Nightmoth had agreed to join with Bergin, a Fjerdan Grisha, to locate Jarl Brum's secret laboratories, all under Tamar's command.

Fjerda's crown prince had sanctioned the covert operation, and he was in attendance at the wedding too—along with the woman who would be his bride, Mila Jandersdat. She wore a gown of cream silk with a neckline that could only be described as scandalous and opals the size of walnuts at her throat.

"Fjerda suits you," Zoya had whispered to Nina when they'd managed to steal a few moments alone outside the chapel.

"The food is still terrible, but we manage."

"Your prince isn't at all what I expected from our intelligence. Far kinder and less arrogant."

"He is all that Fjerda or I could want in a ruler."

Zoya didn't need to let her dragon's eye open to sense the conviction in Nina's words. "I'm sending you back to that Saintsforsaken country with a gift."

"A chef and two pounds of toffees?"

"A plant. It's from my garden."

"Your . . . garden? Zoya Nazyalensky likes to root around with worms?"

"Wretched girl," said Zoya. "I hope it will bloom for you. And I hope you bloom too."

She knew Nina wouldn't return to them. At least not for a long time. Zoya would miss the sight of the dahlias in the summer, but maybe they were meant for different soil.

Among the other honored guests in the chapel were a group of Suli, dressed in silks. Some wore the jackal mask. Others wore their hair braided and decorated with flowers. They were seated beside Nikolai at the front of the room, along with a couple in simple peasant clothes, the woman's gleaming white hair hidden beneath a beaded shawl.

There were ghosts in this room, phantoms who would never be laid to rest. They would walk this new path with her—Liliyana, David, Isaak, Harshaw, Marie, Paja, Fedyor, Sergei. The list was long and would only grow longer.

You cannot save them all.

No, but she could try to be a good queen. The little girl would always be there, frightened and angry, and Zoya would never forget her, or how it felt to be powerless and alone, even if she was not alone now. She had her soldiers, her Grisha, her friends, her prince, and, she supposed, she had her subjects now too.

Zoya of the lost city. Zoya of the garden. Zoya bleeding in the snow.

"Rise, Zoya, queen of Ravka," the priest said, "wearer of the dragon crown."

Zoya stood. She raised the scepter in her hand. She listened to the people cheer, watched her dragon banner, wrought in Ravka's pale blue and gold, unfurl. The task before her felt overwhelming.

None of this had been fated; none of it foretold. There had been no prophecies of a demon king or a dragon queen, a one-eyed Tailor, Heartrender twins. They were just the people who had shown up and managed to survive.

But maybe that was the trick of it: to survive, to dare to stay alive, to forge your own hope when all hope had run out.

For the survivors then, Zoya whispered to herself as the people before her knelt and chanted her name. *And for the lost.*

The rest of the morning was a whirlwind of greetings and congratulations, wishes for the future, and even a few veiled threats from the Kerch. The throne room was packed with guests and miserably hot, a fact not helped by the weight of her velvet gown, but Zoya endured it all with Nikolai and Genya to help her.

Still, there was something on her mind. "Genya, will you find Alina before she vanishes with her tracker? I need to talk to you both. Meet me in the king's chambers."

Genya planted a kiss on her cheek. "*Your* chambers."

Nikolai appeared at Zoya's side as Genya disappeared into the crowd. "There's someone I'd like you to meet."

He was accompanied by a Suli girl, tiny in stature, her hair worn in a thick braid.

She curtsied with a dancer's grace. "Queen Zoya, it's an honor."

Zoya studied her a moment, noted the glint of knives discreetly hidden in her pockets and beneath her embroidered vest. "Captain Ghafa," she said quietly, making sure her voice didn't carry in the busy room.

Inej grinned. "You know my name."

Zoya glanced at where the Kerch dignitaries had gathered in a corner. "A great many people are looking for you."

The gleam in the tiny girl's eye was wicked. "They'd best pray they don't find me."

"If there's anything you need—"

"She will have it," said Nikolai, with a smart bow.

"It's been my dream to visit this place," Inej said, "to walk the same paths as the Sun Saint."

"Then we'll have to show you the Little Palace, where she trained to use her power."

Inej's grin widened. "*Bhashe.*"

"*Merema,*" Zoya replied in Suli. "You're welcome."

A crease appeared between Inej's brows. Her dark eyes focused on someone moving through the crowd. "That woman," she said, "in the shawl. Her hair—"

"Friends from the country," said Nikolai briskly. "Now let me introduce you to my sister Linnea. She'll want to hear of these new cannons you're using."

Zoya would have liked to follow along and listen to them talk ships and sailing and whatever else privateers and pirates liked to discuss, but Tolya was already whisking her off to meet with a group of Kaelish aristocrats. The Zemeni followed, then powerful merchants from West Ravka, Fjerdan nobility, and Count Kirigin, who had dressed in vibrant tangerine, his tiepin a gold dragon with a lump of turquoise in its claws.

Zoya wasn't sure how much time had passed or how many people she'd met when at last she glimpsed Genya across the room.

She excused herself and hurried through one of the palace's many passages to Nikolai's chambers—*her* chambers, damn it. Genya and Alina were waiting in the sitting room, both of them seated by an open window, the cool air a blessing after the heat of the ballroom.

"Well," said Alina, setting down her glass of kvas as Zoya closed the door. "It does look good on you."

"Was there ever any doubt?"

Genya laughed. "I told you she's the same Zoya."

"You looked so serene up there," Alina protested.

"All an act," said Zoya. "Mostly I was hoping I wouldn't faint. This dress weighs more than I do."

"Beauty isn't supposed to be easy," Genya said with little sympathy.

Alina nodded. "The real question is how you're going to outdo this gown for the royal wedding."

"Don't get ahead of yourself," Zoya said. "Nikolai hasn't asked."

"Can you blame him?" Genya said. "He hasn't had much luck with proposals."

Alina snorted. "Maybe he should have offered me a dynasty and not a piddly little emerald."

"Poor boy," said Zoya. "But I do intend to dangle the possibility of my hand in marriage in front of every eligible politician, merchant, and minor aristocrat while we forge our new trade agreements and treaties."

Genya rolled her eye. "Very romantic."

"I can't just *stop* being a general," said Zoya. "It's good strategy." Her romance with Nikolai would never be bouquets of flowers and pretty declarations of love. It lived in the quiet they'd found in each other, in the hours of peace they were stringing together one by one.

"But you *will* get married," Genya insisted.

"I can't help but notice," Alina said. "The too-clever fox gave up his throne, but still managed to stay a king."

"A prince," Genya corrected. "Prince consort. Or is he your general?"

Zoya didn't really care what title he took. He was hers, and that was all that mattered. Her eye caught on the blueprints she'd found waiting for her on her desk that morning, designs for an extraordinary structure Nikolai had designed to protect her garden. The plans had been bound with her blue velvet ribbon and accompanied by a note that read, *I will always seek to make it summer for you.* Zoya had been courted by men of wealth and power, offered jewels, palaces, the deed to a diamond mine. This was a different kind of treasure, one she could not believe she'd been lucky enough to find.

She turned back to Genya and Alina, and leaned against her desk. She wanted to sit and rest her feet, but she was too nervous about what she had to say. "You know what we did in the mountains."

"Yes," said Alina. "You saved the world and doomed Ravka's most deadly enemy to an eternity of torture."

"Very efficient questing," said Genya.

Zoya tapped her fingers against the desk. "I've . . . I've been having nightmares, about the monastery, the thorn wood." When she had touched the ancient tree, she had felt the Darkling's pain. The dragon hadn't let her forget it.

"What happens in the dreams?" Alina asked.

"I become him."

Genya worried her lip. "You're being tortured?"

"Worse than that . . . I have everything he wanted. The crown. The power. I'm a conqueror of cities, an empress, a killer." In her dreams, she stood on the prow of a ship with a beautiful city before her. She raised her hands and the Fold rushed forward in a black tide, drowning Novokribirsk. She woke each night bathed in sweat, hearing her aunt's screams. "I'm not certain we can just leave him there."

Genya crossed her arms. "No?"

"Not if we want to rule justly. Not if the future is meant to be better than the past."

"Do you have a fever?" Genya asked.

But Alina's expression was knowing. "You're afraid you'll become him. You're afraid you'll be the avalanche."

Immortal and unstoppable, another tragedy to befall Ravka.

"What are we meant to do?" Genya said. "Free him? Forgive him?"

"Grant him death," said Zoya.

Genya stood and walked to the mantel. "Does he deserve it?"

"That's not my choice to make," said Zoya. "Not on my own."

Alina rested her head on the back of the couch. "Why are we even discussing this? From what I understand, the Darkling knew the bargain he made. He stands at the doorway between worlds. If he dies, the Fold ruptures again and the void comes pouring through."

"Yes," said Zoya. "But the monk told me that a heart as strong as his could free him." She'd spoken Liliyana's words. She'd wanted Zoya to listen.

Genya looked aghast. "Someone to take his place? Unless you're volunteering Jarl Brum—"

"No, I think it was a riddle. Not someone, some*thing*. The first heart to be pierced by the thorn wood. The heart of Sankt Feliks."

"You're talking about a relic." Alina sounded skeptical. "As someone whose finger bones are on sale in villages right now, let me tell you, they're all fake."

"She's right," said Genya. "If Sankt Feliks really existed and his heart was somehow preserved, no one knows where it is."

"True," said Zoya. "And whoever has it won't be eager to part with an object of so much power."

Genya made a kind of humming noise. "So, *if* we decide he deserves the mercy of death, where does that leave us?"

Zoya touched her fingers to the little wire ship on her desk. "A priceless object, impossible to find, no doubt under lock and key, and most certainly in need of stealing? I know a thief who might be up to the task."

Genya groaned. "You can't be serious. You can't stand the man!"

"Because he's insufferably rude and utterly without morals. But he has his uses."

"You think he'll do it?" asked Genya.

"For the right reward."

There was a long silence in the room. At last Genya reached for Alina's glass and took a long sip. "I don't believe the Darkling has earned forgiveness. I don't know how many years of pain buys that, or when we become the monsters and he becomes the victim. But I don't want to spend the rest of my life doing that math. If there's really a way to accomplish it, let's be rid of this burden once and for all."

"All right," said Alina.

Before she could talk herself out of it, Zoya rang for a servant to fetch Nikolai.

"Has a decision been reached?" he asked. "I can't decide if you all look ruthless or beneficent. Maybe just hungry."

"Is Captain Ghafa still here?"

"I believe she left an hour ago in the company of Prince Rasmus and his betrothed."

"Perhaps that's a sign," Zoya ventured.

"Zoya," Alina said warningly. "We did agree."

"Oh, all right," Zoya said. "I need Sturmhond to take a message to Ketterdam for me."

"I hear he's very busy these days."

"I think he'll appreciate the reward."

He lowered his voice. "If it involves you out of that dress, I have no doubt I can convince him."

"You won't stop until you've created a scandal, will you?"

"The demon made me do it. What vital message will the world's most handsome privateer be taking to Ketterdam?"

Zoya sighed. Tragic to think a woman might have everything she desired and still have need of a thief.

"Get a message to the Crow Club," she said. "Tell Kaz Brekker the queen of Ravka has a job for him."

ACKNOWLEDGMENTS

Rule of Wolves is the seventh novel I've written in the Grishaverse, a story that began with a girl trying to find her way through the dark. As Zoya would say, it's not a metaphor. But I'm still grateful to all the generous people who helped light the way.

Thank you to everyone at Imprint: Dawn Ryan, Hayley Jozwiak, David Briggs, Raymond E. Colón, the meticulous John Morgan, Camille Kellogg, my talented editor Erin Stein, who lets me pitch her wild ideas, and Natalie Sousa, who has worked so hard to make these books beautiful. I'm deeply grateful to the wonderful marketing, publicity, and subrights teams at MCPG: Kathryn Little, Melissa Zar, Teresa Ferraiolo, Julia Gardiner, Lucy Del Priore, Allison Verost, Mariel Dawson, Kristin Dulaney, Kaitlin Loss, Jordan Winch, and Team Triple M: Molly Ellis, Morgan Kane, and Madison Furr. Thank you to the remarkable sales team of Jennifer Edwards, Jessica Brigman, Jasmine Key, Jennifer

Golding, Mark Von Bargen, Matthew Mich, Rebecca Schmidt, Sofrina Hinton, and Taylor Armstrong. Also to Jon Yaged, who didn't fit into any of these lists.

As always, I am glad and lucky to be a part of the New Leaf Literary family. Thank you to Hilary Pecheone, Joe Volpe, Veronica Grijalva, Victoria Hendersen, Meredith Barnes, Abigail Donoghue, Jenniea Carter, Katherine Curtis, Kate Sullivan, the always on-point Jordan Hill, the relentless Pouya Shahbazian, and my agent, Joanna Volpe, who somehow saw the destination before I did—and managed to get us there.

Sarah Rees Brennan and Holly Black lent me their extra-ordinary brains and helped to shape the earliest drafts of this book. Marie Lu and Daniel José Older steered me through to the end with kindness and insight. Thank you to Kyle Lukoff and Jesse Deshays, who aided me in telling Hanne's story. Robyn, Rachael, Ziggy, Morgan, Michelle, Sarah, Theodora, Jimmy, the Platinum Patties and the Pajama Pals—united in alliteration, all kept me going with humor, smarts, and the occasional delivery of ceramic ghosts. Thanks and love to Christine, Sam, Emily, Ryan, my beautiful mother, and Wally, who makes everything better. And E, I know you don't like me to make a fuss, but thank you for being my friend, my familiar, and the only person I could love more after eleven hours in the car. A final thank-you to Jean, who is loved and remembered.

EXPLORE THE
GRISHAVERSE

THE SHADOW AND BONE TRILOGY

THE SIX OF CROWS DUOLOGY   THE KING OF SCARS DUOLOGY

THE ANTHOLOGIES

grishaverse.com

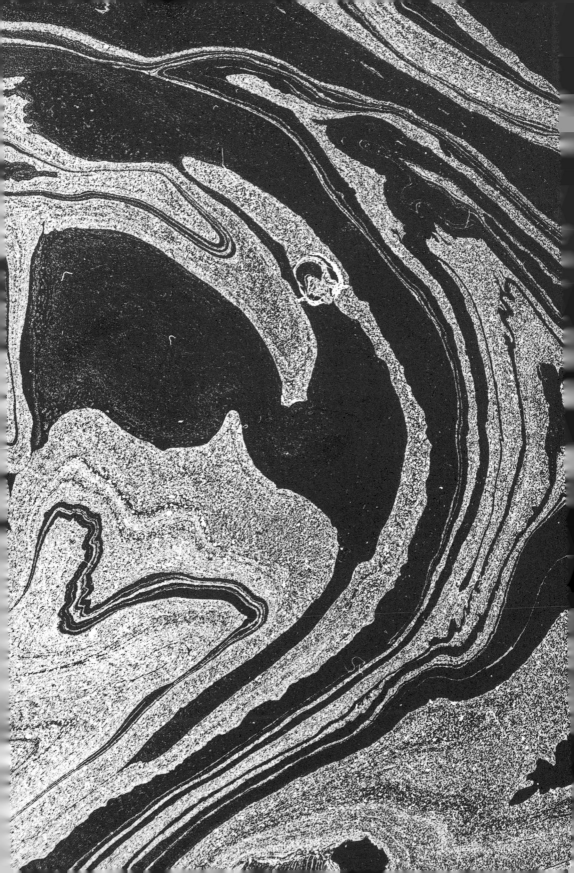